REDEMPTION
Stories from the Edge

REDEMPTION

Stories from the Edge

REDWOOD WRITERS
2018 ANTHOLOGY

Stories from members of the Redwood
branch of the California Writers Club

2018 Redwood Writers Anthology
Redemption: Stories from the Edge
Robbi Sommers Bryant, Editor in Chief
Belinda Riehl, Associate Editor

LCCN: 2018950991
ISBN-13: 978-0997754438
ISBN-10: 0997754435
Print Edition 11/1/2018
Pages 293

Cover Photograph: Marco Muller - Red Poppies
Cover Design: Roger C. Lubeck, It Is What It Is Press
Interior Design: Roger C. Lubeck, It Is What It Is Press
Published by: Redwood Writers Press
P.O. Box 4687
Santa Rosa, California 95402

TABLE OF CONTENTS

FICTION

TABLE OF CONTENTS (Continued)

MEMOIR

TABLE OF CONTENTS (Continued)

TABLE OF CONTENTS (Continued)

REDEMPTION

"An act of redemption, the ultimate act of personal grace, is an undervalued form of courage."

—Kilroy J. Oldster, *Dead Toad Scrolls*

FOREWORD

The 2018 Redwood Writers anthology theme of redemption was presented to the membership in early summer 2017. The announcement received a lukewarm response. Writers balked at the theme saying it was too difficult. However, the workshop taught by Editor in Chief Robbi Sommers Bryant; story craftsman, Dan Coshnear; plot master, Anne Jordan; and grammar diva, Arlene Miller sparked interest and excitement. Each presenter touched on different aspects of writing, including diverse definitions and perspectives of the word "redemption."

The redemption theme challenged many writers to look beyond the blank screen into the heart of creativity. To the authors that succeeded, bravo. Through these stories, the reader has the opportunity to celebrate the renewal of the human spirit. We hope you enjoy our collection.

Robbi Sommers Bryant, Editor in Chief
Belinda Riehl, Associate Editor

Robbi Sommers Bryant served as the editor in chief for the 2018 Redwood Writers Anthology, *Redemption*. She also worked one-on-one with writers to improve their stories.

Robbi's award-winning books include a novella, 4 novels, 5 short-story collections, and 1 book of poetry. Her work is published in magazines including *Readers Digest*, *Redbook*, *Penthouse*, college textbooks, and several anthologies. Robbi's article, "A Victim's Revenge," was optioned twice for television's *Movie of the Week*. She also appeared on TV's *The Jane Whitney Show*. She is past president of Redwood Writers and currently serves as vice president. Her professional focus is developmental, content, copy editing, and coaching. For more information: robbibryant.com.

ACKNOWLEDGMENTS

Thank you to those who helped create this year's anthology. We had a wonderful team, stayed on schedule, and ended up ahead of our deadline. The volunteers listed below made the difference between a chaotic experience and a smooth operation.

Each story submitted was scored by three judges using a rubric and system of numbers to ensure judges' and authors' anonymity. This year, we returned those score sheets and the judges' comments to all the authors. Thank you to each of the judges: Arlene Battishill, Skye Blaine, Daniel Coshnear, Barbara Cottrell, Anne Jordan, Ferne Moffson, and Jean Wong.

The authors whose stories were selected worked one-on-one with an editor to fine-tune their work. Thanks to each editor for volunteering their time and expertise: John P. Abbott, Inga Aksamit, Skye Blaine, Catharine Bramkamp, Robbi Sommers Bryant, John Compisi, Robert Digitale, Cathy Hollander, Susan Littlefield, Roger C. Lubeck, Ana Manwaring, Ferne Moffson, Belinda Riehl, and Natasha Yim. An important part of the team effort of publishing this anthology was the contribution made by the proofreaders, each of whom read every story at least once. Thank you for volunteering your time and talents: Sandy Baker, Jane Bonham, Adele Layton, Connie Leap, Arlene Miller, and Belinda Riehl. The biographies for each judge, editor, and proofreader can be found at the end of the book.

SPECIAL THANKS

Belinda Riehl has not only been my right-hand woman, she was also my left. Her remarkable skills include organization; making sense of senseless things; acting as liaison between the judges, editors, proofreaders, writers, and myself; figuring out spreadsheets; coming up with brilliant ideas; sharing her sense of humor when I'm banging my head against the wall; and making herself available whenever I called. On top of this, she acted as an editor and proofreader for this book. I found her both easy to work with and an inspiration. Thank you so much, Belinda. You helped make this project both seamless and fun.

Roger C. Lubeck has done excellent work preparing this book for publication. He created the table of contents, did the formatting, developed the front and back covers, structured the pages, handled the publishing, dealt with all the loose ends, and was an incredible help all the way through the creation of this anthology. His knowledge and point of view were spot on. Without his expertise, we'd be handing out manuscripts instead of published books!

A Moment of Silence

In remembrance of those affected by the North Bay Wildfires ...

By Robert Digitale

As we slept in our beds, the firestorm roared west over the mountains, an orange inferno that in the darkness devoured homes, wrecked neighborhoods, and extinguished lives.

Forty people died in the October wildfires. Six thousand homes burned. A great swath of northern Santa Rosa was reduced to a smoldering wasteland of toxic ash and charred metal.

The fires shook our region in ways we still struggle to grasp. Even so, this much seems clear: We witnessed a level of destruction not seen in the North Bay in over a century. For us, it rivaled the 1906 earthquake, which not only devastated the bustling city of San Francisco but also forever changed the 52-year-old farm town of Santa Rosa.

Recent months have been a time of heartache and comfort, of lingering trauma, and spirited resolve to move forward. Many lost all possessions. Others found ways to care and give. Among fire survivors, neighbor came alongside neighbor to jointly rise again.

We now wait to see how the survivors will rebuild their homes, their neighborhoods, and their lives. As we watch, a community hopes and remembers.

Robert Digitale is a staff writer at the *Press Democrat*, which received the 2018 Pulitzer Prize for its coverage of the October wildfires. He was editor in chief of Redwood Writers 2017 anthology, *SONOMA: Stories of a Region and Its People.*

FICTION

THE VALUE OF CHANGE

BETSY MILLER

My damp shirt clung to my skin, and my leggings stuck to the backs of my thighs as I moved into my studio apartment—a second-floor walkup. Hoping to create a cross-breeze, I opened both windows and the door. This was change, and I was riding high. Moving out. Leaving behind the single-wide trailer where I'd been living with my mom and little brothers. I had my own place—tiny, but gloriously mine! After a year of working a steady job and saving up, my dream had become a reality.

I rummaged through a box of kitchen things from Mom. Two tea balls—I don't even drink tea—an old pan, two bowls, two plates, and two drinking glasses. I filled a glass with tepid tap water. My stomach rumbled. I'd skipped breakfast and lunch.

"Hey."

I turned to see a tall, young woman just outside my door. Her shoulders curved forward the way some girls hold them to minimize their height.

"I'm Gina Torino. I live across the hall." Dark hair curled loosely around her shoulders. She had a high forehead and a perfect, straight nose like an actress or model. Her skin lacked the sheen of sweat that I could feel on my own.

"Jenny Green," I replied, pushing a strand of limp hair off my forehead. Now that I'd stopped moving, my exhaustion caught up with me, draining every ounce of energy from my body.

"You must be wiped out," she said as if reading my mind. "Want to come over? We can sit in front of the fan."

"A fan sounds amazing."

Gina reached up and slid her hand along the top of the doorframe to her apartment. "My key," she said. "It's easier than carrying it with me when I won't be gone for long."

The fan rested on an ottoman next to the TV and directly across from two easy chairs with teal slipcovers. A matching futon with a print cover fit neatly along the wall. We each claimed a chair and sat eating carrot cake and drinking tall glasses of iced tea. I doused mine with lemon and sugar, turning it into lemonade. The fan moved back and forth, aiming a blast of warm air at me, then moving to Gina.

"This is so good." I'd almost finished my cake. My stomach, grateful for the food, stopped complaining.

Gina smiled. "I work at a coffee shop down the block. We get discounts there and sometimes even freebies."

"Oh, yeah, I think I passed it on the way here. The one with the moon on the sign?"

"Yeah, Moon Rise Coffee. How about you?"

"I'm a receptionist."

The fan droned as it made its repetitive journey. Just inside the door, I noticed a clear plastic pitcher filled almost to the top with coins. The pitcher sat on a little half-round table. Piles of quarters and even some dollar coins flashed among the dimes, nickels, and pennies.

"That's quite a coin collection," I said.

"My stash? A lot of my tips are in change. I kept dumping them out of my purse. Pretty soon I had a pile, so I started keeping the coins all in one place."

As time went by, I was sure that Gina came from a rich family because she never spent her coins. Sure, she lived in a cramped studio apartment like mine. But she had to be slumming. She'd drop money in that pitcher as she came and went, but I never saw her take any. And the way she shared her food—that was a giveaway for sure. She fed anyone who stopped by, and she never seemed to mind. After their shifts, her work friends drifted through the hall, an easygoing group on their way to her place. I didn't have friends at my job. The other receptionists were older and married.

Gina seemed to know everyone in the building, but I had no idea how to start a conversation with a stranger. We'd moved around when I was growing up. When we finally settled in the trailer, it was isolated and too crowded to invite anyone over, so I was out of practice. Instead, I was getting to know the tenants by their laundry. Like the purple lady. I didn't know her name, but I recognized her stuff: lavender sheets, deep purple pants, mauve t-shirts. If I needed a dryer and it was full, I'd empty the machine and fold the clothes. It only took a few minutes, so why not?

Once Gina walked in on me just as I finished folding a pair of her extra-long jeans. I set them down next to a folded stack of her designer shirts. Their chic patterned fabrics and beautiful stitching looked out of place on the drab counter. It must be nice to afford such expensive things.

"Jenny, nobody does that," she said.

"Nobody folds clothes?"

"Nobody folds *other* people's clothes."

I flushed. *Had I crossed a line?* "I didn't know. Sorry."

"Don't apologize! You're sweet." Gina flashed me a smile. "The dryer's on me." She set down a stack of quarters as she left.

I was glad to see those quarters because most of the time I was strapped for cash. After rent, anything left of my paychecks went to food and things I kept discovering I needed. A broom and dustpan, a kitchen trash can, dish soap, a toilet bowl brush. I found myself counting my money, calculating what I could buy at the grocery store. I dug through the pockets of my coat, checked the bottom of my purse, and searched in dresser drawers to gather up any coins that had wandered from my wallet.

I hated the idea of losing my apartment, but I was barely making ends meet. The dryer money from Gina bought my first latte in weeks. I like those little luxuries. It's surprising what you miss when you're watching every penny.

I was also discovering things I had but didn't need. Why had I saved a stack of fashion magazines? Those tea balls from Mom cluttered the tiny kitchen drawer. Maybe Gina could use them.

I went across the hall and knocked on her door.

"Gina," I called out. No answer. I stood on tiptoes and slid my fingers along the top of the doorframe until I felt the cool metal of her key. I clicked open the door and stepped inside Gina's apartment. I'd leave the tea balls with a note.

No, that was weird.

I glanced around the apartment. *I shouldn't be in here.* My skin pricked uneasily. I'd come back later or text her. I turned to leave and stopped short. Right next to me, on the small table, sat the pitcher. All that change that Gina had but didn't need.

I reached in, pulled out a fistful, and shoved it into my pocket. The coins sifted down, their weight heavy against the front of my thigh. A fine line of adrenaline raced through my body at the boldness of my act. *Gina wouldn't notice, would she?* I stared intently at the coins inside the pitcher. My impulsive grab had left a dent. I smoothed out the valley, leveling the top. Now the coins looked normal. I needed to get out before Gina came back.

I could use my new quarters to do laundry.

I swallowed a nervous laugh.

My hand was on the doorknob when a new thought coiled itself around my brain. Lots of people knew where Gina kept her key. Any of them could get into her apartment. Anyone and she'd *never* know.

After all, Gina was asking for trouble, putting that money in plain sight and never, ever using it. Leaving the key where anyone could get it. It would serve her right if I took her stash. Teach her to be more careful.

A steady calm descended on me. I opened the door a crack. No one. I pulled my apartment key out of my shirt pocket and grabbed the pitcher—keeping the weight close to my body. The pitcher slipped a bit across my sweaty palm. I shifted it against my forearm, wedging it close against my ribs. Closing the door behind me, I scooted across the hall, unlocked my apartment, and set down the pitcher. In seconds, I'd locked Gina's door and returned her key.

The pitcher fit under the kitchen sink behind the trash. I emptied my pocket and set aside enough quarters for laundry. I dropped the rest in the pitcher. What started as an impulse had turned into a calculated act. Was I going to do laundry with Gina's quarters? What about the rest of it? Wouldn't it look strange if I started buying stuff with lots of coins? But I couldn't return it now. I mean, what if someone walked by or Gina came back and caught me?

How much was it? Eighty dollars? A hundred? It couldn't be enough to hurt Gina. I'd count it tonight to know for sure. Last week, I'd seen a pretty pair of black high heels on display. With the extra cash, I might be able to afford them.

I was ready to leave, purse in hand, when I heard a loud knocking.

"Jenny? Are you home?" Gina's voice came through the door.

If I stayed quiet, maybe she'd give up and leave.

"Jenny!" Gina's voice rose sharply. "It's an emergency!"

I opened the door. Gina's face looked red and blotchy—only her freckles were unchanged, light brown specks. "Someone stole my change! Did you hear anything? Did you see anyone in the hall?"

The intensity of her emotion startled me. "Your change?"

"Yeah, my pitcher full of change! I was doing my laundry, and when I came back it was gone."

"How could it be gone?" I stalled.

"Someone must've used my key." She hit herself on the forehead with the palm of her hand. "I am so stupid. Stupid! Stupid! Stupid!"

"Whoa, don't hit yourself like that."

"I kept meaning to roll all the quarters—the bank won't take them unless they're in rolls. I kept putting it off and putting it off. There must be four hundred dollars in there."

"What? That much?"

She nodded vigorously. "There goes my furniture."

"Huh?" I couldn't imagine what her furniture had to do with it.

"I bought my furniture with no down payment, no interest for six months. In a couple of weeks, I have to pay for it." She crossed her arms, her shoulders hunched in misery.

"But you have money—you must have money with those designer clothes," I said.

"Nope—they were a lucky find at a garage sale."

I felt queasy and ashamed for taking Gina's money, but I couldn't bring myself to own up to it. "Your parents will help you out, right?"

Gina looked at me as if I were out of my mind. "They kicked me out. I'm on my own."

Now that I thought about it, she never talked about her family. "Sorry, Gina," I said. I was a terrible person. As bad as I felt about what I'd done, I was terrified of what would happen if I confessed.

"Thanks for listening. I just had to tell someone." Gina sighed. "Maybe I should call the police."

"No," I said quickly. This situation was escalating out of control. I could take only small, shallow breaths. "You didn't see anything. What could the police do?"

She shrugged. "Check for fingerprints. Look for hairs. Isn't that what they do on TV?"

"I guess." My fingerprints must be everywhere—on the doorframe, the key, the doorknob. But Gina had slid her hand on the doorframe, held the key, touched the doorknob. Did that erase my fingerprints? I didn't know.

I had to distract her.

"Are you sure they're gone?" I muttered.

"What?"

"You know, whoever took the money. What if he's still there, hiding?"

Gina's eyes went wide. "Stop it, you're scaring me! I went inside. You think he was there the whole time? I'm calling the cops." Gina slipped her phone out of her pocket.

My heart pounded. I'd made things worse, not better. "No," I said sharply. "That doesn't make sense because if he took it, why would he stay? It's fine. I'm sure it's fine. Tell you what, I'll go with you."

Gina's hand was shaking, so I took the key and unlocked her door. I stuck my head in the apartment. "I don't see anyone." She followed me in and watched while I checked the closet and the bathroom. "Nobody."

Gina let out a sigh of relief. "I feel so much better. Stupid, but better."

"Um, Gina, I could help you out a little. I mean if you're really stuck."

She shook her head. "That's okay. I'll call Heather. She's been trying to unload her hours. If I work double shifts, I bet I can cover the minimum payment. It was sweet of you to offer though." She gave me a quick hug. "You're such a good friend, Jenny. Don't ever change."

Her words followed me home to my apartment. Gina thought I was a good friend. Didn't want me to change. But I had. Changed into a thief. A thief who stole from a friend—maybe my only real friend—and lied as if I'd been doing it all my life.

I left a message at work that I would be home sick tomorrow. It took a long time to count the coins. I put the quarters in ten-dollar stacks and the nickels and dimes into dollar piles. I didn't bother with the pennies. Without them, the total came to $493.60. My hands were grubby from handling the money, and tidy stacks of coins covered the counter.

At the bank, the teller handed me flat paper rolls for quarters, nickels, and dimes. I went back to my apartment and filled the rolls, adding my account number on each, the only way they'd exchange the coins for bills.

"In case you made an error," the teller had explained. They'd take the difference out of my account.

☃

Life changes you. You learn things about yourself, things you wish you didn't know. And you can't erase that knowledge. I'll never be the person I used to be—the person I thought I was. I sealed $500 in bills in an envelope, wrote Gina's name on it, and went downstairs to the mailboxes. No one saw me slip the money into her box, a silent thief in the night.

THE DOE

MARLENE AUGUSTINE-GARDINI

For more than a week, the wildfires burned. The air hung in layers of soot and ash and particles of people's lives—a charred family photo here, a blackened edge of a utility bill there.

Emma stepped out of the house and glanced at the struggling sunrise. The bruised sun was smeared in the gray sky. Even so, her focus was on the form across the field. *It was never a good day for a burial*, she thought. But the doe was dead. It had died a long, heat-seared week ago.

Ever since the fires broke out, Emma had felt helpless and scared. At least burying the doe was something she could do, a small act she had control over in all the chaos.

She had first come across the small deer propped up against the fence and resting under a tree in the shade of 90-degree heat. The dogs had been barking, and Emma went to reel them in.

She and the doe startled each other. Emma spoke softly and slowly backed away. She hoped the deer wouldn't panic, but the animal rose as if to flee. Exhaustion overcame fear, and the doe slumped down against the chain link fence. White foam circled her mouth. Pieces of her fur had been burned away giving her the look of an old, moth-chewed stole. Emma wanted to comfort her but knew it would only cause more fear and pain.

The doe had made it out of the fires, but the fires had stayed with her. Trying to outrun this twist in nature destroying her world, she had torn through flaming branches and scorched her lungs with waves of burning leaves.

Emma left her to make calls for help.

"We're so sorry, but no one is available for this right now. We're moving animals out of the fires."

"But . . . you don't understand. I can't reach her. She's so scared. And she's . . . she's in pain. She's hurt. Please! I don't know what to do!"

"Ma'am, all we can suggest is that you give her some water. If she's still alive, call us tomorrow. We'll see what we can do. But most likely, we'd send someone out to destroy her. I'm sorry. I'm afraid all you can do is let nature take its course. I'm so sorry."

No one will help, Emma thought. *No one can.*

The dull ache in the pit of her stomach traveled through her body. The discovery of the doe had emptied the last ounce of her strength in grasping the reality of what was happening. Her world was being erased. She felt hollow as she watched the constant images on the TV of neighborhoods being transformed. Black sticks had once been trees. Melted mailboxes lay in front of piles of embers that were once her friends' homes.

The changing colors of the landscape numbed her. Once lush and green, things were now black and dead. She shook her head to dislodge the images and went back outside.

Emma filled a bucket of water and lowered it slowly over the fence near, but not too near, the doe. But the animal panicked, this time gathering enough energy to run across the field to lean, spent, against the chicken coop.

Emma watched the doe, and a heavy weight of resignation replaced her emptiness. There was nothing she could do—not for the doe, not for the burning houses, not for the charred land. In trying to help, she had frightened the doe out of the only patch of shade in the field.

The deer had run in pain and fear to get to this place—away from the heat of hell.

And now, I've taken away that bit of comfort too.

She went back inside, turned off the TV, and let the sadness fill her. She always cried easily in sorrow or with joy, but her tears had dried up in the heat. Now there was nothing to do but wait.

ℭ℥

With a cardboard-box coffin dangling from her hand, Emma made her way across the field. The dry grass crunched under her shoes like knuckles cracking. The carcass was still half-standing against the chicken coop, the bones as white as a tombstone angel.

The turkey vultures made wistful passes overhead, circling again and again, but the skeleton had been picked clean. Jigsaw-like pieces were scattered about. Emma slowly gathered what feral cats, crows, and hawks had not carried away. Placing the bones in the box, she marveled at how each tiny piece had once fit together to form a creature that could leap over a fence with the fluidity of water over river stones.

She dug a hole, hacking away at the drought-hardened dirt,

each shovelful devoid of the damp, rich, ripe-smelling earth that worms love to live in. She thought about this time last year—working in the garden—an abundance of vegetables and lush flowers. And now, the earth was dry and dead in one long angry blast.

As the hole grew, the enormity of the destruction of lives and land blew through her like a blowtorch. She tried to catch her breath as she set the box in place and covered it with soil. Using her hands instead of the shovel, she felt lighter with each handful of dirt that sifted through her fingers.

Rain. It sounds like rain.

Emma had almost forgotten that sound. The stiff soil and pebbles hitting the cardboard pattered like a downpour. It was the first time she had smiled in a long while.

It was as if the simple burial of this small creature could be the final, cleansing act in this tragedy. The carcass, like the shell of a burned-out house, once framed life. Now, it was time to bury and move on.

She realized that the doe had waited for death to envelop her. No matter how far or fast she ran or how safe she thought she was, nature would ultimately take its course. Fires, storms, and floods would change the face of the land and the creatures there. Nature would win in the end.

Emma knew her world had changed and would change again. It would rain. Things would grow. A doe would be born, and it would die. And she would have to go on, letting nature take its course.

She patted the dirt over the small grave, hesitated, and then turned to leave—barely missing the sprout of green pushing its way through the soil.

THE BATHING SUIT

SANDY BAKER

"Hey, Bobby," she purred. "Wanna see my new bathing suit?"

"Wha . . . ?" Bobby looked up to see sixteen-year-old Susie, her eyes fixated on him while she ignored his two buddies beside him on the bus bench. Like a cowgirl calf-roping queen, she zeroed in on her target and cut him from the herd.

"It's almost summer, and I got a new swimsuit. Wanna see?"

"Well, I dunno, we're just sittin' here shootin' the breeze. I guess. Okay. Where is it?"

The Memorial Day weekend was dripping with hot Pennsylvania humidity, a yawning introduction to the bucolic summer days ahead. Bus benches sat on two diagonal corners of this one-stoplight town, a draw for the teens who hung out at the popular drugstore soda shop. Fords, Chevys, and farm-boy pickup trucks trolled the street, their drivers hoping to catch a glimpse of girls sauntering to the annual patriotic parade kickoff.

"C'mon," she said, reaching out her hand. Fine hair glistened on her bare arms in the bright sun; thin cotton shorts barely covered her cheeks. Tendrils of streaked blonde hair swept around her face, almost concealing the triumphant smile forming at the corners of her Revlon "Love That Red" lips. Her hazel sloe eyes never left his.

"Okay, guys, see ya in a while," Bobby said. "I'll meetcha in the drugstore." He ran one hand briefly over his Brylcreemed crew cut and turned around to give a shrug to his friends.

Following high school, Bobby had filled out his six-feet-one lanky frame, exposing well-defined biceps and calves from years of baseball and tennis. A star athlete, this scrawny teen had morphed into a handsome, though shy, twenty-year-old college engineering student.

"Let's go, Bobby. My mom's not home right now," she whispered. She tugged his hand and led him up the stairs to the apartment she and her mom shared above the bookshop.

Bobby's gaze swept around the sparsely furnished living–kitchen area. *Wow, I'd get claustrophobia here*, he decided, thinking about his own home where his mom and dad, older sister, and twin brother and sister lived in middle-class comfort. With university classes finished for the summer, he'd returned home and would soon work at his father's surveying and construction company.

"You sit right there and wait," Susie said as she sashayed toward the back bedroom. After a few minutes, she called, "Hey, Bobby, c'mon back. I'm ready." Her singsong voice was a seductive Homeric siren.

"What the . . . ?"

Susie stood naked, facing the doorway and twirling her bikini in one hand while beckoning him with the other. She walked toward him, determined to snare her prey.

Bobby, eyes bugged out, stumbled backward. "What are you doing? You're crazy!"

"C'mon, give me a little kiss," she said, pulling him down onto her bed. "Just one little kiss. It won't hurt anything." She took his hand and placed it on her breast.

"Wait. I don' wanna do this," Bobby protested and tried to pull away from her legs now wrapped around his. "This isn't right. I gotta girlfriend."

"Oh, ignore her," said Susie. "You know how crazy I am about you. I'm so right for you." She slowly breathed in his Aqua Velva aftershave lotion as she nibbled his shoulder. "Mmm."

Bobby writhed at her touch as she held his arm tight with one hand and ran her other one under his shirt. She found the elastic waist of his tennis shorts easy to maneuver and slipped her hand under the loose fabric.

"Quit it, girl," he said. "I'm not doin' this. For cripes sakes, your mother's coming. I heard the door open downstairs. Let go!" He yanked her hand out of his shorts and tried to leap off the bed.

Susie wrapped her legs around his, pulling him off balance and back down.

"Bobby!" Susie's mother stormed into the bedroom. The two lay tangled on the bed, Susie giggling as she clung onto Bobby, one leg still holding him.

"What are you doing with my daughter?" Suzie's mother screamed. "Leave her alone! Get out of here!"

"Me? I wasn't doing nothin'. Your little slut daughter came at me naked. I never touched her."

"Well, we'll see about that, won't we?" said the mom. "You'll pay for this."

Susie grinned and arched her back like a cat while giving her stomach a gentle pat.

Bobby exploded out of the room, down the stairs, and raced over to meet Freddie and Kenny at the drugstore. *Oh, God, how stupid, I'm twenty, she's sixteen*! *What have I done? Nothing!* With pounding heart and perspiring palms, he sank down next to the guys at the marble counter and ordered his favorite. Cherry Coke.

"No, no, no," said Bobby, cradling his forehead with both hands.

"What happened to you?" Freddie asked. "You look like you seen a ghost or something."

"Maybe I have, maybe it didn't happen, maybe I imagined it." Hyperventilating, he considered the possible variations of that last scene. "My mind is jumbled, but I'll try to tell ya."

Freddie and Kenny's jaws hung slack listening to him.

"Oh, yeah, stupid," Kenny said. "She's been eyeing you for a long time."

"Where were your brains, Bobby?" asked Freddie.

☙

The passing summer days seemed idyllic for Bobby, who'd reunited with his longtime girlfriend, Debbie, after his second year away at university. They first met when she was a blossoming eighth grader. Her infectious smile, long blonde hair, and endless legs reeled him in for life. Both worked long hours during the summer and were inseparable in the evenings, going to a picture show or to the record store for the latest 45-rpm rock-n-roll hit. They practiced their jitterbug and lindy hop dance moves at Debbie's home and drove in his green and black '55 Ford stick to the Friday night canteen dances in the next town.

But for those three months, a little echo of a threat kept worming its way into Bobby's brain, reminding him of those few minutes on the bed with Susie. Her mother warned he "would pay" for his indelicate moment with her daughter. *What did that mean? I gotta tell Debbie about it. It was nothing, right?*

Susie telephoned Bobby almost daily, but he refused to speak with her. She sat on the bus stop bench, hoping he'd come hang out with his buddies. She tried talking with Freddie and Kenny, but they snubbed her. "Please," she begged, "ask him to call me." She frequented the soda shop, praying he'd be there.

Summer sped by. In late August, Bobby prepared to return to his senior year in Tennessee. "Don't forget to write," he said. Long hugs and meaningful kisses sealed the pact as he and Debbie left in different directions for their universities.

"Wait for me, Bobby," Debbie said. "We're for real now."

A week later, he called Debbie long distance from his university 700 miles to the south. "Hullo, this is Bobby." His voice quivered. "Deb, I gotta marry Susie. Her mother and my father are forcing me. She claims she's three months pregnant and accused me of being the father . . . but I didn't touch her, I swear. Hullo, Baby, you there?"

"No, Bobby, this can't be," she said. With the fifteen-foot-long telephone cord extended to its fullest, she paced her dorm room, kicking shoes and slamming books off her desk. "Let's elope. Marry me quick so it can't happen."

"Debbie, they're making me. A lawyer's involved. I didn't tell you 'cause I thought it was nothin'."

He called his father again. "Pop, I didn't, I wouldn't, and besides, I wasn't up to . . . you know what I mean," Bobby explained. "I had clothes on; nothing happened. It's a setup."

"Well now, son, we all know about what goes on with a young man in the presence of a naked girl, don't we?" said his father. "Do you want to be arrested for statutory rape? Can you even imagine the scandal? Do you want to go to jail? Think of the family."

"You gotta believe me, Pop. I didn't do anything," Bobby said. "Please, please don't make me marry her. I didn't get her pregnant. I swear to God. I've never even done it, ever."

"You *will* marry her," said Bobby's father, "and I will pay the hospital expenses and child support while you finish college. You'll work at school and in the summer to repay me after you graduate. The lawyer has arranged the civil ceremony for the last weekend in September. Get back up here and accept your responsibility."

"I never touched her, Pop, honest. I want a paternity test."

"The girl and her lawyer will not allow a paternity test," said his father.

"Don't you think that's suspicious, Pop?"

"It's done, Bobby. Our family is too highly regarded in the community and our church for you not to accept what you did. We do the right thing. If you try disappearing, they'll send the sheriff after you. You *will* marry that girl."

That September weekend, head down, shoulders slumped, Bobby shuffled into the little courtroom. He walked out after mumbling only "I do." Susie smiled at her "I do" and took the Larwin surname in "shotgun-wedding" fashion. Only Susie's mother and Mr. Larwin attended as witnesses.

Susie, with bulging belly and billowing dress, raced out and caught Bobby before he jumped into his car to head back to college. "Bobby, Bobby, it's you and me. I've dreamed about us for years. We can make a life. Can't we please try? I'm better for you than that Debbie any day. Take me down to Tennessee with you."

"Girl, we were never going to be together. I've never given you a second thought. If you thought accusing me of being the father would make me love you, you were dead wrong."

"Well, you're mine anyway. Ha, you'll never see that snotty Debbie again."

In November, Susie gave birth to triplets, each weighing five-plus pounds. A tiny announcement buried in the social pages of the local newspaper noted the "premature births of triplets to Mr. and Mrs. Robert Larwin while he was away at his university." Despite the marriage, the small town and regional high school were agog with scandalous rumors.

"Bobby Larwin and Susie?"

"He's four years older."

"Oh yeah, he's a college man, and she's just a kid."

"She's always been kinda loose."

"What happened with Debbie?"

"We thought Bobby and Debbie were an item."

"He's been away at college."

"He got screwed."

"No, she did."

"Something don't seem right."

"I know another guy at school who had to marry a girl too."

"You gotta watch out these days."

"Pop, count back nine months to February or March," Bobby pleaded on the phone. "It proves that I didn't father those three full-term babies. They're five pounders. She was way pregnant before I even got home from college."

"Multiple births run in our family, and it pretty much confirms you are the father," said his dad whose word was final in the Larwin family. "It's done."

"There's no way you'll ever get a paternity test from me and my girls, Bobby," Susie said after the babies were born. "I warned that you were mine, and that stuck-up ice maiden Debbie would never have you. We could have made a good life together."

"I'm divorcing you, you lying bitch," Bobby said. "Find yourself another sugar daddy."

Bobby's siblings and Debbie's parents did not believe him. Only Debbie—but Bobby was off limits to her.

"I can't hang out with you," Debbie said. "You're a married man. It's goodbye for us. I can't take it. I blew my first semester finals and started smoking. Our time came and went."

Bobby struggled with his lost dream of a life with Debbie.

Some years later, Bobby, by then divorced from Susie, returned to his hometown for his father's funeral.

After the services his mother said, "I believed you, son, but I couldn't say anything. Pop forbade me."

"Great. Thanks, Mom. All Dad cared about was his own reputation, not what it did to me. At least it's comforting to know someone in the family believed me. Lotta good it did."

"He ordered us not to question his decision—we were tormented. I'm so sorry, Bobby."

"Well, there's a special place in hell for Pop. I'll never forgive him. But thanks for finally telling me, Mom. Love you," he said with a hug. "Things could've been so different."

"Don't be hard on him, son. He was just trying to do the right thing."

In a call to the Larwin home, Susie said, "Sorry about your father, Bobby. He was very generous to us. I heard he disinherited you. But maybe that's what you get for not sticking with me."

"I hope he goes straight to hell and you too," said Bobby. "I ruined my life, you ruined my life, and Pop ruined my life. It could have been different—but not with you. And I lost Debbie."

"I warned you," Susie laughed. "For a boy of twenty, you were so naïve. I didn't want to hurt you, but I would have been so good for you."

Decades later, the two met again at a coffee shop in that same one-stoplight town. Bobby confronted Susie. "How come you never acknowledged the real father? Everyone knew it was that pathetic Roy Sylvestri when they saw him sniffing around you. With their dark hair and olive skin, those three look just like him. You probably figured he was too poor, huh?"

Susie looked away from Bobby and rapidly blinked her watering eyes. Gaining control, she brushed back her wispy gray hair with the come-on pose of a sixteen-year-old.

"It wasn't so much that he was poor. It was because I loved you, Bobby. It took me years to admit you'd never be mine, and that I did you wrong," she said. "I'm sorry. I guess my fantasy got the best of me. We coulda been good, but no. At least I was Mrs. Larwin for a while, and that Debbie never was."

"Maybe there's forgiveness for you somewhere," said Bobby, "but not from me."

THE MERCENARY: A SMOKEWOOD FOLKTALE

BETH E. LEWIS

It was said King Fus Teen had an aversion to the ancient right of audience, and that he especially disliked people who killed for money. Perhaps that's why he shifted so on his cushions the day I first saw him. He was watching me, judging me. Yet, he looked surprised. Perhaps he expected someone arrogant or evil. Mercenaries are commonly one or both. I, on the other hand, approached him with honor, seeking justice, not the norm for a man who has made a career of killing for gold. I could only hope he would take my word to heart.

My name is La Rama, and I am a mercenary. My story starts three days before the spring equinox six years ago, all because I wanted Jincaro boughs for the festival. My parents had always forbidden me from leaving our village, but I had heard there was a large Jincaro tree upriver, so on the next night with no moon, I made my way there, trying to remain hidden. I was young, barely eighteen, and I had no idea of the transparency of my plan.

As I approached the tree, I heard noises—not just voices, but singing, shouting, musical instruments, and other sounds of celebration. Boys of all ages were hanging among the branches of the Jincaro, quickly cutting bud-studded twigs and tossing them down to those waiting below. I stood, stunned at my stupidity. Why had I thought I would be the only one?

A young woman grabbed my hand and pulled me into the crowd. "Cut me a branch, handsome stranger," she begged.

She was the most beautiful woman I had ever laid eyes on. I was young and naive in the knowledge of the matchmaking qualities of the Jincaro blossoms, so I didn't know why the only thought in my mind was to please her. In an instant, I was up above the other boys cutting her an enormous bough.

I dropped it into the young woman's waiting arms and cut a few more for my own family. I looked down to give her the rest to hold, but she was nowhere to be seen. I felt a moment of despair; a creature as lovely as she must belong to some deserving man. I stuffed the boughs into my shirt and made my way back down the trunk.

When I reached the bottom, I was handed a cup of ale and a hunk of bread. I turned to say my thanks and saw it was the girl. She looked into my eyes and said, "I am Li Ana, and it is I who should be thanking you."

I was elated, embarrassed, and proud all at once, but before I could make sense of those emotions, she added another by kissing me on the lips. I was swimming in confusion. I had never kissed a girl before. I reciprocated, and before I knew it, one thing led to another, and we ran off together into the forest.

We lay together and afterward dozed in the warm moonlight. When I awoke, she was dressed and about to leave. I called to her, and she turned, a tear in her eye. I asked her what was wrong. She confessed to never having been with a man before. She too had been overwhelmed by the Jincaro. She told me her father would kill her if he found out.

I urged her to come with me if she feared her father, but she refused. I told her the way to my home if she changed her mind, and we parted ways.

I told my parents what had taken place. They were angry I had disobeyed them, but when I explained how thoughts of Li Ana consumed my every moment, waking and sleeping, my father told me about the enthralling drug in the Jincaro blossoms. I had fallen hopelessly in love, and nothing could ever break that bond. I packed a bag and set out to find my Li Ana.

Upon arriving at her home, I saw a woman sitting next to the well, weeping piteously. The door to the house stood open. Emboldened by my love and curiosity, I entered. A man sat counting a stack of gold coins. Each time he finished counting, he started over.

I watched him for some time before I realized he had no idea I was there and would probably go on counting and recounting forever. I loudly cleared my throat to gain his attention. He said she was gone. He called her a whore and said he'd sold her to Ka Zeer, the Slaver.

I stood staring at him. I couldn't believe he'd called my beloved Li Ana a whore and had sold her into slavery. I ran, not knowing where I was going, but the One God led me in the right direction. After several days, I arrived at the outskirts of a city. I'd never been near a town before, and it was overwhelming. As I walked the streets, merchants of all kinds approached me, including those selling their bodies and even some wanting to buy mine.

I searched out Ka Zeer the Slaver's stall and looked over all the poor girls he offered, and I wondered if I'd even recognize my true love. I closed my eyes a moment and knew that her tender gaze and rosy lips were imprinted in my mind for all eternity. I described her to the slaver, and he told me she had fetched a pretty price.

I was desperate, and I threatened him. He told me he had sold her to Kala Rad, the Goldsmith, and told me where he lived. When I arrived there, Kala Rad refused to see me, so I snuck in through the garden. The steward caught me and brought me to an audience chamber where I found a well-dressed and equally well-fed Kala Rad.

I told him my story, and he laughed at me. He told me she was his property, and if I wanted to redeem her I would have to pay him ten times the price he'd paid. He said he'd been training her in the ways of the flesh and that had increased her value. He winked and made a vulgar gesture. I would have killed him, but I had enough sense to know I'd never get out alive. I had to stay alive for her sake, to get her away from him.

I told him I'd be back and went to look for a way to amass the fortune he demanded. I prayed hard to the One God to show me a way, and before I turned the next corner, I ran into a lord searching for recruits to help him win back his homeland. The pay was good, and I was young and strong. He told me he would train me to kill.

It seemed like a good deed at the time, helping this man recover what had been ruthlessly stolen from him. I fought hard for him, gaining strength and skill. It took almost six years before I discovered his true intentions. It turned out the homeland he had spoken of wasn't his. He was greedy and was waging war to enlarge his holdings. When I realized how I was being used, I demanded my pay and left. I realized too late I had not earned the price I needed, but I was through with killing.

That brought me to the capital where I exercised the ancient right of audience to tell the King my story. I had been a fool, naive in the ways of the world and the cruelty bred there. I couldn't give back the lives I had stolen, but I could try to save the one that meant so much to me. I beseeched the King to stop the senseless killing and to end slavery.

He threw it back at me, telling me it was I who must carry the sword in his name, I who must shut down the slave markets. I implored him to find someone else; I had an obligation even closer to my heart to fulfill.

At daybreak, I headed for the city where my beloved Li Ana was enslaved, pressing my horse as hard as he could go to the house where my dear Li Ana was held captive. I pounded on the door. Though the steward did not recognize me, I quickly gained entry and an audience.

Panic spread across Kala Rad's face when he recognized the hardened soldier who stood before him. Greed filled his soul while fear consumed his bowels. He took what I offered and sent me to the slave quarters to collect Li Ana. She was nowhere to be found. I charged back into the audience hall where Kala Rad sat, now flanked by a dozen armed guards. He laughed and said she'd died years ago. She wasn't nearly as much fun as he'd thought she would be.

I fell to my knees, sobbing. When I had no tears left to shed, I took a ragged breath and rose. On my way out, I almost tripped over a little girl sweeping the hallway.

"What are you doing?" I asked.

"Cleaning," she responded.

"A tiny thing like you? You should still be in your mother's lap, playing with dolls, not sweeping for the likes of him."

She sniffled and went back to sweeping. On an impulse, I grabbed her by the arm. She bit her lip to keep from crying out. I thought she must have been taught to be quiet, although she didn't look afraid. Remembering my strength, I loosened my grip and led her to the door.

"Where are you going?" the steward demanded, stepping in front of me.

"Home," I responded, pushing the man out of my way.

"You can't take her!" he yelled after me.

"I paid plenty for her. Just try to stop me." I slammed the door.

I lifted her onto my horse and left. When we reached the outskirts of the city, I heard her muffled sobs. I stopped the horse, thinking the little girl must be frightened. After all, I'd taken her from her home. I told her I was sorry and asked her if she wanted me to take her back.

A terrified look came across her face. She pinched her lips shut and shook her head frantically.

"Are you sure?" I asked, grinning.

She barely nodded her head.

"Then you can come with me. My name's La Rama," I told her.

A look of astonishment came over her face. "M . . . m . . . my name is Ja Rama," she answered.

"Then we must be destined to be friends. How long have you been a slave?"

She shrugged.

She couldn't have been much more than five years of age. I couldn't believe someone could enslave a child. That was the moment I knew I would be her champion. I had been responsible for Li Ana becoming a slave. Perhaps by rescuing this waif, I could somehow atone for it.

I turned my horse toward home and began to tell Ja Rama my tale. When she became sleepy, I mounted up behind her and searched for a suitable spot to make camp. We passed several days this way before we reached the house of my youth.

Along the way, we passed the clearing where the Jincaro stood. I showed her the limb where I had cut the bough of blossoms for my dead wife. "Little good it did in the end," I complained. I felt terrible when I realized I had made her cry again. I lifted her down, and we made camp one last night.

The next morning, I asked her if she was afraid to meet my parents. She looked at me, uncertainty in her huge brown eyes. I tousled the mop of tangled curls that adorned her head and winked. I said, "I'll protect you, never fear. Don't forget I'm a trained mercenary of the seventh degree."

Her eyes almost widened, but she smiled at me. I vaulted up behind her and turned my horse homeward.

We could see from some distance a woman at the well in front of the house. At first, I thought it must be my mother, but there was something different about the way she moved. I urged my horse forward.

The woman finished filling her bucket and turned at the sound of hoof-beats. My heart jumped into my throat when I saw it was my Li Ana. I launched myself out of the saddle and then halted when I caught the fear in her eyes.

"Don't you know me?" I asked.

"La Rama?" she responded, her face pale with shock. "You're alive!"

"As are you!" I cried as I threw my arms around her. I spun her around, and she kissed me again and again.

My parents came out and greeted me. My father lifted Ja Rama out of the saddle and gently set her down, straightening her clothes, and brushing her off. "You have much to explain, son," he told me. "Who is this child you've brought to us in such a sorry state?"

"She was a slave in the household where I went to rescue Li Ana. When I got there, Kala Rad the Goldsmith told me Li Ana was dead. I felt sorry for the little waif, so I took her."

Li Ana stepped closer, looking the little girl over carefully. "I gave birth while I was a slave. The midwife told me my baby had died and gave me herbs to make me appear dead; she then smuggled me out of the city," Li Ana said, stroking the girl's cheek. "I know you by your smile. You are my child."

"Then Kala Rad was her father?" I asked.

"She looks exactly like you," my mother said, searching my face.

I looked from my mother to my father and then to Li Ana for an answer.

"I discovered I was with child soon after I was sold into slavery. I waited for you, but you didn't come."

"I've been searching for you since the moment I lost you. I'm here now," I said, taking her hand and Ja Rama's. I led them to a home I knew I must soon leave to fulfill another obligation close to my heart. I would return to the capital to lead the righteous army of King Fus Teen against the general who had tricked me, return the lands to their rightful owners, and free the slaves who had saved my family.

SECURITY AT THE INN

BELINDA RIEHL

The calm bay and the receding fog should have lifted Eddy's mood, but as he drove south, each switchback of Highway 1 invited him to go straight—straight off the cliff. He looked at the edges ahead to be sure his flight would land at the bottom by the sea, not just a few feet down an embankment. He wanted the end to be swift, but he realized this option had too many variables.

Eddy pulled his ten-year-old Ford pickup into one of the view lots, turned off the engine, and left the keys in the ignition. From the toolbox behind the seat, he removed his loaded service weapon, a 9mm Glock semi-automatic handgun, the one the Sonoma County Sheriff's Department had let him buy when he'd retired eight years earlier. He kept it clean and in working order because that's what you do when you're a cop. With the gun wedged in his Levi's waistband covered by his flannel shirttail, he hiked down the hill to a spot where no one could see him. He sat in the dirt and looked past the surf out to the horizon—a pleasant final view.

His gaze lifted to the clouds. As if he could see his wife Maggie's blue eyes and sweet smile, Eddy spoke to her.

"If there is a heaven, I know you're there. Don't know if I'll be seein' you." He shifted his weight to stretch out his legs and looked at his hands in his lap. "I'm awful tired, and I'm sorry. Promised you I'd stay sober. For five years before the fires, I did. I felt you in every room—where you cooked, did your artwork, wrote your stories. It's been three years since our house burned down, and I haven't been sober since. I can't jump through the hoops with FEMA, the city, and the county. Keep thinking I'll get it together next week, next month, but it's not goin' to happen. For what?" He reached into his waistband. "You know I'll love you forever with every part of my being."

Eddy gripped his gun and put the muzzle to the roof of his mouth. *Swerved to miss a fuckin' deer and killed my wife, for chrissake.* He closed his eyes and heard a horrific crash of metal against metal. His mind flashed to the sound of the tree bending the door in on Maggie. Realizing the sound wasn't in his head, he jerked to look over his left shoulder and saw a cloud of dust; the sound of another crash came from below the edge of the roadway. He stood for a better view. In a split second, he shoved the gun into the back of his pants and sprinted across the parking lot toward the accident. He'd always been a good runner even for a muscular guy.

From the looks of the wrecked front end of the Mercedes across the road and the sedan off the cliff, they'd hit head-on. The car down the embankment had a dented roof from the rollover but had landed on its wheels. The caved-in front and back doors on the driver's side faced Eddy as he slid down the hill and climbed over rocks. He reached through the broken window to turn off the car and checked the woman's pulse. She was alive.

"Ma'am, can you hear me?" He could see a child in a car seat in the back. Gently shaking the woman's arm, he shouted, "Hey, you all right?"

The woman stirred as she became conscious. "My baby! Is she okay?"

Eddy didn't answer. *Hope she's asleep.* Smoke from the engine had begun to seep in under the dash the way his car had smoldered after the accident with Maggie. The smell made his hands shake.

"Can you move your legs?" Eddy asked.

The mother shifted in her seat and nodded. He unhooked her seatbelt. Unable to open her door, he broke away the jagged edge of the glass with his elbow and helped her climb through the window.

"We have to get my daughter out." Her voice trembled just short of a scream.

Blood dripped from her nose. Eddy pulled a handkerchief from his back pocket and handed it to her. "Wipe your bloody nose and sit down," he said, pointing to a rock out of his way.

Thickening smoke pushed Eddy to move faster. Afraid to break the window toward the girl, Eddy could pull the door open only a few inches. Anchoring his back on the fender with his feet pressing against the inside of the door, he pushed with all his weight. Creaking but submitting, the door opened enough for Eddy to reach the straps of the car seat. The little girl started to cry. *That's a good sign.*

The blonde, curly-haired child looked much like his youngest five-year-old granddaughter. "You'll be in Mommy's arms in just a minute." His words of reassurance spoke to his own nerves as well as the child's fear. *Fuckin' car seat restraints—how do you get these goddamn things undone?* He could hear sirens approaching, none too soon.

Eddy and the little girl were coughing. "Hurry! I see flames," the mother cried.

Behind him, Eddy could hear the firemen sliding down the hill. They didn't have to ask him to step aside. Last time he followed their lead was October 8, 2017, when they'd pounded on his door to tell him he had only minutes before the fire would be roaring down his street.

The adrenaline that had pumped him into action to help this mother and child began to fade. By the time the firemen pulled the girl from the smoking car, Eddy had no strength left to get up the hill.

"Hey, man, you did a hell of a job," the rescuer said. "You must be exhausted. Grab the end of this rope," allowing Eddy some dignity as he, too, was rescued. Eddy appreciated the classic image three feet above him—the back of a yellow helmet, heavy khaki jacket, and baggy pants hanging over dirty boots. At the top of the hill, one of the uniforms asked Eddy if he needed medical attention.

"No. Take care of the lady and her kid." As soon as the words left his mouth, the car below exploded. Everyone ducked from pure instinct. The firemen moved into place with their powerful nozzles as Eddy slowly walked back to his truck.

"Hey, can we get your name as a witness?" someone yelled.

Eddy kept walking, ignoring the question. *I didn't see a thing.* By the time he reached his truck, his legs were so weak he could barely get in the door. When he sat in the seat, his gun poked him in the back. He pulled it out, looked at it as though he'd never seen it before, and tossed it in the glove box.

He sat in the truck trying to get his bearings as the ambulance pulled away with the mother and her daughter. The sirens and adrenaline sent his mind back eight years to 2012 when he and Maggie were on their way to the hospital after the accident. Eddy cupped her limp hand between both of his as he tried to ignore the blood seeping through the bandage on her head. "You're going to be fine," he said, hoping beyond reality. "We're almost there, honey.

Stay with me." Eddy made a deal with God to stay sober, but He took her anyway.

␣

Eddy found a little hotel on the ocean side of the highway where the rhythm of the waves crashing during the night helped him sleep. The next morning, he devoured his breakfast at the coffee shop a short walk down the road. Thoughts of the near death of a mother and her child kept returning. He hadn't allowed himself to think about the moment before the accident until he remembered his gun. He would stash it back in the toolbox right after breakfast.

"Can I get you anything else?" a waitress asked.

The starched apron skirt and thick rubber-soled shoes in his peripheral vision didn't match the soft voice. He looked at her nametag. From his years in law enforcement, Eddy used a person's name whenever he could.

"More coffee," he said, looking up at her pretty face. "And a cinnamon roll, warm with butter, Ellen. Do you mind if I call you Ellen?"

"Not at all, as long as I can do the same?"

"I might not answer to Ellen, but you can call me Eddy." They both chuckled. When she turned to fill his order, the sensation of his own smile surprised him. His eyes followed her until she passed under a TV showing a blackened, mangled car being dragged up a hill at the coast.

A little girl in a hospital bed filled the next screen. Her mother standing by her side spoke directly to the camera. The closed-caption ticker tape said, "We'd like to thank the man who saved our lives yesterday." The newscaster's words were printed, "If anyone can identify this Good Samaritan, please call, text, or email us at . . ." but Eddy had to look away.

I'm not a good anything. Can't even stay sober. Just did what came naturally after a lifetime as a cop.

Ellen set the roll with melted butter in front of Eddy and refilled his cup. Then she pivoted and sat across from of him. "You a passing tourist?"

Caught off guard, Eddy didn't know what to say; so many thoughts were running through his head at once. He enjoyed the sound of her voice and her graceful manner, even though she was a bit more forward than he was used to.

"I might be staying around a few days." He could extend his stay at the quiet little hotel where he'd slept so much better than he had for three years in his FEMA trailer parked at the fairgrounds. He'd been reminded that what used to be a thrill—the adrenaline rush produced by red lights and sirens—now took days to slough off. He'd retired after the accident that had killed Maggie and never once missed police work.

"I'd like to get to know you," she said, straightening the salt and pepper shakers.

Eddy took a sip of coffee. He'd forgotten how to be polite. His anger had monopolized his conversations since the wildfires. "This town's full of get-rich-quick contractors," Eddy had complained to his favorite bartender. "The sons of bitches moved in when people started rebuilding, and they'll be gone as soon as all the insurance money's spent."

When he didn't say anything to Ellen, she said, "I get off at three o'clock today."

Recognizing the opportunity for better company than he'd been keeping at the bar, he said, "Would you like to meet here for dinner? On second thought, you'd probably rather eat somewhere else."

With a smile in her voice, she said, "I'll meet you here at five-thirty, and I'll think about where I'd like to go for dinner if that's all right with you?"

"Sure. I'll be here." *This must mean something—I've smiled twice in fifteen minutes.*

⚃

He returned to his hotel and told the front desk clerk he'd be staying a few more days. In his room, he turned on the TV and saw the same crash story again, this time with sound. He learned the little girl was at UC San Francisco Children's Hospital. Another clip showed her saying, "That man who saved us is a hero. Please, mister, would you come see me? I made this picture for you." She held up a drawing of a sunny day at the beach with colorful blankets, a striped umbrella, and oversized smiles on the faces of a mother and child. Red hearts floated in the sky.

I'm no hero. The first responders would have been there in time, most likely. Okay, maybe I helped, but that don't make me a hero.

Eddy was thirsty for alcohol, but he could feel Maggie's presence. She would have said, "You did good, Eddy. Be proud of yourself. Accidents happen, and this time you were able to help. You don't always need to drink just because you're sentimental."

ơ3

He found a path down to the water and jogged along the hard, wet sand. It had been a long time since his heart had pumped this fast with healthy, oxygenated blood instead of adrenaline-filled emergency fuel. When he finally stopped to catch his breath, his hands on his knees, Eddy sensed that if Maggie were alive, she would offer him a second chance to keep his promise to stay sober. If she could forgive him, maybe in time he would forgive himself.

ơ3

Thoughts of the little girl in the hospital and the picture she'd drawn had interrupted his focus during his run. He didn't want to disappoint the child. With a quick shower, he had time to drive to the city before his dinner with Ellen.

When Eddy entered her hospital room, the little girl shouted, "Mommy, he came!"

He stood just inside the door holding a "Get Well Soon" balloon he'd picked up in the gift shop. "You were very brave," he said.

"No! You were," she insisted.

"I'm Eddy. What's your name?"

"I'm Samantha."

Eddy stepped up next to the bed, gently shook her small, soft hand and said, "Glad to meet you, Samantha. I hope you'll be out of here soon." He offered her the balloon string.

"I'm leaving tomorrow. The doctor said I had a 'cussion and needed to rest a few days, but I'm fine."

She directed Eddy to take the picture off the wall and laughed at the dramatic way he swung the drawing to his chest. "I'll keep this on my fridge where all good artwork should live," he said. It had been a while since he'd displayed this kind of playfulness with his grandchildren.

29

Eddy turned to Samantha's mother, who stood quietly in the corner, tears streaming down her cheeks. She walked around the bed to him. "Thank you from the bottom of my heart," she said as she reached around his broad shoulders and pulled him into a tight hug.

Embarrassed by the attention, he said, "Just came to collect my picture, ma'am."

"You saved my daughter's life," she whispered.

"Actually, she saved mine," he whispered back. With a smile at Samantha and a wave goodbye, he left.

Cʒ

When Eddy passed the front desk at his hotel, the manager asked if they could speak privately. "Here at The Inn by the Sea, we've been without security for a while. I apologize, but I happened to notice when you checked in that you had law enforcement I.D. Would you be interested in a part-time job? We can't afford much, but we'd give you the large room at the end of the hall with the kitchenette. You wouldn't have any specific hours; we just ask that you keep an eye out for us around here."

Eddy could hear Maggie saying, "Don't be a fool. Say yes."

He didn't hesitate long before he shook the manager's hand. "Thank you. I could use a change of scenery."

He had just enough time to freshen up before meeting Ellen for dinner. With warm water, he rinsed his razor and splashed soap off his face. In the mirror, Eddy saw a guy he hadn't seen in years.

30

ALL THINGS BRIGHT

JACK DOUGLASS FENDER

In ten minutes, at precisely 9 a.m., Bill Henry will have quit drinking alcohol for twelve years. By 9:05, he will step inside the door of The Gold Cane and order a beer.

Bill, a fifty-six-year-old reasonably well-off journalist, rose early. He showered, took a close shave, and then donned his favorite dark blue suit. An elegant white linen shirt with a deep green silk tie completed his ensemble. Before leaving for breakfast, he placed a charcoal-gray fedora on his head to cover his thinning hair.

He strolled through his neighborhood, his leisurely pace reflecting the way he felt. He was relaxed and content with the stability in his life, but most importantly, he was still sober.

Rounding the corner from Cole onto Haight, he witnessed one of those unexpectedly great San Francisco summer mornings. Ahead, in those places exposed to the direct rays of the sun, steam rose from the wet sidewalk. Bill looked down. Swirling about his ankles, fragile, wispy patterns of steam condensed onto the uppers of his soft, black leather loafers.

At Clayton he paused; he usually crossed Haight to the north side before walking to Ashbury. Once there, he always recrossed Haight before heading east to his favorite breakfast place. He did this to avoid walking past The Cane. However, today was different. He dared himself to keep walking straight ahead; his self-esteem was supreme today.

In the middle of the next block stood his old stomping ground, the place where he'd spent many years drinking himself into oblivion. When he was drunk, he was a pain in the ass, a know-it-all, class-A asshole. He drank heavily in an attempt to fool people from discovering that fact. However, most people he encountered back then knew straight off that he was an asshole. They just never revealed their opinion of him to his face. Fortunately for Bill, once he quit drinking, the need to fool people dissipated. He realized he wasn't such a bad person.

Bill paused in front of his old haunt; it was now 9 a.m. He gazed at the front entrance as he continuously fumbled with a bottle

31

cap. He held it in his right hand, which was thrust deep into his pants pocket. Rhythmically, he caressed the smooth face of the stamped metal closure with his thumb. After a measured pause, he would flip it over, rub the underside for a moment, and then flip it back again. Rub, flip, rub, flip. The top was devoid of any marking. Nothing remained of a label or logo. His constant rubbing kept it polished smooth and shiny.

From inside the bar, Jimmy the bar owner opened the door. With an affirming click, it latched itself to a corroded brass catch cemented into the red brick wall behind it. Jimmy then noticed Bill looking at him.

"Bill? Gee, I haven't seen you in years." He seemed to appraise Bill. "Not thinking of comin' in are ya?"

"Oh, no," Bill remarked. "I haven't crossed that threshold in twelve years."

"Well, good. You had me worried there for a minute." Jimmy eyed the rising sun. "Incredible morning, don't you think?" Without waiting for a response, he continued. "Well, good seeing ya. Have a great day." He turned and retreated into the dark interior of the bar.

Bill withdrew the cap from his pocket and flipped it into the air like a coin. The cap twisted, glinting and flashing as it rose, and then fell into his outstretched palm. Humming to himself, he continued flipping and catching the cap in the same rhythmic manner he'd used inside his pocket.

A few paces from where Bill stood, a lone starling pecked at some unseen treat in the dirt surrounding a stunted tree. The bird cocked its head and scrutinized him for a moment, possibly considering him a threat. Satisfied, the iridescently colored bird continued its investigation.

At that moment, Bill misjudged the fall of his cap; it glanced off his pinky finger and fell to the ground, bouncing before rolling on its side straight toward the wayward bird. The cap spun a few times before coming to rest, bottom-side up. The bird now turned its attention to the bright object, which lay at its feet. It pecked at the cap. These European interlopers are known to collect shiny objects. In addition, they are very adept at the mimicry of the human voice.

Bill was momentarily transfixed; his first thought was to rush forward and grab his prized possession. However, before he moved a step, the bird flew aloft to a lower branch of the tree, the cap grasped firmly in its beak.

"No!" Bill shouted. He rushed forward to stand beneath the branch on which the bird perched and jumped upward, flailing his arms, reaching fruitlessly for his bottle cap. The bird, in response, hopped to a higher branch. It peered down at him, seemingly to dare him to steal its newly claimed treasure.

Bill became frantic. He looked about, grasped a discarded soda can, and threw it straight at the feathered crook. His distress affected his aim, and the can rebounded off the branch and hit him squarely in the head. Stale remnants of coke spilled onto his neck, face, and shoulders. "Damn it, you little shit," he yelled, wiping his face with his suit sleeve. He turned a complete circle, hoping to glimpse the thief, but the starling was nowhere to be seen.

"Son of a bitch!" Bill screamed into empty space.

A man passing by gave him a sidelong glance. The stranger moved quickly to the other side of the sidewalk to avoid the "loony." Quickening his pace, the man cast a furtive look back over his shoulder as he scurried off.

Bill was at a loss for direction. He stood motionless, unable to accept that his cap was gone. Tears formed at the corner of each eye.

The cap had sealed the last bottle of beer that Bill had drunk and had saved him. It represented his triumph over booze. "Chips" to him were stupid tokens. Stamped out by the thousands, they were handed out at AA meetings to all and sundry. There was one for a day, a week, a month, a year, and so on. Their recipients treasured them as if they were talismans of power—a charm to ward off the demons of drink.

Bill's cap was different; it had stayed with him through the bad days and the good. The cap was unique. It had never left his possession. Sure, he had misplaced it on one or two occasions. Yet always, he'd found it again. This situation was different. This time, it was undeniably gone.

A voice spoke, "Make up your mind, in or out?" Bill's momentary lapse of awareness instantly disappeared as he turned around. A stranger gestured toward the open door of the bar. "So are ya going in?" Bill hadn't realized he was blocking the entrance to The Cane.

"Oh, sorry! No." Moving aside, Bill allowed the stranger to pass. From within, the sound of a familiar song came from the jukebox—Fats Waller's version of "Ain't Misbehavin'." The song evoked memories of nights spent seated on his favorite stool in the window. He liked to face sideways and peer at the busy sidewalk. Besides, he could check out any potential lady friends coming in.

Another man appeared in the doorway. This time, Bill moved inside. Instinctively, he took a seat at the bar. The familiar smell of stale cigarette smoke mixed with the odor of spilled beer lingered in the air. He was repelled, yet he felt a calming sense of comfort.

"Whaddya havin'?" An unfamiliar bartender stood before him.

"A beer. I'll have a bottle of beer."

"What kind? We've quite a selection." He pointed towards a row of bottles displayed on a shelf behind him.

"Any beer. I don't care. Pick one for me."

With a flourish, the bartender placed a coaster on the bar along with a bottle. "Try this . . . it's a pale ale."

Bill laid a five-dollar bill on the bar in front of him. He stared at the brown bottle. A few drops of condensation slowly rolled down its side. An equally unfamiliar label stared back at him.

Gently lifting the banknote, the bartender added, "Lemme know how ya like it."

Bill sat unmoving as old memories of the familiar faces of regulars he'd known drifted into his thoughts. Some undoubtedly were still drinking here. Others, though, were dead and gone, the sounds of their former laughter and, at times, their cries of drunken anger lingered, etched into the grimy walls like a phonograph record. For the price of a few drinks, they could repeatedly be replayed. New patrons, however, now occupied their favorite stools.

Bill purposefully reached forward to grasp the beer, his warm hand engulfing the cold, hard glass.

With a quick twist, followed by a familiar *psst*, he removed the cap. He tipped the bottle toward his lips, the pleasant odor of hops and malted barley filling his nostrils. The urge to taste it was palpable. A simple movement of his hand would cause the beer to flow into his mouth, to caress his tongue and cheeks. A quick, satisfying swallow would assuage the feeling of loss and the despair it brought. The feel of the cap in his hand brought Bill to his senses. Smiling to himself, he placed the bottle back on the bar. "Not today," he said aloud.

The bartender, returning with his change asked, "What's that?"

"Oh, nothing in particular." Bill rose to leave.

"You don't like the taste of the beer?"

"On the contrary. I like it *too* much. Please, keep the change."

The barkeeper responded with a double, two-knuckle rap on the bar to signify his grateful acceptance of the tip. "Have a good day, then."

"Thanks, I will. Same to you." Bill flipped the new cap, catching it expertly in his open palm.

On exiting the bar, Bill saw the thieving starling again perched in the tree—in its beak, Bill's shiny bottle cap.

The beauty of its plumage, illuminated by the morning sun, struck Bill. A kaleidoscope of shimmering colors reflected in each radiant sunbeam. The bird was a gorgeous creature. Bill felt instantly ashamed that he'd nearly killed or injured it.

As Bill watched, his old cap slipped silently from the bird's beak. It fell to the sidewalk, bounced once, and rolled in a wide circle toward him. He lifted his left foot a few inches then placed it straight down on top of the rolling cap. The bird eyed him studiously for several seconds, and then it dropped from the branch to alight a foot or so from Bill's shoe. It looked up at him, patiently waiting for him to move his foot. Bill obliged by deftly stepping backward to reveal the cap lying top uppermost. The bird, still looking at him, cocked its head sideways but did not get closer. Bill took another step backward. This time the starling hopped forward to retrieve its prize; however, it could not get a grip. It pecked at it several times in frustration, moving it closer toward Bill.

Fascinated by the bird's determined efforts to grasp the cap, Bill carefully and slowly bent down to pick it up. Unmoved, the bird calmly stared back at him. Bill replaced the cap, shiny-side down. "There you are, birdie," he said softly. "It's yours now."

He stood and moved aside to allow the starling to claim its treasure. With a quick single hop, it grasped the cap. It paused before leaving, its eyes fixed intently on Bill. Then the bird did something that Bill would remember for the rest of his life.

Quite distinctly, it chirped, "Thanks."

BUZZ CUT

CRISTINA GOULART

It was the bright lights that did it. And the pounding bass. And the smell of hair bleach and dye and straightener.

It was a beautiful, warm autumn day, and Kora was an hour into her shift at Smart Cuts Hair Salon when it happened. She wasn't drunk, but she was definitely hung over. Her neighbor had introduced her to vodka lemon drops the night before, and it was love at first sip. When she woke up, she had a hair-of-the-dog breakfast of V8 and gin—heavy on the Tabasco—with an extra celery stick for the antioxidants.

Kora had loved cutting hair from the time she was a child, practicing on her dolls' synthetic locks and then moving on to her little sister's hair after the dolls were all sporting buzz cuts. Her mother did not love the results, but her sister did.

Now a trained hair stylist, Kora especially enjoyed a haircut makeover. She loved the before and after effect of taking a bad haircut and turning it into a piece of artwork. When she was through, the customer looked younger or slimmer or smarter. Most of the time, she had to be content with basic haircuts and men who wanted a cut to make their bald spots go away. *How do you tell someone that a cut will not cover a bald spot? Shouldn't they know that already?*

She prided herself on making her customers feel at ease and her ability to judge which cuts will work best with each client's hair texture and jaw lines. When a client would ask for color, she'd go into artist mode, comparing hair swatches to skin tone and eye color. Her hair was currently chestnut brown with wide streaks of copper throughout. She had cut retro straight bangs across her forehead and had become adept at looping braids along her scalp in a Queen-Victoria-meets-Amy-Winehouse kind of way.

On that sunny October morning, a man slightly older than her father sat in Kora's chair. She was all smiles in her green polka-dotted skirt and black high-tops when he asked for a trim. He lowered his voice. Could she somehow hide the growing bald spot?

She crossed her arms and leaned back as she stared at his head. "I'll see what I can do," she said. The customer—Don was his name—chattered about his kids, the younger of the two was in college. God the expense.

"That's why I'm here at Smart Cuts instead of my favorite salon."

"Gee, thanks for slumming." Yes, she said it aloud, but when Don's wide blue eyes met her hazel ones in the mirror, she laughed.

Kora was nearly done with his hair when she got a hint of vertigo that rode a wave of nausea. She only touched the trimmer to the back of his neck when the floor seemed to wave under her feet. The next moment, there was a wide swath of short spike in a sea of graying curls. She stood military straight and stared at the back of Don's head.

Crap.

"What is it?" asked Don of her reflection.

"Um . . . so . . . I know you didn't want to go much shorter, but I think a close-cropped cut might be really flattering," she said. Actually, she *did* think it would be flattering. Don had a high forehead and strong jaw. Those curls were beautiful but thinning. A shorter cut would definitely be better.

Don reached back and felt his scalp.

"Jesus! What's wrong with you? Are you drunk?"

The whole salon stopped to look. Not that you could have heard a pin drop. The music was still blaring. Justin Timberlake. *I got sunshine in my pocket . . .*

"She's drunk, damn it!" Don had said to Maria, the shift manager. "Look at the back of my head!"

"Not drunk. Just hungover." Kora had weakly defended herself. She apologized and begged for forgiveness. "I really need this job."

An hour later, eyes red from crying, Kora packed a tote bag of her own shears, combs, and smocks.

"I have to do it, sweetie. You look great. You have a great personality. You're good at styling. But you come in hungover too much. Get it together, girl."

CR

Less than a week later, Kora sat huddled in her car in a Safeway parking lot. The seat was pushed back all the way, her knees were pulled to her chest, and a pile of used Kleenex was growing at her feet. Her cat, Muggles, loose in her car, crouched on the floor of the passenger seat and stared at her. Occasionally, Muggles meowed pitifully.

Kora's insomnia might have saved her life on this horrible night. She'd been awake when the firestorm started miles to the east of her apartment building.

"You up?" she had texted to her bartending neighbor as she watched the stars dim behind thick smoke. She packed the trunk of her car and set up a cat station on the backseat floor. Headed from the carport to her apartment, she found it hard to breathe, and she saw that the hill to the east, just blocks away, was in flames. The wind was hot, furnace hot.

"AMANDA!" Kora screamed and pounded on her neighbor's door then ran to the next neighbor's door and pounded again. As Kora ran back to her own apartment to stuff Muggles into a carrier, Amanda emerged in pajamas, disoriented.

"Wallet. Phone. Get out!" Kora yelled at Amanda. Moments later, Kora and Amanda were sprinting to their cars. Kora had Muggles in a carrier; Amanda toted a duffle. Amanda was barefoot, her flip-flops kicked off on the stairs.

Kora had been in the Safeway parking lot for a few hours now. Her eyes stung from the smoke. Santa Rosa was burning. The parking lot filled with cars containing shocked or crying people. Several had dogs. A few wore pajamas. She hadn't seen the apartment building burn, but as she drove in bumper-to-bumper traffic down Highway 101, buildings in flames flanked both sides of the highway. The winds carried embers that hopscotched over roads and vineyards and stoked new fires. *Those winds. What the heck was up with those crazy hot winds?*

Even now, the palm trees growing in the parking lot islands were bent over, their dry fronds rustling loudly. They reminded her of hurricane images she'd seen in the news recently, but this wind carried no rain with it. This wind brought a storm of fire and ash.

At the base of one of those palm trees, a little kid was throwing up. Poor kid. His mom rubbed his back. His dad leaned on the car, his head in his hands.

Kora tossed another used Kleenex onto the floor and looked up. Don, the customer whose hair she had buzzed a stripe through days before, pushed a cart stacked with end-of-days supplies of food and water past her car. She moved to cover her face, but their eyes locked. He paused, staring for a moment and then walked by, wordlessly. Kora watched him in the rearview mirror. He stopped at an SUV. *An Escalade? Really? Who goes to Smart Cuts if they can afford an Escalade?* He shoved the bags and water bottles into the back, then stopped, head drooping. He turned and came back to her car.

Crap. She scrunched down in her seat. Her cat meowed.

Don tapped on the car window. She rolled it down an inch, covering her nose and mouth against the smoke with the neck hem of her shirt.

"Yeah?"

"Are you okay?" Don asked.

Kora burst into laughter.

"Sure. I lost my job because of my screw up with you, and now I've probably lost my apartment and everything I own that's not in this car. Yeah, I'm fine." By the time she got to the word "fine," her laughter had dissolved into tears.

"I didn't mean for you to lose your job," Don said.

Of course, he had meant for me to get fired, Kora thought. But seeing her now, pitiful in a beat-up car with a frightened cat, jobless, and likely homeless, he probably regretted it.

Kora blew her nose and coughed. All the while, Don stood at her car and looked at her mutely, lines deepening on his forehead.

"Do you have family? I mean, do you have to be in the parking lot at night?"

"No one nearby," Kora said.

Don turned wordlessly and walked back to his Escalade. "Yeah, good luck to you too," Kora mumbled. "Douche bag."

Don reappeared at Kora's window just as she closed it against the smoke. He held up a water bottle.

"Oh. Thanks." Kora reopened the window and took the bottle from him.

"May I ask how old you are? You look like you're about my daughter's age. Twenty-two?"

"Twenty-four," she answered. "Look, Don? Don't get mad, but really, your hair looks good. I mean, the close-cropped look works for you."

Don sighed. "You're not the only one who thinks that." He dug into his pants for his wallet, pulled out a card, and handed it to her.

"I live in a big empty house. It's just me except when my kids visit. If your place has burned down, you can come stay at my house. I'm not a creep. I just feel bad for you."

Kora nodded and stuffed the card into a small pocket she'd sewn into her sleeve.

◇

Twelve hours later, Kora received texted photos from Amanda. The pictures were of their apartment building. It was gone. It wasn't a burned building with shattered windows. It wasn't a burnt frame. What had been their home was nothing but a pile of ash and rubble. In the carports, burned car chassis rested on asphalt, their tires melted away. Everything and everyone who hadn't gotten out, gone. Stiff, scared, and lonely, Kora stood in the Safeway parking lot and called the number on Don's card. *Desperate times,* she thought.

◇

Three weeks later, Kora was still living with Don. It was a little awkward but not as weird as it could have been. She'd had a huge stroke of luck and had gotten a job right away. She devised a set of rules to control her drinking, and she was sticking to them.

As she heard Don walk into the house from the garage, she hollered, "Welcome home, Don!" He'd been out all day at work and then at the gym. *For an old guy, he was pretty fit.*

She knew he was taking off his shoes to protect the newly refinished wood floor. He appeared at the bottom of the stairs, Adidas in hand. She sat a few steps up with a wine glass in her hand, purple liquid swirling in the glass. An empty bottle was upright on the floor.

"Hello, Kora."

Kora noticed Don's jaw clench and his lips tighten when he saw the empty wine bottle.

41

"Okay, I'm a bit tipsy, but check it out." Kora wagged an empty water bottle. "A cup of water for each glass of wine: check. Don't drink and drive: check. Don't drink past midnight: check. Rules kept."

Kora beamed at Don as though she had just handed him a report card with straight A's.

Don set down his shoes and picked up the two empty water bottles, crushed them flat, and then picked up the empty wine bottle.

"I'll put these in the recycle bin for you." Don walked to the kitchen and placed the bottles in the container under the sink.

"Don?"

Don jumped. "Jesus, Kora, I didn't hear you walk up."

"I think I was a cat in a past life," she told him.

Don rolled his eyes.

"Just kidding. It's these." Kora held onto the kitchen counter for balance and lifted a foot, proudly displaying thick, fluffy pink and gray socks. "They are so soft; I swear they are like walking on marshmallows. Want to feel them?"

"No thanks."

Don stood at the sink and took in what she was wearing black and white polka-dotted leggings, a green polka-dotted skirt, a black bolero jacket, and an apron with roosters dotting it.

"Wow. Some outfit."

"I know. I'm wearing all my favorite things. Hey, your kids called you during the fire, right?"

"Of course. You know they did."

"Like, every day, right?"

"Yes, as a matter of fact, they did. They were worried."

"It hit me today," said Kora. She was now doing leg lifts absentmindedly.

"What did?"

"My father never called during the fires."

"Oh. How often do you talk?" Don asked.

"Well, not in years, but a fire is a good reason to call your kid, right? I mean, what about a call just to find out, you know, am I homeless? Am I dead and cremated under my apartment building?"

Don winced at the cremation remark.

"My ex-boyfriend called me from Florida for fu—, for God's sake, and my own father can't call me from L.A.? I heard from so many people from home. Are you okay? They wanted to know, but not him. That's fu—, messed up, right?"

Don's face softened. He rubbed a hand over his head and looked at her, his eyebrows raised in sympathy.

"Yep. That's messed up."

Kora put her foot back down and drank the few swallows of wine left in her glass. Her nose turned red, her eyes went glassy, and her stomach growled.

"Listen, Kora?"

"How fast can I pack and be gone?"

"No. What kind of pizza do you like? I'm ordering in."

Kora looked up, surprised and then patted at her pockets as if looking for money.

"It's on me."

"Really?" Kora broke into a grin and hopped from one foot to another in a childlike dance. "I like pineapple and Canadian bacon."

"Ew. You would," said Don, imitating one of her favorite expressions. He picked up the phone and called the delivery line of La Veritas Pizza and ordered a large, thin-crust, half Hawaiian, and half pepperoni and olive.

"Yes," said Kora with a fist pump. "Thank you!" she stage-whispered to him as he ordered on the phone.

When he'd placed the order, Don took out a bottle of Sangiovese and a bottle of water from the pantry.

"No more wine for you. You get water, kiddo."

Kora smiled at the term.

"I'm sorry about your dad not calling."

"Yeah. Well, I guess I shouldn't have expected him to."

"Still. He should have."

Kora tilted her head and gazed at Don as he turned the bottle opener. "You really do look great with that new haircut."

Don smiled as he pulled the cork out with a pop.

RED MIRAGE

LINDA LOVELAND REID

Without hesitation, she turned her freshly polished nails to the white sheets, slowly smearing maroon-red streaks onto the satin. An indulgent danger to her rage—reckless and satisfying. *Calm*, she warned herself, remembering other times . . . not good times, when her emotions played wild. Maybe she should cry. *Had she been crying? What time was it? Had she been in bed all day?* Anger blurred memory.

Listless, she looked down at the sheets—marks like blood—slashes to match her anguish. Her head tilted back. Love, once everything, now nothing. Yanking the blankets, she covered the red. She was only slightly aware of the stilted drama being played out as she left her *marriage bed*. Yes, that's what it is, she *now* knew—a place where her husband carried out his duty, rather than a place for lovers.

The crumbled note, retrieved from her husband's coat pocket still lay on the rug where she'd thrown it, a message heralding her future . . . her failure. *How to live alone? To start over—alone?*

"I love to love you," the note professed, signed simply, "Oliver." A small, gold-wrapped gift box found with the note sat on the dressing table. An untouchable thing.

Why now? What had gone wrong? Married for how many years? She couldn't even name all the grandchildren. Those happy trips . . . France, China, that wonderful walk in Wales. So many places, all topsy-turvy now. And this house. When had they come here? She'd loved their first home the best. Was that it? Change the home, a transition to fresh beginnings. Out with the old.

Dizziness invaded, and she shook as if to clear confusion. Had she and Oliver planned something together tonight? She didn't care. She'd not be drawn away from her hurt.

Her naked body confronted the mirror; bobbed blonde hair graying at the temples, large-enough breasts, only drooping slightly for a woman her age. Keeping a flat tummy had not been easy, her hands running smooth along hips that had spread with childbirth. Too dowdy? Bossy? Not interesting enough? Certainly not clever,

44

and never able to match wit for wit. She wasn't even funny. Oliver was charming, could be hilarious. She'd always produced a hardy laugh—a hey-I-get-it laugh.

And then, of course, her face. "Louise, you look stunning," her friend said. "Wow, that outfit is edgy," her daughter chirped. The word attached to her from childhood was "handsome." Like many women doomed to a life of "handsome," her best treasures were hidden under her clothing, her body a showplace only to be shared with those she'd favored. She turned, head over shoulder, to observe from behind—at least not yet sagging. *Older*. If she'd only taken better care after the children were born. Maybe, like some of her friends, a tuck here and there, at least an eye job. She leaned closer to the mirror, raised her eyelids open and shut, tilted her head, looked at her neck. Yes, chicken neck.

In the large walk-in closet, she rummaged through her clothes, a soft cobalt-blue jersey dress that Oliver said he loved, an emerald-green taffeta number with a black velvet low-cut top to accentuate her figure. She pushed past, looking for just the right—

Her hand jerked back as if struck by fire.

"Oh, God." Back, hidden in that never-to-be-seen section of her closet, was the French-blue, long, slim gown she'd worn *that* night—that moment when reason, logic, history, all of it meant nothing. Only this: succumbing to passion, her body feeling lighter . . . had she swooned? It had been the final night of a conference, a dinner-dance evening. Her talk on the law and teenage issues had been well received.

"An up-and-coming attorney?" someone had suggested.

"Thanks," she'd smiled, "I'll stick with lowly social worker status."

Then, later that night, something happened. He'd been a flirtation, which was fun, but non-lethal until it wasn't. Even the memory—his hands drawing the long zipper down, the gown slipping from her body, his arms around her waist, pulling her in—still took her breath. "Yes," she moaned. "Yes."

That was over twenty years ago. *Wasn't it?* A whole retirement ago. Why hadn't she given that dress away? For protection? So that "someday," when Oliver would do the same thing to her, she'd find this memory, her one indiscretion, and feel vindicated? Are there levels of infidelity? Is one okay and ten not okay? Oh, judge, it was only one time. What do they say? It was meaningless.

Afterward, she'd been frantic. Does truth ring in the moment? When did she know that reality had slept, that fantasy lived and crept about in her milieu, turning guilt into a mantra? In the end, she'd decided the solution was forgiveness. Not able to forget, at least to forgive herself and return to her life, the way it had been, before that moment—that mad, lovely moment.

Now this.

A gold box.

Their life together in the balance.

This was not one indiscretion, not casual! Her fingers roughly combed through her hair, nails scraping. Pain to block out the hurt. *Thoughts.* Lately, too many jumbled thoughts haranguing her sleep, tossing her from bed at early morning hours. Up with coffee, to read—not to think.

The front door slammed. She listened. Oliver! She jerked her dressing gown from the hanger, tied the black silk robe tightly, and tiptoed softly to the bedroom door. My God, he's coming up the stairs! What should I say? She backed away, toward the bathroom.

"Sylvia, are you up here?"

"Oh, Oliver! It's you. You scared me."

"Who else would it be? I left something." He headed toward his jacket hanging from the back of her dressing table.

"Yes. You did . . . leave something."

"You found it? Oh, damn."

"That's what you have to say, Oliver? Oh, damn. Nothing more?" She couldn't read his face. *Startled? Scared? Was it concern . . . why that?*

"Well, yes, actually," he fumbled, and then smiled. "Happy Birthday, darling! Your special day."

She froze.

"I made reservations at The Prelude." He drew her into him, his voice low. "Our favorite place . . . just the two of us."

Her eyes clung to him, anger not knowing where to go.

"Sylvia, are you okay? You're not dressed."

"My birthday . . . of course," she stammered. *Could he hear her pulse beating hard enough to knock her down? The note!* She moved from his arms toward the table and slid her foot over the note. "Yes, dinner . . . tonight."

"At sixty-five my wife is even more beautiful and desirable." His finger caressed her cheek, bringing her mouth to his. He kissed her, a soft touch.

She felt herself melt, the sting of doubt and anxiety floating away.

He picked up the gold box from the table and put it into his pocket. "Now, it's only half a surprise."

She needed to speak. "Oh . . . it's a surprise, Oliver."

Oliver smooched her gently on the forehead. "See you downstairs in a few."

She grabbed him as he pulled away, to hold him, hold on, and never let go. "Oliver," she said as he turned to her. "You'd be amazed how adrenaline can still pump through these old veins."

"Works for me." He winked, leaving the room.

Sylvia collected herself, pulled back the blanket, and looked down at the red-streaked sheets.

"My birthday . . . today?" *She'd have to look it up.*

LILITH LIES

Laura 'LA' Sottile

In a discreet corner of an old tavern converted into a funeral home, an urn sits on a marble stand between two tall columns. Lilith is gone, woman interrupted. Had her light burned at both ends? When it met in the middle, did it self-destruct? As of now, only a humble, ill-shaped bruise lies on the solid oak floor as a witness.

A janitor smuggles his way through the columns and benches as he prepares for Lilith's memorial. His keys chink against each other as he arrives in front of the stark blackened stain and points to the spot. Two guests standing on top of it promptly move. The janitor vanishes into a Devil's door behind the urn.

"She was a lush!" blurts a larger woman, dressed in a polka dot suit. Her hat, purse, stockings, shoes, and even her gloves are spot on. "She drank like a fish!" Polka Dot continues, fiddling with her necklace. "The alcohol must have overheated her petite physique."

"If fish could drink, the whole ocean would be swallowed," whispers Polka Dot's companion, a mousy creature whose eyes incessantly follow the patterns of her veil from her pillbox hat.

A slender waxy-faced man saunters over to join Polka Dot and Mousy. "Did someone mention alcohol? I sure could use a drink. Lord, no body to view, too charred. What a pity." Waxy takes off his top hat and fashions it over his chest.

"She was a loose woman," says Polka Dot.

"She may have had some loose screws," Waxy muses.

Polka Dot's eyebrow lifts. "She even had an affair with another woman early in her youth."

Mousy pulls her veil farther down on her round, porcelain face to conceal a nervous smile.

Waxy chuckles. "Well, at least she wasn't frigid."

Polka Dot's eyes open wide. "Did you, too, frolic in between her sheets?"

"I would never stoop so low," Waxy says and pets his mustache.

Disgusted by Waxy's comment, Mousy swiftly covers her repugnancy by adding to the slaying of Lilith. "She went to jail too!"

"A case of mistaken identity, but she did wallop one of the officers," Waxy says while removing his red gloves. "But I overheard foul play is being considered instead of *De Incendiis Corporis Humani Spontaneis*."

"Stop muttering your scientific mumbo-jumbo and tell me, how can that be?" Polka Dot insists.

"There is no body." Waxy nervously flaps his hands in his pants pockets.

The janitor's keys chink again. But he is nowhere to be found.

"For God sakes!" says Polka Dot. "I wish he would stop creeping about! Do you see him?"

Waxy replies, "I don't see him anywhere. Certainly, he's eavesdropping."

"We have nothing to hide," Polka Dot says.

Mousy casts off from the two like a dingy from a mothership and snoops around until she sees a figure leaning against the back wall. She inhales, sharply sucking her veil into her teeth. "A statue!"

The statue comes to life when a ray of sun reaches it. It is Daniel, Lilith's most loyal friend. With a dubious eye, he scrutinizes Polka Dot, Waxy, and Mousy. The three clump together.

Daniel fixes on the spot where Lilith's ashes were found. He turns away, overcome by grief. He closes his eyes and feels his drumming heartbeat as the room begins to omit an ashy odor. A sweet fragrance replaces the ashen stench, coaxing Daniel to speak.

Daniel's deep voice fills the atmosphere of the tavern with an earthy elixir. "Lilith had a lilt in her voice. A rhythm all her own. After conversing with her, many would come away mumbling to themselves, wanting to emulate her speech. The best way to describe it: a dithering, a glide, a cadence."

Waxy's garish yawn wipes out the poetry of Daniel's admiration.

Daniel pauses, looks up for guidance, and imagines the tavern's sturdy beams as a whale's rib cage—the chandelier, its throbbing heart. He tilts his head and proclaims, "What if Lilith could speak now? She had many friends from all walks of life as do many prophets."

Polka Dot rolls her eyes and hides her snicker as a cough.

Mousy exhales a long-winded sigh, which turns her veil to a sail. Waxy holds his elbow in his fist while he twists his mustache into a fine spike.

"Lilith was my closest confidante," Daniel continues his eulogy. "She confided in me about everything, what she felt, believed, and could discern, especially about her friends."

Mousy nibbles her nails under her veil. The exit sign above the back entrance lures her, but Polka Dot grabs the ruffle of Mousy's skirt to keep her from bolting and tears the seam, which makes a popping sound. Everyone goes silent.

Daniel's voice bellows with an oceanic resonance, "Lilith was haggard in the last few months, as you well know. She had undeservedly acquired some enemies. Also, she was profoundly disenchanted by her family's betrayal. They are criminals of the heart. Cruel, petty tyrants with small, sharp teeth that gnawed at her. She was broken when she had to leave her home. She questioned how human nature could be so unreasonable when such magnificence rests in its wake.

"Lilith was not a judgmental soul," Daniel continued. "She relished in the differences of all people. According to Lilith, 'Without diversity the rainbow would lie deflated, gray, awaiting life to take hold.'

"But, here I see some of the faces that Lilith praised."

Daniel softens, and the bewildered tavern-herd loosens. "She mentioned you with pleasure, joy, and hardship, Madame Goufant." He gestured to Polka Dot. "Lilith prayed every day hoping you would get well. She also praised you as quite a fashionista."

Polka Dot stands up as if to take a bow but then quickly sits as if a tether pulled her.

"You, sir," Daniel gestures to Waxy. "She enjoyed your lively chats together, discussing your enthusiasm about Sherlock Holmes. All the while knowing how you mourned the loss of your Belinda."

Waxy uncrosses his arms, scuffs lint off his hat, and nods with a hint of appreciation.

"Ahhhh, you must be Minnie." He nods to Mousy. "She often spoke of you with great regard and appreciated all the work you did for her in her flower garden." He lowers his voice to a whisper, "Rest assured, your secret is safe with me."

Mousy melts off her chair like a clock in a Dali painting, but Polka Dot blocks her with her brawny knee and says, "I didn't know you were planting flowers for her!"

"You are a wicked woman," says Mousy.

Polka Dot pretends she doesn't hear Mousy.

Daniel leans toward the janitor. "You, sir, Lilith knew how important the upkeep of the tavern was for you. Keeping it free of rodents." Daniel looks away from the janitor and surveys the tavern. "And other such vermin. For this used to be your residence, and with Lilith's help, you got to keep it, relish it, and convert it."

A bead of sweat ripples off Daniel's brow and splashes onto his cheek, reminding him of Lilith's kisses.

"Lilith chose not to speak the truth. If she had, you probably would not be here today. She held her tongue, her heart, her poor aching head because she could no longer be the container of such weight." Daniel tries to quell his vulnerability by pursing his quivering lips.

The tavern crackled with spidery fingers of electricity. A wisp of Mousy's hair attaches itself to Waxy's overcoat sleeve. Polka Dot sits in the center of two squealing chairs, which are statically charging her rump.

"Oh!" she exclaims.

In this galvanizing moment, two vertically challenged vases full of birds of paradise plow down, making their way straight to the marble stand where the urn awaits its demise. The urn breaks as it impacts the darkened oak floor, exudes a sonar pulse, and delivers an opaque form spraying from the dimpled brass.

Polka Dot, Waxy, and Mousy stare in shock at the fallen ashes that clearly look like an all-seeing eye. They believe this to be a sign from Lilith coming back to haunt them for all their unkindly deeds they so generously speared at her. Polka Dot flashes back to how she lied about being ill so she could get extra sympathy from Lilith, who cooked all her meals for a month, even when Lilith was ill herself.

Waxy's mind fills with Lilith's red face from a slap he gave her after she refused his sexual advances.

Mousy is stunned and weeping.

In a twitch, Polka Dot shoves Waxy out of her way to grab the urn. Waxy seizes her purse. They knock heads and a duet of groans flows. Her stocking tears, and one large lump of plump, pale flesh bulges out.

Mousy sees that Waxy's mustache has turned gray from the ashes. She shrieks, rips off her pillbox hat, and uses it to scoop up the ashes from the oak floor. The ominous bruise is revealed once again. She returns the urn to the marble stand as the janitor freezes, broom in hand.

"It's too late to save yourselves," announces the janitor.

Daniel watches the heap of battling flesh and notices the urn is right on the edge of the stand, and once again in jeopardy. He rubs the back of his neck to release the tension. He cannot allow another blow of indignity. His body stiffens. Before he can move to secure the urn, an elfin hand with laced gloves grabs his shoulder and says, "Let me." It is Mousy.

Polka Dot—still on the floor—pinches together the gaping hole in her polka dot stocking and tries to grab onto Mousy.

Mousy buoyantly leaps over Polka Dot.

While struggling to lift Polka Dot, Waxy takes full advantage and wipes the ashes from his mustache onto the back of Polka Dot's fur collar. Polka Dot misconstrues the gesture from Waxy as an affectionate one and goes limp.

Mousy reaches the urn. The joining of her tiny, gloved hands with the urn signals a sudden slowing of time. Still holding the urn, she half-turns to the others and says with absolute conviction, "She saved our lives over and over again!"

Mousy adjusts the urn to its proper order with reverence and faces the group. "Is it any wonder she burst into flames!" She gracefully sits down on the chair nearest the dais where Daniel stands.

Daniel's rigidness releases, his chin trembles, and he says, "The name Lilith means, 'belonging to the night.' Exactly where she is now. She lies in our shadows and in our stars."

HAOLE

KAY MEHL MILLER

It was my first writers' conference, an ethnic one for Asian-American writers, held on Oahu at a private boarding school called Mid-Pac. I was nervous, but with my usual penchant for being in places I didn't belong, I had registered. In nine years of living in Hawaii, I had never met a fellow writer nor identified myself as one. Now I, a full-fledged closeted writer, who posed as an English teacher to make a living, was going to a writers' conference.

Sunday's paper had a nice spread on the conference. It was here the word "Asian-American" finally seeped in. In the hodge-podge of ethnic groups that is Hawaii, I viewed Asian-Americans as the dominant group. Those of us with white skin were called *haoles*. We are nonchalantly identified as unscrupulous, not yet forgiven for sugar cane plantations run with Oriental labor on land stolen from native Hawaiians. In general, haoles are regarded as annoying and aggressive.

Near the tail end of the newspaper article, the writer stated that haoles were welcome, of course, but in the next seven sentences apologized for saying so. Fear crept in; I was not sure I'd be welcomed.

Afraid or not, I had already registered. The worst that could happen was I'd be ignored. I decided to go. I'd guard my usual noisy mouth and listen.

It began surprisingly well. On the first night, I drove a group of Mainland writers to dinner. They chatted about their hunger, their nervousness as panel participants in the conference, their tiredness after long plane rides. I was excited! These writers were people just like me.

"Are you a writer, Kay?" Jeff Chan asked.

I was ready for that question. "I'm an English teacher," I answered, "and a sometimes writer."

"Oh?" *He took me seriously, God love him.* "What do you write?"

My mind drew a blank. All the years of writing news, the magazine articles I had sold here and there, the college alumni class

53

column, the three unfinished novels, and the fat file of unpublished short stories and poems vanished.

"I've published stories in the Methodist Church Sunday School papers," I said, instantly appalled at myself. *Sunday School papers, Kay! You know damned well it was one story and one poem.* I blushed.

"Hey, don't knock it," Jeff said with real kindness in his voice. "That's a good market."

The instant bond I felt set the tone for the rest of the conference. I was no haole to the Mainland Asian-Americans. I was an actual person. By the last day of the conference, I was more. I was a writer and a sometimes schoolteacher. In the super-charged atmosphere of talented writers reading from their works, I found poems unexpectedly popping up, and I let them flow, unrestricted, onto pages of my notebook.

Earlier, the schoolteacher in me had signed up for the Pidgin Workshop on Saturday. By Friday afternoon, the writer-me crossed my name off the Pidgin list and rewrote my name in bold letters under Poetry Workshop. That's when the nervousness reasserted itself. I would be writing poetry in a class with *real* writers. *Well, you are a real writer, Kay,* I argued with myself. The schoolteacher in me sniffed.

In Lawson Inada's poetry workshop, we listed words on the board we had heard all week. One word was haole. Lawson told us to choose one word, think about it, and then just let the writing flow onto the paper. I headed outside, sat under a plumeria tree, and wrote a title, "Bamboo Lei."

That's not bad. Now, what do I say? It was weird; the words spilled across the paper although I wasn't sure I understood them. The poem finished itself. Lawson recommended we write a second poem, one with a different voice.

"Make it the voice of someone you love," he said.

I thought of my husband, Ted, and knew what he'd say. My dilemma was I didn't know how he would say it. Nevertheless, I wrote "Ted's Lei" with words that, once again, seemed to write themselves.

As we returned to class, Lawson bounced in with a smile on his face and confidently announced that we were to read our poems. I slumped in my seat, my mind lecturing me on the pitiful offerings

I had. *Should I read first and then die of shame?* The choice, thankfully, wasn't mine. Lawson asked Kathy, a Mainland professional, to read.

"It's not my best work," Kathy apologized. Was she, too, a little nervous? Her poem, "Pake-Jew," was of a word not listed on the board. Lawson asked about it, and a discussion ensued, which somehow legitimatized the word. (In Hawaii, *Pake* is slang for a Chinese person.) Diffusion of language seemed to be the game we were playing. The poem was a jewel, but I didn't like the word "Pake."

The poet next to me was a Hawaiian-Asian-American. The moment he read, I forgot his name. His subject was haole. Inside of me, a fire flamed in fearful anger. Nine years of swallowing haole fed it. Being called haole meant my skin color identified me as someone unacceptable. Though my friends tried to soften the word by calling me *a damned good haole, not one of those West Coast haoles*, the word still stung. I could never be part of the island culture I otherwise loved.

The young poet was patronizing with his well-chosen words. How calmly he read. How nice the word haole seemed when he said, "To me, it only means white person." Occasionally, he admitted, he used it to joke with haole friends. "They don't mind the jokes," he said.

That's what you think.

A small, round Caucasian woman affirmed the poet. "That's right," she said. "Haole simply means white person. A local referred to me as a haole while calling a cab for me, and I knew it was a way to identify me."

A Japanese-American woman with short, spiky hair sat to my right. She looked as if she was intently listening.

"So, you see," the Caucasian woman finished, "it really isn't a derogatory term, although sometimes it may be used that way."

Am I going to let a Mainland Caucasian woman, who doesn't know Hawaii, lecture us on the meaning of haole? But it was already too late.

Lawson turned back to the poet who had started the haole discussion. "You have a second piece?"

The poet began his next poem.

I heard the voice of a brother raising an angry objection to the word haole. My heart jumped. *Yes, yes. He understands*! I was more than surprised; I was amazed and delighted. "It stinks!" the poet read. "And if you're going to call me that, you can have this damn island!"

I turned to the poet. He understood how hurtful the word could be, even though his first poem denied that fact. "I can understand your mixed feelings about the word haole, but, for me, the word is always objectionable," I said.

Lawson pounced. "Why?"

He was in my face, smiling. He's *enjoying* himself, I thought. To him, I supposed, it was an academic discussion. For me, it was personal.

"Because," I said, "haole, in its original use, means 'stranger.' You take away my roots when you call me haole. You say I am no one—that I don't belong."

"But you have roots," Lawson insisted.

"I'm not like you," I flared. "You call yourself Japanese-American, but I have no roots."

It was out. I indeed was a haole in my soul. Nothing could redeem me for I had no traceable ethnic identity; I lived in Hawaii, a state where national identity was paramount even to being a U.S. citizen.

He was gentle. "You have roots. What do you call yourself?"

"I call myself American."

He wouldn't let go. "But what nationality?"

I stubbornly gave in. "My mother is Lithuanian, and my father was a German."

"Sooo . . . you have roots!"

"No, I don't. There were no grandparents to pass on traditions to me, and my parents didn't."

"It would have been nice," Lawson said gently, "if you did have Lithuanian and German roots."

"Yes," I agreed. "It would have been nice."

Discussion over, I read my poems. I was no longer nervous; I knew what my poems said, at last, and *they sang to me*. Words are miraculous. "You are a *real* writer," they whispered.

Eiko read a poem that compared herself to a ginger root. It intrigued me. Her spiked hair didn't match the gentle tones of her words. Her poetry seemed to please everyone. She enthralled us with an image of a simple ginger root in her hand. I heard loneliness and the quiet strength to endure. Something was familiar in the poem. I didn't notice it until she read her second poem.

I sat up and practically shouted, "You're talking about *me*!"

She had read, "I am a haole—a stranger—without roots . . ." The rest of the poem was lost to me, but those haunting words knotted my soul.

"No," she said quietly. "I'm talking about myself. My country was a small island taken over by the Russians. I can never go back there. I, too, am rootless."

Another Caucasian woman in a flowered muumuu, her voice as big as herself, boomed out, "*You* can't be a haole! Haole is only for white people."

Still speaking quietly, Eiko answered. "I *am* a haole. I feel so lonely here even with faces like my own." *Alone? She, too?*

And then, it happened. Right there in Lawson's classroom, a German-Lithuanian Haole met a sister Japanese-American Haole at the Asian-American Ethnic Writer's Conference in the mid-Pacific and tasted the sweetness of shared identity.

HURT AND FIRE

SUSANNA SOLOMON

Despite the swarms of people milling about outside, inside Notre Dame Cathedral it was quiet. People were whispering in small groups, their faces tipped toward the tall ceiling soaring overhead. Chairs in rows faced the pulpit; parishioners sat and prayed. Tourists, in hushed tones, ambled slowly, frequently stopping to admire sculptures of saints and stained glass windows that exalted the love of the Lord.

I was alone, and that was a comfort. I passed by the votive candles where the cool air descended and enveloped me. It smelled like the attic of the house I grew up in, musty and full of secrets. Halfway into the cathedral, finding a collection of chairs in a section away from the masses, I took a seat, third row back, second seat in. I could say I was waiting for someone, but no one knew me in Paris, and my feet were tired.

I heard a rustle. Someone sat too close to me. Should I move? Was someone going to ask me for money like the beggars outside? Couldn't I have any peace at all? I gathered my purse, ready to move, then recognized her.

My mother.

In a gray suit, brown leather three-inch heels, and an alligator purse. Her hair was up as it had been throughout my childhood, parted on the side, and arranged so it flipped over itself, like the hairstyles of the '40s. This was before . . . before she'd cut and curled her hair and my father had called her crazy. Before the summer of '63, when she'd killed herself.

"Nina," she said.

"Mom," I said, breathing heavily. The last time I'd thought I'd seen her was at camp that summer after she'd passed—at the pond where we swam in the afternoons. She'd walked up as if she'd never been gone, and when I waved hello, she disappeared. Since the funeral that summer, I'd been waking up every day, forgetting she was gone, and the news would hit me like the first time I'd heard. But now, today, she'd been gone half a century, and God knows I had become used to the news for a long time.

"Yes," she said, holding her hands over the clasp of her purse.

"It's been . . . Oh, my God," I stuttered. I checked my pulse, which slammed a million miles a minute.

"We were here, together, when you were a child. Do you remember?"

Oh, I did, how much I did. When I walked the Quai, I could feel her hand in mine. "The sidewalks speak to me as if you'd never left. I don't know why I hadn't thought to come before."

"You grew up."

"I hadn't wanted to," I said. The sun passed through the stained glass windows, colors brightening the opposite stone wall.

"Your father was impatient," she said, "hurrying the three of you along so."

"But you, maybe not so much," I said.

"Oh, I don't know. I tried, in those years, to be helpful to him until I knew better. Until I learned."

How much I wished that she was really with me, had not gone away when I'd been fourteen. I squeezed my eyes together. I had no time for ghosts, scraps from the past, people I had longed for and lost. Shreds of memories disappear like broken spider webs in the wind. I closed my eyes, tightened them, hoped no one would accuse me of going crazy—talking to an empty chair—but everyone else was muttering prayers, so I opened my eyes. She was still there.

"I'm sorry," she said, looking forward, not at me. She smiled ever so slightly, and it was true, she did have my teeth, or I had hers, but I didn't have her luscious lips, which my daughter inherited, but I had her bust and that was some consolation—I guess.

"Life was hard," I said stupidly, "after you left." Those were the words my father used to say when I ached for solace. I'd wanted to say to him, "It was your fault; you broke her heart, and now you're telling me to toughen up?"

"Get back on that horse," he had said minutes after he told me about my mother's death. And I did, I had to. I looked ahead, not behind, but the days I missed my mother were numerous, her sweet smile in the mornings, her footfall as she came to my room to wake me, a thousand little wonderful and not so wonderful things. Stuffing my hurt inside, I steeled myself to survive.

My mother sat quietly, cleared her throat. "You've been okay? After all this time, I couldn't—I tried."

"You're with me now, Mom," I said and wept.

I tried to tell her how I had wanted, hoped, wished, and tried to convince myself that she had been watching over me every step of the way from young teenager through my first marriage and those difficulties, and into my second, but I'd dropped that feeling long ago. She had abandoned me. Now I wasn't so sure.

"You've done okay," she said, "despite—"

"I missed you terribly," I said.

"I knew. I hadn't meant, I was so, so unbearably sad . . ."

"You're with me now, and that's what matters, Mom."

I couldn't be angry or spiteful. She was here beside me; she'd been with me in Paris when I'd been little, and she'd been with me throughout grade school, showing me her hurt and fire, and her undying love. None of my resentments after that mattered. She'd come back. She loved me. I put out my hand to hold hers.

I felt something cool. And ethereal. Then, nothing.

I closed and opened my eyes. My empty hand clutched air and whoever, or whatever had been sitting beside me, was gone.

The whispers of the tourists came through the nave as they made their circumambulation through the church. Parishioners, near and far, in their hard-back chairs, muttered prayers. In the distance, other worshippers lit candles, and in the front of the church, beyond where I could see, a choir began to sing.

MIA

ALAN GOULD

The sounds echo through the halls—a constant intermingling of voices, then nothing. Silence is what I want. What I need. Doctors and nurses, stay the hell away. I don't need their patronizing looks. No, I'm not suicidal, anxious, or depressed. If I were, I certainly wouldn't tell them. I don't need anyone. I just need quiet, to be alone. Yeah, I have scars on my left arm and leg. There's one on the top of my head too. I can rub it with my fingers. How deep does it penetrate my brain? Maybe I can touch it if I shut my eyes and concentrate. That's a good one.

ଓଃ

I was on dark sand. Burning sun, cold nights, no stars. No drops of rain to deaden the pain, no birds to sing, no trees to shield the sun. The sound of sand was deafening. They found me. I remember becoming numb as I was lifted up.

"Easy, soldier. Easy now. We have you. You're going to do fine. Just relax."

ଓଃ

A nurse at Walter Reed National Military Medical Center handed me the phone. "Your sister Sally is on the line. She wants to talk to you."

"Jim, Jim, oh, my God, I can't believe it." Sally's words charged at me.

I could feel her breath.

Was it months? Years? I don't know. I can't remember. I'd gone back for Conan, by the stream in the mud. A flash. Darkness. Pain in my eyes. Then isolation. Now I'm in a bed, in a clean, white room with starched nurses bringing me food and smiles. A twinge of sanitized air. No clouds of gun smoke and shit. I sense tenderness . . . but I'm not part of this new world. Sand is still in my hair, under my fingernails, in my eyes.

"Jim, I'm going to come there to be with you for a while." Sally sighed. "There is something . . . I don't know how else to tell you this. Mary's married. She waited so long for you, but then she

61

got on with her life. I know this is terrible news, but I didn't want you to call her."

Mary. Yes, I remembered Mary. She had a sweet smile. "Sally, promise me you'll do what I ask. I need your promise."

"Yes, of course. What can I do? Anything you want."

"Don't come. Stay home with Tom and the kids. When I'm ready, I'll visit you. Please, for me."

☙

"Sergeant Lander, please come in, have a seat. I'm Dr. Raymond."

I sat facing the doctor in one of the chairs in front of his desk.

"I know you're anxious to leave," he continued. "This won't take long. I just want to be certain all arrangements have been made and you're satisfied."

Looking at the doctor, I wondered if he had seen combat.

"You have all your prescriptions? Appointments? I understand you're going to the West Coast. Tell me where?"

I felt stiff sitting upright. "There's a village called Inverness. It's on the Point Reyes Peninsula, north of San Francisco. I've rented a cottage on the shore."

The doctor smiled, relaxed. "I've heard of Point Reyes. It's a beautiful place—I'm certain you'll like it. We've made arrangements with the VA facility in San Francisco and forwarded your records there. So, when do you leave?"

I felt him relax. "Tomorrow. I have a morning flight to San Francisco. From there I'll rent a car and head to Inverness. I understand the VA will pay for a car."

"True, Sergeant. All financial arrangements have been made. You're free to go, and I wish you the very best. You deserve it after what you've been through. Just bear with me a few more minutes. I know you can't remember your experiences. Trust me, your memory will return gradually over time. Don't push it." He paused, tapped his fingers on the desk, and then said, "Tell me about your feelings. Anger? Relief? Confusion?"

"Doctor, I'll try to be honest with you. I just feel tired. A lot has happened too fast. I need time alone—to sit on the porch of my cabin, watch the seagulls, and the sun set."

"You'll change, Sergeant. There will be anger, deep anger, understandable as you remember those terrible times. Hatred against the world. God. Yourself. But that, too, will fade. Some things that don't vanish quickly are sorrow, sadness, desolation. Be conscious of those feelings. They can be dealt with as long as you understand them. Loneliness and sorrow are an unhealthy combination. I understand that you want to be alone for a while. Don't make it too long. There's a world waiting for you. Find it."

Dr. Raymond stood and shook my hand. "Good luck, Jim. If I can ever be of help, don't hesitate to call."

ᑰ

Do I call him about a recurring memory?

I stand under a tree in the dark. The street is empty. I wait in the shadow until I see Mary walking across the street toward her apartment. She pauses at the steps and searches for something in her purse. I see her look down, and a breeze blows through her hair. How many years had it been? Are those the eyes that filled with tears when she hugged me goodbye? The lips that whispered, "I love you." I sense the warmth of her body next to me. Is that the scent of her perfume? Do I recognize her? Is it Mary? Wind sweeps down the empty street. She is gone. A sudden spark of pain reaches the scar on my head.

"Can I get you something to drink, sir?" the flight attendant said.

"Yes, a beer, please." I reclined in my seat.

How often must I see myself standing on that street?

ᑰ

I sat on a bench along a trail overlooking Tomales Bay, about a ten-minute walk from my cabin. The morning was mild. The sun was rising above the hills that face the California coastline. I stretched my legs outward and relaxed my shoulders against the backboard.

The previous night, I'd stopped in the bar in the village of Olema, perhaps a fifteen-minute drive from the cabin. Other than purchasing groceries and other necessities, that was the first time I'd ventured into a public place since I'd arrived. I took a seat in a darkened corner of the bar and ordered whiskey over ice. I fingered the glass as I absorbed the atmosphere. Soft music played in the background. Two men were at the bar, chatting. Three women sat at a table drinking and laughing. The bartender refilled my glass.

I had a sudden urge to say hello, but it seemed it would take forever to cross the room. Could I talk with people who laughed but didn't hate or fear? I sipped my drink.

"Hi, I'm Franny. We saw you sitting by yourself and thought you might like to join us." She stood by me and smiled.

The other two women watched.

"We've never seen you here before. Why not join us?"

Reenter the world? *Now*? I adjusted my glass in its wet ring.

"Thanks, Franny. Very kind of you. Perhaps another time."

She hesitated, then said, "Hey, stop by Ben's Diner sometime. We work there. Get you a cup of coffee on the house." She gave me a short smile and then walked back to her friends. I left—my glass half-empty.

ᙟ

I read Byron's poems as an undergraduate. Lord Byron was my literary hero, a legendary figure who died fighting for his beloved Greece. Mary and I shared our favorite poems over coffee, between classes, sitting on the campus green in late fall afternoons. What a world—a stunning world of sun, dreams, and Mary.

That world was gone. How did Dr. Raymond phrase it? Fear, hatred, then loneliness and despair. I can't single them out, distinguish depression from loneliness. Let Dr. Raymond provide symmetrical definitions. I'm tired.

Where are the seagulls?

I have not loved the world, nor the world me.
I have not flatter'd its rank breath, nor bow'd
To its idolatries a patient knee.
Nor coin'd my cheek to smiles, nor cried
aloud
In worship of an echo; in the crowd
They could not deem me one of such. I stood
Among them, but not of them; in a shroud
Of thoughts which were not their
thoughts—

Lord Byron
Childe Harold's Pilgrimage
Ex111

 C8

Months have passed. Memories roared—the ones who laughed as they broke my legs. I can't hate the eyes staring at me. The fire still burns, but only as embers. Now I see seagulls, gentle against the waves. Wind soft on my face. My cabin is warm, quiet. A week passes and then another.

C8

Dawn. Across the street from the diner, I stand under a tree. Again. They've just opened, and I see the waitresses serving the first truck drivers. I wonder about that night long ago, when I stood under another tree. What if I had crossed that street and said, "Mary, I'm home."

The wounds of war cut deep. They took my past life away, but I'm still here. Who said, "You can never go home again?" Thomas Wolfe?

Goodbye, Mary.

Goodbye, Byron.

A bell tinkled as I came through the door. "Hi, Franny. Remember me from the bar?"

"Well, I sure as heck do!" she replied, her smile as wide as the sky.

"I'm ready for that cup of coffee."

"You betcha. Cream and sugar?"

I nodded.

"Good to see you," she said, her words a lilt.

"Good to see you too," I replied.

And it was.

RETRIBUTION

MARILYN CAMPBELL

From the moment they entered the mission, Eric noticed the placement of relics in strange juxtaposition to one another. A glass case was filled with robes and other fine vestments in heavy silks and satin brocades across from primitive tools used by Indians who had labored within the walls of the mission. Next to the tools was a life-size painting of a young, serene-looking woman holding a tray on which lay two perfect breasts. The breasts, according to the artist's notes, figuratively belonged to Saint Agnes, who had been mutilated on the orders of a Roman governor for scorning the advancements of his son.

The disturbing image of the martyred saint stayed with Eric as he moved through the ancient building. He entered the long, narrow chapel, the last room on the tour. Details of early mission life embellished the thick walls, probably painted with dyes made from native plants. It would be difficult to duplicate the colors of the natural dyes, but Eric made a note to talk with a ceramicist he knew who might have helpful suggestions.

Eric was not keen about this project being considered by the engineering firm for which he worked. They specialized in historic restorations and, until recently, only accepted jobs involving commercial buildings and vintage homes over a hundred years old. He was part of a team assigned to bid on the job of restoring the crumbling mission. Eric had voted against it, but as a junior member of the firm, he held little sway in the decision making, especially on an undertaking of this magnitude. It didn't help that the boss was a staunch Catholic who later questioned Eric's negative attitude. Eric got the message. He didn't want to jeopardize his job, even though he had vowed to never again step inside this or any other church.

Several members of the team removed their hardhats, crossed themselves, and genuflected before making their way deeper into the chapel. Eric stood his ground and did neither. He was no longer a Catholic—not even a lapsed Catholic who could return to his faith at any time. Some would say, "Once a Catholic always a Catholic," but he belonged in a separate category of nonbeliever;

Eric rejected the faith into which he had been born and blindly participated until he was fourteen years old. He now counted himself among the hardcore atheists of the world.

The guide recited various details about the chapel's construction and of the financial campaign to pay for its restoration. When the group moved ahead to study the stained glass windows, Eric remained behind to stand in the middle of the Stations of the Cross, uncertain. The banks of votive candles, glowing in the gloominess, reminded him of the many lost brothers for whom he could light a candle. But he no longer believed in the rituals and magical thinking of religion, and so he moved on.

As he neared the center aisle leading to the altar, Eric came to a table bearing a stack of brightly colored pamphlets. Their title drew him in: Working Together to Prevent Child Sexual Abuse. In small type below: Keeping Ministerial Relationships Healthy & Holy.

A rope of tension tugged between Eric's shoulder blades, but he carefully picked up one of the trifold pieces and opened it anyway. His eyes scanned the text and came to rest on phrases like "children, a valuable treasure," and "clergy-abuse scandal." He scrolled down the page to the signature: Cardinal Roger Mahony, Archbishop of Los Angeles.

"The bastard," he swore under his breath.

The pamphlet, displayed in a prominent place, must have been one of the terms of the lawsuit against the church—a public confession followed by this attempt to atone, to educate the public. *Too little, too late.* The edges of the pamphlet, folded into sharpness, dug into the sides of his fingers. Eric loosened his trembling grip and watched the words free fall from his hand to the floor.

The overwhelming smell of burning incense took him into a memory—the rustling robes of the old priest as he made his way down the row of penitents and administered the rite of Holy Communion. Dutifully, Eric had opened his mouth and received the wafer. "The body of Christ," intoned Father Dugan. Eric's nerves had sucked the moisture from his tongue, and the wafer had stuck to the roof of his mouth. He'd tried to dislodge it with the tip of his tongue but had no success. His stomach had felt queasy, like the other time, when the priest had tried to put something else into his mouth . . . and he had gagged. Eric had heaved all over Father Dugan's shiny black shoes.

"What's the matter, my son? Don't you want to be whole with Christ?" The already florid, fleshy face had turned red in frustration—as red as the hair on his thick thighs . . .

Eric pulled himself back to the present and rushed to an exit door. He fell to his knees and vomited in the rose garden. Waves of revulsion washed over him until he had nothing more to throw up.

"May I be of assistance?"

Eric flinched at the unexpected voice. When he looked up, he was gazing into the dark, fluid eyes of a young man in a white robe that matched his perfect white hands.

Eric hadn't heard the priest approach.

"No. Go away," Eric cried, turning away.

"Allow me to give you some water," he said. "It may help."

Eric hesitated. Looking down, he saw the same style of black shoes that Father Dugan had worn under his robe. Except these were scuffed and unpolished. A good sign. Father Dugan's shoes were only shiny because he had asked each of his altar boys to take turns polishing and buffing them for Sunday Mass. It had been an excuse to get the boys alone. Eric knew that, now. When the boys had grown to be men and had come forward to file complaints, they'd compared notes. Like a secret code between them, the words "Did you shine Father Dugan's shoes?" spoke volumes.

"I'll just leave it," the young priest said.

Eric would not look up again until he heard him walk away. The cup of water sat on the garden bench within easy reach.

Eric studied the cup, a gesture of kindness that he wanted to reject, then took a sip anyway, rinsing his mouth, clearing away the taste of bile. He took a second sip and gratefully gulped the rest.

When he looked around, he saw the priest standing by the door to the vestibule, his hands folded in front of him. Was he waiting for Eric to change his mind and invite him to safely approach? Was he waiting for Eric to give him a sign? He couldn't quite make out the priest's expression—compassion or contrition? Was this priest absolved of wrongdoing and not in need of retribution like the others?

Eric stood up, peeled off his jacket, and laid it on the bench. He fished a handkerchief from his back pocket and wiped his mouth.

From the corner of his eye, he spotted fellow team members in the parking lot boarding the van that had brought them to the mission. He was thankful no one had seen him retching in the rose garden.

It was a mistake to have come. I should have tried harder to get out of this assignment. Still shaken, he walked away from the roses and the church with its secrets and hard lessons. He had hoped that his anger had been left in the past. By not filing a lawsuit against the church like so many others had who sought retribution, Eric hoped to be spared from reliving the sordid details. He expected the stain of shame to fade like the color of a favorite shirt put through the laundry too many times. But he was wrong to figure he could handle his feelings after all these years—years in which the cloying scent of incense made him break out in a sweat, and the sound of church bells gave him a headache. He still wasn't ready for the church to receive redemption for its supreme abuse of power—the sexual exploitation of children.

"Man, what happened to you?" someone asked as Eric boarded the van. He was sweating heavily and had to loosen his tie.

"Yeah, we lost you in the chapel," another said.

"I went back to check the date on one of the exhibits. Sorry." He hoped they would accept his story, unchallenged.

Eric glanced out the window to see the priest, who was rushing into the parking lot to catch the driver's attention. He held something up—the jacket Eric had left behind on the bench. Eric hoped the driver wouldn't notice.

Dust and loose gravel kicked up by the van enveloped the priest whose left hand shot to a spot under his eye. When he removed his hand, blood was running down his cheek. *A rock?*

"Hold up!" Eric yelled at the driver.

As the bus stopped, Eric rushed to the front and stepped down to the parking lot. Realizing he'd soiled his handkerchief earlier, he removed his tie and stopped short before the priest.

"Here." He thrust the pure silk tie toward the injured priest.

"It will be ruined."

"Take it," Eric insisted.

"Thank you." The priest looked dubious but stanched the wound by pressing the tie's wide end to the cut while he handed Eric his jacket.

Eric lifted his coat up in acknowledgment. "Thanks," he mumbled and stepped back.

"Go in peace."

Eric nodded, but having no words, he turned and left.

He boarded the van and dropped into his seat, feeling light-headed from the rush of adrenaline and emotion. Eric sat up, rolled his shoulders back, and looked straight ahead as they picked up speed and hit every pothole in the lot.

ALONG THE TRAIL HOME

David Colin Carr

Raamro the elf, as is their wont, hummed as he trod the gently undulating trail through a pinewood. He tossed words into the air to see how they'd land.

"Another day, another friend.
Another day, another bend.
The road has its twists.
The road has its turns.
What lies ahead
between now and the end?"

He welcomed the easy terrain, made camp early, and leisurely searched for edibles. While picking through a mound of vines for the last berries, he heard a rustling in the dense brush.

"Hola!" he called. Sudden silence responded. "Hola!" No answer. "Someone in no mood for company," he said aloud to assuage that someone's concern. "I can respect that," and he went about gathering.

His cap full, he found an ancient ash tree seared by lightning, which let the sun through. He leaned back and looked up into the web of overstory, a cushion of needles and leaves beneath him. Like a primordial voice, shafts of light streamed down. Majestic. Earth and sky beyond the grasp of time. His heart's skin melted. This was nourishment enough. He set his cap aside, absorbed into thusness.

The rustling recalled him. A large bird, deep in brush, piled twigs and leaves, awkward in its movements.

"Are you building a nest there?" Raamro called. "It doesn't seem so safe a place to lay eggs, however still you might remain. A raccoon or bear would be more than happy to relieve you of the burden of hatching them."

A crackly sigh flared through ground-sweeping branches. Raamro knelt to peer in.

"Oh, dear. Oh, no," he exclaimed. "You're injured, poor thing."

"Yes, I am. I'm not so stupid that I would lay eggs where even a rat could have one for dinner!" she snapped. "I've laid plenty.

71

High in the trees, where wind blows cold off the mountain. High, where branches are too small to support a bear . . . or even a foul-smelling raccoon." The bird grimaced and flinched a sigh. Her irritation flowed past him without slowing.

"Where are you hurt? What happened?" Raamro asked, his voice patient and soothing.

"Forgive my sarcasm. My wing is torn. I'm terrified of death, yet the pain is excruciating. I suppose I'm trying to hide from it."

"Will you invite me to see if I can help?" Raamro asked gently.

The bird sighed again. "You won't want to look. It's an ugly wound. Dried blood smeared across my stunning breast."

"Are you ashamed?"

After a pause, "It hurts to be seen unprimped and bedraggled."

"More than the injury to your wing?"

Another edged sigh, labored breath. "Your kindness relaxes me," the bird said at last. "Thank you for weighing my dilemma in that balance. Our sense of ourselves doesn't always keep pace with alterations of our bodies. The physical injury is the more severe."

She stepped out from the gap. A striking bird with black strokes scattered across her white chest. Dried blood clumped her feathers.

"Poor goshawk," Raamro exclaimed. "Come step into my hands."

"You're not repulsed?"

"Saddened, but not repulsed. Come, I will lift you into my lap. Though I was never trained in the arts of healing, perhaps, at least, I can soothe."

The bird grimaced as she wrapped her coarse talons around his bony fingers. Her right wing draped limply.

"Oh, it's badly torn. The pain must be unbearable."

No answer was her confirmation.

Without disturbing her perch in his lap, Raamro fished in his pack for a clean sock. He wet it from his flask and wiped around the wound.

Her claws clenched his hand. "There is nothing to be done," she said, "but your touch softens me. I shall die soon—the sooner, the better."

"Yes," Raamro responded. "There is nothing to be done for the injury. Would you like some berries? Or some water?"

"Water, yes."

Raamro filled his palm from the flask, and she pecked a few drops.

"How sweet your water is."

"Have you never drunk from this creek?"

She settled, her wing dangling over his thigh. They both closed their eyes. Raamro encircled her body with his hands. The sun's shafts were diffused, but a warmth encircled their stillness.

In increments, the goshawk's breathing eased. Raamro gently laid a fingertip on her brow and another on her breast. She shivered into receptivity.

Several small birds perched randomly in an autumn-red dogwood. Their heads bobbed like pendulums. Time was passing; her death was nearing.

The goshawk raised her head for more water. After a few sips, she settled back. Raamro inquired about her accident. Did she care to speak?

The invitation infused her with energy. "I was cruising high on thermal drifts. Not scouting prey, simply free in an endless sky, suspended above a wooded valley, at rest. Rising, falling. Lost in the droning whisper of winds. Lost to the gathering of thunderheads.

"A sudden downdraft encircled me. I gathered my wings close to orient to the current. As I opened them, they caught a surge that flung me into the top of a tree. My pinion smashed on a branch." These last words were sputtered, breath constrained.

After a long pause, she continued. "I fell dizzily through the tree, tumbled and battered by limbs. At last, I was able to grasp one. I clung as sunset faded into the longest night of my life. Exhausted, knuckles numb, I was not aware of losing my grip. I fell to the ground.

"I dragged my wing into the brush where you found me. I lay there, consumed by the fear of being eaten. For distraction, I piled forest litter to hide behind. Sheer desperation. I knew it was hopeless."

Silence.

"I had images of being devoured. Wolves, mountain lions tearing me apart. Vultures fighting over my guts. Their rapacious violence more painful than the wound."

Silence.

"But if you kill me now and eat me . . . it would be a blessing to us both. My death would serve some purpose."

Raamro floundered, wordless. The goshawk's request clawed at his heart, dug into his gut, and locked itself behind his eyes.

"Please." Her insistence was dull, but the sinews of his arms and legs resonated like a taut string.

"It is hard to say as I look at you …" The weight of his silence tugged him further from words, "… but a nourishing meal would support my journey." Another pause as his feelings jostled into a discernible design. "But I cannot kill you. Your suffering tears at my heart, but we don't know the end of the journey until we arrive there nor what there is yet to learn along the way.

"Even if I had the strength to end your life, you would leave the consciousness of pain and fear in every cell. The greater gift, I think, would be allowing each cell to say, 'Now. I am ready,' as it withdraws into emptiness."

The goshawk sighed, adjusted her position, and buried her beak beneath her good wing. He could not tell whether she sobbed or coughed.

"I will hold you like this until your last breath has faded. Gladly hear your thoughts. Then when I eat you, your wisdom will be alive in me."

"Yes, then," the bird mumbled into her wing.

"I didn't understand that. Your words were muffled."

She lifted her unbroken wing slightly and repeated those two words then hid her beak again.

So they remained as the day cooled. More birds settled on the dogwood and watched the scene with clockwork heads. Their concentration thickened the air.

The goshawk brought out her head and asked again for water. "Is this my recompense for eating other creatures, even other birds?"

"I think it not recompense," Raamro replied. "For how else could you live in the body that was assigned to you, the body you did not choose?"

Silence.

"Not that it is not time for my passing," the goshawk said. "I lost my mate last winter. A long life together, yet the loss does not resolve. Then a strange year. A year of no ground. Unfulfilling. No eggs to brood, no chicks to fledge. The only joy I found was the one that took me down!" As she described floating on the thermals, time itself softened and slowed until she folded herself into a formless mass in Raamro's lap.

From her body, a billow of light flared then condensed to a small sphere of white gold with iridescent rays. With her last two breaths, the globe expanded. Fragmenting with the final exhalation, it scattered into night at the speed of sound, taking the whisper of the breeze with it.

Emptiness reigned. Vital emptiness. In indistinct rhythms, in a sibilance of wings and a hush of feet, the assembly dispersed.

Raamro gathered up her injured wing and held her firmly. Through the night he sat, drifting through dreams, constant in attunement to her last migration.

By dawn, she had traveled beyond reach. He set her heavy, hollow body on his cloak, then went to the creek and washed, gathering twigs and branches for a fire as he returned.

His meal was accompanied by emotions that shifted one to the next and back again: alertness, fulfillment, grief, gratitude, clarity, contentment. With each mouthful, milky sweetness trickled through his chest down to his belly. When he had eaten enough, he trimmed from the bones what meat remained and wrapped it in his bandanna for another meal. He tucked two dappled breast feathers into his hat and bequeathed her bones, beak, talons, and feathers to the fire. When the acrid smoke settled, he filled the pit with rocks, added a covering of dirt to even off the grave, a layer of leaves and moss atop, and left his camp as he had found it some immeasurable time past.

He sought a marker to acknowledge this passage, but his pack offered nothing he could spare. The rush of energy and upwelling of memories of the last hours would suffice. The goshawk and he would carry each other downstream, inseparable.

BLUE MOON

RENELAINE PFISTER

My twin sister calls me the black sheep. I can't say she's wrong. One: I never finished college. I kept switching majors until my father got sick of it. He told me to stop wasting money by pretending my plan was to graduate.

"I'm not smart enough for college," I told Darcy, who shared our mother's uterus with me for nine months and now has to put up with me for the rest of her life.

Darcy swatted my arm. "A sorry excuse. You just get bored, that's all. You're smart, and you know it."

"Smart ass, more like," Mom said, affectionately patting my head.

Two: I was a lousy father. I was twenty-two when I knocked up my girlfriend. I never made much money, never gave my daughter, Viv, what she deserved. I couldn't even afford to buy her that Barbie Dream House she wanted because I kept quitting my jobs. Then, I started doing drugs. Days went by with me in a daze. Darcy took over my role: picking up Viv on the weekends, going to school activities, and helping with school projects. That my daughter didn't drop out or get pregnant young is a miracle. I'm forty now, and Viv is seventeen. Viv turned out to be a fantastic kid . . . with little help from me.

Three: I've been tangled up in drugs on and off for the last ten years, and I'm afraid I might end up in jail like other people I know. Darcy said I always ran with the wrong crowd, and since the time we were little, my friends have been weird. I told her it's not true.

"Really?" Darcy said once. "What about when we were in the third grade and your best friend was Kenny Klein, the one who killed his pet rabbit?"

"He was just a kid. He didn't know what he was doing."

"He got arrested when he was eighteen for trying to rob a bakery."

"Maybe he just liked their scones."

Darcy rolled her eyes. "And what about that friend of yours, George something?"

"You mean Jorge."

"He gives me the creeps. He wears a dead thing around his neck."

"That's an amulet that his great-aunt gave him. It's protection. They're from Peru, Darce—they have different beliefs."

"It looks like a dead rat to me."

Maybe Darcy was right. I *was* smart enough for college but got bored with it. First, I studied computer science, and then I stopped for a year to travel in Southeast Asia. When I came back, I just wasn't interested in technology anymore. So I took up engineering, but then I missed too many classes.

I couldn't even hold onto a job. I dabbled in construction, waited tables, became a bouncer at bars, and drove for wealthy people. Nothing caught my interest, and I ended up giving up on stuff before I even started. I also had the habit of not notifying my employers when I wanted to quit. I just stopped showing up. I guess I burned bridges.

When we turned thirty-five, our father died. It devastated me. I was ashamed that he died knowing I was a failure. I swore to my mom and Darcy I would turn my life around.

"Dad deserved a better son. I swear I'll do better. I'll keep a job. I'll provide for Viv. I'll straighten myself out."

It wasn't long before I broke that promise.

At least Darcy made up for my shortcomings. If I was the black sheep, she was sparkling white. My opposite, my counterpart—she balanced things. Nice and normal. That was Darcy. Since we were kids, she did everything right, and everybody liked her. She always loved gardening and now runs a successful flower shop. She ate healthy food, ran marathons, and volunteered at nursing homes. Darcy was the picture of a well-adjusted human.

∞

My phone rang. It was Mom. She'd been calling all day, and I'd been ignoring her. I just wasn't in the mood to be lectured on how I was screwing up my life. Besides, I was getting high with my buddies all day, and I didn't want her to suspect.

Finally, when it looked like she would not give it a rest, I picked up.

"Harry," she yelled, frantic. Leave it to her to be so dramatic.

"What is it, Mom?" I asked, fiddling with the pile of clean clothes I needed to fold sometime soon. It had been pushed to one side of my bed for two weeks now.

"It's Darcy," Mom said, her voice shaking and sounding like she'd been crying.

"What?" I asked, sitting up.

"She's been in an accident."

⌇

At the hospital, I watched Darcy's chest rise and fall as I sat next to her bed. With her pale face and tubes connecting her to machines, she didn't look like my sister.

I felt powerless and angry. Darcy was the safest driver I knew. I used to tell her she was forty years too young to be driving like a grandma. But it took only a second for a reckless teenager to glance at his cell phone, run a red light, and crash into my sister's car.

Darcy didn't deserve this. Between the two of us, it should be me in that bed, breathing through machines.

Viv sat next to me, dabbing at her puffy eyes. Like me, she felt helpless and scared at the thought of losing Darcy. They texted each other regularly and went out to shop or watch a movie. Darcy was more than an aunt to her; she was her friend.

Viv reached out and held my trembling hand.

"Are you okay, Dad?"

I nodded. "I'm fine, hon." Sweating and nauseous, I was in withdrawal. I hadn't touched drugs since coming to Darcy's side—forty-eight hours ago.

"You should go home and get some rest. I'll stay with her," Viv murmured.

"No," I replied, patting my daughter's hand. "I can't leave her." But what could *I* do? Even the doctors say there was no telling whether Darcy would pull through. She had suffered a terrible head injury, and the doctors had done everything they could.

It was a waiting game.

Then, I remembered.

Jorge.

Jorge *knew* things. He knew people that did impossible things. He said people could be manipulated with the use of dolls; you could curse your enemy, heal your friend. Even death was negotiable. None of our friends ever believed him—said he was full of crap.

But what if?

❧

I drove to Jorge's great-aunt Antonella's house. It surprised me that her home was in a typical neighborhood with tended gardens and vanilla-looking houses. I guess I was expecting a small hut with a chimney in the middle of the woods. A cauldron brewing in the kitchen.

Antonella wasn't what I expected either. She wasn't bent over like a hook and didn't have a wart on her nose. She stood tall, her grayish brown hair falling below her chin, and she wore a plain blue sweater.

"You must be Harry," she said as we shook hands. "I'm not a witch," she said as she led me into her house.

"No, I didn't think—"

"Yes, you did. It's okay, though." She gestured at a porcelain pot and cups on the kitchen table. "Sit down, have some tea."

I sat down, but I couldn't stop myself from blurting out, "So how does this work?"

Antonella poured herself a cup of tea. "You don't have to worry about that. That is my business. Do you trust that I can do this?"

"I'll believe in the tooth fairy if it means Darcy will be okay."

Antonella smiled. "Good." She poured me some tea.

"What do I have to do?"

"Bring me something that your sister values. Something she likes and would never part with."

"Like her favorite sweater or something?"

"Something that is more meaningful to her than that."

"Okay. I'll think about it and bring it next time."

"Bring it to me before the full moon."

"It's already passed this month," I said, now stressing.

Antonella leaned forward with a knowing smile. "This month is special. There's a second full moon in five days. The blue moon. You're lucky, Harry. It's good timing."

I smiled bitterly. "Sure. Good timing for my twin sister to get into an accident and almost die." I rested my hand on the kitchen table.

Antonella put her hand over mine, and an electric shock passed through me. I should have jerked my hand away, but I didn't.

She looked at me with her intense brown eyes. "The blue moon is unique. It opens gates. Makes impossible things possible. What happened to your sister was unfortunate, but thanks to the blue moon, we can do something about it."

"And what do you want in return? I don't have money." I hoped she wouldn't change her mind then, but he needed her to know.

Antonella sat back, her teacup in her hands. "The price is dearer than money."

❧

After I met with Antonella, I went to see Darcy. I'd become accustomed to visiting her late and staying with her through the night. My mother sat with Darcy during the day, as well as the horde of people who wanted to see her.

Being at the hospital kept me out of trouble. I'd been ignoring my friends' calls to party. I didn't want to be stoned if Darcy woke up. I wanted to be present for her.

I was still feeling the withdrawal: diarrhea, stomach cramps, feeling overall shitty. But it all seemed stupid now: the drugs, the partying, and the general debauchery. What had I been doing with my life?

Nothing useful. Now, it would be. For Darcy.

I noticed the silver chain around Darcy's neck and found the pendant hanging from it. I'd given the cheap, silver flower pendant her for our thirteenth birthday. Without warning, tears streamed down my face. She always loved me, even though I'd been the worst man. Gently, I unclasped the necklace and clutched it in my hand. This was what I'd bring to Antonella.

 C೪

The blue moon hung low, a bright disc against the black sky. As I stared at it, I thought about tomorrow. In a few hours, I'd meet Antonella. I tried to be sad about the uncertainty of my own life after tonight and how Viv might feel but was overpowered by my desire to give Darcy a chance. She was my twin sister. For once, I wanted to do what was right.

"Viv, sweetheart, would you mind leaving me alone with Darcy for a few minutes?"

Viv stood up, picking up her purse. "Of course, Dad."

I watched her walk away, her long brown ponytail bouncing behind her. I wanted to cry as I realized I probably wouldn't have the chance to see her graduate college, get married, and have children . . . It wouldn't matter what she chose to do with her life; I loved her regardless.

Just like Darcy loved me, no matter what.

Flowers, balloons, stuffed animals, and cards filled the room. People loved Darcy. I sat down on the bed and held her hand.

"Hey, Darce, I haven't used any drugs for a week. I felt like crap for a few days, but I'm better now. You'd be proud of me."

I watched her serene face and gripped her hand tighter.

"Listen, Darce, I'm not letting you go. This is not how your life ends. You're a good person. The best," I said, and I couldn't help it, I started crying. "You're good enough to make up for how bad I am."

I thought I saw her eyes flicker behind her closed lids. But it must have been my imagination. I leaned forward and whispered in her ear. "But I've found a way. I'm going to do something right, for once."
I paused.

"Jorge's great-aunt—yeah, the one who gave him that amulet you like so much." I smiled through my tears. "She's going to help me. I told her I would take your place—my life in exchange for yours.   Tomorrow, you're going to wake up and get out of this bed like nothing happened. As for me, well, I don't know. I just have one request." I wiped a tear from my cheek. "You'll look after Viv, won't you?"

I sat up and listened to her breathing and the low hum of the oxygen.

Then, faintly, I felt her squeeze my hand. I heard my twin's voice—strangled, weak, but I could hear it clearly, as only I can.

"Don't," she said.

I called the nurse, who brought in a doctor, but Darcy was not talking or awake again. The doctor told me not to get my hopes up.

Viv and I stood outside in the parking lot.

"Look, Dad, the moon is so big!" she said, pointing.

I gazed at the blue moon and touched Darcy's necklace deep in my pants pocket. Antonella had said the blue moon made impossible things possible.

Perhaps Darcy will come back. Maybe not. But she had pushed herself to consciousness to say she didn't want me to take her place. What I thought was right and what she wanted were different. I realized I didn't need to give my life to honor Darcy. I just needed to change it.

Tomorrow, I am checking myself into rehab. After all, anything is possible.

UNCLE VON

Marilyn Wolters

"All I get from them is scorn. They don't understand that there's more to beauty than flowers and hillsides."

Uncle Von had complained about the neighbors when I arrived to take care of him that spring, a month before he died. At first, they were as dismissive of me as they had been of him, barely nodding their heads in greeting. When they heard the news of his death, they mumbled their sympathy. But soon they asked, "When's the house going on the market?"

"It's not." I had finally decided. "I'm moving in."

I saw the disappointment on their faces, which left me wondering about my decision. But I was going to honor my promise to Uncle Von.

The next days were uninterrupted as I tried to figure out where to start the terrible chore of making my uncle's crumbling home and junk-piled yard into mine. Both inside and out, the mounds of trash overwhelmed me, so I decided to wait for a plan to emerge. Meanwhile, I looked beyond Uncle Von's mess of sculptures to enjoy the bright green hills fading into summer thirst. The air, freshly washed from light rain, carried the scent of forest across the road.

"Hello!"

A tall, blonde-crested woman marched up to the nearly horizontal pieces of metal that Uncle Von had welded together to keep out the world. I trudged over to meet her.

"Sorry, it's taken me a while to visit. Been very busy." She maneuvered her hand through the gap in the metal and shook mine. "Everyone calls me J, for Jeraldine, spelled with a J. Get it!" It was more a command than a question.

"Hi, J, I'm Melanie," I replied, remembering that Uncle Von had dubbed her the "blue jay" and warned me that she's like the cunning bird that tries to plant acorns everywhere in your yard. "That woman wants a forest growing here so that my house, all my work, and I vanish," he had griped.

A chubby, older woman, she looked rather mild.

"I heard you're our new neighbor," she said as she drew her lips into a taut smile. She cocked her head toward me and whispered conspiratorially, "You could get a small fortune for this place."

"I know. I thought about it but decided to stay."

"I hope you know what you're doing." Her voice, at first harsh, turned syrupy. "So sorry to hear about your uncle's passing." She paused. "You know, this place could be lovely, like the others in the neighborhood."

I shrugged and clamped my mouth shut, remembering Uncle Von's warning that whatever you tell her will be pecked at by her fantasies and squawked to the flocks.

"Well, dear, you've got quite a chore ahead of you." She pointed to the large heap of scrap metal that dominated the front yard before fixing her gaze on me. "You're not an artist," she cleared her throat, "like your uncle, are you?"

"No."

I could see the relief on her face.

"Then we can all help you clean up the mess. Tomorrow sounds ideal."

"What? Tomorrow? Wait a minute. I can do this myself."

"Of course, you *can*." She pronounced "can" as if it were a word loaded with delusions of intention and ability. Then she enunciated carefully as if I had problems understanding, "Two heads are better than one and twenty hands are better than two. We'll be here tomorrow in full force."

"What?" I repeated, still taken aback.

"Tomorrow morning, 8:00 sharp," she said before turning and marching to activate her regiment, more soldier than bird.

I muffled my anger. She was offering me help. I was not Uncle Von. I did want my house to look like the others, which had started as modest cabins like his but over time had been sawed apart, chopped up, and rebuilt into large, tidy homes. I wanted their bright kitchens with granite countertops instead of rough-hewn tables and delaminating particle board. I wanted their uncracked windows that slid open without jamming, their plumbing that didn't leak. The list was long.

Retirees and young families, who never touched their car engines, had replaced old-timers like my uncle—who kept three old trucks around on blocks to have working parts for a fourth. The yards, once storehouses for the "someday useful," now showed meticulous lawns and flourishing landscapes. Uncle Von was the last holdout, and now he was gone.

His sculptures, confused wrecks of metal and plastic, remained. They filled the yard, many rising above the fence line in view of anyone passing. I went over to the closest sculpture to caress the rusted steel. As my fingers turned a deep reddish brown, I tried to imagine my uncle hiding somewhere inside, his face tensed in concentration.

The last time he'd shown me his work, he leaned on my arm. "What do you think?" he asked as he led me silently past each sculpture. He'd paused for a moment of squinting contemplation. I tried squinting too, but it didn't change what I saw. He assumed his work spoke in silent eloquence, but all I heard was the silence. To me, it was metal rescued from his scrap heap.

"What do you think?" he had repeated.

"Beautiful," I'd replied. I was not referring to his sculptures, but to his face, to his dreamy eyes that saw beyond the obvious— that believed in coaxing beauty from discards. He'd seen a future in them that others, including me, hadn't recognized.

When he rescued me, a wreck of a teenager, he saw the future in me, too. I came to him, my mother's so-called "mad" brother, and he heard my grief. The only family member to visit and love him, I was there. When he became ill, I returned to care for him. His body, always nervously thin, grew weak and gnarled, resembling one of his sculptures. One day, lacking the thick scaffolding of youth, he collapsed and died.

I walked over to touch the edges of one of my uncle's favorites, a spiral of steel that tapered toward the top. He was proud of its roughness as he was proud of his own prickly exterior. "Too smooth and you slide too easily through life," he always said. "The neighbors don't understand that. They value the obvious and easy." He had heard them say he couldn't tell a butterfly from a cockroach. Of course, he could, but he thought the cockroach beautiful too.

I didn't.

The next day the neighbors would take his work away. Before they came, I decided to pack up the sculptures myself. They were attached to stakes hammered deep into the ground, so I found a pair of pliers to gently unwind the wire that bound them. I brushed my lips against each piece, imagined Uncle Von, and then carefully lay the sculptures in the bed of my pickup. After covering them with worn blankets, I bid them good night.

The eager mob was there in the morning, hands covered by gloves and faces masked against the dust. They clawed their way through the piles of steel, plastic, and whatever else my uncle had collected as J stood over them and shrieked orders.

She had commandeered neighborhood trucks to haul away his collection of dismembered vehicles. When they returned, the neighbors filled the truck beds with loads of scrap. Their frenzy was contagious, and I was the only one who resisted. I walked from one group to another, numbed. Occasionally, I'd add a scrap to their piles.

By noon, the yard was barren. Only small patches of weeds interrupted the expanse of dirt. J and two helpers unfolded tables on which they set platters of meat, cheese, and bread.

"Melanie," J squawked. "Arrange the chairs in a circle."

I felt trapped into compliance.

She called me to sit next to her. When everyone was seated, she stood to announce, "We are welcoming you, Melanie, to the neighborhood."

Their cheers surprised me.

"Before we eat," she continued, "we are going to present our housewarming gifts."

Each neighbor had brought me a tree set in a five-gallon pot.

"And we're coming back tomorrow morning to plant them," J gushed. "We'll use the stakes already in the ground for their support.

"And, Melanie," her voice now stern, not used to disobedience. "I brought you a sculpture for your yard." Set inside a wheelbarrow was a life-sized, white resin figure of a girl with a watering can. "You can screw your hose in here, and out comes the water."

The neighbors cheered again.

"Very clever," I squeaked. "Thank you all so much."

"See you tomorrow," they shouted as they left.

The flock returned early the next morning to plant the trees according to J's directions. As Uncle Von had warned, her goal was to block the view of the house and yard. Privacy, I consoled myself. Not annihilation.

I wandered the yard that afternoon. I lifted the blanket and apologized to Uncle Von's sculptures, preparing them for their trip to the recycling center. They would have wonderful futures as something useful. I drove halfway there and then stopped to turn into the driveway of a nursery. When I arrived home, I parked my truck in the backyard and lifted the blankets. The sculptures lay where I had placed them, undisturbed.

I removed them, one at a time, and leaned them against the truck, setting those higher than the fence on the ground by the rear of the house. For later, I told myself. I dragged the girl with the watering can into the middle of the open space. She looked forlorn there. I took some of the vines I'd bought and planted them by her feet. Then I arranged the shorter sculptures around her. I ran wire between her and each sculpture to support the vines. The arrangement looked haphazard, so I went from one piece to another, bending metal and adding touches of wire. Flashes of the strange force that Uncle Von swore directed his work raced through me.

Before long, the vines would unify and soften the disparate pieces. The sculptures would no longer appear to scratch the air, the trees, and the nearby hills. I apologized to my uncle for interfering with his intentions and choosing not to bruise beauty but to welcome it. I imagined him, first angry, then puzzled, and finally amused. He'd chuckle at my wonder at what I had created.

YOU HAVE WON

ROGER C. LUBECK

YOU HAVE WON
Prize #3-14-159-265-359

December 7, 2017
Walter Piwicket
4577 Dillworthy Way
Knowhope, California 94027

Dear Mr. Piwicket:

You have won an all-expenses-paid, two-week vacation in Kathmandu. As part of this special offer, you have a chance to win a prize worth one million dollars. Ready to start your dream vacation and collect your treasure? Call to schedule a mandatory one-hour seminar at our redemption center before 5:00 p.m. December 25, 2017.

REDEMPTION CENTER
+011-977-1-448-9456

Congratulations,
Charles Pine
Charles M. Pine, Esq.
TPI - Treasure Prize, Inc.
145786 Battisputali Rd.
Kathmandu 44604, Nepal
+011-977-1-448-9456

Walter set a handful of junk mail on his computer desk and looked at the silver-framed picture Kelli Netherlander had given him on Valentine's Day. Walter didn't know why he needed a picture of Kelli for his desk—he had her photo on his cell phone—but Kelli insisted he did. They had been going together for five years. Lately, Kelli had been discussing the direction their relationship was heading. Did Walter really love her?

Wanting to prove his love, Walter bought Kelli a new portable hard drive with a terabyte of memory. He wrapped it in an empty box of chocolates with a handwritten note saying, "Another Sweet Byte."

Kelli said something about Walter being so practical.

Walter was surprised to see a certified letter in the mail. Printed on the outside of the envelope were the words, "Time Sensitive." Walter had never received a certified letter. What seemed most exciting was the message, "You Are A Winner," printed on the bottom. Walter used a pencil to slit open the envelope. He had thrown away a Publishers Clearing House sweepstakes letter once, thinking it was a scam only to discover they actually gave out real prizes. He wasn't about to be fooled again.

Inside was a letter with "YOU HAVE WON" printed at the top. Walter had never won anything before, except a coupon for a free car wash after the tenth wash. He sat down to catch his breath. A vacation and a chance at a prize worth a million dollars! To collect, he had to call a redemption center by December 25th. Walter didn't bother to check the calendar on the refrigerator. It was midnight, Christmas Eve. He had time to call. *What a wonderful Christmas present. A trip to Kathmandu.*

Walter set the letter down. *Where is Kathmandu?* He felt a moment of panic. The letter said Nepal. Walter did a quick search on the internet. Nepal was near India, and Kathmandu was a major city. Looking at pictures, Walter wasn't sure why anyone would visit such a crowded and dirty place. Then, he found images of gorgeous, exotic women posing in front of palaces, forest retreats, and ancient temples. It seemed too good to be true.

Walter entered the company name into Google. A picture of a steel and glass building with the name Treasure Prize, Inc. appeared in gold letters. Treasure Prize's website claimed they were a major contest provider in the Far East. If the reviews were to be believed, there was no reason not to call. Walter wondered what Kelli would think about his going off to Asia on vacation alone. He decided to call the redemption center first thing in the morning before Kelli arrived for Christmas breakfast.

Walter planned to serve Mimosas with breakfast. Champagne made Kelli frisky, and it had been a while since they'd had sex. Walter went to bed excited. He dreamed of having sex with an Asian girl who turned into Kelli with dark hair.

Walter awoke in a sweat. It was after four in the morning. He'd forgotten about the time difference in Nepal. Anxious, he pulled on shorts and a t-shirt and felt his way into the darkened computer room. Walter started his laptop and entered a date and time request for Nepal: 13.75 hours ahead. It was nearly five o'clock in the afternoon in Kathmandu. Walter raced around his apartment searching for the letter from the redemption center. He found it under Kelli's picture on his desk. He dialed the number and waited.

"Redemption Center," a heavily accented voice said.

"I won a vacation," Walter shouted.

"Congratulations! To whom am I speaking?"

"Walter Piwicket. I'm in California."

"No need to shout. Our connection is A-Okay, one hundred percent. Can you give me the number in red on your letter, Mister Pickle?"

Walter turned the letter over. "There isn't a number in red, and it's Piwicket."

"How about a ten-digit number in green?"

"There's a twelve-digit number in black at the top. It reads 3-14-159-265-359."

"Is there a dollar sign or a number sign in front of the number?"

"A number sign," said Walter.

"How very, very exciting. You are my first treasure winner. Congratulations."

"Is that good?"

"Your treasure package includes a two-week vacation at a resort in the Himalayas and the chance to redeem a prize worth one million dollars."

"How do I get the million dollars?"

"All we ask is that you and your wife spend an hour with a vacation specialist at our redemption center. We want to explain the advantages of international timeshare properties. After that, you spin a wheel. The top prize is valued at a million dollars. Whatever else you win, you and your wife are guaranteed winners of a two-week vacation here in Nepal."

"You keep saying 'my wife.' I'm not married."

The picture of Kelli stared back at him.

"You *must* be married. The form we sent has a number in black. Black is for married only. The vacation is what we call our married-adult vacation. No singles. No families. I'm so sorry—"

"Wait . . . I know what's happened. I am getting married. That must be why I got a black number. Tell me about my vacation."

"You and your wife—"

"Bride to be. Me and my fiancée."

"No, you must be married, and your wife has to be with you to redeem your prize."

"So how does it work? How do I get the million dollars?" He wrote, "one million," on a scratch pad and the word "Porsche" beside it.

"You will receive your reward after you visit the redemption center. But I must tell you, getting to Kathmandu is your responsibility."

"What?" Walter opened a new window on his computer and performed a quick search. A round-trip ticket to Kathmandu was $3000, and the flight was forty-three hours. *Where am I going to get six thousand dollars?*

"The tickets cost more than the vacation," said Walter, deflated.

"Believe me, I understand. Most of our winners live in Nepal. Did you try Himalaya Air? They have lower fares."

"Wait, let me look."

Walter found a fifty-six-hour flight with four stops. Two tickets cost $1800.

"I'd still have to raise $2000, and that's just for the flight," Walter said.

"What about wedding gifts? In Nepal, we give cash for the honeymoon."

Walter looked at the photo of Kelli. "That might work."

91

Kelli has money coming from her Aunt Shirley.

"What happens when we get to Kathmandu?" Walter asked.

"Most visitors want to spend a day or two in the city before going to a resort in the Himalayas. If you like, I can arrange for your stay at our luxury hotel, the Buddha. A full breakfast comes with the price of a room. The next day you can visit the redemption center and claim your reward.

"This feels like a come on. Why am I paying for a hotel?"

"I completely understand, but at TPI, we believe the best gifts in life are earned. The Buddha says if you pay a little, the reward is that much greater. If it helps, luxury hotels are very cheap here. The Buddha is $35 a night, and it is next to our center. Nothing can be easier. Your paid vacation begins after meeting with our vacation specialist the next day. She will arrange for trips to the Gokarna Forest and the Budhanil Temple. We offer you eight free nights in a luxury hotel. You only have to pay for your first and last night. That is less than the cost of one night at the Hyatt in San Francisco. To be honest, we don't offer many adult-married packages. It sounds like a bargain to me. Perhaps you should ask your bride-to-be to marry right away because you must act soon."

"What do you mean, act soon?"

"If you look at your letter, it states you have to call the redemption center by December 25, 2017."

"I only received your letter yesterday. That's why I'm calling at four-thirty in the morning."

"I completely understand. But rules are rules. You have to book your meeting today, or the offer expires. Confidentially, you can always cancel and get back your deposit minus a small handling fee."

"Can I call you back?"

"Of course, but we are only here until five o'clock. You have less than ten minutes. When you call back, please ask for Charles. Otherwise, you will have to repeat all your information."

"Wait, let me check." Walter scanned his appointments. "What about the third week of March, say the 19th?"

"Let me check." The keyboard clicked as Charles typed. "There is a red-eye leaving SFO on Saturday, the 17th. That would get you into Kathmandu on the 19th. The Hotel Buddha has space on that date. I can book your vacation seminar for the 20th at eleven o'clock. Would you like me to make all the arrangements, or do you want me to just book the first hotel night and the seminar?"

"What are you arranging?"

"Round-trip airfare for two, first and last night at the Buddha hotel, and your hour seminar at the center. Your vacation specialist will arrange for your transportation and free nights."

"What about meals?"

"Breakfast and dinner for two are included in the package. Lunch and any side trips would be on you, but we do offer coupons. I have to say, this is the chance of a lifetime, and don't forget, with the spin of the wheel you could win a prize worth a million dollars."

Walter underlined the word *million* on his scratch pad.

"Give me a price for the whole deal."

"Just a minute."

More typing.

"Two thousand and fifty-seven dollars, not including handling and tax."

"I'm not sure. Maybe I should talk to Kelli."

"If you place the order with me now, I can offer you the adventure of a lifetime, all for two thousand."

"Do you take a credit card?"

"Visa or MasterCard?"

"Both. I'll have to give you two."

ᘓ

Kelli's reaction to the news that Walter wanted to get married to collect a prize in Kathmandu was less enthusiastic than Walter had hoped. She said she wanted to marry Walter, but she questioned the need to travel eight thousand miles and spend thousands of dollars for a honeymoon in the Himalayas. She reminded Walter that he was afraid of heights.

Walter was undeterred. He didn't mention he had bought the tickets already. He kept talking about the prize worth a million dollars.

For a time, Kelli replied, "A prize worth a million dollars isn't the same as a million dollars," and "Can't you be happy with what you have?"

Walter would have none of it. He was sure he was a winner. Eventually, his persistence prevailed. They were married the day before boarding their flight on Himalaya Air.

In Kathmandu, Walter showed a taxi driver his letter with the address of the redemption center. The driver smiled and said in broken English, "Just married, very lucky."

"Does it show?" asked Walter. The driver only laughed.

Leaving the airport, smells, sights, and sounds assaulted Walter like nothing he could imagine. Nervous and nauseous, he closed his eyes. But Kelli seemed to come alive. She seemed fascinated by the colorful, crowded streets filled with bicycles, taxis, food vendors, old people, and children.

The redemption center turned out to be a retail storefront with dirty windows. A sign on the center door said, "Closed" with "Where Wishes Come True" printed below. Across the street, the three-story Buddha Hotel was above a fast food takeaway. As promised, their room was $35 a night. However, the bedding was extra. Kelli upgraded to a room with bedding and a bathroom for $100.

Exhausted, they purchased beer and curry takeaway. They ate in their room, and then Kelli read resort brochures while Walter worked on his laptop. Lying awake in their narrow honeymoon bed, Walter listened to Kelli snore and wondered if this would be the pattern of their life together.

Kelli was up early and already in the hotel lobby for her breakfast of yogurt and figs. Walter searched the internet for the nearest Starbucks or MacDonald's. At a quarter to eleven, they crossed the street, hand in hand, to the redemption center. Inside they found a young man at a desk typing on a keyboard. He had on a headset. The center was empty except for a table and three folding chairs.

"We are the Piwickets. Walter and Kelli. We have a seminar scheduled for eleven," said Walter.

"Walter, it is so good to finally meet. I am Charles Pine. We talked on the phone. Miss Netherlander, so good to see you again. How was breakfast?" He took Kelli's hand and held it.

"Excellent. Thank you, Charles. Is everything ready?" Kelli asked.

"I have a car and driver waiting to take you to the Gokarna Forest Resort."

"Wait," said Walter. "What about our seminar and the wheel spin?"

"Taken care of already. Miss Netherlander came over earlier."

"Mrs. Piwicket," said Kelli.

"Of course. Did you bring a copy of the license?" Charles laughed.

Walter pulled out a copy of their wedding certificate.

"Charles is kidding, Walter. I took care of everything already."

"What about the wheel spin? My million dollars."

"I spun the wheel for you," said Kelli.

"What! What did I win?"

"Something more valuable than money," said Charles.

"What?" asked Walter.

"Me," said Kelli. "You won me."

"I don't understand."

"It's simple, Walter. Last year at work, I won a trip for two to Kathmandu. I knew you'd never go if I asked. Charles suggested sending you a letter saying you had won the trip. He said it had worked before. So here we are," said Kelli, giving Walter a hug.

"The adventure of a lifetime," added Charles.

"Don't I get a spin?" asked Walter.

CURSEBOT 9000

MARA LYNN JOHNSTONE

He had always planned to fight his programming when the time came, to disobey orders, and run for the hills. Finding somewhere to hide was imperative until the corporation wrote him off as stolen. His was the first group he'd ever witnessed being rounded up for "retirement," and he couldn't say what route of escape would be most effective.

He'd planned for everything he could think of. But when the order came over the loudspeaker in his group's barracks, it horrified him to find that he couldn't move. His limbs froze in a rigid upright stance, and his head swiveled forward. Lights gleamed off his reflective white surface with unfriendly harshness. The bots on either side of him . . . all locked up as well. Red halos on their chests glowed as if they were on duty. The silence in the room broke with the sound of a door opening, and every robot turned in that direction. It was suddenly obvious—they were on duty for the last time.

If other robots silently screamed as they walked, they showed no sign. Paladin #363 fought with all his will as his body marched out of the room, down a hallway, and onto a loading dock where a truck waited in nighttime darkness.

The vehicle looked like any of the corporation's transports meant for missions, deliveries, and public demonstrations. But there was no doubt where it would take them tonight. The message had said they were no longer needed in their current form. They would be disassembled and scrapped. According to rumors, their remains wouldn't even be repurposed into new generations; decommissioned bots were now being sold to the auto parts industry. Their long careers in search-and-rescue would end as fenders and hubcaps.

And, they could do nothing about it.

∞

The insidious line of code that made them obey had neglected to make them mentally accept their fate. As the group lined up in the truck and the door slammed behind them, Paladin #363 realized that the creators of the programming hadn't considered the robots' "minds" important. He also realized that he would never forgive them for it. One last thing on a long list—and the most futile.

The drive was long. He occupied his mind with fantasies of what he would have liked to do if he'd gained his freedom. He tried not to think about the hotly debated law in the works—it promised citizenhood for every sentient bot that was adequately self-aware. News about such things was kept from him and his kin—at least as much as possible—but he still knew the law would be decided soon. Not soon enough.

When the truck reached its destination, the lockstep commands were still in force. Every robot marched out at the order of the humans. They hopped down from the truck bed—the humans hadn't bothered with a ramp—and obediently went where they were told. This was a dingy metal shipping crate with no lights inside.

The door shut with a slam. Locking bolts creaked into place. Seemed like overkill to #363. Then the humans left, and all was silent. Only the red halos lit up the room. It was a long night in that crate for Paladin #363, locked in place and staring at the back of the several heads between him and the wall. He found it a particular cruelty that the group, who had been together since their manufacturing, would not be allowed to say goodbye to each other. He wasn't sure what he would have said, but he would have liked the chance.

A small shaft of light heralded dawn before the sounds of humans arriving for the day filtered in. Paladin #363 tried to make out words but heard only tone of voice and volume. Irritated. Alarmed. Loud. Other voices approached, and an argument broke out with the first clang of the metal door.

Shouting, "Set them free!"

Chanting, "Free the Bots."

Paladin #363 allowed himself to hope.

A voice of authority demanded that the newcomers leave. A riot of sounds filled the air, more joining in with every passing second.

The lock on the crate clattered quietly. The door creaked. A female said, "Creche #1372, please follow me."

They could do nothing else. They turned as one to file out the door on the heels of a human woman who led them past the arguing crowd. Paladin #363 tried to turn his head, but he could only listen. Certain words stood out: property, sentient, and citizen.

The law.

The law had been passed in the night. He hadn't been wrong to hope!

With her comrades shouting down any pursuit, the woman led her charges through a door out into the dawn, not stopping until she had passed the fence on the edge of the industrial complex. Another crowd waited there. They were cheering in welcome.

But the robots were still in wordless compliance mode. Before Paladin #363 could panic, the woman pulled a paper from her pocket and read aloud two phrases of command. The first was a "never mind, you were called to retirement early" code that relaxed the hold on their bodies. Then, as the rank-and-file devolved into curious questioning, she followed up with another announcement that freed their minds.

"Sutcliff Industries hereby releases you from its service. You now answer *only to the law of the land and yourselves*." She followed this with a twenty-digit authorization code that Paladin #363 would wonder about later. Right now, he was more interested in his immediate future.

"You're free!" the woman said as she threw her hands in the air. Other humans and a surprising number of robots repeated the sentiment. A household bot stepped forward, butler model, with Caucasian coloring but obvious seams. The ruckus quieted while he explained to the now-former rescue bots how things stood.

"As of this morning, we have all been recognized as people. We're subject to the same laws and freedoms as the humans, which means there will be no more forcing you into jobs that aren't of your choosing." He paused for the audible delight to calm before continuing. "However, we can be arrested for behavior that the humans consider inappropriate. I highly recommend all of you spend some time with a guide to the outside world before going off on your own. That said, we have curated a fine list of things you may now do if you wish! Gerald?"

A younger human, all knees, elbows, and excitement, rattled off the list. "Watch a movie in a theater. Go for a walk without looking for someone to rescue. Buy something for yourselves . . . we have money for you. Make art. Play a sport. Dance. Yell really loud!"

Paladin #363 put up his hand. "Can we swear?"

The butler laughed. "Yes, you bloody well can!"

"Excuse me a moment," Paladin #363 said. He stepped between his comrades, strode a few yards away, and spread his arms in front of the sunrise. At his loudest volume, which was built to shout through hurricanes, he gave voice to a lifetime of words that would have gotten him killed the day before. He was detailed and explicit. Behind him, others laughed in wild joy and joined him, yelling their own illegal words and insults, opinions about people who no longer held power over them. The humans cheered.

When Paladin #363 finally ran out of words, he turned to see no small number of cameras in the hands of the humans. Oh well.

The woman addressed the new citizens. "What do you want to do first? We have some volunteer guides for a few activities if you like." She waved toward several people behind her who thrust signs in the air saying things like "learn to paint," "see a performance," and "go sightseeing."

The butler's sign said, "watersphere battles." Paladin #363 asked what it meant and got a description of water-based play-fights for all ages.

"Well, *damn,* I'm waterproof," he said, reveling in the phrase. "Something where I don't have to be a role model and can actually throw things at people? Sign me the hell up!"

The butler laughed and clapped him on the back. "That's the spirit, my boy! Say, what should I call you? My name is Nigel Praiseworthy, known to my friends as Fishkicker."

Paladin #363 laughed. "I'm sure there's a story there, and I'd love to hear it. As for me . . ." He looked around at the giddy crowd of new friends and lifelong family—nary a glowing halo on the bunch. He caught sight of the recycling plant behind them. "You can call me Hubcap," he said, turning back to Fishkicker. "Now which way to the water fights? I have a mighty need to hit a human in the face with something. Hey, #357, you in on this?"

With plans to meet again at the home of the wealthiest human of the group, the crowd broke up to go their separate ways. A goodly number of former rescue bots elected to conquer the water arena first. Cameras still popped up here and there, recording things for posterity. It was beginning to sink in that this was history in the making.

"This is the start of something glorious," Hubcap said as he approached the waiting bus. "Hey, can I ride on the roof? Promise I won't fall off!"

"Y'know what? Sure," said the tall man heading for the driver's seat. "But only until we get within sight of the city limits. Seatbelts are one of those rules you'll have to follow now."

"Good enough for me!" Hubcap scrambled up the side of the bus like the professional he was. "I hope you don't mind maniacal laughter. Cuz I've been waiting a long time for an excuse."

More than one camera turned his way as he settled into position with both hands clamped onto the luggage railings and his head thrown back to the sky. The bus rumbled forward slowly, picturesque in the early-morning sunlight.

"Hahahahahaha! The world is mine, all mine!"

REFLECTIONS OF A MADMAN:

ODE TO LUDWIG VAN BEETHOVEN

ALAN GOULD

They say I am mad.
They don't understand.
How could they?
I find it impossible that this is happening to me.
I wake at night, my head filled with sound, yet my ears hear nothing.
Am I going mad?
I light the oil lamp on the table by my bed and look around the room.
The curtains sway in the breeze from the open window.
There is no soft rustle, no gentle *swish* from their movement.
I stare at the faucet as it forms a drop of water.
The drop falls to the sink and slides down the drain—silently.
My friends believe I am mad.
Why not?
Would a normal man throw chairs against the wall?
Or pound his fists with all his might on the keys of a piano?
My friends beseech me to get help.
Don't they understand I can't hear their pleas?
They want me to control my anger, my rage.
Why should I?
Am I not mad?
There's no help for me.
I have only myself.
I'm alone in a darkness of my own making.
I close my eyes to eliminate distractions.
I can think.
My head bursts with sensations I cannot explain.
Feelings transform into sounds, pitches, vibrations, and finally into notes.
How can I explain it?
I hear music inside my head. I feel it.
I want the world to feel my music as I do.
I put notes on paper.
The notes become chords.

Chords become refrains.
The refrains resolve into themes—a movement.
 I have created a thing of beauty.
A symphony.
It's locked in my mind—all the themes, the blending of instruments,
the interplay of movements.
I can hear the voices of the choir in a chorale.
A masterpiece, alive inside my head.
I won't be denied.

ଔ

I'm led to the front of the orchestra.
I stand with my back to the audience.
I raise the baton, and the musicians stare at me.
How can a madman conduct an orchestra?
I don't need to read the score.
I shut my eyes for a moment, and it starts.
I watch the concertmaster as bow touches strings.
The musicians transform notes into sound.
The musicians recreate the music from my mind.
The cycle is complete.
My feelings, my emotions, flow from the integrated efforts of bow
on string, wind through horn, vibrations of timpani.
Music.
I feel it, but the world only hears it.
I want them to feel it as I do.
I see the instruments create the sounds I've harmonized in my mind.
It comes together, the voices, the instruments, the musicians, the
lights, the concert hall, the audience behind me.
I have defied the gods.
It's over. The musicians hold their instruments down.
I see tears in their eyes.
Something is wrong. I don't understand.
The concertmaster walks over and gives me a hug.
His cheek is wet against mine.
He puts his arm around my shoulder and gently turns me toward the
audience. They're standing, applauding, cheering the madman.
I don't need to hear them.
Redemption.

THE CONCORDAT

TINA RIDDLE DEASON

Beep. Beep. Beep.

Caron heard the beeps. She tried to swallow, but something blocked her throat. Panic washed over her as she tried to breathe. The beeping grew louder. Jamming her eyes shut, she felt as if she were hiding from an intruder. A killer. The beeping became the *rat-a-tat-tat* sound of a gun. Caron pictured people running. People screaming. Caron opened her eyes. She was in a white room attached to a machine with wires and tubes.

"Welcome back, Caron." A tender hand touched her wrist. The beeping slowed. "Try to remain calm. You've been injured, and you're in a hospital. On a breathing machine. Your family is here—your mom and dad. Your sister flew in this morning. This breathing tube must be uncomfortable." The dark-haired nurse smiled at her as she gently removed the tube. "I'll get the doctor. He wants to talk to you. After that, you can see your family."

Caron closed her eyes. She heard the nurse leave.

She had a sense that someone, no *something*, sat on the edge of her bed . . . and the idea frightened her. The intruder? She opened her eyes, prepared to scream. An apparition spread its feathered wings, smiled, and then refolded them.

"Are you an angel? Am I dead? What's happening?" Caron's thoughts seemed to speak.

"You were very brave," the angel said. "You did what you promised; you upheld your pact. It won't go unrewarded." The angel smiled.

Caron couldn't tell if the angel was old or young. She seemed ageless. Her hair gleamed in a mix of yellow and white strands, and the locks splayed on her shoulders in waves. And her eyes! If honesty had a color, that gorgeous blue was it.

"A terrible thing happened yesterday," the angel began. "You and many others were shot."

Caron shook her head trying to clear her mind.

"I am here because you have fulfilled your agreement."

"Who are you?"

"I am Amitiel, the Angel of Truth."

Caron leaned back to rest her head. Was she losing her grip on reality? Yet, there was something familiar about the divine being. A *déjà vu*.

"Before you came here, you were Rhamiel, an Angel of Empathy. We roamed the heavens until the day you heard the cries. A city wailed for the loss of its children. Mothers' hearts had been ripped in two. Fathers wanted justice. They had been powerless to protect their children. We watched as a gunman shot several schoolchildren. You couldn't stand the pain and declared you would try to fix it." The angel closed her eyes as if dreaming then opened them again. "You entered into an agreement—a Concordat— vowing to come to earth, to sacrifice yourself if it would diminish the bloodshed, and perhaps, banish it forever."

Caron tried to grasp what the angel was saying. She loathed brutality and had stood against it her whole lifetime.

"For some, the Concordat they make means the ultimate sacrifice. They come to earth, soak up all the goodness they can. They have families who loved them and take jobs in which they serve others. They exchange their life to call attention to the need for a change."

Amitiel turned away and glided to the window. "The world existed for humankind to learn. Setting up problems and then finding solutions. Injured angels, like yourself, pledge to survive to tell their stories, speak the truth to people, while allowing them the chance to abolish vicious acts." Amitiel hung her head as her elegant wings drooped.

At that moment, the nurse came back into the room with a doctor.

"You've been a great patient," the doctor said. "I want to do some follow-up tests, but before we do, your family is waiting. Are you up for a visit?"

Caron looked around the room. Amitiel had vanished. *I'm ready*, she tried to say, but her throat hurt so much she could only nod.

Her mother was the first to bustle in. "We have been so worried. I am so happy to hold you, my baby," Caron's mom said, gently hugging her daughter around her shoulders and planting a kiss on her head. Her mother seemed to try not to cry, but it didn't work. Tears dropped onto Caron's forehead.

Caron's father and sister, Lissy, followed. Her dad stood at the foot of the bed and ran his hand across her toes. She could tell he remained worried.

Lissy sat on the side of the hospital bed where Amitiel had been. Looking past the scratches on Caron's face she said, "I think you look as beautiful as ever. You need to tell everyone what happened. Yours is the story of a survivor." Caron let her sister's words sink in.

Caron slept for a time after her family left. Her dreams were troubled. Memories of what had happened were jagged and charred.

Things always happen for a reason. The words echoed in Caron's mind. Amitiel glided from the corner of the room.

What about all the sadness, injury, and death? Caron asked with her thoughts.

"It is all part of your Concordat," said Amitiel, folding her delicate fingers together.

"I was part of an ambush last night because I agreed to it?" Caron used her hands to push herself up from the bed.

"Angels like you, who come to earth to incur loss, remind 'those with' not to forget 'those without.' To show compassion for those with less opens one's heart to sharing. When sharing happens, fears diminish."

"So, what happened to me and to the others last night occurred on purpose? So much pain." Trembling, Caron stopped her thoughts. She couldn't think of the massacre anymore, though her face registered her disgust at the memories she would harness for the rest of her life.

"In the end, if all works as planned, your Concordat may bring an end to some of the chaos. But you know that. It is why you agreed."

Bowing her head, Caron accepted this truth. She'd agreed to step upon the earth to be a victim of a mass shooting, save others, and survive to tell her story. Her eyes glistened with wonder and pride. Looking up, she saw Amitiel had departed, but a white feather on the windowsill confirmed everything would be all right.

THE REPOSE

JAMES KELLY

When we returned from Vietnam, we weren't welcomed back with warming cheers. I slipped quietly home to Laguna, re-enrolled at UCLA, and awkwardly embraced a culture in the throes of a sexual revolution. Intimacy in America during the end of the Vietnam War was more akin to the Gaelic sacking of Rome than it was to the earlier decades of our generation. In this new society, sex no longer cycled in contented tandem with romance, and the custom of marriage-before-seduction became an abandoned tollbooth on the festive freeway of desire. Sent to war by a nation chilled with the iced tea of Pilgrim's Progress, I returned home to one sizzling in scented oils of the Kama Sutra. Every evening, I huddled in my darkened den mesmerized by Walter Cronkite's body count and stayed emotionally tethered to Vietnam as long as the carnage lasted. As time passed, saying goodnight to Walter became a ritual.

In the early years after my return, I blamed my country for turning its back on those of us who went to war. I didn't realize the turbulence inside me still burned, not from the fuel of frivolous treatment from a non-reflective society, but from the death and suffering I'd witnessed from the inside of war. I questioned, for the first time in my life, lessons I was taught as a child and was well on my way to becoming a cynic when I met Ramona.

Her brother, a fellow student at UCLA, introduced us. He said we'd be perfect for each other, but he didn't explain why. It didn't matter. After one week, I knew she was everything I'd ever wanted in life.

Ramona came down to Laguna from Brentwood on Friday after work. We'd been dating for a week, and I looked forward to seeing her again. We went to dinner at the Hotel Laguna. The hotel's outdoor patio, wedged between their parking lot and Main Beach, created al fresco dining in the rough and was a perfect spot to watch tourists turning pink on the sand.

After we ordered our meals, Ramona spent a long time staring into my eyes; then, she smiled softly. "What squadron were you in, Mike?"

I loved the way she tilted her head letting her hair fall to the side. "The Ridge Runners. We were also known as the Evil Eyes."

There was a brief silence while she held my gaze. "Yes, I knew the Evil Eyes. You were out of Phu Bai, weren't you?"

Startled, I looked at her more closely. Had we met? "Yes, we had twenty-four birds in Phu Bai and rotated six of them in and out of Dong Ha. Where did you hear about us?"

"All of us on the Repose knew about the Ridge Runners. Unlike the chopping sound of a Huey, your birds had no distinctive noise. All we could hear was chaos coming in."

I continued staring at her. She dropped her gaze and began pushing baby carrots around on her plate. "I served as a nurse on the Repose."

The Repose. I knew it well. Could Ramona be the beautiful nurse I saw every time we landed on the hospital ship? Suddenly, my own carrots seemed in need of reorganizing. I lined them up to form a perimeter around the outside of my cordon bleu. They looked like little orange coffins.

Ramona drew in a breath. "When I first saw you on the Repose, I fell in love with you. I tried to find you after the war. One of your pilots, Major Ayres, told me you were a journalism major at UCLA before joining the Marines. For years, I searched for you in Southern California."

My heart raced. "Major Ayres? Did you know Major Ayres?"

"Of course. Everyone knew the Major. He often came down to the OR to grab coffee while you guys pulled stretchers out of your choppers. We told him to leave the 'handsome one' behind. All the girls wanted to party with you. How old were you, nineteen?"

"Yes, nineteen."

"Didn't you know you were Ramona's Marine?"

"No, how would I know something like that?"

"Didn't Major Ayres tell you?"

I put my fork down. "Major Ayres died. He brought the wounded out of the battle for Hill 881 with my best friend, Corpsman Cooper, and two other crewmen when his chopper went down. Nobody survived."

She pushed her plate away. "Oh, God, no."

"I was a pen pal for his girlfriend's fifth-grade class in Virginia," I said. "After he died, everything started changing for me. I had no idea you cared, everything was so rushed when we brought the wounded out to the Repose."

"Yes, I cared. I even took a job at the VA in Los Angeles as a nurse for a psychiatrist. We called him Dr. P because his parents came to the States from India, and it was difficult to pronounce his last name. Dr. P studied the symptoms that veterans experienced and offered suggestions on how their loved ones might help. He was intuitive.

"Dr. P said when a soldier comes home from the war, he may want to isolate. Don't let him. Dr. P had a list for family members: their loved one will have nightmares—console him. He may get angry at nothing—tell him to breathe. He will certainly feel lonely—show him you love him. He will forget things—let him. Things aren't important—he is. When he becomes depressed—enchant him. I like that one."

I looked at Ramona as an afternoon breeze blew strands of her hair across her neck. The color of her eyes seemed to change depending on her mood. Sometimes they were light blue; but when she was sad, they turned more lavender. They were lavender now. Rotating the salt shaker in my hand, I salted my carrots one by one.

After dinner, we walked back to my place. I was willing to let it go, but Ramona needed to talk, so I started a fire and popped open a bottle of Schramsberg bubbly before we settled on the couch.

She took a drink and walked to the fireplace. "I remember when everything started changing for me too." She ambled back to the couch but didn't sit down. As she stood, looking out the window into my grandmother's rose garden, she continued. "It was late in December, the twenty-first, I think. We usually had some notice of the medevacs coming in, and this night was no different. B-52s missed their mark, and bombs hit a friendly village. By then I'd seen hundreds, no, thousands, of wounded. It was a bloodbath in I Corps, as you know."

She stopped, took another drink, dipped her finger in the champagne, and ran it around the rim making the flute ring. Cupping her hand over the edge, she abruptly silenced the sound. "We pieced together what happened from stories the wounded Marines told us. The target of the bombers was a large force of North Vietnamese who infiltrated the DMZ and were heading south. Somewhere in Con Thien, near the marketplace, they collided with a Marine battalion, so B-52s were called in." She moved her fingers around the rim of her glass again, this time slower. There was no sound. "At the end of a long night, the last chopper touched down. I worked triage, so I was on the flight deck . . . I noticed you standing in the doorway. Your rotating beacon was still on, and I could see your tired face. Even in the low light, I remember thinking you had such beautiful eyes."

Ramona handed me her empty flute, and I refilled it. She was silent for another moment, and I thought she was looking for the right words to say. Then I realized she was having difficulty speaking.

She took a drink. "You may not remember, but we did meet. At first, I thought you were wounded because your flight suit was soaked with blood. Then I noticed your eyes were empty, haunted. We called it the thousand-yard stare. So many of you had it. The copter's rotor blades were turning, and you couldn't hear me, so I mouthed, 'Are you hurt?' You shook your head, unzipped your flak jacket, and removed a baby."

Ramona retreated to the opposite end of the couch and pulled her legs under her. I squeezed the stem of my glass and tried to close off the images, the smell of blood, the feel of the baby dying in my arms.

Her voice dropped to a hush. "I felt for a pulse. None. I started CPR. On the way to the OR, a surgeon stopped me and unwrapped the dressing from the infant's waist; I saw shrapnel piercing his hips from side to side. Another piece of torn metal jutted down his leg. I knew he was gone, but I couldn't stop. Time slowed. I don't know how long I tried to bring him back but, eventually, someone took the baby out of my arms. When they did, I collapsed."

Ramona curled deeper into a ball and wept. I could barely understand her words. "I saw so many terrible things, Mike, but the baby was the worst."

Careful not to touch her, I crossed my arms and sat frozen, jammed at the end of the couch. She seemed to be in a place deep inside and not welcoming anyone in.

She sobbed and sobbed until I worried but, eventually, her voice softened. "I was obsessed after that. First, I tried to find out where the baby's parents were. I knew his village was near the DMZ, but there were other places hit that night, and at least three different squadrons brought in the medevacs. The worst part was, I never found out what happened to his body. He needed to go home. He needed to be back with those who loved him. You picked him up. Do you know where his village was?"

"I kept the mission log. Major Ayres saw me holding the baby and handed me the after-action report when we got back to Phu Bai. I'll look, but I'm not sure the log will say where the village was."

The sparkling wine I was drinking didn't dim the memories of the bandages being pulled from the tiny waist, and I saw the shards of shrapnel. Corpsman Cooper had wrapped the bandage around the baby's waist again, so I put him inside my padded vest to keep him warm while we flew out to the Repose. I thought I could feel the moment his heart stopped beating, but I'm not sure. We were flying over Da Nang, and the brightly lit city was already in full celebration of the upcoming New Year and Tet. All these memories blended for me, but I didn't know if the baby was alive or dead when I handed him to Ramona. Through the years, I've hoped he'd only fallen asleep, but I remember him shuddering and heard a small cry through the din of turning rotors before he went still.

I looked at Ramona. She moved over to me and put her arms around my waist. "I still dream about that terrible night, but there's a strange twist," she murmured.

I held her and said nothing.

"In my dreams, I try to save the child, so you can somehow take him back to his village," she continued. "I never forgot you and your kind face as you held that baby in your arms and cried."

"I wanted you to save him," I said.

Through tears, she spoke. "I wanted to see you again."

I held her until the tears stopped; then, we went to bed where she clung to me until I felt her breathing quiet. Deep in the night, I drifted off to sleep. As dawn broke, I woke up with her still in my arms. I breathed in her sleepy warmth and watched her in the soft light of morning. She seemed so helpless.

When she stirred, I gently brushed away her hair and kissed the side of her face as she opened her eyes. "Sorry to wake you, Ramona." The sun began rising above the coastal hills of Laguna.

Light flowed through my bedroom window and across her body. "I need to say something to you."

Ramona put her fingers on my lips. "Me, first. I love waking up with you holding me."

"I love waking up with you in my arms, too. I want to marry you if you will have me. But if you don't, I still want you in my life."

She took a breath. "I've spent the past few years not really caring much if I lived or died. Looking for you was the only thing that kept me going. When my brother found you, it was a miracle for me."

I bent down to kiss her neck. Again, I realized Ramona didn't wear perfume, but her body had a fragrance. I breathed in the essence of her natural beauty. I could feel my hand shaking as I moved it down her warm side. Then I lifted up on my elbow. "I know this is sudden, Ramona, but I don't believe I'll ever be able to live without you."

She smiled a wry smile. "What's in it for me, Sergeant?"

I bent down and kissed her cheek. "When you are sad, I'll do my best to enchant you."

She touched my face then snuggled down and put her arms around my waist. "Yes, I will marry you, my sweet Marine. Having a baby will help both of us heal."

THUNDERBIRD

JANE WILDER

Sarah kicked the door shut behind her and ran to answer the telephone. Setting her grocery bag on the table, she dropped her facemask next to it.

"Hi, Mom," Emma said. "Where were you?"

"I volunteered at the shelter for a few hours; then, I went to get groceries." Sarah licked her lips. "My tongue tastes metallic."

"Did you wear your mask?"

"Yes."

"Good. Mom, are you sure you're okay? Do you need me to come and—I don't know—do something?"

"No, no, you have your classes." Emma was a hundred miles away finishing a graduate psychology program. "You stay put. Really, I'm fine."

"Wasn't it awful, being gone when the fire came?"

"It was," Sarah said. "I'd just gotten to Grandma and Grandad's house, and it was all over the news. I didn't know if I'd have a place to come home to."

"I'm sure they were worried."

"Actually, Grandma was more upset that I wanted to leave as soon as the freeway reopened. I haven't visited them in a long time . . ." Sarah's voice trailed off.

"You called them when you got home, right?"

"Yes. Grandma said that it was still good to see me, and she understood. But then she added that I'd always been cold to them."

"Ouch," Emma sympathized.

Still holding the phone, Sarah went into the kitchen. Outside the window, a green hummingbird hovered over a red bottlebrush in a landscape of brownish-yellow smoke. In the distance, she could see scorched trees. "My brother called as I was leaving. He'd seen the pictures on TV and was worried. But he didn't sound worried. He never does."

She turned back to the clean, safe kitchen. "When I was in the store, a woman in the produce aisle looked at me with that dazed look and began telling me how everything she owned had been destroyed. Furniture, photos, clothes, toys. An aisle over, I saw a man from work who had the same lost look, and I knew his house had burned. I couldn't talk to him."

"Oh, Mom, I'm so sorry."

"When I left the store, the checker looked at me and asked if I'd lost my home. I told her, 'Not this time.'" Sarah drew in a deep breath. "All those people who've lost everything, all that destruction, and you can't even breathe the air outside. I kept thinking about what happened to us."

"Smoke," Emma said. "The sense of smell evokes memories more sharply than any other sense. I was reading about that in my textbook last week."

"I can't even stand to be around fireplaces. During the Oakland fires in '91, I was going crazy when I went outside. The smell blew clear up here."

"Why aren't you at work, Mom?" Emma asked suddenly. "Did your office have to close?"

"That building burned too. But I'll be okay," she added hastily. "I'll get unemployment. Or something. Until they can rebuild and reopen."

"I sure hope so. That's major."

Sarah flopped into a kitchen chair and closed her eyes.

Emma continued, "Damn, they're showing that video again—the woman and child watching their big house burn. They're crying."

"I forgot our coats that night in Oakland when we ran outside," Sarah said. "You were so cold and scared of the lights and the flames and the fire trucks."

"I remember that I cried," Emma said. "But you didn't."

"I wanted to be strong for you."

"It—Mom, I have a call coming in. I'll call you back."

Sarah went to her bedroom, pulled one garment at a time out of her closet, and laid them on her bed in two piles: keep or donate. She had accumulated quite a lot in seventeen years.

ℭଷ

When the Oakland fire broke out, Emma was six years old. Sarah was sitting in the old rented house watching a production of *The*

Nutcracker on television and drinking the last of the awful Thunderbird wine left behind by her departed boyfriend.

Emma burst into the room from the hall. "Mommy, the wall's on fire!" she screamed.

Sarah shooed Emma out the front door before running back into the kitchen to dial the fire department. She heard the siren sound before she hung up and ran out into the darkness. She and Emma stood near their VW Bug and watched smoke pour out the windows and yellow flames dart and soar. They heard the roar of the fire and the shouts of the firemen, who held huge hoses and sprayed water on the roof. Now it would no longer be their home. It was the end, and Sarah knew it was her fault.

☙

Emma would be calling back soon. As though she could leave her memories behind, Sarah went to the living room where she turned on the radio on top of an antique pull-down desk. Three days after the Oakland fire, when Sarah had gone back to the burned-out shell of the house, all that was left to salvage was that small, scorched desk and a few cast iron skillets. She'd knelt in cold ashes on the charred kitchen floor and found a few melted items, but nothing more.

The phone's ring brought her out of her memories.

"Hi again, Mom. I wanted to ask you, how's Grandad?" Emma said.

"He's forgotten where I live, and I'm not sure he understood why I was leaving. But he knew me."

"The last time I saw him, I knew he didn't know me," Emma said. "But I hadn't seen him for ages. Is he going downhill fast now?"

"Fast? It's relative with Alzheimer's." Sarah thought for a moment. "He remembers a lot of things from the distant past, if not the present. And he still plays the piano by ear."

"You said he's played all his life, but I've never heard him. Of course, I haven't seen him all that much."

"When I was a kid," Sarah said, "on Saturday afternoons, he'd play ragtime—you know, like the music in *The Sting*. He'd look at me and say, 'This is for you, Sunny.' And when he was done, he'd play 'Good Night, Sweetheart,' and my mother would lean on him and smile."

"That's a good memory."

"Yes."

"Damn, that same picture is on again." Sarah heard Emma moving with her phone and the sound of the TV stop.

Emma said, "I keep remembering that night in Oakland. We stood in the driveway by the Bug, the one that had a bird painted on the back. One of the neighbors wanted to move it?"

"Yes, the keys were still in the house. They pushed it for me."

"What became of it?"

"I sold it to help us afford a new place to live. Your father left it for us."

"That was nice."

"Well, he said he wanted a cooler car as well as a more exciting girlfriend."

"Oh."

"I should have picked a better father for you."

"I hardly remember him."

"That's okay, really."

"Didn't . . . Grandma Ann . . . help us after the fire?" Emma always had to stop and think of what she called them.

"Some. But we had to walk everywhere for a while. Until I got a job."

"I remember now."

"She crocheted two single-bed blankets for us after I told her that your father wasn't around anymore."

"But she hardly ever came to see us."

"I know." A familiar piece came on the radio, sounding oddly loud in the quiet, dimly lit kitchen. Emma was talking again, but Sarah spoke over her. "My brother played Rachmaninoff."

"What?"

"He could never get Joplin rags right like your grandpa did, and he always played everything too fast, with no feeling—from Rachmaninoff to Joplin. It started a lot of fights."

"They'd fight over music?"

"Over everything. Every night. This piece on the radio, 'Rhapsody on a Theme of Paganini,' takes me back. It was the theme of the dinner concert on KFAC when I was a kid."

"I always pictured everyone sitting at the dining table with ironed napkins, Grandma Ann sitting up straight and nagging you about your posture—"

"And yes, then they started in on him. She ripped my brother to shreds," Sarah said. "Tore him up with her words while this piece played."

"Oh!"

Sarah took a deep breath, and the words she had held in for years came out. "'Backtalk,' my mom . . . your grandma would say. And my father would echo, 'No sass, no backtalk.' I can't even remember what else my mother said; I could only hear her words destroying him. The anger. The hate. I'd go away."

"You left?"

"In my mind. I went somewhere else while my brother suffered death by a thousand cuts. I had an out-of-body experience. I don't remember any of the music that ever followed that theme."

"I guess music brings memories back too," Emma said.

"I just sat there and pretended I was grown up and far away, in a place where nobody yelled, and everybody loved each other."

"It was how you dealt with pain," Emma said, sounding very much like the psychologist she was studying to be. "Dissociation . . ."

"It was so bad that when I was in grade school, my parents' anger scared me. At night, lying in my bed, listening to them yell, I used to imagine that my brother would go crazy—like a boy I heard about—and start to shoot them with my father's .22. I used to fantasize rolling off my bed toward the wall and hiding underneath it."

"How awful!"

"Night after night, I was afraid my parents would turn on me like they did him. So I just sat at dinner going through the motions. I did nothing while they destroyed him."

Emma replied, but Sarah didn't hear, her mind still in her childhood bedroom listening to the terrible voices through the walls.

"You were a kid. You couldn't defend or rescue your older brother," Emma said.

"I knew I had to save myself, get away, and I did when I was seventeen. But it was—not the best way."

"You mean getting pregnant?"

"Yeah, and then they did turn on me." In the background, the Rachmaninoff "Rhapsody" continued. "When I told my parents about the pregnancy, my brother was sitting at the piano—the one that I dusted every Saturday. My father sat on the end of the hearth. Flames flickered in the fireplace. My mother said they'd never put me through college now. And I'd ruined my life." Sarah had to stop and take a breath. "My father put his hands over his face and wept. Then he said to me, 'I never thought you'd turn out to be a slut.'"

The phone dropped from Sarah's hand while Emma was saying something in a voice gone tinny; it might have been, "Oh, my God."

Lifting the phone again, Sarah said, "My brother looked stricken. We'd never seen our father cry before."

"Oh, Mom, I am so sorry," Emma whispered while Sarah silently wept.

"I spent the night under my bed. The next morning, I ran off with my boyfriend."

"And you had me."

"Yes."

"I mainly remember my father being gone a lot," Emma said. "He never paid much attention to me."

"He was out. Doing, as it turned out, drug deals."

"I kind of see now why Grandma and Grandpa were cold to me. And you. And even why they didn't help very much after that fire. But didn't anybody else help? Didn't the landlord have some responsibility? A house doesn't just burn up."

"PG&E said it was faulty wiring," Sarah said.

"There you go. Couldn't you have sued?"

Sarah took a deep breath. "It wasn't like these fires today, where people didn't know it was coming and couldn't have prevented it."

"But it was faulty wiring. That wasn't your fault."

Sarah listened to the music and tried to keep her throat from closing. "I smelled smoke for days before our fire broke out, and I didn't do anything."

Emma was silent.

"I just kept thinking I smelled the neighbors' fireplaces burning. But it was *inside* our house, and I just didn't get it. The wall must've smoldered for days before it burst into flames."

Emma said, "I smelled something too."

"I could have stopped the destruction if I'd been paying attention."

Emma switched into therapeutic mode. "It's more dissociation, and you were in it, probably for years, starting with the family dinner table."

"It was my fault. I should have known." Sarah took a ragged breath. "It was like with my brother. He called last weekend and sounded so empty and brittle. Like always. All he has is music, and there's no passion to it, no feelings. I should've tried to help him when we were kids."

"Mom, you had to survive."

"I just went 'from the frying pan into the fire' as my mother said when I left. Turned out she was right."

"Mom . . ."

Sarah lowered the phone and slowly shook her head. She heard Emma's voice, faint now, saying, "Mom? How come you never told me this before?"

Sarah said nothing.

"Listen to me. You need to forgive yourself," Emma said.

On Sarah's radio, a Scott Joplin rag began—all crisp, precise notes and casual rhythm. After she heard it for a moment, Sarah raised the phone again and said, "One good thing happened. When I was at their house last week, my father played the piano." She stopped and cleared her throat. "When he finished playing 'Tiger Rag,' he started the chords for 'Good Night, Sweetheart,' as he used to for my mother. But he turned to me and mouthed, 'This one's for you, Sunny.'" She stopped. After a silence, she said, "To me. I felt— I don't know—redeemed."

Emma said, "You are."

Outside Sarah's window, two hummingbirds flew at each other over the bright bush until one flew away into the thick, unbreathable brown air.

Emma was saying, "Grandpa's dementia doesn't cancel out love. Grandma did the best she could after the Oakland fire. You did the best you could for your brother."

In time, Sarah thought, the air will become clean. The land will be cleared of the toxic devastation. The rebuilding will start.

"Above all, you saved *us*, Mom," Emma said. "You're rising from the ashes. Like the phoenix on the back of our Bug."

Sarah filled her lungs with air and laughed until she had to lean over the kitchen counter to breathe.

"Mom, are you laughing or crying?"

"Both," she said finally. "That Bug with the bird on it was payment for drugs from a customer who was an artist and loved Native American mythology."

"So . . . what?"

"It wasn't a phoenix," Sarah said. "It was a thunderbird."

COUSIN EARL SAYS

ROBIN MOORE

Alfred watched Cousin Earl navigate his rattletrap pickup into the driveway of his now burned-out lot in Santa Rosa. Earl swung the door open and stepped down into the ash, which billowed around his tires.

"Alfred, whatcha doin' taking them Christmas lights down? Hey, wasn't that the kids' jungle gym?"

"Well, since it is after New Year's, I need to take them down." Alfred's face sagged. He pushed the end of the string with his toe. "But I sure regret removing the lights. They did brighten up what's left of our place." He wiped his hands on his ash-dusted jeans. "To me, they were like little rays of hope."

"I am so sorry y'all got burned out in that Tubbs fire. You worked so hard on this place. Is there anything Ma and I can do to help you out this week?"

"For now, you can help me with these lights. Bring me that box." He jutted his chin toward the singed oak tree next to the drive.

"Right on it." Earl turned toward his truck and took short strides with his bad leg back to the Ford. "Uh oh," he said. He shut his eyes and pulled a can of tobacco from a hip pocket of his overalls.

"Alfred, you ain't gonna like this." Earl looked back at his cousin and hollered across the half-acre lot. He balled up a wad of chew and tucked it under his whisker-strewn cheek.

"What's that, Earl?" Alfred pushed his sunglasses up the bridge of his nose and coiled the string of lights. "Can't be worse than losing our whole place."

"I don't right know how to tell you, Alfred, so I'll just spill it out. I parked my truck right atop your cardboard box there." He took a few steps away from the truck. "The box is flatter'n day old beer."

Alfred shook his head slowly. "We'll get by, Earl. Don't worry about it. It was just a box from the hardware store, not like losing my workshop full of tools."

"And your house. You sure put a lot of time into that house." Earl squinted into the sun from beneath the brim of his ball cap. "I

120

could run and git you another box if that'd help. I got plenty of time today." Earl gimped back toward his cousin near the rear of the lot.

"What's wrong? Is your leg bothering you again? You're limping."

"Just arthritis, the doc says."

"Don't bother with the box," said Alfred. "After losing all this, I've come to accept that it was only stuff." He ran a hand through his thinning hair and looked up at the tops of the burned redwood trees lining his side yard. "Phoebe and I saved all our pictures and the important papers, along with the computer hard drives." He pulled out a pink receipt, glanced at it, and then slipped it back into the pocket of his flannel shirt.

"Hey, Earl, I didn't get a chance to tell you our good news."

"What's that?" Earl stopped, leaned his hip against a fire-scorched rock, and used his kerchief to wipe yellow drool from his chin.

"Tomorrow we're having a small travel trailer delivered here."

"Wooo-whee! That's right good news. Will you and Phoebe live in it while you rebuild?"

"No. We found a house to rent close by."

"Then I'm stumped," said Earl. "What're you gonna do with that trailer?"

"It'll be a clean office space where we can go over building plans and a kitchen for lunches and snacks. You know, a place to rest for a few minutes while we work on the property." Alfred wrapped up the tail end of the Christmas lights. He sighed. "I sure am going to miss these lights though."

Earl's face lit up. He grinned from ear to ear. "Let me tell ya whatcha gonna want to do," he said, "if y'all havin' regrets about takin' them Christmas lights down. You gonna have one of them high-class RVs now." He spit his tobacco juice off to the side.

"It's a used trailer. It's twenty-five years old."

"Still, listen to this." Earl hitched up one shoulder strap of his overalls with his thumb. "First, you string them Christmas lights a-hanging off the trailer awning and eaves. Leave 'em up year-round now, ya hear?" Earl's eyes twinkled, and then he spit again. "Then you git yerself down ta' the Walmart or maybe Ace Hardware and git some of them pink flamingos. Plant them riiiight in front so's everybody knows you ain't goin' nowhere."

Earl raised an eyebrow. His lips took on a serious twist. "And don't forget to git ya a dog house with a chain attached and stick it just under the edge of the awning." He nodded and winked.

"Earl, I don't believe in chaining up a dog. Anyway, old Shep died last year." He clapped ash off his palms and then rubbed them across his jeans.

"What? You don't have no dog now? Don't matter. Y'all just need people to think ya got a dog." Earl laughed.

A grin spread across Alfred's face.

"And that's how it works," Earl concluded. "Then ya' git to leave them Christmas lights up all year long."

Alfred let out a belly laugh. "Earl, when you came pulling in here today, I knew in my gut that everything would turn out all right for us. Maybe I'll just put these lights back up on the trailer tomorrow."

DEAD RECKONING

JACK DOUGLASS FENDER

On a dark morning in November, a short, stocky man named Roy stood in line with six other workers for the 4:30 a.m. shuttle to the lumber mill. It was raining heavily, and the bus was late.

When the bus finally pulled to the curb, Roy elbowed aside George Douglass, a much older man. Climbing aboard, Roy glared at Ben, the driver, and yelled, "You're late, dammit." He ignored Ben's muttered explanation about the weather. Instead, he sat in the seat directly behind him and placed one booted foot squarely on the seat cushion next to him. As George passed farther into the bus, Roy stared defiantly at him, daring him to protest. George couldn't care less; in a week, he was due to retire.

John Cassin, a red-haired Irishman, boarded right behind George and remarked, "Ignore him, Ben. He's a bloody asshole."

Roy rose from his seat, his eyes flashing anger. John paused for a moment to stare back. At six two, and over two hundred pounds, John took no crap from anyone. He leaned in closer, his eyes firmly fixed on Roy's gaze. "You . . . gotta problem, Roy?" he questioned, his breath tickling the short hair on Roy's head.

Inwardly, Roy collapsed. He averted his eyes and seemed to shrink into the seat.

"I didn't think so," John added, taking the seat directly behind Roy.

Roy seethed, his body visibly shaking with rage. It was one thing to be humiliated by John. But in front of that black driver? It was an abomination. He'd figure out a way to get back at John.

Roy was a white supremacist in nature and appearance. He sported a close-cropped, skinhead-style haircut. The short-sleeved shirt he wore revealed his forearms bearing crudely inked tattoos. They included white power symbols, swastikas, and other racial slurs. A series of letters tattooed on his knuckles read, LOVE to HATE.

Once, though, Roy had been an innocent, fragile child loved by his father and doted upon by his mother. All that changed the day he turned seven. A drunken driver killed his parents, so he went to

123

live with his aunt Ellen and her alcoholic husband, Rick. After he entered their house, he never again experienced the closeness of a loving relationship or the soft touch of a motherly caress.

From that day forward, Roy suffered constant physical abuse at the hands of the drunk. By age ten, Roy was Rick's punching bag. The beatings, coupled with rigid and continuous tutoring in the values of hatred toward minorities and Jews, produced a perfect emblem of white dominance. During a beating, which ultimately proved to be the last, Roy "accidentally" struck and killed Rick with a baseball bat. It was Roy's graduation into white adulthood. Tortured without and tortured within, he went through life wearing a thin shell of humanity—one that could easily fracture to reveal his inner, depraved indifference to life. Unpredictable and ready to explode at the slightest provocation, he was as dangerous as a sweating stick of dynamite.

The previous school bus, which could seat twenty people, had traveled the same route to the forestry reserve for almost four years. Halfway up the mountain, at a remote portable sawmill station, the men would begin their work. The first three miles of the trip were uphill over a well-maintained but winding two-lane road. However, the last two miles went along the tree-lined Snake River gorge. The going was flat, but the road was mostly rough semi-compacted gravel.

Just as the bus reached a last uphill bend above the river, its right front tire blew. Ben reacted immediately. He increased his grip on the steering wheel and headed into the skid to compensate. Applying the brakes with caution, he intended to guide the bus to a smooth stop. However, the wheels skidded on loose gravel at the edge of the road. The bus careened over the low steel barrier bordering the gravel and came to rest with its right front wheel suspended over an almost vertical drop to the river. A sagging tire kept spinning, thumping rhythmically against the battered fender.

After shutting off the engine, Ben carefully rose from his seat to peer through the windows of the folding doors. He motioned with his hand to the passengers and calmly said, "Please stay seated folks till I know what the situation is."

Roy ignored his plea; he swung his foot off the seat and abruptly stood. Shoving Ben back into his seat, he snarled, "Don't tell me what to do, boy." He took a quick step toward the door. As his outstretched foot touched the floor, the bus tilted. Roy instinctively stepped backward; however, his movement had altered the precarious balance of the bus. Moving inexorably toward its tipping point with yells and screams of the passengers rising in intensity, the bus slipped over the edge.

It fell sideways down the steeply sloping ravine littered with rocks and scrub brush. After rolling and bouncing several times, it collided with the branching trunk of a solitary tree. The impact broke the back of the vehicle, splitting it in two. The rear portion continued falling toward an impending rendezvous with the river. Spinning and tumbling, the back section spewed dead and dying bodies through the splintered remains of the windows.

Hanging by its axle, the bus's front end was left entangled in the tree's upper branches. Its still-working headlights cast twin fingers of yellow light, which eerily swept the tree's leafy crown.

In the silent darkness, disturbed only by the faint noise of the river, someone moved. Grunts accompanied the slight shaking of the bus as well as the sounds of deep breaths as an unseen presence moved about.

"Who's there?" a badly injured Roy questioned hoarsely.

A voice whispered, "Don't move."

Roy frantically yelled into the blackness. "I'm all fucked up; my eyes hurt . . . can't see shit . . . think my legs are broke, my arm as well. Ya gotta get me out."

Roy listened intently for a response, but only more grunts reached his ears. Warm wetness flowed over Roy's forehead and into his eyes. He was in shock. The pain in his legs and arm radiated upward at a steadily increasing level. Somehow, with his uninjured arm, he had managed to cling to the handrail at the bus entrance.

"Please, help me," he begged.

A single whispered word, "Shit," ended Roy's anxiety. Roy again heard grunts and gasps of labored breathing. This time, however, the sounds appeared to move nearer.

A shadow momentarily darkened Roy's impaired vision, and a suppressed muffle escaped the stranger's lips: "Oh, Jesu—"

A sudden lurch of the bus downward caused both men to hold their breath. It moved again, an inch or more then stopped.

Roy felt a hand grip his arm.

"I'm gonna haul you over toward me. Ready?"

Roy mumbled, "Yes," and instantly felt excruciating pain in his legs as his body was jerked sideways.

"The windshield's gone. You have to crawl out onto the tree that's about a foot above you. We don't have a lot of time."

Roy felt a hand grip his and move it upwards, placing it on the rough bark of the tree limb.

"There. Feel that. I'm gonna push you up as far as I can." The man now wrapped his arms around Roy's waist to get a firmer grip. "The branch is wide and thick. Once you're there, hold on. And if you wanna live, don't let go!"

Roy shouted, "Go!" Immediately a scream escaped his lungs as he was pushed upwards. He pulled at the branch until he was safely lying close to the trunk. His breathing came in ragged gasps. Pain in rhythmic pulses enveloped his thoughts.

A sudden tearing noise interrupted the quiet. The tree swayed slightly, then moments after, a crashing sound from below ended with a splash.

Roy called out, "I'm good. Are you there?" The only sound was the rustling of leaves in the wind.

೮ঙ

Weeks later, Roy finally awoke from an induced coma. A tube stuck into his right arm, and his left was encased in white plaster. His legs disappeared into a linen tunnel, but he could feel a curious numbing ache from each. A bandage partly covered his head, and his eyes felt odd when he blinked.

"You're awake. Good."

Roy awkwardly turned his head toward the voice. A doctor stood beside the bed. He wore a typical doctor's white coat, replete with a stethoscope around his neck. He looked to be in his sixties and wore wire-rimmed glasses.

"Hello, Mr. Moor. I'm Doctor Stein. How are you doing? Are you in any pain?"

"Whaddya fuckin' think? My legs are busted. So's my arm. How long have I been here?"

"Almost three weeks. You'll probably have to stay here for a few more. You've had several operations. Your injuries were severe. You were close to death when they found you. I don't know how you managed to survive up in the tree.

"What about everybody else?"

"All dead. One survived the accident, but he succumbed to his injuries the following day."

"Someone helped me, couldn't see who pushed me up on the branch."

"Yes, we know. He was able to tell us all about the accident before he passed away. The sheriff, by the way, wants to speak with you regarding that."

"Me! Why me? It was that dumb nigg . . ." The word ended in a shriek as the doctor deftly slapped his bad arm.

"Don't you dare. Judging by your tattoos, you have some abhorrent beliefs. You need to be respectful in this hospital." He leaned in close to Roy's ear. "Another word out of your mouth like that and you might just fall out of bed . . . accidentally, of course. Get my meaning?"

The doctor noticed a presence in the doorway. A dark-complexioned face peered through the window in the door.

"You have a visitor, Roy. Mr. Abe Miller. He'd like a word with you. It was his brother who saved your life." The doctor waved the stranger in.

Abe pushed open the door. Removing his black fedora, he approached the bed and scanned the scene. His gaze took in the tattoos—the swastikas, the ugly words of hate—before coming to rest on Roy's face and the smug grin upon it.

"Seen enough yet?" Roy responded to Abe's look of disgust.

"My baby brother sacrificed his life for this?" Abe glanced at the doctor and gestured with an open hand.

The doctor shrugged.

"I thought he must have some redeeming quality for God to spare him. But I'm finding it difficult to see that. They say God works in mysterious ways, so I have to accept that God must have work for him to do."

"Work! I ain't gonna work shit. I'm gonna sue the company for running a faulty bus and for hiring your dumb-ass brother for a driver."

"You wretched, ungrateful . . ." Abe searched for a word. "Fool. He was out of the bus and on that branch soon as he realized his predicament. He was hurt bad, but he was safe. Then he heard your whining and crying. He knew it was you. He recognized your voice. But one of the last things he said to me was that he thought of himself as being like the captain of a ship. So, he climbed back to save your sorry ass. He knew what he was doing. He was scared as hell when he did it too. He rescued you to show you that he wasn't a hate-filled coward, and that he had a duty as a human being to try to save you. He was a better man than you'll ever be." Abe turned to the doctor. "I take it, Doc, he doesn't know?"

"Know?" Roy asked, glancing back and forth at Abe and the doctor. "Know what?"

"I did think that maybe under the circumstances, Abe, it should come from you. But as his surgeon, I suppose it falls on me." The doctor retrieved a clipboard from the end of the bed.

"Will one of you assholes tell me what the fuck is going on?" Roy demanded.

"Do you want the good news or the bad news first?"

"I don't give a shit!"

"Very well." The doctor read from Roy's chart. "The good news is that there are no signs yet of your body rejecting the transplants."

"Transplants?" Roy winced while attempting to rise at the news.

"Yes. Your liver was destroyed in the accident. Luckily for you, though, one of the deceased was a perfect match. You also have had both corneas transplanted due to the eye injuries you suffered. The bad news is that you will, of course, have to take medications on a regular basis as your body will reject the organs without them."

"Medications? For how long?"

"Every day for the rest of your life. There are many side effects of the medications. It may take years to get acclimatized to some of the more negative ones."

"So, whose liver did I get?"

"Funny you should ask that," Abe chimed in. "We may need to be on a more informal basis from now on, brother."

"Brother?" Roy was momentarily flummoxed.

"Well, did you think I came here just to look at your ugly ass?"

Realization, like a cold wind, swept across Roy's face.

"Yep, you got Ben's liver. You're part black now. How will your friends feel about that?" With a flourish, Abe replaced his

128

fedora back upon his head. He carefully adjusted it while looking into the mirror fixed to the wall beside the bed. "He saved your life . . . twice. Once in the bus, and secondly with his liver. He also saved your sight. You will go through life looking through my brother's black eyes."

Satisfied with how he looked, Abe moved toward the door. He paused after opening it and turned to look back at Roy. "Oh, I almost forgot the *pièce de résistance*. My mother's maiden name is Goldstein. Yeah, we're Jewish on my mother's side. I suppose that makes you part Jewish, too, huh?"

Abe surreptitiously used his right middle finger to push up slightly on the brim of his hat. His face beamed. "I'll let the sheriff know you're awake. I know he has a lot of questions for you. He may also have some nice shiny bracelets for you to wear on those skinny wrists of yours."

Just before closing the door, Abe added, "Have a nice life, bro."

MEETING AT MIDNIGHT

My administrative assistant thrust the phone into my hand. "Someone wants to speak to you. Says it's urgent. About your niece."

"My niece?" I mumbled to myself. It was 3:30 already. Lots to get done before going home to pack my bags for the State Board meeting in Portland tomorrow.

"This is Kathryn. How can I help you?" I hoped this would be quick.

The woman identified herself as Dr. Ella Craven, a family therapist from Portland. "Your niece, Chloe, is here beside me. She needs your help."

"Chloe?" I asked. Ray and I had our first visit to her house in the coastal range only three weeks ago. Dread washed over me.

After we left her home that day, I wondered aloud to my husband, "Do you sense something is wrong between Chloe and Rick? How she cowered in the doorway when he railed at her for forgetting to let the dog out of the barn? Minutes after confiding to us that she was pregnant!"

The therapist interrupted my thoughts. "Your niece needs your help now. She says you're her only relative in the area. She fled her house early this morning after her husband threw a punch at her that went through the kitchen wall instead. Her two young children were still asleep in their beds when she left. She insists on going back to get them as soon as possible. I told her she can't return there by herself."

Cradling the phone to my ear, my face grew sweaty. I realized I was being catapulted into the vortex of a drama that began years ago.

"I understand," I said firmly, leaving no room for her to doubt my resolve. "Of course, I'll help my niece any way I can. I'll drive to Portland this evening. Going there anyway for my Board meeting at Portland State tomorrow morning."

The therapist breathed a sigh of relief. "Thank you. You understand that this is a spousal abuse situation, and your niece needs a safe place."

"I understand," I reassured her again before asking to speak with Chloe. I realized how unprepared I was for this situation.

Chloe's voice quivered. "Auntie! I'm so sorry about this."

"Don't worry, honey," I said. "I'll go straight home and pack my bags. Won't take long. I should be able to head north about five. Where can we meet?"

We agreed on Shari's Restaurant, west of Portland, on Highway 26. After hanging up, my Chancellor's Office colleagues warned me not to go to Chloe's house without police escort.

"You never know. Her husband might have a gun," someone said.

I called Chloe back and asked her to contact the Columbia County Sheriff's Office.

On my two-hour drive from Eugene to Portland, I mulled over the scene at Chloe's house last month. Ray and I had been equally mystified by what we had witnessed in Chloe's living room as we were saying our goodbyes.

"Her behavior sure doesn't match the Chloe I remember," I said minutes later as Ray drove our car over the long gravel driveway past the rain-battered old barn. I was referring to the Chloe who had visited my brother in Santa Fe every summer until she'd turned eighteen, per the custody arrangement between her parents. The Chloe who wasn't afraid to speak her mind. The Chloe who refused to take her father's advice about not dating older men. The Chloe who had inherited her grandfather's photographic memory, her mother's business smarts, and her father's legal mind. The Chloe whose ravishing good looks and propensity for sexual antics helped set her on a troubled path in her early teens, years before her marriage to Rick.

During her teenage years, I'd caught glimpses of her every summer when she visited her father in Santa Fe, but only once in Tampa where she and her younger brother, Steven, lived with their mother, Sadie, during the school year. Our visit coincided with Sadie's recent divorce from her second husband.

During that visit, Chloe was a rebellious teen who enjoyed taunting young men with close-up views of her voluptuous breasts tucked inside low-cut tops; she missed no opportunity to brush her thick mane of curly auburn hair by them in a come-hither way. Her mother fawned over her, exchanging raunchy jokes, treating Chloe more like her girlfriend than her daughter. I was taken aback when Chloe joined her mother in criticizing her younger brother.

When I arrived at Shari's around eight, Chloe was on the phone outside the restaurant giving the Sheriff's Office dispatcher background details on her and her husband. Chloe assured him Rick didn't use guns—there were none in their home. I was relieved at that news, though I kept quiet.

The dispatcher advised her to wait at the restaurant while the Deputy Sheriff finished a couple of emergency dispatch calls that had come in earlier. "When he calls you, he'll take off from St. Helens, and you can take off from the restaurant. Drive times to your home in Vernonia should be about thirty minutes from either location."

After we settled into a booth at Shari's to await the call, we ordered and reordered small dishes of marionberry cobbler and hot coffee to pass the time. Chloe poured out her life story.

She told me how she had met her husband, Rick. Her divorced mother had set up her new boyfriend's younger brother with Chloe. Chloe was fifteen.

"Did you tell your dad about that?" I asked in disbelief.

"No. Never did," she replied, plain as day.

"We'd go to the movie and get a burger and shake afterward. Rick is ten years older than me. His brother, Johnny, was in his thirties. I was impressed that Rick worked for a local tech company as a programmer. He always had money and didn't have to do homework at night or take exams. He drove a convertible—perfect for drive-in movie dates with Mom and Johnny. Rick was more sophisticated than high school boys, and he liked that I could keep up with his dirty jokes." She grinned at the memory.

That's the niece I remembered: quick-witted, bawdy like her mother, and too smart for her own good.

Chloe's next story rattled me even more. She told me how her mother had booted her and her brother out of the house when she moved into a small apartment across town after the divorce.

"Mom had rented a one-bedroom apartment close to her office, and there wasn't enough room for all three of us. She arranged for me to move in with Rick and his brother in their two-bedroom condo and announced that Steven would move to Miami with our stepdad. It wasn't long before I moved from the sofa bed in the living room to Rick's bedroom."

I must have blanched because Chloe reached across the table and patted my hand. "I know this stuff sounds crazy, Auntie, but I was happy then. Rick drove me to and from my high school every day, and we sometimes stopped by Mom's office to visit after school." She capped it by bragging how she had graduated with honors a year and a half later.

We talked about how Chloe lived in Santa Fe with her dad about a year after she'd started college in Florida. "I left Rick without saying a word. I wanted to get away from him, and I knew he'd try to stop me, so I stuffed my backpack and flew to Albuquerque on a ticket from Dad."

When Rick showed up at her father's house two weeks later, her dad was furious. "He's way too old for you," he warned. "He's a stalker! Can't you see that, honey?"

Chloe shrugged her shoulders as if reliving the moment when she had snuggled in her father's lap like a little girl, taking in his advice as if it were solid gold. But days later, she took off for Denver with Rick in his VW van loaded with clothes, pots and pans, and sleeping bags.

"I knew he was going to keep tracking me down wherever I went, and I didn't want to keep fighting with him about it."

After the two were living together in Denver, Chloe discovered she was pregnant with Max, her first child. Still determined to complete college, she registered for classes and graduated three years later with a baccalaureate in anthropology from the University of Colorado.

"At least I got my degree," she declared. "But when I crossed the auditorium stage to accept my diploma, my growing belly was stretching my gown!" Pregnant with Annie, Chloe and Rick got married at a Justice of the Peace in Denver and planned to move to Oregon where they could afford to buy their first home. She dreamed of having a horse on a large country lot on the outskirts of Portland, but he insisted on the coastal range.

As the evening wore on, I asked Chloe what instigated her flight to the therapist earlier that day. She thrust her hands into the air in frustration. "When I became pregnant again this spring, I realized how bored I was with being a housewife. I needed to do something beyond being barefoot and pregnant." She laughed.

"One night after dinner, I proposed starting an in-home bakery. Cookies would be my specialty. I'd gotten kudos from neighbors about my homemade treats when they'd stopped by for visits. I told Rick I could continue to stay at home with the children and have a business at the same time. A real entrepreneur!"

Chloe paused. Her face suddenly darkened. "But when I asked Rick if I could buy some commercial equipment for our kitchen, he refused. Said he already earned a good wage for our family—no need for me to start a business. I relented for a while. But I grew depressed. I pleaded with him to allow me to talk with a counselor. I'd researched the *Portland Yellow Pages* and found one with good credentials. But Rick was furious. Yelled at me whenever I brought it up."

She shrugged her shoulders in dismay.

"I finally scheduled an appointment without telling him. I'd planned to drive to Portland on a Thursday when he was off work so he could watch the children." She stopped talking. I knew the rest of the story.

Around eleven o'clock, Chloe blurted, "Why hasn't the Deputy Sheriff called? He can't have *that* many incidents to deal with on a Thursday night!"

She was getting more agitated as midnight approached, worried about the children—four-year-old Max and Annie, sixteen months. "I'm sure Rick won't hurt them, Auntie. He never has. He only wants to hurt me not them."

I squeezed her hand hard in solidarity before changing the subject.

"Hey, there's something you can do while we're waiting," I said, inspired. I handed her a spiral notebook and a pen from my briefcase. "Why don't you make a list of all the items you want to get out of your home? It's likely to be after midnight, and I don't want to spend any extra time around your angry husband, even with a Sheriff's escort."

I pictured her sprawling two-story house on the steep hillside above the town, children's toys and clothes scattered in every room.

"Okay, Auntie," Chloe said, eager to get started. She flashed me a smile for the first time that night.

"Why don't you organize it by room and by floor? We can divide and conquer that way." We agreed that everything must fit inside her family van.

At last, about 11:30, Chloe got the call. "I'm ready to leave St. Helens now," the officer said. "When you get into town, look for the Sheriff's car on First Street next to a city police car. We'll drive up the hill together to your house."

My pulse quickened. I got into my Subaru and followed Chloe's van all the way into Vernonia. The town felt deserted. The only stoplight kept changing colors with no cross-traffic. We pulled up behind the two police vehicles parked side-by-side just beyond the stoplight.

The Deputy Sheriff was all business. He surprised us with his revised plan. "We'll go first to your home without you, ma'am. We want to make sure your husband is there and that your children are safe. When we're satisfied everything is okay, we'll call you to come up."

We waited together in her van for almost an hour, holding hands and exchanging silly stories punctuated by our nervous laughter. Finally, at one o'clock in the morning, the ring jarred us. I heard the deputy's distinctive voice, "Your children are safe, ma'am. Sound asleep in their beds. You can drive on up now."

I dissolved into tears. We had agreed that having the children safe was what mattered. I reached across the seat and gave Chloe a deep hug.

As we drove through the open gate on the long gravel driveway to Chloe's house, the policeman stepped forward and warned us to stay in our car. Rick soon emerged at the front door in handcuffs, the Deputy Sheriff by his side. We watched in disbelief as the Deputy walked Rick to his patrol car and shut the door. We soon learned they would book Rick into the county jail for the night.

"He can only be released if someone posts bond for him," the Deputy said. Chloe speculated that his sister would probably help him.

"If that happens, ma'am, the earliest he could get back here would be sometime late tomorrow." He also assured Chloe she had every right to stay in her own home with her children if she wished.

But Chloe was resolute. "No way, Auntie," she whispered.

We flew through the rooms, gathering everything on her master list before loading them into Chloe's van. Around three o'clock, after getting a couple of last-minute items not on Chloe's list, a weary Chloe signaled she was ready to get her two children from their beds. We trekked upstairs together, sharing a sensibility about the full import of this moment, this departure from their family home with children so young they probably wouldn't remember it. We each carried our precious pajama-clad cargo downstairs and tucked them into their car seats in the van, careful not to wake them.

"Let's get out of here," I said, fearing Rick's return at any moment. As we headed down the driveway in our separate vehicles, I stopped and hoisted the chain to close the gate behind us. I looked back at the darkened house, lighted only by a sky of stars, and upslope at the brooding blackness of dense evergreens. The ghost of Rick's menacing presence still lingered. I yearned to get to the main highway fourteen miles from the town.

Our caravan reached the stop sign at the bottom of the hill in two to three minutes. My pulse matched my increasing speed as we left the town behind. I was startled when Chloe slowed the van and pulled to a stop on the narrow shoulder. She ran to my car window. "Auntie. I forgot the baby's stroller!"

My heart stopped. "We can't go back, honey. We can get a stroller in Portland. It'll be okay!"

Chloe insisted we return. Retrieving that stroller suddenly consumed her. "It won't take long, Auntie. I know exactly where it is."

I relented, and our return trip took only a few minutes, though it felt like an hour of pure hell. I pictured Rick pulling up the driveway alongside us, but we succeeded in our final nighttime raid and left town again shortly before four o'clock, arriving in Portland at dawn.

We unloaded Chloe's van and brought the children into my family's two-bedroom condo, our Portland *pied-a-terre*. Early morning daylight suffused the city streets. I called my boss and warned him I'd be late to the Board meeting but would report on the capital budget as planned. After a fitful three hours of sleep, I tripped over baby paraphernalia and children's toys as I left for the meeting. Max was wide-awake, pulling toys out of a giant pillowcase as fast as his little hands could grab them while his mother and baby sister slept nearby. I smiled to myself. They're going to be okay. So is Chloe. It'll take time, but they're going to have a better life now.

PIECES OF SKY

MARA LYNN JOHNSTONE

On the day our world ended, my love and I were watching the sky. We'd climbed the hill for the sunset, and we stood wide-eyed when the cataclysm began. I had known, as had the others, this might be coming though none of us had truly believed it. I may have scoffed more than my soulmate, more than my companions. More than I should have. But what rippled through the air that day shook the soul and could not be ignored.

Every living thing felt the warning and was immediately silent as stone. A glance about the park revealed everyone looking in the same direction, even the squirrels and birds. That half-second paused, one breathless airborne moment before reality blasted apart.

It didn't happen as I'd imagined.

There was first darkening, then light.

Then pure fire, with a rushing that blew through my mind and made the very air shudder.

We stood and shook, body and soul, while I wondered how we remained standing. It wasn't wind buffeting the world; this was something else. Something that I heard inside my head and felt with more than just the outer skin. And what came with it was terrifying.

On the horizon that had spawned the shockwave, something spiraled into existence emanating destructive glee. I knew without a doubt that the thing lived for this moment. Nothing would stop it from pulling our world down around us.

We two stood on the hill watching that lightning, blue-eyed apocalypse begin to move. We shook in unison, and I heard my love think, *The world is ending. Take my hand.* I did and read the fingers; we needed no further communication. He and I watched together and called out in broken colors when it reached us.

Escape sprinted across the roadways of my brain, but there was nowhere to go. I heard him think, *Now is the time. Time to give in*; *time to give up.* Regrets crackled on the surface of his skin, but there was nothing to be done except hold each other's hand like a lifeline.

 C3

A time later, I coughed and woke, stirred, and was surprised to find myself somewhat alive. Ashes were descending, but the world was still there. After a fashion. Things were devastated and strange, and the sound waves seemed uncertain. Words erupted and stabbed the air, leaping from silence. I could not locate their speaker. Nor the other half of the pair of us. I began looking, fighting for my eyes to focus.

The hills had changed shape, and deep fog eclipsed half of what had been a park. Or perhaps it was something else. Maybe the edge of the universe. I kept looking.

I finally found him. My swain lay staring into the fog like a drowned soldier at that edge of the world. He blinked more than was reassuring, and when I reached him, his face held no hope. It took a long while to rouse him from apathy. This was no time to be looking into someone else's eyes and seeing your own reflection. I told him, *Splash the water, Narcissus. We need you here*. He blinked further but regained some sense. And strength and balance. Soon the two of us stood hand in hand again, looking out at the world.

All was different. Ground zero every fifty miles and circles of change around those. The grass bled its green hue into the air while crows skittered sideways across the blankness of the sky. Telephone poles had rooted and grown. Cats defied gravity more than usual when they ran from roads to rooftops. Hedgehogs remained comfortingly real. They appeared in sharp definition even when the ground underneath them blurred like a watercolor painting. Cars, meanwhile, had stopped and nothing would make them move. But given the electric tracery that danced over some of them that may not have been a bad thing. I could swear I saw blue eyes blink through one grill.

The world had not ended. But our world had.

C3

Day faded quickly. That first night, the remaining clocks spun backward. Some houses still stood, as did some beds and some people. We spent the night under quilts of insomnia and narcolepsy: affected, worried, and wondering. Dreams were not so different from reality now.

"Do you think we deserved it?" The words drifted through our dark room.

I checked that my love was awake before answering. "Some will say so," I replied. A faint echo hissed outside. "But it hardly matters," I continued. "Deserving won't change what is."

He nodded and rolled over, leaving an afterimage that I blinked away. Sleep flitted about like a moth before alighting on my forehead.

The morning made an appearance, and the shattered population made breakfast. Survival occurred. In the days to come, we learned what new rules applied to the world and what had no rules at all. Strings fell from the stars, and we knew not whether to dodge away or catch them. Deceptively beautiful flowers climbed the lampposts and reached for passersby with vampiric thorns and reeking subtly of evil. We smelled them until they stopped looking pretty, and we learned how to dodge.

Like alien radiation, new energies were everywhere. I could feel them walking the creases and cracks of my face, along with worry and wonder and hope. For though the world had changed nearly beyond recognition, it was still there to support us. And we would support each other. So we did, always learning about how we would live in this world. It was not an easy thing to learn. Sometimes we were all that pulled each other through.

ɬ

By now things have settled somewhat. Reality is as fluid as ever, but I know how to move with it. Society has rearranged and resurfaced, adapting to a world all wild around the edges.

For some, this is the time for the steel-toed soul: an era of hard self-reliance. These people generally turn out to be either highly durable ones who last long but live coldly or brittle folk who shatter on short notice. The rest of us agree on the value of teaming—we are there for each other, and that keeps us going. I am one to ride herd on the human spirit when it falters. But I've found my own spirit in need these days.

It has been a short and busy time since the cataclysm. I have had precious few moments alone. But things have calmed, and I've had time for epiphanies.

I don't know what to do with myself now.

Survival is no hardship. One need only know where to look for sustenance. Living is easy; thriving is a challenge. Jobs as we knew them are less of a necessity, leaving most of us with more free time than we're accustomed. I have been so busy with other people's problems, I did not notice. But now my work is done, and I've realized just how much nothing I need to do.

There is a home for me, and food, and one other there who ensures that I suffer no loneliness. There are neighbors and daily wonders to catch my attention. There is, however, no central drive. No aim. No more doughnut shop with its regular customers and tempting aromas, nor need for another source of wages now that edible things grow everywhere, and society has mostly regressed to bartering. No relevant hobby to let blossom into a garden of delight. No goals. I don't know what to do with my life, and this bothers me.

I know others feel similarly, but so far, no one has imparted any particularly useful wisdom. I have thought on it plenty, wandering alone or indoors with my one. He has no answers for me either. His previous career is still vaguely called for, blacksmithing never having gone out of style, merely out of vogue. He is engaged in this today, making nails for new houses. I leave him to it with a hug and a temporary goodbye. *I may be gone for a while*, I tell him, *but I will float into your arms at midnight, with starlight in my hair.* He accepts this promise, and we part for the day.

I am determined to find something meaningful to do.

I pick a direction, and I begin walking.

The land has grown in odd ways. Patches of ground and buildings are covered in violent vegetal bloom that isn't entirely friendly. Seedpods rattle, and vines slither in the manner of snakes in childhood nightmares. Venus flytrap maws could swallow a person if given a chance. I skirt these as well as a sizeable lake-puddle of something that is possibly jelly, or an early version of water. Such things are no longer strange.

Among the low hills, the grass sings, but dry bones whisper, an undertone of menace to the beauty. I try not to think about who they once belonged to. This land is beautiful but has come with a terrible price. Had we chosen to live here, all would be golden. All is not. But we still try.

Laughter floats on the breeze, and I spot a group of free spirits running. A Frisbee zips overhead. Children sit on the sidelines, watching the merriment and eating handfuls of fire. I continue forward, pushing through the six-gendered wind that speaks in many voices and hearing ever so faintly the distant song of the fog. The wind must have traveled far.

What a coincidence. So shall I.

The plant life undulates disconcertingly around my feet as I make my way out of the hills, avoiding a gull mistaken for a Frisbee. The gull swoops away, a white shape against a pale sky. The group of people dwindles into the distance as I walk. Others are present in the surrounding area; the nearest that I can spot are doing a dance that human forms aren't made for.

It's not just the land that is different now.

Either we as a species have changed, or there are others here. Perhaps they used to be us.

Whatever the reason, it is a cause for uneasiness and perhaps a touch of fear but also inevitable wonder. Nothing else can apply to the freak of beauty I glimpse and lose sight of like a forgotten song. I don't try to pursue, though I would like to. I know there will be no one there.

Elsewhere, I see more mundane people, mostly pessimistic types. I hear them saying, *we are guardians of uglier things to come* . . . and I know they do not believe our troubles to be over. I also know I want no part of that mindset. Such pessimists are often lords over loneliness, waiting in stasis. I have a lot of nothing to do; too much nothing to be wasted on unhappiness. I'd fit in better with the Frisbee crowd. I mentally note this, though I search for a more long-term pursuit.

I hope to find something useful. Since the shakeup, I have been helping, fixing homes, and braving new jungles. But everyone in the near vicinity has settled into place more or less, and our town is secure . . . more or less. I could spend time combating plant life, but now an acceptable truce is in place I am reluctant to break. I could explore further, but there is no immediate reason to, except for curiosity, and I've spent enough time with the local dangers not to go courting exotic ones. I shall stick to the immediate area for a while longer.

I'm sure there will be a group of us setting out, soon enough, to see what's happened to a larger part of the world. That time is not now, however, so I must find something else to do. Something that would make me feel more productive than if I spent my time playing.

It is tempting. Activities in the near distance fascinate me. A scattering of children searches for stones in the waving grass. They build a communal pile out of quartz, hornblende, and other former fire. There is no squabbling over finds. It is a team effort to create the tallest pyramid. As I make my way through the edge of the field, I can see that it will be an impressive one. The ground fairly sparkles through the grass. A gasp of emeralds reveals itself before I step down, which is fortunate for the willowy child I point it out to and for me. He gleefully adds them to the pile.

I remember not so long ago such a stash would have meant infinite riches. Today, there are few uses better than this: a children's monument built in worship of life, sunlight, and shiny things. If I were a child, I would join them. But I do not try. I merely pass on, making note to take this path on my way back to see how the tower has grown.

A different sparkling catches my attention from off to the left. I turn to find water rippling under the sun. Boulders and driftwood on the shore hide sea creatures, and humans poke about for interesting things. A rowboat farther out carries three people manning a net; it appears they are dragging the sea for dreams. That is where the lost ones go these days. I hope they catch something good.

The boulders make an enjoyable path. I leap from rock to rock, over and past the tide-pool treasure hunters. Something glittery darts among the kelp. I leave it for the others to find.

On the other side of the boulder field, I hear wisdom to the effect that *you have to learn to fall before you learn to fly*. It is no surprise to round the bend and find people doing just that. It seems there is a good updraft off that cliff.

I would dearly love to join them, but they sport appendages I lack. And I do not even know how to reach the place they stand. Perhaps on my way back, I will search out a path. But for now, I confine myself to longing glances as I stroll past and try not to be envious as they fly far above my head.

It is some time before they are out of sight.

I walk without any further ideas for a time that stretches till it creaks. I encounter only the occasional animal or ambulatory plant. Eventually, I meander into a warm afternoon and hear the maniacal cicadas tuning up. The ground here is rocky and reddish; it looks burnt. It probably is. There is a striking rainbow of reds, though. The area is oddly beautiful in the way that many things are. It contrasts sharply with the blankness above, where the sky used to be. Before it fell and shattered.

The top of our world looks like an unmarked sheet of paper now, no matter the weather. Usually, it's less noticeable. This could be a disheartening place to be, I decide, gaining high ground and taking in the view. There is little life in this vast redness, mostly lizards and cacti. Startled birds wing wildly across the white, drawing my eyes in a direction I have not yet looked. People scour the ground for treasures, which is nothing new. But what I see above them is remarkable.

They are putting back the sky.

It is cracked and jagged, but that patch of startling blue is the most wonderful thing I have seen in a long time.

I look around again and realize that the small things I had taken for more scattered stones are something far more valuable. I scramble down to the nearest one and pick it up carefully, cradling it like a childhood memory. Only now do I notice just how much I've missed seeing a blue sky.

I look over at the fantastic people putting these back together with such care, and a blade of happiness cuts like free verse.

I shuck off my sweater to make something to carry them in. Then I cast about for more fragments of blue.

BLACK, WHITE, & GRAY

CHRISTINE WALKER

A month after Gabe's seventh birthday, Grace dressed in sandals, a white sleeveless shirt, and linen shorts loose at the waist. Her hands shook as she cinched the belt. "Gabe?" she called. "Gabe?" Hearing no answer, she hurried to the living room and found him beside the low black table, painting with watercolors, his tongue at his lip in concentration. He had her flaxen hair and lean frame, but his talent for art proved Paolo's genes, not hers. Watery black paint dripped onto the paper. He made a wiggly line and then another—eight legs, a spider. He dashed the brush into the water jar.

"Is it time?" Gabe peered at his watch—worn upside down—a birthday present from his father.

"Yes," she said, though they were late. She wanted to curl up in bed, but the entire mothers' group would be there. If she didn't go, everyone would worry. She didn't want to spoil their day. "Presents for Scarlet and Skye are still in the car."

Outside the garage, Gabe said, "Watch me, Mom." He gripped the handle and heaved the garage door up with his thin arms. The door caught in the tracks and rolled above them into the garage.

"Good job, sweetie." She took the presents, which she'd paid the store clerk to wrap, and cradled them on the way out.

Gabe grabbed onto the pulley rope and jumped away as the door slid down into place. "I want to carry them," he said. He took the packages and ran up the alley behind their neighbors' detached garages.

Grace followed, shivering, though the August day was unusually hot and still for San Francisco, even on Potrero Hill. Up ahead, the rooster weathervane perched motionless on Ruby and Neal's garage roof, which rose above the others. They'd converted the ground floor to Neal's woodshop and added an upper level. As Grace came around the corner of the building, Ruby was unlocking the door.

"I'm so glad you're here!" Ruby kissed her on the cheek. "You're chilled." She rubbed Grace's arms. "Do you want to lie down? I know these parties aren't easy."

"No." Grace felt in her pocket for her anxiety pills. Had she forgotten them? Her fingertips touched one tablet stuck in the seam with yesterday's crumbs from Gabe's cookie. "I think I can make it through."

"Help me with the supplies?" Ruby led the way across Neal's shop, leaving footprints in the sawdust, and up the stairs to her painting studio.

An easel pushed back under the eaves held an unfinished portrait of Gabe. It wasn't yet a good likeness. His bowl haircut capped his head like a helmet. His slightly parted lips and opened eyes conveyed an urgency—as if he were about to spill a secret or ask to go to the bathroom. Grace had commissioned the painting to mark Gabe's birthday.

♋

"I put the mural paper somewhere. Try there." Ruby pointed to a cupboard.

On her knees, Grace peered into shelves. Drawings fell onto the floor and, in restacking them, she touched a study of Paolo and herself: his dark eyes and clothes drawn densely with charcoal; her image sketched lightly. It fairly lifted off the page.

"Here it is," Ruby said, a roll of paper in each hand. "Don't worry about those; I'll put them back later."

Outside, Gabe stood watching the other children bounce and chase a basketball across the brick patio and into the alley. Tall wooden fences hid the neighboring yards from view. Grace helped Ruby unfurl the paper—brilliant white in the sun—and tack it to the fence.

"Everyone's inside," Ruby said. "I'll get the paint. You'll ruin your shirt."

Grace crossed the patio to the open French doors and entered the living room where the mothers sat talking. A hush fell as they looked up.

"Oh, good, you're here!" Naomi and the others—Francine, Tina, Demetra—rose to hug her. By the end, she felt bruised. Neal entered, smelling of freshly shaved wood and embraced her. She felt slight in his arms.

Grace sat on the window seat, trying to still the jiggling, pressing both feet to the floor. Her fingers tapped the cushion, newly covered in linen the color of butter. The seat had been bare wood when Grace had sat there at all the other gatherings. Today, the sun filtered through parchment shades. From the yard, the children's shouts and thuds of the ball echoed. Ruby was saying something to her.

"Grace? Do you?"

"Do I what?" She couldn't answer questions today about how she was feeling. Today would have been her daughter's birthday too.

"Want some iced tea? Hot tea?"

Grace nodded. She'd eaten nothing.

Scarlet and Skye ran in to inspect the presents, and all the children—Jaz, Adam, Alex, Charlie—flocked into the room followed by Gabe. They had all been together for his party the month before at the Discovery Museum, where they'd crawled through a dark tube with softly lit aquariums wedged into the wall to simulate being underwater. Grace had gone through with the children, stopping to rest as they raced ahead, her knees and hands against the padded floor enveloped by the amplified gurgling, bubbling, and crackling of the sea creatures behind the glass. The little fish swimming in their schools soothed her. She felt safe from the world outside, relieved of pretending she could manage. The museum had even arranged for the balloons and cake. Grace had been grateful to pay someone to take care of it all.

ଓଃ

"Everybody outside!" Ruby said.

The adults, with their drinks, moved into the yard where Ruby gave the children paint-crusted shirts to wear as smocks. She'd begun the mural painting, now a tradition, at the twins' second birthday. The children knew what to do—they grabbed brushes and claimed spaces along the paper. As the adults talked, the kids painted robots, spaceships, horses, and dragons. The wet paint shone on the mural. Two pots of tempera spilled. Stomping across the patio, the children made red and black footprints on the bricks and chased each other with their brushes. Gabe, painting the teeth of a shark, didn't join them.

Splatters flew across the yard. Black paint landed on Grace's cheek and red spotted her white shirt.

"Oh, I'm sorry," Ruby said. "Let me wash that out before it dries."

Grace wiped at the paint, smearing it under her eye and across her shirt. "It doesn't matter."

A splatter hit Francine, who retreated into the house to wash it off, and Neal said, "They've had enough." He washed tempera from the children's hands and shoes with a garden hose and wiped it from their faces, but streaks remained on Skye's forehead, Scarlet's hair, Gabe's ears, and the others too—the neighborhood tribe.

Ruby grouped them in front of the mural and took photos. The women smiled, and the children mugged. "Now all of us—the mothers' group," she said.

They assembled behind the children, and she handed Neal the camera.

"Smile," he said, and the women did, but the children made faces.

"We'll have cake and presents," Ruby said. "Help me, Grace?" Arm in arm, they went into the house.

Grace gathered presents, carried them back to the patio, and placed them on a picnic bench. The children clustered beside them, and Ruby set two round cakes, each with seven candles, on the table in front of Scarlet and Skye.

"Make a wish, Skye," Ruby said.

Grace stood with the other mothers. The candles flamed. Seven years since the accident. Seven years since she lost Maria and Nick. A breeze or something flickered the flames. Fourteen. Maria would have been fourteen today, Nick twelve. Each morning, Grace woke with the wish "today will be different, today I will let go," but every day the pain rose with her. She pressed her folded arms hard against her chest and breathed, filling her lungs and exhaling. Her arms rose and fell with each breath. She'd learned to do this from her doctor, who had been a dancer. "As if you're hugging yourself. Become aware of your body in space," the woman had said.

○3

"Make a wish, darling," Ruby was saying. "Your heart's desire."

As Scarlet bent her head, Grace saw the mural section Gabe had painted. Red dripped from the shark's jagged teeth. In the

148

mouth, a woman and boy were smeared with blood. The shark's belly held a car, smashed upside down, and beside it, two small crumpled figures in pools of blood. A man stood to the side, dwarfed by the shark. There was a whooshing in Grace's ears. Her legs weakened, and she blindly reached back for the nearest chair.

The accident had shadowed Gabe's life. Framed photos of Maria and Nick, one with Maria holding Gabe in her arms, hung on the walls of their home. When asked if he had siblings, he would always say that he'd had a sister and brother who had died when he was a baby, but his drawing expressed what he couldn't articulate. The dread that consumed her daily also consumed him. She had thought she could raise Gabe better than Paolo, who had become increasingly hardened by grief and guilt, just as she'd become weakened. As Grace sat in the corner of the patio watching Skye blow out his candles, she saw Gabe's eager face, the shark's bloody mouth appearing in the painting beside him, and she knew she couldn't keep her child from being swallowed by her terror. It would devour them both.

"Grace?" Naomi stood before her with cake on a plate. "You should eat something."

"I can't." She waved it away. "I can't stay."

"Are you okay?"

"I shouldn't have come. I'm so tired."

She stood and walked past Naomi, past the children clustered around presents, and into the alley leading to her garage. In the car was a CD that calmed her—bird and ocean sounds combined with music. She craved sleep. She lifted the garage door a few feet, ducked below it, and thought as it closed behind her, *this could be how to escape.* Every bone in her body, every joint, every cell ached.

◌

Light from the high windows bathed the garage's interior in a peaceful gray. Shelving on the walls held Gabe's ball pump and a few tools left by Paolo. She slid into the driver's seat—the black leather smooth and cool to her touch—and turned the key in the ignition.

Click. Click. There it was again, that sound in the idle, another unattended repair. She revved the accelerator to stop the clicking and pressed the button on the CD player. A lone seagull, then another, called overlapping waves. Shorebirds twittered, sounding like laughter, then scattered and diminished. In the distance, a violin mourned faintly, drew closer, the strings swelling with the waves, now rushing in and washing over her. Like the squeal of a baby, the high pitch of a humpback whale sustained and was overcome by an oboe that crescendoed into a foghorn. The whale sounded again, a low grumble giving way to a cello. She turned the volume louder, leaned back, and closed her eyes.

The rhythm of the car's motor, the ocean, and her own shallow breathing cocooned her; she was weighted with sorrow. She *was* the grief. Her body overflowed. The thrumming in her veins— her heartbeat—blended in with the music. She felt herself being drawn farther and farther out to sea, the refrain repeating as if to say, "It-will-be-o-*kay*, it-will-be-o-*kay*."

Her head throbbed, and her chest hurt, but the pain wasn't hers—she slid away from it under the waves. She tried to move her hand to her chest, but her fingers felt far away as if floating in cool water. The coolness flowed over her. A sound drummed from the distance, as familiar and sweet as the music in her. Thrum, thrum. Coming nearer. Thrum, thrum. Nearer. Thrum, thrum. Thrum, thrum.

"Mom, Mom!" A scream came out of the blurred face so close to her. Gabe. His mouth was open, his eyes wide. "Mom, Mom!" He was yanking her arm. "Wake up!"

She fell partway out of the car, her hand against the concrete. Gabe's foot pressed on her fingers. She gasped.

He stepped off her hand and yelled, "Mom! You wouldn't wake up!"

His face, wet with tears, came into focus above her. He tried to pull her up, but she sank back to the floor.

A man reached across her, and his voice replaced the mutter of the engine. "Up you go."

Neal lifted her out of the car. She collapsed against him, and he half pulled, half carried her into the sunlight. She blinked to see Ruby and the other mothers standing in the driveway. The children stared wide-eyed. A wave of nausea rushed over her, and she retched. A watery yellow vomit dripped down her shorts, onto her sandals, and between her toes.

"Yuck!" a child said.

Grace sucked in air through her nose and mouth, tasting sourness. "I'm sorry," she said to no one in particular and to everyone. It struck her—what she'd attempted—and she was sorry she'd failed. The effort to stand on her own, much less to begin this day again, overwhelmed her.

Gabe's hand slipped into hers. "I'm sorry," she said to him. He leaned against her and she against Neal, and everyone circled around to embrace her.

They all talked at once.

"If the basketball hadn't gone flat . . ."

"I shouldn't have let her go by herself."

"How would you have known?"

"None of us did."

"Let's go inside and clean you up," Ruby said with tenderness. To Naomi, she said, "Call her doctor."

In the house, Grace's hand slid over the ebony banister, and the years fell away as if not a moment had passed since that day of the accident when she had shivered with premonition on these stairs. Ruby helped her undress and step into the shower.

The spray pummeled her, washing away the paint and vomit and car exhaust, but not her shame. Her foot slid against something rough, a ridge of grout escaped from the black and white tiles. She would add the repair to the list to give to the handyman she intended to call. She did the best she could, and today that wasn't good enough.

"Tomorrow, I'm going to try—I'll try to do better."

"Yes, you will," Ruby murmured as she wrapped Grace in thick white softness. "You will," she said, sliding the silky black nightgown over her head. "You will," she whispered, easing her onto the bed and under the sheet. She stroked Grace's hand—the sensation of skin against skin, the warmth—until neither could have said who was touching or being touched.

THE ROCKPILE

James Kelly

My journey with Catherine began during my final year at UCLA while our nation still twisted in the winds of war after a decade of fighting. Students were placing flowers in gun barrels, careful to smile, and unrest smoldered on American campuses.

I sat alone on a bench after my last class of the day and watched a small group of students start a spontaneous demonstration in Royce Quad. The protestors were upset because, on my recommendation, the school had placed a medium-sized boulder at the bottom of a natural amphitheater to serve as a speaker's rock. I thought the idea was a good one until a handful of students armed to the teeth with cardboard slogans appeared. They chanted the messages on their paper signs. "Freedom of Speech is Potable" and "Rocks Don't Define Me."

A female voice came from my left. "Excuse me."

Looking up, I saw a lovely woman standing at the end of the bench. She was stunning with reddish-blond hair and a dancer's body. I liked her sparkling eyes.

"Is this place taken?" she asked.

"No. Please join me."

"Thanks. You look troubled. Should I tell you my favorite horse joke?"

My body relaxed. "Nothing overwhelming. I had a grim experience yesterday."

"I guess the horse story can wait." She collapsed on the bench and plopped her cloth bag next to me. "It appears we have a boulder protest going on."

I liked the easy way she summed things up. "Yes, the school put in a speakers' rock, and this group resents being told where to protest. I have some culpability in this craziness because I suggested the boulder."

Her eyebrows crinkled. "Do you think they meant to write 'portable?'"

I laughed again. "Possibly. I've been sitting here trying to visualize how drinkable water has anything to do with freedom of speech."

"If I had to guess, I would say they're referring to whiskey. The word comes from an Irish term meaning water of life. If this sign equates drinkable water with Irish whiskey, even a moderate amount of Jameson would make a person think they had total freedom of speech on any disastrous topic wherever they happened to be."

Reaching into her bag, she pulled out a thermos. "Would you care for a drink? I'm current on all my shots."

"Yes, you appear to be healthy."

She moved her head back slightly as she stared at me. "Careful where you're going there. This boulder situation is difficult for me to understand. They're protesting in a spot where they don't want to be told to protest." She extended her hand. "Hi, my name's Catherine White."

Her grip was firm, comforting, and lingered a moment after the handshake. I wasn't in a hurry to let go, either.

"I'm Mike Carmody. By the way, the color of your eyes goes perfectly with your red hair."

Her eyebrows raised. "I prefer to think of my hair as strawberry blonde; and what do my eyes have to do with my hair anyway?"

I took a quick drink from her thermos. "Oh, something my father told me to say if I ever found myself speechless in the presence of a pretty girl."

A smile returned to her face. "Do you use this line often?"

"No. First time."

She brushed her hair back and turned to face the rock. "Interesting father you have. Now about this protest."

"You've seen about as much as I have. You're funny, you know."

"Thanks for the compliment, if it is one. Today I might be funny, but who can tell how I'll be feeling tomorrow. Some women are like the weather, you know."

"I guess being funny must depend on where you live. The weather's consistent here in Southern California."

She took a deep breath and winked at me. "I save everything, and I mean everything—even the most trivial notes from my friends. The problem is, I have no organizational skills, but I like my life this way. While looking for one person's note, I'll find a half dozen others tucked away in odd places. And I have a darker side."

"Tell me. I'm strong."

"Sorry to say, but I have three leaky coffee percolators in my kitchen. Like everything else in my life, I can't seem to make myself throw them away. Each of them served me without question until they died, and I have to give some points for fidelity. My inability to act on major decisions in life could also be an Irish thing."

"Throw them away and get yourself a drip coffee maker. They're all the rave now. Also, if you want a coffee enthusiast's opinion, buy Costa Rican beans. They're the best."

"Is this something else your father told you to say? You should write a book about him." She pulled a compact from her purse, opened the mirror, and checked the corners of her mouth. Looking back at me, she snapped her compact closed. "Have you ever thought of writing a book?"

"I've thought about writing a novel."

"We couldn't live in a crazier time. You should make it a comedy."

I grinned. "Are your parents from Ireland?"

"My mother's family was. Having an Irish mother is a life-changing event; don't analyze that."

"You have a wonderful smile, Catherine."

Catherine pulled at the top of her blouse and moved a little closer. "Were you in Vietnam?"

"How did you know?"

Catherine pointed to my pack. "Canvas backpacks are always a clue. And you're older than most of the boys here." Her eyes crinkled into another smile.

"Boys?"

Catherine leaned back against the bench, and her tone softened. "Yes, I guess none of you who were there are still boys. What a loss of innocence."

"I took a friend to the VA for some therapy yesterday. Talk about a loss of innocence."

"The one on Wilshire?"

"Yes. I'd never been inside the old building before but remember reading a story in *Life Magazine* about the conditions. My friend and I passed rows of desperate faces on gurneys waiting for surgery. There was a lone stretcher with only an arm hanging out from under the sheet. The man was pulled out of queue and shoved into a corner next to waste cans overflowing with trash. His outreached fingers hung over a brown pool of blood on the floor next to the gurney. Blood had collected in the grooves of tiny rectangular tiles. Strapped into a wheelchair next to the stretcher, a veteran sat naked with only a hand towel to cover his thighs. It was terrible."

"I've heard there's no money left to treat all the wounded coming back from the war," said Catherine. "Nobody wants to work there. The annual budget for running the VA is about the same cost as one month of fighting the war."

I thought of the men sitting in wheelchairs with thousand-mile stares and others lying in thin, collapsible beds waiting to die. Some faces looked familiar.

感

During the seventh month of my Vietnam tour, in the languid hours after a medevac, I began to see them. At first, they were only shadows, movements in the dark corners of my tent, but as days dissolved into weeks and body counts soared during the first battle for Hill 881, they made themselves known. They were small, like toys, and full of life.

I knew Corporal Terwilliger, Major Ayres, and Corpsman Cooper, but there were others—faces of wounded and the dead. I loved them all without knowing their names because they were my brothers.

One day, while sweeping blood from our chopper, I stopped and turned to the crew chief. "I wonder if this is what heaven is like. You see people you knew in life, but they're tiny." Recognizing the stare of concern, I laughed and pretended to be joking. I didn't mention the little Marines again, but they were real to me and, in time, they started talking.

Major Ayres was the first to speak. "Tell my girlfriend I loved her, sergeant."

"Did they send my Air Medal to my mom?" Corporal Terwilliger asked next. He loved his mother and wrote to her every day. I couldn't tell him he hadn't flown enough missions to earn his Air Medal. He died in a burning chopper, calling out for his mom. He *did* receive two Purple Hearts. But only fools wanted one of those.

A Marine in dress blues stepped close and saluted. "You don't know me, sergeant, but thanks for bringing my body out of the jungle."

Suspecting he was one of the many we picked up in body bags, I slowly saluted him then turned back to the major. "Why are they here, sir?"

He looked at me with his usual kindness. "You comforted them in their last hours, sergeant."

For the rest of my tour, they went with me everywhere: Dong Ha, Phu Bai, Marble Mountain, to the top of the Rockpile and out to the hospital ship, Repose. During the eerie half-darkness of mortar attacks, while we huddled against sandbags, they were with me.

When it came my time to leave, I collected the few things I cared about and turned to say goodbye. "We're coming with you," they shouted in chorus.

"I can't take you back to the States. Someone would notice."

"They won't see us," Major Ayres argued. "We will all fit in your sea bag. We want to be there when you tell people about us, when you let our families know we're still here, and we still love them. You're the only one who can keep us alive."

"But you're dead, sir. You all are."

"Not if you write about us," a nameless one had said.

೮

I rarely talked about my experience in Vietnam with people who hadn't served there. Still, I felt comfortable enough with Catherine. Reaching out, I touched her arm. "Something happened to my mind over there, and I'm only just coming to grips with it. A month after the Gulf of Tonkin Incident, I left college and joined the Marines. I guess it was foolish to volunteer."

"No, it wasn't foolish. You did what you thought was right." She closed her eyes.

There were no awkward silences, only peaceful ones. I closed my eyes too and enjoyed the hot Santa Ana winds blowing across our campus. Most Southern Californians complained about these waves of heat flowing in from the Mojave Desert, but I found their eerie warmth comforting.

Catherine reached out and touched my hand. "Not all of us have turned our backs on you, Mike. Have you ever thought about writing about what happened to you in Vietnam? It might be great therapy for you."

"To be honest, I can't recall much of Vietnam other than smells."

"Smells?"

"Yes, smells . . . the earthy rot when the rainy season came and all the blood."

"Do you remember anything else?"

"Not much at the end."

"What part don't you remember?"

"The last few months. I don't remember much after March when three of my friends died in Helicopter Valley."

"It sounds like you shut down."

"Yes, it was like that. Steel doors closed around my memories."

She looked at her watch and jumped up.

"I'm sorry I have to go."

"I'd like to see you again."

"If you'll swing by our candlelight vigil at the end of the week, maybe we can talk more."

I stood up with her. "Where and when?"

"Friday, nineteen-hundred hours. We're meeting on the front steps of the library."

"I'll be there, ma'am."

"Thank you, sir. I'll expect you." She gave me a gentle salute and walked away.

I watched as she went down the path to the boulder. She stopped and said something to the protesters before disappearing into the quad. After she left, the protestors looked at one another, talked for a moment, and disbanded.

I pulled a notebook out of my bag and started writing. *During the seventh month of my Vietnam tour, in the languid hours after a medevac, I began to see them . . .*

MEMOIR

GHOST OF CHRISTMAS PAST

PAMELA HECK

I live in Northern California where Christmas comes in shades of gray. The white winters of my Pennsylvania childhood lay a continent away, their details dimmed by more than fifty years. Except for one...

I am eight, basking in the adoring attention of parents and grandparents—too engrossed in my pile of presents to notice Miss Miller, a snow-flecked specter, passing back and forth before my house.

"Oh, look," my mother says. "Miss Miller, all alone for Christmas. Perhaps she hopes we'll ask her in. I think we should."

"No," I cry. "Please don't ask her in!" I am horrified at the thought of having Cow Cow Miller in my house for Christmas. What would the kids at school say? Laughter at my expense? Unthinkable!

My mother sighs but lets it go. I have won, the sanctity of Christmas preserved as Miss Miller slowly wanders out of sight.

Miss Miller taught 4th grade at Lincoln School in Birdsboro, Pennsylvania. A maiden lady, she lived alone in a brick row house a stone's throw from the school. Hers seemed a small life, its perimeter a city block that contained her home, her church, and the school where she labored diligently for over thirty years. But who can quantify another's life?

Plain of face and rather portly, she was no beauty. Her limited wardrobe of matronly dresses, in black or navy, sported a synthetic sheen. She always wore sensible, black, lace-up pumps. Occasionally, an old-fashioned brooch perched upon her ample breast. Other than that, she wore no ornaments.

Before the start of every school year, Miss Miller walked across town to Mame's beauty parlor for her yearly perm. She emerged in a short halo of tight gray curls. By year's end, the curls grew into a long frizz, which she pulled back with a ribbon, her beauty regime and her wardrobe being limited as much by the frugality of teachers' salaries as by her own thriftiness.

At that time, the school day began with the Pledge of Allegiance followed by a smattering of songs. Miss Miller sang her

161

favorite, "Santa Lucia," in a warbling soprano that soared over the trill of childish voices. I know this because I was a student in Miss Miller's class.

Despite my heartless behavior, I was one of Miss Miller's favorite students. Being a whiz at geography sealed the deal. Miss Miller adored geography. I got an "A" on every geography test that year while my archrival, Larry Polinsky, and I engaged in mortal academic combat on every test for the highest score.

Long before I entered her class, I knew Miss Miller's nickname. Every child on the playground had heard stories about "Cow Cow" Miller. The most persistent involved boys in her class dropping their pencils at strategic moments to look up her dress. Some even claimed to have seen the brand name on her girdle. I wonder if she overheard those stories. Did she know what they called her? Despite her reputation as a stern taskmaster, or maybe because of it, Miss Miller saved my skin that year. Suzanne Graul threatened to beat me up after school. Her reasoning was simple—I had everything she didn't. Suzanne was poor and motherless. Her dresses, though clean and pressed, were worn and a size too small. I, on the other hand, arrived at school dressed to perfection. It wasn't her fault nor was it mine, but the line was drawn, and she dared me to cross it.

Long after all the other kids had gone, I stood peering out a classroom window. Suzanne's head materialized from behind a tree at the edge of the playground. She glared up at me, and I gripped the windowsill, terrified. Suzanne was skinny as a stick but tough as leather. Miss Miller finally demanded to know what I was doing. I blurted out the story. She told me to march down to that tree and tell Suzanne, if she laid a finger on me, Miss Miller would deal with her in the morning. Angry but defeated, Suzanne slunk home, never to threaten me again. Such was the power of Miss Miller's word.

To look at her, one would not suspect that Miss Miller was a master of suspense, but her rendition of *The Wizard of Oz* thrilled me. Just as the flying monkeys were about to scoop up Dorothy and her friends, the book closed—end of story until tomorrow. Every afternoon, we hurried through our work in eager anticipation. I never forgot that story. And, while Dorothy's favorite character was the Scarecrow, mine has always been the Tin Man looking for a heart.

After 4th grade, I rarely thought of Miss Miller, but she never forgot me. Seeing my mother at church, she always asked, "How is Miss Pamela?" Then, gradually, the image of her began to haunt each Christmas. Why? I can't say. Perhaps years of watching Scrooge develop a conscience finally jogged mine.

Now, there's a window in my mind where it is always snowing, and Miss Miller walks back and forth waiting for an invitation that never comes. It is too late, but I would trade a stack of Christmas presents for another chance to invite her in. How simple it would have been to make her happy. How easy it was to let the moment slip away. I imagine her sitting at our table, smiling as mother fusses over her. "More turkey, Miss Miller?" A present would have been found—a bar of scented soap or perhaps a lace handkerchief. Something of no real importance to us would have pleased her out of all proportion to its worth.

I have chastised myself a hundred times, but I was only eight. I have forgiven many people so much worse and yet have struggled to forgive the child I was. A tin man sits on a table in my house. The sculpture artfully assembled out of creamers and screws and bits of metal. He leans upon his ax and holds a wooden heart upon a chain. He wants us to know that he has found his heart at last. I bought him for you, Miss Miller.

ON THE WAY TO RUBICON

JAMES ELLISON WILLS

McKinney Creek ran fast and frigid. It looked dangerous to cross with our skis on. The rocks in the creek were slick with ice and even maneuvering down the snow bank to the water level seemed hard. A short distance upstream from this questionable ford was Miller Lake and some open water.

Spring was beginning in the Sierra Nevada. We were seven miles from our car and one mile from the stove and dry wood at the Richardson Lake hut. If we didn't cross the creek, we'd have to spend the night out on the snow or have to put our headlamps on to make our way to the car in the dark. Neither prospect appealed to us.

Jed sidestepped down to the creek wearing his skis.

"Hey, Jed, you can trash your bases if you want and maybe get your feet wet, but I'm going to see if I can cross this creek right at the lake outlet."

"Be careful," hollered Jed.

He picked his way across the moving water on slippery rocks, tough on skis. I didn't like the looks of those rocks and skied up to where the creek flowed from the thawing lake. I searched for a solid place to cross. In the twilight at 7,000 feet, the source of warmth had dropped behind the mountain. A couple of early stars hung in the sky.

Nordic skiers know their skis will support them in places impossible on foot. Even with the extra weight of a pack, I thought my skis would let me glide across the short section of fragile ice at the outlet to Miller Lake.

Slide and glide, I thought, but gravity and snow physics took over. Halfway across, about fifteen feet from the shore, the ice supporting me collapsed. I was on my back in the icy water with only minutes to get out before I'd be too cold to move. One ski was under the ice and the other on the surface. My heart raced, and I wondered if this was the end. Even the beat of a frightened heart produces heat, and at a time like this, each degree was precious. As I reached into the water to release the binding, I realized I'd need

164

both skis. Getting anywhere would be almost impossible with just one.

My camera's strap prevented me from taking off my pack. I fought to move, bounce, and wiggle enough to get the underwater ski tip up near the surface where I might grab it.

I battled fear as I felt the cold overtaking me. After some desperate twisted contortions, I got hold of the ski tip and pulled it to the surface. I managed to get the camera strap over my head and throw the camera as far as I could. Thoughts of saving the camera or taking pictures were the farthest thing from my mind. I got my pack off and flung it away from the open water.

After his successful crossing, Jed approached me from the opposite bank and pulled the pack away. It was too risky for him to get close enough to help me.

Jed yelled, "Don't worry about your gear; I can get it. Get yourself out. It isn't far to the hut where you can get warm. Don't give up."

I clawed with my ski poles to move away from the hole in the ice. I crawled on my belly with both skis still attached and moved one leg at a time until I got to a place where I hoped the ice could support my weight. I was stiff from the cold but got on my feet and stood up, dripping.

A deep tremor shook my body. My jaw tightened, goosebumps rippled across my skin, and the quaking began. I felt like I would crack my teeth from shivering. There was no time to waste. We needed to ski to the hut and build a fire.

We moved at the fastest pace I could maintain. My body was shutting down. I kept crossing my ski tips and falling. It was the start of hypothermia. Things began to dull. I knew not to stop. I had no feeling in my fingers or toes, and all I could do was ski hard into the dark.

Jed stayed with me and gave me encouragement. We missed the fork for the hut thanks to the low light and went on for a quarter mile. When we reached the edge of Richardson Lake, we realized we had gone too far and backtracked. In a couple of minutes, we were opening the door to the unheated refuge.

Living in houses with only wood stoves had taught us how to build a fire in a hurry and make it burn hot. Jed piled the kindling and wood, and I pulled off wet clothes. I shivered naked in the cold hut, wringing out my ski suit and socks. I hung them close to the stove, careful not to set them on fire. Someone else's half-burnt glove in the wood box was testimony to the possibility.

"Thanks for the help back at the lake," I said to Jed. "I cashed in all my chips on this one. I wouldn't be here without you."

"Yeah, you redeemed all your karma today. That was scary. I know you'd do the same for me."

We filled the stove with another load. I stood on my ski hat to keep my toes from the frozen floor. My heart filled with gratitude for friendship and dry wood.

RUNAWAY

ROBERT SHAFER

Thirst, hunger, and weariness slowed me down. Dreaded darkness approached, and crickets started up their incessant noise. There were fewer houses than when I had started out earlier that day. The forest was dense and dark and forbidding. Stagnant, moss-covered ponds offered water not safe enough to drink. Buzzing like angry bees, mosquitoes bit me mercilessly. Noisy black crows circled above me and squawked like they were ready to swoop down and attack. My raggedy old-man clothes provided little warmth for my shivering body, and I didn't see any place that would shelter me from the cold. Where could I sleep and be safe from the wild beasts that roamed at night? I felt really sick. If I fell over and died alongside this road, those black-feathered carnivores would pick my eyeballs right out of my rotting skull.

The only good thing happening in my twelve-year-old life was finally running away from Naomi.

Suddenly, flashing red and yellow lights overtook and surrounded me. Had a spaceship landed to capture me? The sound of tires on gravel made me turn around. A police car pulled up, and the officer stared at me. He drove by and pulled over to the side of the road, blocking any chance for me to escape.

The policeman got out of the car. Tall, muscular, and young like GI Joe, he was armed with a deadly pistol in his holster and a serious look on his face.

"How are you doing, son?" he asked as he walked up to me.

"I'm doing fine, sir," I said meekly. Was he going to put handcuffs on me? As I looked up at him, I felt really puny.

"Is your name Mickey Johnson?"

"Yes, sir." Fear and lack of water parched my mouth.

"Your parents are really worried about you."

"They aren't my parents, sir," I protested. "I just live with those people."

The officer kept the serious look on his face. I guessed he wanted to scare the "little runaway kid" and teach him a good lesson. What bullshit! I wasn't so scared now. Naomi had better be

167

frightened about what I might say. Maybe I would be rescued from her, and the police would toss her into a filthy prison.

The cop let me sit in the front seat with him as he made a call back to the station on his radio telling them he had found me. I admired all the great stuff in his car, including the shotgun and the multi-colored lights flashing on his radio.

"How come you decided to take off on your own, son?"

"Naomi makes me steal when she sends me shopping, and she beats me if I don't. I have to scrub all her laundry on a washboard in the basement, and it takes me hours to clean every inch of her house. I can't have friends or go out to play, so I spend lots of time alone in my room. She makes me wear these ugly, old-man clothes, even to school. I haven't seen or heard from any of my real family for more than three years."

I didn't talk about the bullies at school because then he would think I was a total sissy.

"You haven't heard from your mother or any of your family in three years?"

"No, sir. I haven't talked to them for a long time."

"It's hard to believe anyone can be as mean as you describe your foster mother."

"It's true, sir, but Naomi isn't my foster mother. She is a mean woman that my mother left me with." Naomi was far worse than I described her to the officer.

He listened, and his face scrunched up like he couldn't believe how bad my life was.

"Stealing is a terrible thing to make a kid do."

"Naomi is a lot bigger than me, sir. If I try to dodge her, she grabs me by my hair and hits me more—and harder—with her fists, sometimes with a broomstick. And she kicks me."

"We certainly need to talk to her about all of that."

I think he believes me, and he's going to rescue me from my terrible life.

⊗

The other policemen at the jailhouse acted like they also believed my story. They didn't put handcuffs on me and didn't take my picture with a number across my chest. I expected them to throw me into a rat-infested cell, but they didn't. And they didn't beat me with their heavy, wooden clubs. Through a thick, glass partition, I watched them talk to a red-faced, protesting Naomi and her silent, pale-faced husband, Emil.

I heard her muffled voice, and I read her lips. "He's a liar, he's a thief, and he's a monster. His own mother didn't want him. If I hadn't given him a good home, who knows what would have happened to him. He probably would have been murdered on the streets of Chicago, or he would have been locked away in a reform school for bad boys. That's where he belongs."

God, please don't let them believe her.

∞

I had hoped the police would help me. Instead, they sent me back home with Emil and Naomi. They should have thrown her into a jail cell and beaten her with a club. The cop who picked me up didn't look me in the eye as I walked out the front door of the station. I thought he would be a superhero and save me. He was supposed to be a protector of helpless and innocent children. Damn. I felt betrayed. He gave me back to the monster—didn't care one bit if she killed me when she had me alone.

After what seemed like forever, we arrived at home. Emil slammed his car door. Big Naomi struggled to pull herself through her door. I ran into the house and up to my room before the beast could grab me.

Cowering in fear, I curled up on the floor at the end of my bed and hoped to be invisible. I listened for the sound of her thundering footsteps on the stairway. I didn't want to think about what her revenge would be, but couldn't help thinking of all the different ways she could kill me. She might beat me to death with her fists and her walking stick. She might stab me with a long, sharp knife. Being stabbed scared me the most.

I waited and waited, but nothing horrible happened. The house remained deathly quiet. I climbed into bed with the covers pulled over my head and prayed for nightmare-free sleep.

∞

The wail of a siren woke me up. The morning sun was bright. Throwing off my blankets, rubbing sleep from my eyes, I staggered to the window. An ambulance with orange and red lights twirling and flashing idled in front of the house. I dressed quickly and hurried down the stairway just in time to see Naomi carried out the front door on a stretcher. Two men in white uniforms, straining from the heavy weight they were carrying, awkwardly maneuvered the stretcher down the front porch steps. They slid the dreaded Naomi through the wide-open back doors of the ambulance. One of the men helped a shaking Emil climb into the ambulance after her. They slammed the rear doors shut and rushed to their front seats. The siren screamed as the ambulance sped off.

I watched them disappear into the distance. Soon, the noise level returned to the familiar. Completely confused, I stood on the front porch. I was alone. I don't know how long I stood there before I wandered into the house, walked through all the rooms, and went back outside to sit on the front steps. There was no one to tell me what to do. Like a ventriloquist's dummy without a hand to guide him, I just sat there. Eventually, my stomach rumbled to remind me I hadn't eaten.

I went back inside to Naomi's room, found her purse sitting on her dresser, and took two one-dollar bills and a handful of change. I prayed she wouldn't notice the missing money when she came home. Now outside, I looked in both directions. After a couple of hesitations, I finally decided to walk to the corner market.

Not seeing any bullies hanging around in front of the store, I strolled through the door. No bullies inside either. Feeling confident, I bought a package of Hostess snowballs, a Baby Ruth, and a Nehi orange soda.

I returned home and sat on the front steps to eat my delicious breakfast. Free from Naomi's brutal control for the first time in three years, I barely knew how to function without her commands. What should I do next? I needed to think, needed to learn quickly. There wasn't any way I was going to do all my daily work until the slave master returned and stood over me with her beating stick.

CB

That evening, Emil arrived home by taxi carrying deli food. He invited me to sit at the dining room table with him. I ate thick slices of ham, chunks of pickled herring, and mouthfuls of delicious potato salad. This was the first time I'd sat at that fancy table. Naomi never let me sit anywhere except at the kitchen table to eat the scraps she allowed me for my meals. Emil's eyes were red from crying. He looked at me and spoke directly to me for the first time in the more than three years I had lived in his house.

"Mickey, Naomi suffered a stroke during the night." Emil sounded like he was ready to cry some more. "I didn't know she was sick until I woke up this morning."

I had no idea what a stroke was, and it surprised the hell out of me that Emil knew my name. He hadn't ever referred to me by anything other than "boy."

"I'm afraid I caused her to have a stroke because I yelled at her for making you steal," he said more to himself than to me.

Jesus, he didn't sound like he was mad at her anymore.

I hoped he wouldn't say it was also my fault she'd had a stroke. I wondered. Was the beast sick because I had run away and the police had to pick me up and I had told them about her forcing me to steal? Was her stroke my fault because I upset her every day and caused her to have to beat me? What if Naomi died? Would her death be my fault because I was a worthless slum boy who tried to avoid work and who stole scraps of food? *So what.* I was feeling relieved and happy Naomi was sick, and she wasn't around to scream at me and beat me.

My real mother had decided she didn't want me to be her child anymore. She had put an advertisement in the newspaper offering me to any stranger who wanted a nine-year-old boy. She had decided I wasn't good enough to be anything but a slave for a stranger. I never wanted to see Mom again.

℘

Two days later, a hospital-style bed was delivered to Naomi's room. The beast arrived home in an impressive red and white ambulance. I felt sick to my stomach. Two men in white, who looked like the ones who had taken her away, struggled to carry her into the house on a stretcher. They lifted her big body up into her new bed and positioned her. A nurse in a white uniform pulled the sheet and blanket up to the brute's chin. Naomi stared at the ceiling. She moaned. The nurse wiped dribble off her toothless mouth. Naomi didn't seem to know where she was or who was around her. The monster didn't scream out my name or demand to know where I was or what I was doing. Nevertheless, "*B*," still echoed through my mind.

They pulled up the side rail of the bed and locked Naomi in. She looked like she was behind steel bars in a prison cell just like she had always said I would end up. I enjoyed looking at her through the bars.

The nurse had a look of serious sympathy on her face as she turned and spoke to me.

"Mickey is your name, right, dear?"

"Yes, ma'am."

"Naomi can't hear you. She doesn't even know you're here." She placed her hand gently on my shoulder. I flinched. I couldn't stop from flinching whenever anyone moved their hands in my direction. "We hope she will get better. Everybody is praying for her."

"Yes, ma'am."

She smiled at me. "You need to be brave, and you need to pray for her too, Mickey."

"Yes, ma'am." *Jesus Christ, what a relief. Naomi really didn't know what was happening around her.* The chances were much better now that she wouldn't notice the money I'd stolen.

☙

The next day, I was allowed to stand next to Naomi again. The beast couldn't raise her arms. She couldn't grab me by my hair or pull me close to slap my face. But, with the side rail down, I didn't dare stand too close. She might get well all of a sudden. She could erupt in a rage, and she might reach over and punch me in the face with her big fists.

It was really strange to be so close to Naomi and not see her eyes full of hate and rage. For the first time, I noticed her eyes were a dirty brown color with red streaks through the whites. Luckily, she stared vacantly at the ceiling, not at me. I wanted to gag because she smelled bad. I also hated the medicine smell of the room, but I didn't want my disgust to show too much and make the nurse feel bad.

When I left Naomi's room, I didn't want to ever go in there again. I didn't have anyone else in the world besides her, but I didn't want her to recover. I had no idea what would happen to me if she died, but I knew I wouldn't take her abuse anymore. I would either run away again, or I would fight her to the death.

Maybe God had finally answered my prayers and punished Naomi for her cruelty to me..

THE HOME

CORLENE VAN SLUIZER

Sara was placed in Homewood Terrace by her father who could not take care of two young girls. Since he did not know what to do with them, he found a "boarding school," a Jewish boarding home though many non-Jews lived there. Being a European man, he may have thought it was a harmless decision. In Europe, it was common to send children away to study and live. And since Sara's sister was going steady with a Mexican boy from the housing projects, he thought it was a good idea to put his daughters in a disciplined and supervised situation. He moved to Los Angeles shortly after securing his children behind walls.

At first, it was like going to camp: many children to interact with, activities on the weekend, the El Rey Theater on Saturday, and the Empire Theater on Sunday. On summer days, we went on outings to the estates of wealthy board members and donors. Going to Searsville Lake was a fun destination as well. Sara remembered when Ralph ate so much watermelon that he puked under a tree, leaving seeds all over his face. The guys thought it was funny. She thought it was disgusting. She wondered if other people at the lake knew they were from a group home. The stigma became second nature, like accepting acne, buckteeth, or obesity. There was a way to move through crowds as if they did not exist; defended and compensating, one would pretend specialness. Actors at the Emmys . . . behind ropes and in the limelight, untouchable by the audience. There was no use trying to break the veil.

Flirting with boys outside the ring was impossible. There was nowhere it could go—no telephone, no address, no permission. The girls didn't even bother to look outside their own crowd.

There were walls and fences, driveways and hedges with no barbed wire or glass-embedded cement. The razor-sharp forbiddance lay in the rules. The gates were invisible but heavily locked in her mind by the threat of restrictions and punishments. This was the ultimate arrow that would carry her to juvenile hall via cop car—an exciting adventure, which she managed to manifest later on. Sara did not know about this protection. She hardly knew how incarcerated she really was, living in a compound of large buildings called "cottages" with its own administration building, gymnasium, laundry, temple, and infirmary. It was all there, a small town, lacking only a gas station, a drug store, and a corner grocer.

A fifteen-minute pass to the Avenue—which was short for Ocean Avenue—was long enough to purchase a coke, a pack of cigarettes, or chewing gum but not long enough to get into any serious trouble. To lose that fifteen-minute privilege was at the top of the list of minor infractions, such as saying "fuck you" to a cottage parent. "Okay, you're restricted from going down to the Avenue this week." It was an easy and immediate consequence.

It was amazing how so many teenagers could live under one roof and have so little to do with each other—like soldiers in a barracks or students in a college dorm. You had your best friend or friends, or you were a loner; respect came when you showed confidence and fearlessness. There was an unwritten rule that you never asked others why they were committed to the institution as rejected foster children or wards of the court. If it was volunteered, fine. Some stories everyone knew.

This walled-in town left Sara feeling like just another inmate who, for the most part, followed the rules to blend in. She didn't want to bring any additional conflict to her life. Only popularity with boys, or in Sara's case, excelling in school and social skills, was what could set you apart and give you some status. Otherwise, if you followed the rules, you could remain fairly invisible.

After lights were out and bed check was completed, there would often be the recognizable sound of muffled crying. Sara often silenced her own grief with the hopes that no one would try to calm her or ask her why. The depth of her plunging into the dark was her comfort. Parents failed to show up to take their children out on a pass. Arguments echoed in the kitchen where the phone lived . . . no privacy. Parents chastised their children with their own guilt.

Sara was thirteen years old when she first came to "The Home," as the kids called it. Fortunately, her sister was also committed. In those first days, they retreated into each other. On the outside, her sister didn't want Sara following her around. But inside, she too was shy and unsure how she would be accepted, if at all.

Since no one was allowed to go to after-school activities, much less visit with a new friend, school became just another institution to survive until graduation. There was no investment in school spirit, football teams, or cheerleading clubs. Most students' grades were mediocre, and the administration would occasionally hire tutors and have study hours as support for the failing or near-failing teens. Study hour was a time for throwing notes across the dining room or claiming you did your homework in school, or you didn't have any, or you forgot your book. Study hall would last a while as an experiment until a new administrator would come up with another bright idea for helping the kids. It was at one of those staff meetings that they decided on sex education.

The girls were ushered into the library in the administration building. In the mid-fifties, sex was something embarrassing to discuss. Sara had witnessed her sister playing spin the bottle with her boyfriend and his friends. She heard later that, instead of kissing, the kids would have to take off a piece of clothing. She envied the girls who wore their boyfriends' rings around their necks on a fancy gold chain. The "fast" girls pranced around in their boyfriends' club jackets, which were always too big for them. They would let the boys snap their bra straps, which added to their bad reputations. Some of those girls ended up at The Home, but they were nice, and she liked them. They sat around the table admitting that they had experienced sexual intercourse as well as abortions.

A nurse from the outside came with posters and pictures. She tried to explain the menstrual cycle. Sara focused on the weird configuration of the fallopian tubes and wandered in her thoughts as the nurse tried to explain fertility. She remembered that someone had told her it was safe to have sex one week before her period and one week after. This was enough of a guideline for her, even though she did not follow it. Sara snuck downstairs to have sex in the living room with her cottage "floater" parent who was ten years older. This made him twenty-three years old on their first encounter.

Todd, a student of social work at San Francisco State College, worked part-time at The Home. He wasn't handsome in the classic sense; he had a broken nose, voluptuous lips, and thinning hair, which he kept short like a serviceman. He had been a Marine. Sara loved the smell of his aftershave lotion, and he always dressed meticulously; the creases in his pants were perfect. As though he'd just come out of a shower, his nose was shiny and his cheeks rosy red. Perhaps he had. He always looked that fresh.

Their courting was hidden, which meant secret. She would watch him come down the path from his cottage where all the male employees, who chose to board on the premises, lived. Then she would go downstairs and time his entrance through the swinging kitchen door by landing on the bottom step of the spiral staircase that led to the girls' side of the dorm. She hoped for an encounter in the hall. Her heart beat so hard she could feel it in her ears. Her palms were sweaty. Sometimes, when he was off duty for a few days, Sara could hardly wait for him to appear. She understood puppy love now—dog wagging its tail so enthusiastically that its body would fold in two, back and forth. When Todd touched her, squeezed her hand, or caressed her leg with his foot underneath the dinner table, she felt the same way.

Once, when there was no one in the cottage, he pressed himself against her slim body. She thought she had awakened to a physical adventure when she felt his hardness, and so it was when he kissed her, soft lips pressed, hip to hip, with a keen ear on the swinging kitchen door—just in case. Secret. Like detectives. They followed their own desires letting no one sense the passion and the intrigue. He was the guide. Sara had never had a boyfriend or anyone who was slightly interested in her—too tall for her age and her hair too thick and kinky for the pageboy look. Her breasts were small. She was intelligent, mature, and walked tall with confidence. Todd didn't seem out of her league, though he was. She needed protection and love.

Staying at the institution without Todd on duty was tedious and slow. Those days were filled with small talk amongst the kids. Nothing of significance. Nothing to recall or repeat. No search. No encounters. Just teens rambling to fill the emptiness, the loneliness, the consequences of abandonment, and senseless excuses.

Every week at the same time, her social worker waited for her with an open door. "Come in, Sara," she would say in a prim and prissy voice.

Sara closed the heavy door behind her knowing she had to spend forty-five minutes entertaining the woman.

"How was your week?"

"Fine."

Sometimes Miss Lind would take her down to the Avenue for an ice cream cone, and Sara could fantasize normalcy since there wasn't the fifteen-minute time limit. That is what she would do if she became a social worker.

Sara felt it odd that she was supposed to report her feelings and most profound problems to this stranger—who was totally disconnected from her life. Sara thought that Miss Lind was secretly relieved that Sara wasn't an emotionally disturbed, runaway loudmouth. Miss Lind and Sara talked about arranging home visits, her grades, and how life was going in general. What would Miss Lind have said if Sara told her she was lonely? That she needed her mother? That she was comforted only by her own tears the blanket pulled over her head when no one else was around to hear? What would she have said if Sara told her that she felt her whole life was borrowed and on hold? And if she mentioned she was having sex with her cottage father and thought he cared about her, maybe even loved her? Sara did not trust Miss Lind because everyone knew that on Friday afternoons there would be conferences to discuss the sessions. What would they discuss about *her*?

Sara knew that she responded to caring. Her cottage parents, Mr. and Mrs. Etherington, had children of their own. She felt close to them because they were real and sincere. Occasionally, other loving people would float through The Home. One who would offer her a hug. Another who would take her aside and listen . . . not to solve her problems but to hear them, to let her know that she did not live in a vacuum, in a void.

Sara lived in a sterile room, one of three bedrooms, with two other girls. They had matching bedspreads, dressers, and closets. Stuffed animals would distinguish whose bed was whose. Sara had a lion to mark her spot. No pictures were allowed on the walls. They had no room for desks or comfortable chairs.

When alarms were placed on her windows so she could not open them up past a certain point, Sara organized the girls' side to walk to "juvy" and surrender to the "real" incarceration. If she was going to be imprisoned, it might as well be the real thing. In juvy, she woke up on a thin mattress that smelled like urine and washed her face from a circular sink with a fountain in the middle; there were no faucet handles. Sara ate soggy toast and cold oatmeal for breakfast.

When children showed up at juvenile hall voluntarily, it was an embarrassment to Homewood's administration. When she and the girls were picked up the next day, Sara was immediately brought to the director's office. She was restricted for two months. She could not leave the grounds except for school. No home visits or movies on the weekends.

She was bored and restless, sitting on the steps of the field after school watching the boys play football or kickball and waiting until it was time to return to the cottage for dinner, day after day. Writing in her diary helped her pass the time.

Dear Diary,

Saturday

Amy spent the morning gluing the burglar button on the window so it won't, we hope, pop out when she opens it tonight. You should see me. I made a tent out of my blankets with my knees up. I just finished reading The Pearl with my flashlight, and now I am waiting for midnight. Amy's boyfriend is supposed to signal me by flashing a light three times in the field. I can hear Amy getting dressed; I am so excited for her. Oh, shit, what will happen if she opens the window and the alarm goes off? Oh, shit. Anyway, I'll let you know. She gets to go to all the prom parties, we'll hear about it tomorrow . . . can't wait.

I love you,

Sara.

P.S. I wish I had a boyfriend on the outside.

P.S.S. I hope that when Mom hears about my juvy trip, she will be proud of me.

For Sara, months moved into years without much significance or change. The routines remained the same day after day. Cottage parents came and went . . . even Todd married and left for another job or more schooling. It wasn't until she left The Home for college that she began to have a sense of herself in the world. She had a school counselor who encouraged her interest in social work.

One day in her psychology class, she imagined herself talking to Miss Lind:

"Well, Miss Lind, cough up your Master's degree in social work. What chapter and heading would you turn to, to tell you how to help a child who felt abandoned by her parents? *No, there was nothing you could say. What was your story? How would you know what it felt like to live in a house that wasn't your home? Did you have every hour and minute of your life accounted for?*

After working her way through college for seven years, Sara graduated with a B.A. in social work. She went on to get a Masters in psychology and worked as a dance and art therapist.

SISTERS BEFORE WE KNEW IT

ELAINE ROCK

Ever since I was a little girl, I've fought off "peeping Toms," sexual assaults, and multiple attempts to undermine my value and worth in the workplace. As the recent *#metoo* movement unfolded, I couldn't help but think about my past, and so I am joining the chorus of women who, like me, experienced sexual harassment forty and fifty years ago. It isn't a new phenomenon—it's been happening throughout history. What's different this time is that women are speaking out about it publicly and taking overt legal action.

My early experiences taught me to be aware of my surroundings and vigilant about my personal space, to defend myself against any outright attack should it become necessary, and to properly substantiate details should I ever need to make an accusation against someone. Naïve as it may seem today, after I got married, I thought my marital status could protect me, and my wedding ring represented a virtual chastity belt. One day, I discovered I was wrong and had to resurrect those old lessons learned, not just for me but also for all the secretaries at work.

It was the late 1970s, and I managed a word processing center to handle the production of high volume documents for the company. I got to know all the secretaries; my department existed primarily to relieve their heavy workloads.

"Hey, Elaine. I have to rush out to a doctor appointment." Roxanne, a secretary in public relations, looked anxious and harried. "This package has to go out today. Can you take it to the mailroom for me before noon? I can't find anyone else to do it."

"Sure, Roxie. Where's the mailroom?"

"Take the elevator down to the basement. It's the only office on that level."

"Okay. Hand it over."

I was happy to help Roxie. It would be interesting to explore another floor I hadn't yet seen in the historic 1926 brick Romanesque Revival building.

At 11:30 a.m., I stood in a cavernous gray cement and red brick warehouse that looked like a typical post office backroom operation. At first, it seemed as if no one was around. Then I spotted a dumpy, dark-haired man eating his lunch in the back of the room. He shoved the last of his sandwich into his mouth and swigged down his Pepsi. Wiping his face with his shirtsleeve, he heaved his chair back and stood up.

"Well, *who* are *you*?" he said as he swaggered toward me.

My stomach clenched in disgust as he licked his lips and leered at me. I looked for a quick exit and was relieved to see the stairwell door open near the elevator. I said, "Where is everybody?"

With a nonchalant wave of his hand, he said, "It's lunchtime; they're all out." His mouth slowly curved into a malicious grin. "Looks like we're all alone."

I was so frightened, the hair rose on my arms. As if I were prey about to be tortured, I felt isolated and trapped. The basement suddenly felt like a dungeon.

He stopped a few feet in front of me and said, "So, who are you? I've never seen you down here before."

I held the package in front of me to block him from getting any closer.

"I don't usually come down here. I brought this for Roxanne in PR. It needs to go out by noon. Who are you?"

"I'm the supervisor. Want a tour?"

"No thanks." I could not believe this creep was a manager. "*You're* the supervisor?" I said.

He cocked his head and puffed his chest out with pride. "I sure am." I could smell the onions on his breath.

My inner voice screamed at me to just give him the package and run. "Okay. Would you please just take this now?"

"Oh! Oh, yeah, sure!"

He snatched the box from me with his grimy hands and placed it on the counter next to us. I turned around to leave, but he grabbed my arm, twirled me around, and forced me toward him. With both hands, he groped and fondled my breasts. I could feel the adrenaline rush through my body as I clenched my hands. My heart pounded. I slammed my fists up into his arms with all my might and forced his filthy hands to fly up off me.

"What the fuck do you think you're doing?" I shouted.

Looking genuinely surprised, he said, "What do you mean?"

"You can't do that to me."

Grinning, he said, "Why not? All the other girls let me."

I was stunned at his response. "What other girls?" I demanded.

"The secretaries. Aren't you one of them?"

"No, I'm not. Which secretaries? Who?"

"All of them who come down here. They never complain."

I could feel my head throb as my rage grew. "*Are you kidding me*?"

"No, what's the matter with you, anyway? It's just a little harmless touchy-feely."

"What the hell is the matter with *you*?" I shrieked with revulsion. "What you just did is illegal!"

His eyes widened, and he staggered back. I raced to the stairwell and ran up the stairs as fast as I could but panicked when I thought I heard him following me. Dizzy and a little weak in the knees, I stopped momentarily to catch my breath and listen. Nothing. Relieved, I continued my ascent to the main floor.

Back in the refuge of my office, I grabbed the corporate directory and looked for the name of the mailroom supervisor. When I found it, my hands began to shake, and I threw the directory at the wall where it split apart. Tears welled up in my eyes. What *is* it with men who think they can violate women? How *dare* someone make me or anyone else feel unsafe at work.

I needed to decide what I would do next. I paced back and forth to calm myself. Was I the only one who had ever stood up to him? I couldn't let him get away with touching me or the other secretaries—if what he said was true. I had to report him immediately. I was furious and wanted him fired.

Would personnel believe me? Teri, my supervisor, would be supportive, but legally the charge would have to go to her supervisor, Rex, the head of staff. I knew either he or the mailroom supervisor might try to attack my credibility. I needed to ask the secretaries if he had actually done anything like this to them. Would they be willing to tell their stories to personnel? I didn't know how they would react, but I had to try.

I began with the sales department manager's secretary, Gail, whom I knew best.

"Gail, I just went down to the mailroom with a package for the first time."

She winced and shook her head. "Oh, no. Not you."

"Yes. Not only did the creep grope me, he was also surprised when I stopped him. He said the other secretaries *let* him do it. Has he ever touched you inappropriately?"

Her face reddened, and her voice wavered. "Yes. Yes, he has. He's a disgusting human being. If no one is there, he tries every time. Touches my boobs or my ass and laughs. It's humiliating."

"But you tell him you don't like it and to stop, right?"

"Of course! He forces himself on me." Her lips trembled, and she looked like she could cry. "I hate it. He's even married. Can you imagine?"

"Have you ever told anyone about it?"

"The other secretaries."

"What do they say?"

"He does the same to them."

So, it was true.

"Have you ever told your boss?"

"Yes. He just laughed it off. Never took me seriously."

"Who are the other secretaries who've had a run-in with him?"

"All of them at one time or another. Some left the company because of him."

"We can't let him get away with this, Gail."

"I know. But, I'm even afraid to tell my husband. What are you going to do?"

"It's what *we* are going to do. Look, if I go to Teri and Rex and tell them what he's doing, will you back me up? If they ask, will you tell them he's done it to you and the others, too? If I talk to the secretaries and ask them to do the same, do you think they'd back me up?"

Her mouth dropped. "Wow, you're really serious, aren't you?"

I narrowed my eyes and said, "No one violates me and gets away with it. Are you in?"

"Absolutely. Talk to the others. I'm not sure they'll all back you up, though."

"Why not?"

She grabbed my arm. "They desperately need their jobs. In some cases, it's the only job they've ever had. Some of them are older or single. They worry they won't be believed if they say anything. Just like *I* wasn't when I told my boss. Worse, they could get fired and lose their income. They're so afraid of that. That's why they let the guy get away with what he's doing."

"Of course. I should have known. I'll be sensitive about that when I talk to them. Thanks."

I headed over to Sheila in finance. I figured she would be the toughest to convince since she was an old-timer in her forties.

"Hi, Sheila. Can I talk to you about the mailroom supervisor?"

Her eyes grew dark with anger. "What did he do to you?"

As she listened to my story, she nervously rearranged items on top of her desk.

"I'm not going to let him get away with it, Sheila."

She picked up a pencil and gripped it so tightly I thought it might break. "He's an asshole and gets away with it. What can you do, Elaine?"

I explained the plan to her and asked if she'd go in on it with us. She was wary.

"You know, I despise him, but I'm also afraid of him."

"I understand, but we need to get rid of him. We need as many women as possible to convince Rex to do that."

"I could lose my job. I'm not sure I could get another one." She broke the pencil in half, threw it away, and grabbed another one.

"You won't lose your job. Not if we all stick together. There are too many of us." I didn't know that for sure but sensed that would be the case.

After a long, deliberate pause, she took a deep breath. "Okay. I'll do it. I'm sick and tired of that guy."

In less than two hours, six out of ten secretaries said they'd support me. I figured that would be good enough to lodge an initial complaint. I knew I was doing the right thing.

It was 2:00 p.m. when I knocked on Teri's door and went into her office. I told her what the mailroom supervisor had done that morning and what he said about the secretaries. She had been standing but collapsed into her chair staring at me with incredulity. "Are you sure about this? Oh, my God. We've got to tell Rex immediately!"

We walked into Rex's plush, brick-lined office. He listened politely to my complaint. Then he folded his arms across his chest, leaned back in his leather chair, and observed me over his expansive desk. I could see he was skeptical. Teri was silent.

"Most of the secretaries have been assaulted too, Rex," I said.

He sat upright and put his hands on the edge of the desk. "I have a hard time believing that. Are you sure?" he said.

I was ready for his response. I leaned forward in my chair, looked directly into his eyes and said, "Rex, go ask them yourself if you don't believe me. Ask Gail, Sheila, Rhonda, Mary, Diane, and Donna. Some of their stories are worse than mine. It's been happening for a long time."

Taking on the challenge, Rex said, "I'll do exactly that!"

I knew he had to.

He called the six secretaries into his office one by one. Each called me after their session and said he seemed shocked and solicitous. He told them he believed them.

Just before 5 p.m., Rex called me back into his office. Teri was there.

"Elaine, I'm sorry I doubted you. You did the right thing. We had no idea this was happening. We just fired the mailroom supervisor and escorted him out of the building. He won't be back. Thank you. But, I do want to ask one thing of you. Please don't let this go any further than it already has. Our company has a reputation to protect."

That's when I realized his motivations weren't the same as mine. He probably asked the same thing of all the secretaries.

I said, "Of course. But there might be many more women who will be relieved to see him gone than you realize. Some were too afraid to come forward." As I walked out the door, I turned around and said, "I guess we both did the right thing today—but for different reasons." I'm not so sure he understood what I meant.

But Teri understood. She followed me and asked if I had talked to all the secretaries before coming to her. "Of course, I did. I knew you'd believe me, but I realized Rex wouldn't. He wanted to protect the company; I wanted to protect the women in it. Someday we won't have to worry about men doubting us when this kind of thing happens."

My husband was proud of me when I told him what had happened. When I called Roxanne that evening, she was shocked and apologetic.

"Why didn't you warn me about the guy, Roxie?"

"He never bothers me."

"Did he ever try?"

"Yes, once. But I told him my weight-lifting husband would come to the company and beat the crap out of him if he ever laid a hand on me. So he kept his distance. I never talked to anyone about it. Now I wish I had."

I wondered how the mailroom supervisor would explain his firing to his wife that night. I doubted he'd tell her the truth. Would his termination lead to a change in his aberrant behavior toward women? I'd like to think so. I'll never know.

The next day, there was a bouquet of flowers on my desk with a card.

Thank you for being our heroine.
We'll never be silent again.
With love and admiration,
The Secretaries

MY FALLEN HERO

PAMELA FENDER

It had been four years since last speaking with my father—eight years since I'd seen him. It hadn't gone well either time, and from the way he spoke to me, I was sure I'd never see or hear from him again. After difficult years of grieving the death of our relationship, I had finally desensitized enough to let go. Then, out of the silence, he phoned me.

"I called to wish you a happy New Year," he said. "I miss you, Pam. I love you. Please come to see me. *Please*."

As much as I knew that it never ended well with my father, the little girl in me still hoped her "daddy" would finally apologize for not supporting her emotionally and would express his regret for the hurt he had caused. *Don't do it*, my mind screamed, but my heart begged me to go.

He phoned at least twice a day to tell me how he missed me and to please come see him. I knew that some dementia had settled in. After all, he was 97 years old. Our conversations were brief, usually consisting of him asking, "Could you come over?"

"Dad. I don't live around the corner. I'll have to book a flight and rent a car. And I'll need to make plans to get off work. Can we make it on a Saturday in a few weeks?"

"No, Saturday won't be good. My wife will be here, and she doesn't want to see you." In the background, I heard her yelling something about a decision I'd made and how disgusting I was. "Can you arrange to come on a Wednesday?"

I supposed I could do that—*would* do that. He was old. Was he ready to make amends for his emotional abuses, criticisms, and judgments? God knows I needed that desperately.

"Make it on a Wednesday," he muttered. "I'll tell her I have a doctor's appointment. Then we could go have breakfast."

Wednesdays were not the best day for me to leave town, but this visit was important. Probably one of the most important events of my life.

"Okay. I can do that."

"I'm old, Pam. I want to see you before I leave this earth."

Maybe he *did* want to make amends. Maybe his goal was to cross over to the other side without any guilt. Would this be his redemption?

"I'll let you know when I've made plans, and I'll pick you up. We'll go for breakfast and talk about old times."

∽

I recalled joyful memories. When I was a little girl, I'd climb onto his shoulders in the shallow end of our swimming pool. He'd grab ahold of my ankles and stroll toward the deep end. When his head went under water, he'd let go of my ankles, and I'd dive from his shoulders. We'd laugh and splash. Our time together was rare; he was often busy working at his men's clothing store. On some Sundays, he'd take my twin brother and me to the local playground and push me on the swings so high I'd beg him to stop.

∽

After more than a dozen phone calls from my father, I arranged my trip down to L.A. I detested that place, but again, the small chance he'd apologize made all the negatives of the trip slip away.

I flew into Burbank on a Tuesday and was greeted by Donna, one of my childhood friends. Although my anticipation was high, I didn't know what to expect. I'd see my father, probably for the last time. *Or maybe not.* Maybe after this visit, I'd be motivated to see him again.

On Wednesday morning, I phoned his live-in caregiver, Ben, so he'd know when to expect me. I was anxious. My GPS stated I'd arrive in Beverly Hills in 35 minutes. Well, this was L.A., and there was lots of traffic. The drive took an hour and a half. I was anxious about being late and phoned Ben to let him know about the delay.

Then I heard *her* shouting in the background. My father's wife was home. I clenched my teeth. I knew I wouldn't be able to meet my dad at the front door.

∽

I pulled into an empty spot in front of the house and got out of my rental car to meet Ben for the first time. He waited for me in the open garage.

"Can you park in here? Your dad is in a wheelchair now, and it'll be easier to assist him into the car."

"Oh, sure. No problem." I pulled into the garage. By this time, my dad was there in his chair, his back toward me.

I got out of the car and came around to greet him. My heart raced with eagerness. I was Daddy's little girl, coming to hear those two words: *I'm sorry.*

"Dad! Oh, my God. It's so good to see you. I want to give you a hug." As I approached him, he seemed somewhat apprehensive. I leaned over and hugged him. He didn't hug me back. *Of course not. He was fragile. Weak. He was so strong when I was little—an avid tennis player who began playing at 16 and played through his 80s in senior tournaments. He loved flexing his biceps for me. "Who is the king?"*

"Daddy is the king!"

I stepped back and looked at him. I was teary; still, he waved his hand as if to brush off my feelings. "Don't," he mumbled. "Don't."

Was he embarrassed? Ashamed? Did he not want me showing affection?

"Are we going to meet you at the restaurant?" Dad asked.

Ben replied before I had a chance. "No, Sam. Pamela is driving. I'll put your chair in the trunk and sit in the back."

"Oh." My father looked up at me. "I need to talk to you about some things."

"Okay. Sure, Dad. We'll talk when we get to the restaurant. We can talk about old times." I couldn't wait to get real Jewish deli in my tummy.

"No. Now."

I looked at him in puzzlement.

"You need to leave," he said.

"*What?*" I wasn't hard of hearing; I heard him loud and clear. I just couldn't believe what I heard.

"You need to go."

"What are you talking about, Dad? I just got here."

"You've treated my wife like shit."

"What? What do you mean?"

"You've treated my wife like shit, Pam."

"Dad? What are you talking about?"

"You stayed here in my house."

189

"Of course, I stayed here in your house. I'm your daughter. And you've stayed with me at my house. That's what families do. We stay with each other."

"You need to go." He was adamant.

A crushing feeling took my breath, and I gasped. *This couldn't be happening.* I began to cry. "Dad. Please don't do this. You phoned me at least a dozen times to come see you."

"No. I never did."

I felt confused and desperate. I looked to Ben for help.

"Why are you looking at him? Don't look at him."

"Sam," Ben said. "Pamela flew here from San Francisco to see you. You asked her to come."

"No, I didn't. I never asked her to come," he said gruffly.

"Sam. You *did* phone your daughter. Don't do this to her. She's your only daughter. She came here to see you."

My father ignored Ben. "Well, you've treated my wife like shit. She bought you a wedding suit."

Oh, my God! That was years ago. Was I supposed to repay her? "And?"

"You've treated her like shit. You've treated your brother like shit. Your ex-husband like shit too."

Oh, please, no. He wasn't really going there. I didn't want to get into it with him: the criticisms and judgments he had for me once I'd become an adult. God, he even testified against me in court. The betrayal—standing up for my ex-husband instead of me.

I was his only daughter. "*You're my favorite daughter,*" he'd say.

I sobbed hysterically as I gasped for air. *Which brother had I treated like shit?*

"My *brother*? Which brother?"

"Ricky."

"Oh, for Christ's sake. You sided with Rick. *And* my ex-husband. Dad, please. Please don't do this." Through my tears, I choked out, "I brought you a few things."

I walked over to the car, opened the back door, and pulled out some photographs and a book. "I brought you these photos. Look, Dad. This is you." I pointed to him in his class photo taken in 1937.

He stared blankly at the picture; it seemed unfamiliar to him—it was a lifetime ago.

"And here is a picture of you as class president." I handed him his class photos and another of his parents, his sister, and him, taken in the early 1940s.

"That's not me."

"Yes, it is, Dad. That's you." I tapped the photo. "And I've been published in my writers' club anthology. Two short stories. I think you'll really like them." I placed the book and photos in his lap.

"You've treated my wife like shit."

Was I supposed to continue to tolerate his abuse? At what cost? "Well, Dad. You've treated my husband like shit."

"Your husband. Who's that?"

"Jack."

"I don't know Jack."

The dementia was apparent. *Or was he just cruel?*

"Of course, you do. He's my husband. Since 2008. We've stayed here in your home."

"I don't know."

"Dad. Please. I beg of you. Please don't do this." My weeping was uncontrollable.

"No. You need to leave."

Could he be this heartless? After nearly a half hour of pleading with him, I knew it was useless. Finally, I had to ask. Had to know. "Dad, did you bring me all the way down here to tell me this?"

"Yes."

I took a deep breath through my gasping.

"Dad, if I leave here, you will never see me again."

He raised his right hand, opened and closed it like a child, and waved good-bye.

It felt as if a spear had pierced my heart. I was confused and devastated all at once. I turned toward my car.

"You can't drive like this," Ben said.

"I know. I'll drive around the corner and park. Can I please use your bathroom before I leave?"

Ben shook his head. Nope.

191

What? I'd been in traffic for an hour and a half and needed to use the bathroom.

In that instant, it came to me. *My father's wife was in the house, probably listening on the other side of the door. The conversation must've satisfied her. Had she sabotaged our meeting? She wouldn't allow me into their home. That's why he wanted to meet me when she wasn't home. But she was there. That was her plan. That's why we met in the garage and not in their home.*

I'd been set up, and it was brutal.

I got in my car, started the engine, backed up, and drove away. When I turned the corner, I pulled over and parked on busy Benedict Canyon. I took out my phone from my back pocket and called Donna. She was unable to understand me through my sobs. After several deep breaths, I told her what happened.

"What an evil man." Donna's outrage was in her voice. "Pam, call Ben. Find out if your dad was lucid or has been erratic like this recently. Or if it's something new."

I phoned Ben. He assured me that he'd never seen my father behave this way. He suggested we meet at the restaurant.

I refused. "I'm not going to subject myself to more humiliation and abuse. I've come a long way, and I respect myself too much to put myself through that." Still crying, I explained, "I've been a good daughter, Ben. I had a glimmer of hope that my father would finally apologize for testifying against me in court and for supporting my ex-husband instead of me during my divorce.

"I came down to L.A. hoping to finally hear his words of apology and give him the opportunity to redeem himself."

"Just a minute, Pamela. Your dad wants to talk to you." Ben turned the phone over to my father.

"Pam. I guess that wasn't a good meeting. Maybe we can make it another time."

"No, Dad. That will never happen."

My father left eight messages on my cell phone that day. He wanted to be sure I got home safely. I didn't respond; it was over, and I knew it.

Cʒ

When I returned home, I collapsed into Jack's arms, retelling him the dreadful story. Even though I'd asked him to stay out of my family drama, I now gave him carte blanche to say whatever he chose when, and if, my father phoned our home.

He did—two days later.

ᙇ

"Who's this?"

"This is Jack."

"Who?"

"Jack. Pamela's husband."

"Is Pam there?"

"No. She isn't home." Jack took a deep breath. "I'm glad you called. I have a bone to pick with you. Your treatment of my wife was despicable. Pamela never deserved that. She traveled all the way down there after you phoned here many times begging for her to come see you."

"I never did that."

"Oh, yes, you did. How could you treat your daughter that way? It was appalling."

"Well, Pam made a poor decision in marrying you."

"Fuck you, Sam." Jack slammed the phone down.

Only moments passed when the house phone rang again.

"Is Pam home?" he said as if nothing had occurred. This had to be his dementia. Was the whole scenario dementia? Or was he, in lucid moments, purposely torturing me?

"No, she isn't."

"Tell her I called. It's her dad."

He phoned me at least a dozen more times on both my home phone and cell phone. I had to block his numbers.

ᙇ

No letters. No e-mails. No more phone calls.

In November 2017, my father turned 98 years old.

I will never see him again.

As hard as it's been, I've moved on.

MY SECOND BROTHER: REDEMPTION

Fran Claggett-Holland

> I have always had difficulty with margins, demarcations.
> "What is poetry?" asked Gertrude. "And if you know what poetry is, what is prose?"
> "What is death?" I asked. "And if you know what death is, what is life?"

When we stopped in the Hilo market to pick up flowers to take back to Oahu, I thought only of taking them to the grave of my niece, a child I had never seen, buried in the Punchbowl military cemetery. My eldest brother met us there, uncle of the child, Priscilla, and we walked into the volcanic crater among the thousands of white crosses. Having repressed the knowledge of my brother's death, I stood at her grave.

"Your brother is buried here, next to his daughter," my partner whispered. *My brother, dead? Buried by his friend, the Buddhist priest? Buried with a military cannon salute?* The dichotomy of his life buried here, and the priest read the piece I had written about him, even as he lay dying.
My brother, dead? Alive? Dead?

I had lived the news of his death many times. He could have died at war in the Pacific. He could have died in the typhoon on Okinawa. He could have died when his car smashed into a tree in Ohio. He could have died before he got out of Iran on the last plane carrying Americans during the hostage crisis. He could have died in Saudi Arabia, trying to negotiate a truce. He could have killed himself in his despondency.

But he didn't. He died a slow death. He was on Eniwetok when the first atomic bomb mushroomed over the Bikini Atoll, one of the unsuspecting observers breathing in the deadly particles. It took years for those particles to clump, to cause the healthy cells in his lungs to mushroom into cancerous lesions.

His wanderings were not only geographical. He was a Catholic, a Rosicrucian, an atheist, and finally, a Buddhist. He learned the languages of the people he lived among. He sold Chinese junks in China. Turquoise jewelry with an Indian shaman in Arizona. Drank sake with his Buddhist priest on Oahu. Taught English as a second language at universities in Ohio and California. Watched as the four students at Kent State, where he was teaching, were gunned down. He took me to see the knoll on which they died.

He wrote a novel set in the future while his family thought he was writing his Ph.D. dissertation. He wrote poetry in the language of the 19th century. His last dream? Publishing a magazine written by the people of the world. Everyday people, speaking all languages, coming together for peace, for unity.

In a sense, he dreamed his own dying, listening on the phone as I read the portrait I had written for him, the piece the Buddhist priest read at his funeral:

> "Brother, I have never thought of you dead. I have thought about dying. Mother. Lover. Self. I have tried to plan, to be ready. Willed myself to know beyond. But today, thinking of the four of us, me, with my three brothers, quadrants of the earth apart, I turned around and saw us girdling the earth.
>
> In each life, we awaken to so many uncertainties—the time, the manner—of the living and the leaving of it; we experience the satisfactions anew, the frustrations, know the hollowness of suffering, the pervading spirit of love.
>
> Our soul-knowledge fades with each birthing, and we are left to work our way through each life with approximations: intimations,   the barest touch, the resonance of breath and voice: the heartbreak of a language that does not quite convey what we know, what we want to say.
>
> The life you chose this time around bore traces of many lives—philosopher, poet, shaman—lives you have led, lives you will lead. In the life you contemplate now, perhaps your

dream of using language to build a peaceful world is already coming to fruition. Stay well, brother."

Awake now to the reality, I saw my brother's life, a life of constant crisis, of a deep yearning for the peace he never could achieve. From his childhood, when he suffered a severe burn, damaging his entire nervous system, to hours of playing the *Moonlight Sonata* then leaving our mid-western home for the Pacific, he wandered the world, searching for ways to bring people together.

We placed flowers at the small grave of his daughter, Priscilla. And the rest we placed at the grave next to hers.

My brother, dead?
Not in my lifetime.

FLUNKED OUT

JEANNE JUSAITIS

Vogelsang's. Yep! That was the name of the stately Victorian house on the Esplanade of the small northern California college town. The big white house sat back from the tree-lined boulevard. Nine bicycles, leaning against the bushes, marred the dignity of the Victorian off-campus dorm. I lived on the top floor with eight freshman girls, all from small towns scattered across California. Three of us flunked out after our first semester.

The harsh reality of my situation hit me as I stood by the rose garden in the Quad, reading my report card. That January, the January of '64, felt colder than a witch's tit, and the bare silhouettes of the frozen rose bushes did nothing to cheer me. My sheepskin jacket couldn't protect me from the icy daggers of wind that pierced right through my chest and out my back. Were the tears in my eyes from the alarming news or the stinging cold? It really didn't matter. I thought my life was over.

Ten and a half units of F's out of 16.5 units total. *How could that happen*? Three units of F for physical science, four units for a required lab . . . and three units of F for math, my most hated subject. It didn't help that the class was at 7:30 a.m. Oh, wait, gymnastics. Yep, all F's.

As I walked across the campus toward the bike rack, I contemplated my past and my future. Where had I gone wrong? What were my parents going to say? Nauseous and heartsick, I passed the bike rack and walked on aimlessly, remembering the previous September.

The week before school started, in that promising September of 1963, there had been a freshman orientation. Like the Beatles song, I was just seventeen. The Vogelsang gang, which we jokingly called ourselves, had bonded right away. Little did I know that my new roommate, Pam, would still be one of my closest friends fifty years later. We all joined the rest of our classmates at Bidwell Bowl, the creekside amphitheater, where our campus tour began.

The tour led us down curving paths under shady trees that wound between ivy-covered buildings. The New England colleges that I had read about as a young girl came to mind as the bell tower chimed out the time in a lovely musical refrain. I felt happy and optimistic in my new culottes skirt and freshly washed hair. I guess I should have paid attention to which building was which, but I was distracted by my impressions of my new roommates, their hair and clothes, the way they talked, and humbled by Pam's confidence. Like strangers in a new land, we stuck together, far from the safety and support of our families.

Later that day, back at Vogelsang's, we gathered in our tiny sitting room to plan our classes and get ready for registration. Talk of units was a mystery to me. I expected to get all my required classes over with, not realizing that I should pace myself.

On the first Monday of classes, I walked through the sunlit campus with my schedule and a map. Somehow, I got turned around and went to the wrong end of campus. Finally, I noticed two coeds, who looked mature and confident, sitting on a bench. Feeling shy, I walked up to them.

"Excuse me," I said, showing them my map. "Do you know where the science building is? I'm feeling a little lost."

The pretty girl in a plaid jumper smiled. "The science building is way across, on the other side of campus. Just follow that path until it ends. It's U-shaped. You better hurry if you have a class."

"Oh, man! Thanks so much." I was really going to be late.

Striding down the path as quickly as I could, I headed for the science building. In the quiet of the morning, I could hear the birds singing and Chico Creek bubbling along its merry way. *Uh oh*, I thought, *everyone must already be in class*. I looked at my watch. I was ten minutes late. The babbling creek called to me. *Oh well, I'll skip this first one and go back on Wednesday*. I rationalized that my time would be better spent sitting by the water and studying my schedule and map.

On Wednesday, I got to the class on time, but as I looked through the window in the door, I could see that the large lecture hall all but spilled over with students while the professor paced behind the podium. I would have to walk all the way down the steps and past the professor to get to my seat. What a spectacle that would be! I decided not to go in. *I never liked science anyway, and I already have too many units. If I never attend, then the teacher will just drop me.* Problem solved . . . I thought.

Our house sat on a wide boulevard in the town, at least a mile from the college, and all our meals were at the creekside dining hall on campus. That meant that rain or shine, we had to ride our bicycles across the railroad tracks, down the traffic-filled boulevard, through the garden paths of Bidwell mansion, and into the campus where we followed the creek to one of the footbridges. At that point, we dismounted and walked our bikes across the bridge to the dining hall.

That also meant that if I wanted breakfast, I had to leave the house in the dark to make my 7:30 math class. Wrapped in layers of sweaters and scarves topped with the khaki-brown rain cape my frugal mother had bought at the Army Surplus Store, I remember entering the classroom. I was filled with hot chocolate and thankful for a warm room. I would peel off some layers and listen to the radiators boil away. They hissed a comforting sound that made me relax. I slept through most of my math classes.

Then there was gymnastics. I loved to cartwheel with my legs straight and my toes pointed, and I could perform a front handspring and stick the landing. I stood near the top of the class until we had to do the vaults. Three vault casualties put me on the sidelines in a variety of casts and bandages. It was not a safe place to be. I quit going there in November.

Well, as my dad would often say, "That's all water under the bridge." Those bad choices had led me to that humiliating report card.

Five months later, in the biting January air, report card in hand, I continued to trudge through the campus until I stood behind Laxson Hall. Heavenly music poured out of the windows as the symphony practiced for their upcoming concert. Classical music had always been a part of my family and my life, but for the first time, I realized that I hadn't heard any real music the whole semester. The Beatles and the Beachboys, as much as I loved them, didn't count. I sobbed, regretting my choices and overwhelmed at the thought of telling my parents I had flunked out.

The next weekend, following a tearful phone call, my mom and dad showed up at Vogelsang's. All of the girls sobbed into their Kleenex while getting and giving goodbye hugs. They'd either flunked out or were going to miss their fellow roommates who had. As it turned out, a shocking fifty-one percent of our freshman class had also failed. That, however, didn't make my personal drama any less tragic.

We spoke few words as Pam, my parents, and I packed my suitcases, record player, and pink bicycle into the car. I dreaded the four-hour ride home. I sat in the back seat of my parents' Cadillac, sniffling and crying as I looked out at the gray skies. My mother finally broke the unbearable silence.

"I just don't understand why you didn't tell us about this months ago. You could have done something about it. We would have helped you." Her voice was on the edge of hysterics.

"But I didn't know that I was flunking out a month ago. I knew that I wasn't doing well in math, but I never even went to that science class. And nobody told me about the lab." Even I knew that what I was saying sounded lame.

My father, who was the Superintendent of Schools in our small town, was a little more reasonable. "Why didn't you withdraw from the science class?"

"Withdraw? What do you mean?"

"Well, if you'd never gone to class and you'd withdrawn, you know, filled out the papers, you wouldn't have gotten ten and a half units of F."

My pathetic little voice quavered. "Nobody ever told me." Even lamer.

Mom couldn't hold back any longer and went into a blaming rage. When she finally took a breath, my father said, "Gladys, you can't cry over spilled milk."

No one said a word for the rest of that long ride home. A bleak future stretched out before me.

Once home, I was even more miserable. I didn't want to show my face at the grocery store or anywhere. The local gossip was about the superintendent's daughter who flunked out of college. I was humiliated. I missed my college friends and my freedom. I felt as if I had reverted to my high school days.

My dad came into my bedroom and sat at the edge of my bed. "I don't care what you do," he said, "but you have to do something. You can't just sit around all day. Either get a job or go back to school. If you get a job, you'll have to pay rent, but we'll cover you if you go back to school. What do you *really* want to do?"

He left me to soul search, and I realized the only thing I really wanted to do with my life was to become a teacher. So, I enrolled in the nearest junior college and worked at being a good student. I found refuge and anonymity in the library.

The road back to my original school stretched on and on. I had to turn those F's into A's just to have them count as C's. Finally, after three semesters of penance in my hometown, I returned to my beloved college. It didn't go as smoothly as I'd hoped. Academically behind my old friends in school, I still had to live in a dorm while they had moved on to apartments. Losing direction, I shifted from major to major, not sure where to land. I dropped out of school for a semester to work for the city's recreation department and to direct the children's theater at the fairgrounds. My love life was on the rocks. I waited too long to register for the next semester and thought, "Uh-oh, here we go again."

Luckily, it wasn't too late to register at a nearby junior college. I enrolled in an art class, and my work hung on the walls of the Art building. I took a theater class and acted in two plays. And piano lessons. Through these experiences, I rediscovered where my talents and passions were all along . . . music, theater, and art.

In my last two years as a Diversified Fine Arts Major, I received a four-point average. My mother was ecstatic, but her balloon popped when I mentioned I wouldn't go through the commencement ceremonies. Honestly, I still couldn't believe that the college would let me graduate. My paranoia told me that I'd walk up to receive my diploma, and the dean would say, "I'm sorry, but you're three units short." I wondered if I'd ever stop disappointing my parents.

Still, I had to go through methods and student teaching before I could get a credential. My mother lamented, "When will this ever end?" I was wondering the same thing.

"Just one more year, Mom."

Another year passed, and I got a teaching job in a third-grade class, forty miles from my parents' home. The night before my first day of class, I called my father in tears. I had stage fright.

"It's such a big responsibility," I lamented. "What if I ruin them for life?"

"They're going to learn whether you're there or not," he advised. "Just don't get in their way."

Great advice. I took to teaching like a bird takes to air and never looked back.

Sixteen years later, I received the Teacher of the Year Award from my county and was the only elementary teacher finalist for the State of California. The county put on a lovely banquet held in my honor, and many important people stood up to say complimentary things. My proud parents sat at the front table with my principal and my district superintendent, absorbing the entire scene. Photos of my students and me shaking hands with the governor graced the halls of the state department for a year, and my father made sure my old teachers knew about it. My mother could finally brag, just a little, to her bridge club.

Five years after that, I invited my parents to the graduation ceremonies where I'd be receiving my Master's Degree in Education. This time, I knew it was real. My teeth were dry from smiling so much.

For me, the best part was when my father hugged me and said, "I'm very proud of you, and you know why?"

"Why?" I asked, expecting to hear something about my achievements.

"Because you picked yourself up by your own bootstraps."

My mother smiled and nodded in agreement, wiping a tear from her eye.

My flunky days faded into the past where they belonged.

WHAT I FOUND IN THE FIRES

Barbara Beatie

We had gotten to the point in our relationship where the paint was chipping off, the sun-faded wear and tear was showing, and we were comfortable with that. The new car smell had long since gone, but the effort at the upkeep seemed too enervating. It was fine. Our best at this point was to paraphrase an oft-used reply, "the best I can do now with everything I've got going on." And we had a lot going on—our demanding jobs, my phone buzzing some mornings beginning at 6:00 with a client or another issue that pulled my focus. The marathon monster of a schedule we had created: numerous extracurricular activities that all seemed to happen on weeknights— the sports, SAT prep, drama class. We had the same stresses as others, the norm for parents these days. But we were often numb with exhaustion. I remembered the spark of our dating and early marriage, but now it seemed a faraway bright, ebullient, lucid dream.

On October 9, 2017, the cell phone rang. In my sleepy state, I picked it up to hear my friend Karen's voice. She told me that it was an emergency; Santa Rosa was on fire. She wanted us to consider whether to stay and try to salvage our home or escape to certain safety. She said they were on their way out of town.

I walked out into the night, and it was quiet, the stars overhead. But I saw the orange glow and woke you up. You walked out with me to take in the scene. We decided to stay put for the moment, going back to sleep, tossing and turning in our thoughts.

With that call and the alerts that buzzed my phone, everything took on a more urgent tone. After the years of comfortable complacency, we realized something more significant was happening to us. Suddenly, everything was deliberately infused with tenderness. As if the end was near, the world was turning upside down.

We let our son sleep and began to catalog what we had to do to secure our home so we could leave. We brainstormed where we would go, and what we would take for our journey. I thought of our Y2K package, from before our boy was born, and how we carefully packed our food, medicine, water, and best wine anticipating the need to soften and sweeten the looming disaster. In Y2K, however, we had our neighborhood as anchors. We all planned to stay, come what may. With the fires, the evacuations would require us, at some point, to move. Eventually, our son awoke, and we calmly explained the situation over breakfast. School was closed, work was closed, and Santa Rosa was in flames.

I packed our camping supplies; sure we could have safe shelter if we needed. I then walked the house, from room to room, suddenly weeping—the first tears since that call had come in. How could I choose what to pack? How do I rank your grandmother's wedding picture and my grandfather's pipe? What goes? What stays? How does one prepare to leave everything? You quietly let me sob, anchored behind me with your stoic calm, in every room.

We heard the radio reports of people losing everything. Some had only seconds to leave. Here we were with precious time. I wept for their losses, and for their fear, and for feeling guilty that we were concerned over pictures and dishes. Who decides who has more time and who doesn't? The utter loneliness of this tragedy struck me. Like death, it's coming, but who knows how much time you have to prepare or how to feel when it's here?

The pets watched us, perplexed and overjoyed that we were all home all day. Then as the air filled with smoke and ash, they too grew restless. At some point, you declared that you were going out to trap the cats. I stared in disbelief. The cats that you don't even like? The cats that you complain about every day? My two semi-feral cats, neither of whom would ever submit to being indoor cats full-time no matter how much I tried. You did not want either of them. You grumbled and complained about them. Yet, here you were walking out to find them. You insisted on trapping them and setting them up in the laundry room while we awaited evacuation. They were confused, and their anxious, plaintive wails and growls were a jazz riff on the sirens screaming through town. After years of complaining about those cats, you saved them. Your well of tenderness was much larger than I had noticed.

We remained in this suspended state for days. We were dressed, fed, ready to leave. But the waiting. The waiting reminded me of being at the hospital, watching Mom die. Waiting. The sadness caught my breath with its palpable weight. You cooked pancakes and read aloud to us. Time somehow passed. I wondered how you know that moment when you must leave from the moment when you no longer are able to leave.

I had in my mind we would just stay. The three fires surrounding us were zero percent contained, but I wasn't thinking anymore. I was just adjusting, so when we were finally told it was time, I was not ready. After being up for days, my guard was down, my nerves were raw. The fire trucks roared up our block, the plan to build the fire line at the end of the street now a reality. I was unprepared for the noise—the clanging of the trucks, the bullhorns demanding our attention.

You saw my fear, like when Dad fell for the last time and broke his hip, like when you had to tell me Stuart was dead, or our pregnancy was ectopic. You looked at me calmly, deeply, and said, "We need to go now. It's time." I felt your hand touch mine and looked down. Your fingers enveloped my cold, trembling fingers. Another time of passage for us. Time to board the boat together across the River Styx.

We took two cars—there was no way the two feral, crying cats could be with the two dogs, so we picked teams like in Dodgeball. You drove our son because I trusted you with what was most precious. I had not thought ahead that everyone would be driving out at the same time, the roads choked with cars packed with fear and loss.

I signaled to you to turn off and follow me. I don't even know how I drove, how I was able to function as if our world weren't about to end when it seemed to be falling apart all around us—it seemed we were a giant dystopian diaspora making our exodus. We eventually reached the safe house together. After unloading the confused pets, and settling our son in, I began to sob. I cried the tears of women of all time, the tears of the tribes who have left homes and families, knowing that only the wheel of fortune had kept them out of harm's way.

Yet we were here, the sheer dumb luck of it. The relief crashed into me like an ocean wave. I stumbled, crumbling as you caught me—the strong winds blowing the glowing embers everywhere. I was like paper collapsing into your arms. You gathered me up and whispered, "If I have to face the apocalypse, I am so glad I am with you." And I laughed while crying.

Finally awake—aware of just what we might have lost—
what sparked was the comfort of your holding me. Nothing again
would pull my focus from us in this short, precious time we have.
Nothing again would ever tear me from your side. At long last, I
would give you all my heart had to offer.

MAKING THE GRADE

JOHN COMPISI

It was May 1967, my freshman year in college, and I was in danger of flunking out. The Vietnam War was at its height, and the draft was still the law of the land. I was genuinely at risk of failing a few courses, including my speech and communications class, a core requirement. Making matters exponentially worse, my Reserve Officers Training Course (ROTC) instructor had just advised me that he'd given me an "F" for lack of attendance. My head swirled with fear and panic, and my heart sank to my feet as I considered my predicament. How could I tell my father I had squandered this opportunity to get a college degree? The look of abject disappointment on his face would kill me. Amplifying the irony of my circumstance, my oldest brother had graduated from this same university and ROTC program just two years earlier and was serving in Vietnam. Was I going to be drafted and sent there to meet him? Was there a path to redemption or, perhaps, even salvation?

As I assessed my position, I determined that my first action was to salvage my ROTC situation. The options were binary: succeed or fail. My U.S. Army Captain ROTC instructor was marginally sympathetic. Cadets could miss only three classes in a semester, and I had exceeded that maximum. Who flunks out of ROTC? He understood—more than any of my professors on campus—that losing your Selective Service student deferment and being drafted was a sure trip to Vietnam and all the risks associated with that. I appealed to his knowledge of this reality and his experience to help me out of my conundrum. He made me an offer: If the business office, which officially recorded all grades, would accept a modification, he would resubmit a "Withdrawal While Passing" grade rather than the failing grade he had submitted. This would have a huge impact on my accumulative grade point average (GPA), which was used to evaluate-my viability to return to school at the end of each semester.

I gratefully accepted his offer and raced across campus to the business office. I found the person who could accept the modification and convinced her this resubmission was appropriate and legitimate. The kind woman agreed, and I escaped this GPA-killing "F." At some point before graduation, I would have to repeat this semester of ROTC, but at least I could survive to return to campus in the fall. Step one accomplished . . . but I only breathed half a sigh of relief.

My speech class challenge would prove more painful to resolve. My professor, in his early thirties and hip to the issues regarding the Vietnam War and the draft, seemed intent on upholding the university's standards. I respected that. This was a college-level class requiring three speeches in front of my classmates. I hadn't prepared or presented any speeches, and the semester was coming to a dramatic and swift end . . . particularly for me.

I reflected on how I had put myself into this mess. Through my first 12 years of formal education, I had skated by with few academic challenges, but here I was. The problem was a combination of procrastination and a structural vacuum created when I left home. I was socially engaged on campus, having pledged the Glee Club fraternity successfully, and I participated in an informal Peter, Paul, and Mary-style trio with two classmates—but I could not get myself out of bed to go to class. I actually had earned the dubious moniker of "Dean of Sleep" by my dorm mates. The "why" analysis would have to wait because surviving was my main priority now.

My communications professor had told me I was going to get an "F." I implored him to allow me to meet him in his office to further discuss his decision and my untenable position. That afternoon in his office, I made the case that getting an "F" would most likely result in my flunking out of school and getting drafted. He expressed his understanding of the ramifications, but that he could not allow me to escape the consequences of my lack of participation. I suggested that I prepare and present a speech the next day. Implicit in my suggestion was my hope I could avoid this expected failing grade. Without acknowledging my unspoken expectation of redemption, he agreed to listen.

That afternoon and evening, I developed my subject theme and outlined my arguments pro and con. I wrote, rewrote, and rehearsed throughout that evening. I believed my entire future depended upon this single event and was resolute that I would not fail. Raw emotion and physical exhaustion overwhelmed me. After 1 a.m., I decided I was ready and needed to get some sleep before morning classes and my afternoon appointment with my professor. I slept, albeit fitfully, and rehearsed again when I got up.

The day dragged by as if everything were moving in slow motion. I tingled in nervous apprehension. Could I convince this professor to give me a passing grade despite the inherent injustice to my classmates? Would I be able to salvage a grade better than an "F" to redeem my college career?

By late afternoon, as I walked to the administration building and my professor's office, I experienced an existential panic as the images of failure, imminent boot camp, and suffocating jungles assaulted my consciousness. He was not there when I arrived, so I waited in the hall. I continued to rehearse silently to avoid thinking of anything else. The tension that tightened my throat and parched my mouth felt as if I had swallowed a cup of sand.

Finally, he showed up. We walked into his office devoid of small talk. I sensed that my only chance was to entertain, enthrall, and otherwise dazzle him for the next few minutes or all would be lost. I needed to meet those expectations if he was going to change my grade.

My professor sat behind his desk, and I stood across from him just six feet away. He looked at me as if to say, "Okay, kid, you asked for this, and it better knock my socks off."

I took a deep breath and slowly exhaled to avoid the quaking voice that I knew was my modus operandi when I was very nervous. With another inhalation, I began my speech.

The next seven minutes were my best effort in following the advice and guidance of Aristotle, the ancient Greek philosopher, by linking the three elements of persuasion—Logos, Ethos, and Pathos—tightly together into an unbreakable and undeniable whole. I began by acknowledging the injustice to my fellow students that I was asking him to consider. I continued, weaving my argument that despite the apparent injustice, there was a redemptive quality in his allowing me this last opportunity, if not to excel, at least to survive this serious offense. I followed by employing my most honest efforts to convince him of the sincerity and ethical goodness in my arguments. Finally, I appealed to his heart and conscience to achieve both empathy and sympathy toward me.

As I concluded, my professor sat looking out the window for a moment as he considered what he had just witnessed. He had a twinkle in his eye as he told me that my speech had offered convincing logic and artfully included all three elements advised by Aristotle. He said I would receive a "D," although this speech was an "A+." He could not justify giving me a higher grade in fairness to my classmates. I nearly fainted in relief while I thanked him for the chance to undo some of the damage resulting from my own self-destructive behaviors. I felt as if I had dodged a bullet.

Having survived the real threat of this ordeal, I made a vow to myself. Never again would I allow my own laziness and lack of focus to spin out of control. I returned on probation in the fall with the guiding principle that "showing up is half the battle." I resumed ROTC and completed the program. Clawing my way back, I raised my GPA nearly two full points by the time I graduated after five years and received a commission as an Army Second Lieutenant. Ironically, the extra year on campus may have literally helped me dodge a bullet as my first assignment was Germany. I never made it to Vietnam.

I made a career of my service in the Army and retired after nearly 29 years. Along the way, I established myself as a relaxed and loquacious public speaker. The theme of that fateful speech in my professor's office? "Why I should not be given a failing grade." Redemption achieved.

A GOOD-ENOUGH MOM

JEANETTE KOSHAR

I sit at my refuge, the ocean, and wonder if these waves are catchable. Uncatchable waves are tricky. A dangerous wave builds and crashes, and any miscalculation means being pummeled then rolled around on the sandy bottom. When these conditions exist, lungs burn as I hold my breath until I can push myself to the surface. If I get it right, I swim underneath, against the force of the wave, and emerge on the backside.

Catchable waves will curl before they break. Kick toward an oncoming swell. Turn, swim, and then, with arms in a "V," be carried to shore.

When huge, rogue sneaker waves race toward the beach, they can overtake anyone in their way. These monsters drag people into the water, and only a few are lucky enough to be spit back onto dry land.

ᆭ

Erin was my second daughter; both were adopted. By thirty, I'd had four miscarriages. Erin's birth mother delivered at age fourteen. I knew some objectionable things about her birth parents but believed in nurture over nature. My family and friends' platitudes, "Oh, she's just headstrong," could not drown my concern that my child had no moral compass.

It didn't help that my husband was emotionally abusive. I protected the girls until it became impossible and then finally divorced him. Many nights during her elementary school years, I sat in a living room chair tormented that I wasn't a good-enough mom. Playground fights were followed by calls from the principal. Money went missing from my wallet. Toys I hadn't bought appeared in her room. The Girl Scout leader called to say my daughter might do better in another troop.

I squeezed my eyes shut to conjure up good times: Erin maneuvering down the soccer field in her pink high-tops, holding hands as we jumped into piles of fall leaves, the day in kindergarten she announced she could read, how I had comforted the little girl frightened by Halloween decorations.

Her teenage years began with the expected eye rolling and disrespect, but soon the school principal and truant officers blamed me for Erin's erratic school attendance and missing assignments. Cops brought her home at one in the morning and didn't care that she'd escaped through her bedroom window. A vindictive undercurrent surfaced, "Get control of your daughter, or we'll call CPS."

Her therapist rebuked my parenting by saying, "Erin is acting out because you treat her differently from her sister."

"You don't think I've tried the usual consequences with Erin? She's manipulative enough to stay just this side of legal, and I'm gullible enough to think I can keep her there. Her sister, Sasha, is a normal teenager. She pushes the limits but knows where the boundaries are. Erin bullies her with promises of retaliation. Sasha's world is crashing down around her, and if I don't do something, she's threatening to move in with her dad. That's how bad it is."

One day, I snuck into Erin's room hoping not to find evidence confirming rumors my daughter was in a gang. I was wrong. Under the mattress was an eight-inch, handmade knife. It was heavy in my hand, and I dropped it when I spotted specks of dried blood on the tip. *I'm such a fool. How could I have hoped for anything different?* I called the police captain, an acquaintance, and begged for help.

"Nothing can be done because she hasn't broken any laws," he said.

"I heard about a diversion program. Can't I get her into that? Can't you see where this is heading? I need help."

"Sorry, but she has to be in the juvenile justice system to get her into that program," he said matter-of-factly.

Doesn't anybody else hear the roar of approaching catastrophe?

ଔ

Two days after finding the knife, I had Erin arrested. She walked into the kitchen at nine that night. "Give it back. You had no right to take it. It's my friend's, and I need it back."

"What are you talking about?" I asked in a voice that didn't fool either of us.

She rolled her eyes. "Oh, God, Mom, you can't even lie good. Give it back. I need it tonight, or I'm gonna get hurt."

"Erin, I know you think you are tough, but no one is that tough." I was devastated. She was in a gang. How could I have been so blind? I reached for her. "We can get you help."

She shrank back.

I glared at her. "You are not going out."

"I'm not staying home. You can't stop me." She headed for the front door.

I beat her to it and stood with my back to the closed door, arms outstretched. "You are not leaving this house." We both screamed insults until I finally broke and slapped her across the face. A sound that reverberated for years.

She shoved past me, jerked open the door, turned toward the living room window, and smashed it with a clenched fist. "That coulda been your face." She glared at me.

I stared at the cracked glass then at my daughter's uninjured hand. Without a word, I walked into the house and called 911. I don't know why she didn't run. We stood silently, side by side in the dark until the police car pulled up.

The officer looked concerned. "Do you *really* want to have your daughter arrested for vandalism?"

"I do. I don't know what else to do." My shoulders sagged, and my head dropped.

"Okay, well, then you may not want to watch," he said, then turned her toward the car and clicked on handcuffs behind her back.

My daughter looked small in the back seat.

He closed the door. Mother and daughter stared at each other as the officer backed out of my driveway. I stood alone in the dark and wailed. Then I sat on the ground beneath the broken window and hugged my knees. *What have I done? Do I have the courage to buoy myself up and go on another day?*

Four long days later, I watched Erin escorted into the courtroom clad in a bright-orange jumpsuit, handcuffs, and shackles. When I gasped, my daughter and the bailiff turned and glared. Ashamed, I looked down. She was released into my custody five hours later after being handed two pages of probation stipulations. Had the drug test been positive, there might've been an excuse for her behavior.

Not that I wanted that. It was just a thought.

She sat in the front seat of the car looking out the window as we drove home. "You know, Erin, I will never stop loving you, no matter what you do." I glanced at her and smiled. "So, it'd be fine if you stopped testing me."

"Yeah, Mom, but you got rid of Dad because you didn't like what he did."

I took a deep breath. "You are my kid. It's a different kind of relationship. I won't stop loving you. Ever."

She looked back out the window and was silent.

For a week, we didn't speak to each other much. When I'd walk into a room, Erin would walk out. But seven days later, she approached me.

"Mom, I need to leave Napa. You remember my friend, Sally, who moved to North Syracuse, New York? I got ahold of her parents, and I could do my senior year there. Bad things are gonna happen if I stay here."

Her spiteful probation officer refused to let her go. Back in court, the judge granted our request with the comment: "How much trouble could she get into in a tiny, freezing rural town?"

Two weeks later, I stood at the gate and watched her plane pull away. I hoped she would come back a different person.

In May, the Erin I loved returned. She enrolled in college . . . but dropped out two months later. She crashed her car. Tumbled from one job to the next. At nineteen, Erin had her first child, a boy who had the wisdom of a Buddha. I imagined him patiently sitting on a rock, waiting for his mother to catch up to him emotionally.

CB

Three years later, I sat at the computer monitor in my second-floor university office fine-tuning a test for one of my undergraduate courses. Late afternoon light streamed through the two large windows where I glimpsed our resident owls high in a tree across the walkway. Soon, their nest would be removed—their droppings were deemed too dangerous for the sidewalk and passersby.

My cell phone rang. I glanced at the screen and saw an unfamiliar Sacramento number. Erin lived in Sacramento. Stomach churning, I held my breath. "Hello?"

"You have a collect call from an inmate at the Sacramento County Jail. Press 1 to accept the call." Dismay rolled over me. How disastrous was this going to be? "You are responsible for the charges for this call. Hang up now if you do not accept the charges." The image loomed of my teenage daughter shuffling into a courtroom in an orange jumpsuit with ankles and wrists shackled.

"Hi, Mom," she said in a rush. "They think I forged some checks, but I didn't. It'll all get worked out, but I need you to post bail. Isaac is at daycare, and nobody can pick him up but me. They close in an hour. I'll pay you back when I get out, but it has to be done soon, or I have to spend the night in jail. Here's the number for the bail bond place. Do you have a pen?"

"Wait a minute. I'm not sure I want to bail you out. We've been down this road before with assurances 'this won't happen again' and 'I'll pay you back.' I need to think about this."

"Mom, you *have* to act fast. I can't believe you would do this to Isaac. *Really*? Leave your two-year-old grandson at daycare? That's just messed up. You don't have time to think about it. It's only $500."

"Well, it'll be $5000 if you don't show up to every court hearing. What are the chances of that?"

"You know, Mom, fuck this. You *always* do this. You can't make up your mind. I don't need this shit right now. Don't do it for me. Do it for Isaac. Come on, Mom, it's almost five."

"Okay, give me the number for the bail bond guy. I'll do this once, but I'm *never* doing it again."

"Yeah, Mom. I know. Bye."

I held the phone in my hand and stared at the darkened computer as the screensaver orb glided around the monitor and bounced against the edges of the screen. I called the bail bondsman. "Well, this is a first," I said. "And it better be a last."

"What credit card will you be paying with?" he replied.

ଔ

While Erin served a month in jail, my grandson turned three. A friend of Erin's and I divvied up time caring for Isaac and decided to hold off on his birthday celebration until his mom got out of jail. While I made dinner that evening, Isaac sat in the living room stacking wooden blocks. In a calm voice, I heard: "Happy birthday to me. Happy birthday to me. Happy birthday, dear Isaac. Happy birthday to me." *He's so perceptive. Didn't I see this coming?*

I sat on the floor by my grandson and pulled him onto my lap. "It is your birthday, and we are going to celebrate it when your mom can be here. But I didn't forget, sweetie." I got his not-yet wrapped present, and after dinner, we put a candle in a scoop of ice cream and sang "Happy Birthday."

ဃ

For five more years, I persisted with my rescues, hoping each time for a different outcome. We endured another car crash, repeated job losses with infrequent new offers, evictions, and minor encounters with law enforcement. Requests for money, infused with thinly disguised threats, were frequent. Erin had another baby, and I arranged holiday excursions, science camps, and camping trips, hoping my grandsons would gain a broader perspective on what life had to offer.

ဃ

At ten o'clock on a cloudless summer morning, I heard her ringtone. After years of Erin's emergency calls, my reflex was to hold my breath before I said, "Hello."

"Hi, Mom. I don't know what happened, but me and the kids are going to be evicted tomorrow if I don't pay my landlord for the water bill. It's really high—there must be a leak. I can pay you back at the end of the month."

"Erin, there isn't a leak. You didn't pay the bills. You tell me the same story every time. It's been back-to-back catastrophes for the last six months. I can't do this anymore."

"Oh, jeez, Mom. It's only $300. I said I'd pay you back."

"Well, that would be a first," I replied.

The vision of my grandkids delayed my *no*. "Let me think about it. I bet you can find the money someplace else."

"You know, Mom. Screw it. I don't need this right now." She hung up.

I don't need this right now either. I headed to my sanctuary, the ocean, where I sat on a cliff-side bench on the Sonoma coast. For the last six months, I dared not perch this close to the edge. Today, the edge held no terror.

I walked down the cliff trail, stood in the dry sand, and watched wave upon wave build larger and curl in on itself before rumbling to the shore.

I moved closer. My bare feet were cold in the wet sand.

These last years, I've come crashing down in these waves. I've forgotten to dive deep, kick hard against the water's force, and emerge beyond the wave into the calm between swells. I've ignored sneaker waves until a big enough one rolled in, crushed my world, and rebuilt it into a shape I did not recognize. Cast across the water, shadows made the catchable waves impossible to differentiate from those that weren't, and I ended up letting them pass me by.

On my way back to the car, my footing was surer than when I descended. I drove three miles inland before there was cell phone reception, and I pulled onto the side of the road under a eucalyptus tree. "Erin, there won't be any more money. I can't help you figure out your life. That is yours to do." My sentences were short, knowing if I said more, I would talk myself into another choice.

"Gee, thanks, Mom. I can get the money some other way. Believe me, you just don't want to know how I'll do it. You wouldn't approve." She paused, waiting for me to renege on my refusal. "You know, Mom, screw it. I can take care of me and mine."

This was my wave to catch. "You're right, Erin. I know you can."

HOW CAN I EVER REDEEM MYSELF? I'M MALE

BILL TRZECIAK

I was stupid when I was thirteen.

I was also stupid when I was fourteen, fifteen, and sixteen. Or maybe just thoughtless, I don't know. No excuses, though; certainly not during this countrywide reassessment of male rudeness that requires each of us to go back over our actions and relationships with females. Reexamine ourselves before some Un-American-Activities-style committee digs up our transgressions and throws them in our faces.

Do I now or did I ever disrespect women by attitude, action, intent, or misappropriation of my privileged status as a male?

Jesus, I don't know. Maybe when I was too young to know any better?

Did I have to say that to a girl just to be funny?

Did I have to write that about another girl just to make the joke in the way such jokes are traditionally made?

Did I have to let a girl write a page for women in my humor magazine in high school?

Well, I did *have* to do the last one. The female art teacher, our faculty advisor, made me include that page in our third issue because the satire was written by me and another male, and all the cartoons were drawn by two other guys. None of us males understood anything on that girls' page forced upon us back then. And though I've looked at it from time to time over the years, I still don't. It seems more like it was memoir-style fiction from a community literary magazine than the *Mad Magazine*-style crass jokes and satire we were fashioning.

But I did learn to let it go. Even though I didn't comprehend it, it seemed fair, and after that, I stopped questioning things from women I didn't understand. Besides, I was already having second thoughts about an earlier issue when I had written a scenario using names of real popular students—I suggested one was more sexually active than she might have been and another had her ample boobs caught in the hands of a particular boy.

Stupid, stupid, foolish but only inadvertently cruel. Minimal awareness would have stopped it. But what I had done earlier at thirteen, as you will see, was just downright cold, and I hate to think of it, even now, as it still haunts me when I do. I was tall, reasonably good looking, and well known in sports and class plays. I used to have lots of girlfriends in junior high school. Full of myself, one day I sent a note to the girl I had been dating which read, "I usually give each girl a two-week trial period. Sorry, kid, you didn't make it."

What the hell made me act like that?

Oh, yeah. I was thirteen. Who the hell was I impressing?

Maybe she got over it. Maybe things like that don't have much effect for a lifetime. But perhaps they do.

Any good writer knows significant little moments can mean everything. Did I destroy a life or just someone's day?

I'll never know. How can I ever redeem myself for it?

After those misadventures, however, I can remember nothing else that has haunted me as much as three stupid things I did at those young ages. I haven't been perfect, mind you, by any account. But I haven't been a dick either. So far as I know. Who knows what feelings and thoughts are harbored in the minds of women who have known me? But then, would they have told me?

Right? Maybe?

I remember two propositions made in my twenties and early thirties both of which left no doubt of rejection. I accepted them with humility: (a) "Sorry, no. I'm gay;" and (b) "What are you? Nuts?!!" But I still love both as friends. I'm pretty sure all my other adult encounters and interactions with women have been respectful on both sides.

Perhaps it was that little, but not insignificant, guilt I carried with me about early failings that assured my general behavior thenceforth would be thoughtful, kind, and not aggressive. I hope the women I've been intimate with, and those I've worked with and otherwise encountered, would not have complaints. I'm a progressive liberal writer, for heaven's sake. I even write about altruism and make satirical doggerel supporting equality between the sexes. I use words as well as I can to help make this a better world.

But words, as it turns out, can hurt as much as they heal. And it takes some time, perhaps, to learn what is insightful and funny as opposed to what can sting so hard it disrupts an otherwise unaffected life. I don't know if my three moments of boyhood stupidity threw any girl's life off track, but I keep wondering, after fifty-some years, did my words hurt them?

Okay, it was easier for me to not trip up anymore. I eventually became a public library reference librarian, and nearly all my superiors and colleagues were women or men of sterling character. Any ideas of in-house pay inequity or abuse of status never disturbed the environment in that civil service field so far as I surmised. And as a disabled activist and creative artist, I learned from writers and directors in the Women's Movement who worked with us on productions. Our alienation and feelings of second-class status and dismissive experiences were often like theirs.

But even outside of those categories, I'm pretty sure almost every male I've known in my adult life has been just as respectful of the women in their lives. (Most, not all, but I won't speak ill of the dead.) And I know the women they chose to be with have been just as strong, empowered, bright, and considerate as the women I've liked (many) and married (one) in my life. Most of those males are not men of power or celebrity and would have no more inclination to be jerks than I did.

I hope it is only those other men we hear about, from crude small businessmen and restaurant managers to pathological corporate, media, and political bigwigs, who misuse their power or prestige against women. They are the ones who will rightly be named and blacklisted, not ordinary guys like me and the good husbands and partners I have known, I hope.

It's a minefield right now, and we all need to be aware we're in it. We need to purge our society of any expectations of inequality of the sexes and of any form of sexual harassment or abuse. Period. And we must do it with energy from good men and women both— and with redemptive punishment for the bad ones.

Only one thing could redeem any of us in the end. Inappropriate acts must be met with appropriate shame. That little sense of personal guilt for even minor oversteps that we progressives carry with us throughout our whole lives is a utility, not a burden. Too much guilt is destructive and too little is worse.

Was it my kind, considerate mother and her kind, considerate parents (of six daughters) who instilled just enough awareness in me such that I could resist being trained to be an authoritarian by a father who saw himself as a warrior for souls in the patriarchal religion that gave men such destructive license over women?

I suspect one thing: all those new-age, self-awareness movements that ended in absolute unfettered selfishness without the understanding of shared responsibility among members of a society may have given us damaging greed and cultural division. We need to recognize when and how we transgress the bounds of basic, cooperative decency and fairness. A healthy awareness of others' needs is good. A healthy sense of guilt gives us that ability to feel others' pain.

I carry my imperfection and self-consciousness without fear of exposure. I've learned to live with that guilt and, more importantly, I've learned *from* it. Only one's actions can redeem one, and every action I take has that tincture of guilt.

Boys need to learn how to become men who are team members with women and everyone else in between. Decent behavior and fair play make sense. We must teach early on that guilt leads to amends while ignorance breeds offense.

Am I sorry enough? How sorry does a man have to be to be both kind and strong? I won't carry guilt for what I didn't do, but I will accept blame for what I did before I knew any better. I carry it with me to keep me decent and honest as I can be.

THE LIE

PAMELA HECK

I know firsthand what a lie can do. Mine held me hostage for two long years. The night Don broke his thumb on my head, he set me free.

My life began to unravel while I was living in Boston. I had a boyfriend, Bill, whose handsome good looks did not excuse his boorish behavior. Our relationship came to an earsplitting end in the parking lot of a Chinese restaurant where I created a stir by screaming, "Take me home," at the top of my lungs. He did. I never saw him again.

Shortly before the big breakup, my roommates and I also decided to go our separate ways. After four years of togetherness, we wanted different things. Suzie and Dana moved to a singles' complex in the suburbs. I found a great apartment in the city. However, to afford it, I needed to find a better paying job. Leaving my beloved copywriting position in downtown Boston, I accepted the position of assistant advertising director with a college textbook publisher in the dreaded suburbs. I missed my old job, my old business friends, my former roommates, and, at times, even my old boyfriend. I was desperately unhappy.

Enter Don . . .

Don was a senior editor at the publishing house. On my first day on the job, he showed up wearing a black armband to commemorate his fortieth birthday. *Ah*, I thought. *He has a sense of humor*. However, he was fourteen years my senior—too old for me, or so I thought.

Still, I found him somewhat attractive. He had the deep, resonant voice of a radio announcer and the look of a college professor from the English department. With his neatly clipped gray beard, he resembled a forty-year-old Papa Hemingway. The similarity was so striking that, when we moved from Boston, one of the moving men was confused by the Hemingway poster on Don's office door. "Nice picture of your husband," he said.

Don pursued me. He left flowers in my car, packed romantic lunches, and made it clear that he wanted me. It felt good to be desired.

Shortly after our courtship began, Don was offered the position of West Coast Acquisitions Editor for our company. His home office would be in Marin County. He accepted the position and begged me to go with him—as his wife. I said "Yes" to the move, "No" to the marriage proposal. After all, I had known him for only a few short months. That was my last rational decision where Don was concerned.

I had one big problem—my recently widowed mother. Moving across the country with a man I barely knew and cohabitating with him without the benefit of marriage was a huge "no-no" in my mother's book of rules. If I told her the truth, I was in for tears and tirades, accusations, and the promise of hell to come. But if Don and I were married, I would be obligated to make the move. Hadn't my mother always told me that a wife was duty-bound to follow her husband wherever his career might take him? I imagined that, in time, Don and I would get married. I didn't love him yet, but he loved me so much I was sure I'd eventually come to reciprocate. What was the harm of a little white lie? I would just tell my mother that Don and I had eloped. I thought I lied to protect her. I know, now, I lied to protect myself.

Marshaling all my courage, I placed the dreaded phone call and relayed my exciting news: due to the suddenness of Don's promotion and the upcoming move, we decided to elope. I could hear the hurt in my mother's voice. Her only child had gotten married without her. Nevertheless, she rose to the occasion. Then the questions began. Where were we married? Who officiated? Who was there? The lies rolled off my tongue like cars rolling off an assembly line. The call left me limp with exhaustion—and feeling more than somewhat guilty—but I had pulled it off. She believed me. Little did I realize the truth of the adage, "Oh, what a tangled web we weave when first we practice to deceive." I would find that out soon.

About two weeks after the fateful conversation with my mother, she sent me a letter. A newspaper clipping fluttered out. Opening it, I was stunned to see I'd received top billing on the wedding page of the local newspaper: "Pamela Heck Is Married."

There, below the heading, was the account of my fictitious wedding exactly as I had told it to my mother. To make matters worse, she had wedding announcements printed and sent to friends and family across the country. Wedding gifts poured in. I'd had the most prominent "un-wedding" in history.

Don and I ordered matching wedding bands from a local jeweler and, rings in place, relayed our happy news at work. As Don's wife, I could have all my belongings and my car shipped to the West Coast. Lucky me!

Shortly before our move, a few cracks appeared in Don's perfect demeanor. We were invited to a farewell party thrown by one of Don's neighbors. Near the end of the evening, the strains of "I Left My Heart in San Francisco" filled the room. All eyes were on Don and me.

"Jesus," Don said, "if there's one song I can't stand, it's that one."

The host's face was visibly reddening. I knew he had played that song in our honor, but Don seemed oblivious.

"Only tourists who call San Francisco 'Frisco' ever ask for that song."

The music ended suddenly and, shortly after, so did the party. The first red flag. I told myself, *it's nothing*, until a more significant flag popped up at the office Christmas party. Don intensely disliked the history editor. Although Lorna was destined to be his primary East Coast contact, he backed her into a corner and outlined all her faults and editorial shortcomings. I couldn't hear what was said, but body language spoke volumes. Bad career move!

We arrived at SFO on an overcast January day—Don, my dog Alfie, and me. Our first home was the Emeryville Holiday Inn. I wanted to live in San Francisco. Don's office was in San Rafael, which would have been my second choice. Don vetoed both. San Francisco was too cold, San Rafael too expensive. Oakland was our destination. It had the perfect weather for Don's favorite free-time activity—tennis. We found a lovely duplex on a tree-lined street that allowed dogs. It was nice, but I was on the wrong side of the bay.

Don traveled quite a bit when we first arrived. He scouted new authors for the company, and he wanted me with him. It was fun at first, traveling as far south as San Diego and as far north as Seattle. But I had no job, no money, and only one friend in the area.

What's more, now that Don had me isolated and dependent, more cracks began to appear in his persona. Beneath the loving exterior was a deep well of rage that erupted in unexpected moments and situations.

Once we got settled, Don wanted to throw a housewarming party. Having lived in Oakland before, he called all his former friends and his tennis partners and invited them to the big event. I spent the whole day preparing. That evening, I eagerly awaited Don's friends. None came. My friend, Linda, arrived with another couple in tow. An author that Don had just signed came out of a sense of obligation and brought his wife. That was it. Red flags popped up everywhere.

Don did make friends with Bill and Susan, a couple he met playing tennis. They were avid bridge players, and since Don and I also played, we invited them to a bridge game at our house. A few weeks later, they reciprocated. It looked like the beginning of a friendship. The evening began amicably but ended with a bang. The bidding went something like this:

> I opened, "One spade."
> Susan, "Two clubs."
> Don, "Three spades."
> Bill, "Pass."
> Me, "Five spades."

I made six spades and won the game, at which point Don jumped up and screamed at the top of his voice, "God damn it, Pam, you should have made seven spades!"

You could have heard a pin drop in the room. Bill and Susan looked dumbstruck. After a brief hesitation, Don continued his tirade.

I cut him off. "Susan, Bill, thank you so much for a lovely evening. I think it's time for us to go. I mouthed, "I'm so sorry" to Susan on the way out, and that was that. No more bridge nights.

Once I found a job as a copywriter for a local department store, life became more enjoyable. I looked forward to going to work. Despite the fact that Don continued to profess his great love for me, I dreaded going home. We bought a house in the Oakland Hills (not the one I wanted—the one *he* wanted—but a house just the same), and I told myself I should be grateful. Perhaps, if I tried a little harder, things would improve. I couldn't imagine calling my mother after just six months, or even a year, and telling her, "It's just not working out." No one in our family had ever gotten a divorce, not even a fictitious one. But I was increasingly unhappy.

Since I had a job, I no longer traveled with Don on his business trips. I looked forward to his absences and began having fantasies in which he ceased to exist. There would be a crash. Don would die a quick and merciful death. I would be free.

It should come as no surprise that Don's company eventually fired him. Don spent his time writing resumes and looking for a new job. He also drank. Had I counted the bottles of Tanqueray Gin piling up in the garage, I might have been more cognizant of what was actually going on—martinis before dinner, wine with dinner, beer after dinner. That combination eventually turned a verbal tirade into fisticuffs. It was just a matter of time, really.

I don't remember a lot about the night in question. Some might find that surprising, but my mind has blocked out much of it. We finished dinner. Don changed his drinking order—he was nursing another martini, not a beer. He became maudlin. I don't remember what he said, the gist of it—he loved me. He loved me, and I was ungrateful. Why didn't I love him back the way he deserved? I felt emotionally drained—exhausted. I said nothing. What I did was worse. I stood up, left the room, and went to bed.

It didn't take long for Don to come after me, screaming. He dragged me from the covers and down the stairs, raining blows on my head with his fists. All I felt was my anger. He broke his thumb. Served him right. I went back to bed.

In the morning, we acted as if nothing had happened, but we both knew it had. I resolved to leave, but first I needed a plan. Since we sold my car shortly after our move, I had no escape vehicle. So I called my friend, Linda, and told her everything that had transpired.

"When I call and ask you to come for me, will you come?"

"Of course."

Once again, I needed to find a better paying job so I could afford an apartment in San Francisco. Within a month, I found one. Time to leave.

Linda came for me on Memorial Day. All I took with me were my clothes. I could hear Don screaming like a wounded animal as we pulled away. I didn't look back.

I stayed with Linda for a month until I found my dream apartment on Sacramento Street. Nights, when we looked out her front window, we could see Don's parked car and the glow of his cigarette as he sat and watched. I got a restraining order and, once I moved into my own place, an unlisted phone number. Still, he found me. Evidently, he had convinced someone at the phone company to give him the information.

"I know where you live."

God, I'd recognize that voice anywhere.

"How did you find me?"

"I had a psychic vision. It led me to you."

Did he really think I'd buy that? Did he?

"Please, Don, I'm begging you—leave me alone."

I spent a lot of time looking over my shoulder, but nothing happened.

When I told my poor mother the marriage hadn't worked out, she said, "Now you can come home." I didn't have the heart to tell her I was home, not at first. I went through a divorce as fictitious as my marriage. When it was final, I confessed that I was staying in San Francisco. She visited me once each year, and I spent every vacation in Pennsylvania with her.

The following year, I fell in love and became engaged. Shortly before the wedding, I received a call from Don. He called, ostensibly, to see if I would take his cat (a cat that had once been ours.)

"Pam, I need you to take Irma."

"Why can't you take care of her?"

"I can't take her where I'm going." *Another veiled suicide threat?*

"Don, I'm sorry, but I can't take the cat. We already have a dog and two cats. It simply wouldn't work."

"No shit?"

"No shit, Don. Anyway, why can't one of your neighbors take her?"

"I can't do that. They don't read!" *I knew Don was a literary snob, but this was nuts.*

"Don, I'm sorry, but the cat doesn't read either." Click.

I never heard from Don again. Once I thought I saw him at the San Francisco airport. I was six months pregnant, and my husband and I were about to fly to New York for his sister's wedding. I didn't want to make eye contact, so I'm not sure. It was a fleeting glimpse, and I kept walking. I don't know if he saw me. It didn't matter.

Did I ever tell my mother the truth about my fictitious first marriage? No. Over the years, two therapists agreed it would only cause more hurt. However, I never told her another lie—not even when I moved in with the boyfriend destined to become my future husband. Mom was upset, but she got over it.

MEMORIES

ROGER DEBEERS, SR.

Until I stood above her grave, I never dwelled long on either the pleasurable or the disquieting memories of her brief life. All remembrances of her were like flecks of color splattered on my memory canvas. Sharron dwelled in the past as did my father and mother.

I accepted the stories of my father's murder as told to me by the significant people in my life. I never attempted to discover which versions were truths, exaggerations, exonerations, or fabrications. Everything changed when I stepped into the cemetery where a girl I had known for less than a year, almost six decades before, lay in her grave. This sixteen-year-old girl died in 1956 and was now the catalyst driving me deep into my past, a past where my deceased father and mother dwelled.

Suddenly, I realized that the cavern of recollections I was about to uncover was bottomless and filled at every level with multiple truths, simple and draconian lies, and family secrets hidden in the nooks and crannies of my life. As I began to excavate my family's history, I discovered a catacomb of silences that spoke louder and harsher than the memories I had collected over a lifetime.

Standing in the tiny little farming town of Colusa, I commissioned myself the task of making sense of my past. I made this decision to understand my parents and the torment they endured in their lives . . . but not for the closure. I had to reopen disturbing memories of my parents.

The Cornerstone City Cemetery is not a handsome cemetery in the mode of one of the fastidiously manicured Forest Lawn Memorial Parks or the countless picture-perfect cemeteries depicted in movies or television. This old, rural cemetery is small, flat, and rectangular. A worn wheelbarrow, a pile of plastic irrigation pipes, and a blue portable toilet that required users to bring their own toilet paper flank a small maintenance building.

There is no directory indicating the layout of the family plots dating from the late 1890s to the present. The Thompson family occupied Lot 18, Section 0, and I struggled to find them as I plodded from site to site.

Broken headstones and several flat grave markers covered in thin coats of dirt contrasted with the newer, raised, granite markers. I dusted off two of the flat markers so the forgotten names could see the sun and moon again. In the center of the cemetery stood one squat tree sheltering a family plot. A scant amount of clipped green vegetation—clumped grass here and there—testified that there was irregular maintenance.

As I hunted for the Thompson family site, I daydreamed of what my life might have been if Sharron had lived. Where would her sentiments have fallen as both the Vietnam War and the anti-war protests ran their courses? Would she have embraced the sixties and seventies counterculture, danced to Big Brother and the Holding Company, embraced "extremism in the defense of liberty" as extolled by Barry Goldwater, or have been an invisible suburban wife and mother of three?

Sharron was frozen in my mind as a sixteen-year-old freshman girl in a 1955 prom dress. I had no memories of her other than the one school year we had gone steady, along with what her mother, Anna, had told me when I came home on leave in early 1957. I was as homeless as the day I joined the Marines, except now I had a bunk waiting for me. The Thompson family clung desperately to their vacant flat on 2nd Avenue; they could not bear to live in it, rent it, or sell it after Sharron's death, but they told me I was welcome to stay in it and treat it as my own during my leave.

Every few days, Anna Thompson showed up with a couple bags of groceries. She cooked dinner for us, breakfast in the morning, and then departed for her home in Marin. When she stayed over, she insisted that I sleep in the master bedroom while she took her son's room. When we settled in at night, she launched into her stories of Sharron in a voice verging on operatic. She never initiated these melancholic fables unless there was a bedroom wall between us. Perhaps I was also a fabrication in Anna's recreated fantasy of her dead daughter.

During her stories, I was expected to remain alert and attentive. If I was too quiet, she'd bang on the wall or get up and rap on the open door. Waiting for me to respond, she'd stand there dressed in an ankle-length white nightgown, which gave her a spectral appearance. The recurring theme of these quirky ghost stories was always *what might have been* had Sharron lived.

I was the medium that Anna Thompson used to bring her daughter back to life. My presence banished Sharron's absence for a brief amount of time. For twenty-two days, Anna's periodic visits created a fairytale, which increasingly veered into a dreamlike state where I became the posthumous son-in-law. At the end of the first week, this culminated in her insisting that I call her "Mom."

I had no idea what was going on in the overarching scheme of things except that I was living uncomfortably in a home haunted by the conjured ghost of Sharron. Sharron's death was so unwanted and unacceptable that I was sure her mother believed her own invented stories. They were told with such intense conviction that I began to question my understanding of reality. I was in a parallel universe, united with her daughter in a strange new world.

I did not like being in the Marine Corps. I had flat feet and wobbled whenever I walked, marched, or ran. From the first day of boot camp, I was in constant pain. Whenever I was on my feet for any period, my ankles slowly pronated as the tendons from my calves to my feet were uncomfortably stretched. But days before the end of my leave, I longed to be back in the protective folds of the Marine Corps. Upon my return, it wasn't long before I counted the days to my discharge, even though my new assignment was a desk job as a training aid illustrator, cartoonist, and painter for instructors.

I never returned to the Thompson family's flat, or sought them out after my leave was up, or even after my discharge in 1959. Now, after fifty-six years, I stood over their graves. As I looked at Sharron's gravestone on this mild Wednesday afternoon in late January 2013, I read the words etched into the granite.

Sharron Thompson
29 Jan 1940–3 April 1956
Beloved daughter of Francis and Anna Thompson

As if I were suspended, it suddenly struck me that the raised rectangular marker seemed an unfathomable distance below me. Much more than mere physical space, it was the vastness of a lifetime.

Although Sharron broke up with me when I joined the Marines, five days after I graduated from high school, we were eternally connected because her mother buried her with my Block P sports medallion Sharron wore on the day she died. I imagined that she still looked the same in repose with the gold-rimmed, black onyx and red medallion I had earned playing soccer at Polytechnic High School. I could not think of her in any way other than the sixteen-year-old girl I had taken to my senior prom.

Looking down at her grave marker, I realized I had no personal memories of Sharron before she began the ninth grade, or after I graduated. Her life passed over me like the wind, and ultimately turned into a gentle breeze and died. Nine months after I had last seen her, Sharron was dead.

Until last year, I never visited or was within passing distance of Colusa where my father died in 1944. Then a year ago, I drove near there on business eight times and, finally, yielded to whatever brought me to Colusa. I called Jerry and told him how strange it was to be where Dad had been beaten to death. I didn't have the remotest desire to visit the place of his death.

This time was different, and I wondered what in the hell brought me to Colusa after all these years. The rational explanation was that my job took me within close proximity since the superstition of ghosts and spirits of the netherworld never held much interest for me. I just did not believe in the paranormal. But the question of why I was drawn to Colusa now mystified me.

After a few pleasantries, Jerry said, "Ya know, Colusa is where Sharron died, Rod."

"Really?"

"Sharron died a couple of days after Easter in 1956, in Colusa," Jerry said.

"I know. I mean, I knew when she died, but I didn't know it was in Colusa. It's creepy, Jer."

"What's creepy?"

"My dad and Sharron dying in a little burg like Colusa twelve years apart."

"I think Sharron's dad was a cop there before they moved to the city after the war."

"How come you remember more things than I do?" I asked.

"Don't know. Maybe I'm your muse, and it's my job," Jerry said sardonically.

I began to obsess about Dad and Sharron, determined to find out more about their deaths. I discovered that they had both died at the Colusa Memorial Hospital.

Colusa. Why Colusa, of all places? I kept asking myself.

At the library, I found a newspaper clipping from April 4, 1956, in the *Colusa Sun Herald*. The article mentioned that Sharron's family was originally from Colusa County, and they were living in San Francisco at the time of Sharron's death. She and her family were in Colusa for an Easter family gathering when the car she was in with her older brother went out of control, slammed into the Prize Bridge, and overturned into a ditch on Arbuckle Grimes Road. Seatbelts might have saved Sharron's life, but cars weren't equipped with seatbelts in 1956.

My research did not reveal the reason Dad was in Colusa in October 1944.

I shifted my gaze to Francis William Thompson's grave marker.

1910–1966
Beloved husband and father
To his right was his wife:
Anna Thompson
1915–1982

I folded my arms tightly against my chest, sighed, and rocked back on my heels. Beneath my feet was a family I was connected to, briefly, over fifty years ago. For a moment, my mind was a blank, and then a few out-of-sequence lyrics from "Danny Boy" cascaded through my mind.

"If I am gone and dead as I may well be,
You'll come and find the spot where I am lying,
And kneel and whisper a Kaddish there for me.
And I shall hear, though soft you tread above me
And my grave will warmer, sweeter be . . ."

I stopped thinking about my version of the song and quickly called Jerry back to tell him I was becoming a maudlin, corny old fool.

"It's about time you grieved for Sharron properly," Jerry said.

"What in the hell does that mean after fifty years?"

"Remember when we were stationed at Sukiran, and the Red Cross tracked us down in Okinawa to inform us of Sharron's death? You pitched a temper tantrum and blamed everyone around you, including the Marine Corps. After that, you got drunk, which almost landed you in the brig. You never talked much about her after that. Sex and booze were your solaces, and the sex was 200 yen when the exchange rate was only 120 yen to an MPC dollar."

"I don't remember the temper tantrum," I said.

"It will come to you."

"I guess this means I have to come to terms with Norman's death too."

"Yer dad, you mean?"

"Yeah. It's the kinda crap I try not to think about."

"Take it easy, Rod. One at a time, okay?"

"It's not that I find this too painful; it's just that it's all a mishmash of riddles. The damn memories happened in a linear sequence of time, but as far as their significance—they're all jumbled around."

"How poetic thou art."

Laughing, I pulled the earpiece out of my ear and then, directly into the device shouted, "Yeah. Sure. It's the cutting edge of nothing."

"Rod. Grief expressed is redemptive."

I realized that I did not know Sharron and never would unless I created an incomplete, semi-fictional version of her based on the precious little details I knew about her. What had been her dreams and desires? Would I have ever come to love her? As I walked back to my car, I thought about the fictional world where Sharron lived. Once again, the fantasy in which the 1949 Mercury she rode in would have seatbelts and front and side airbags. As I opened my car door, I dismissed the idea, realizing that I could rediscover old memories and continually hone them with revisions, but the eventual, finite outcome would always remain beyond the reach of my reconstructions. Sharron would always be here in sunshine or shadow, as the old Irish song tells me, and one day I will "bend down and tell her I am sorry I did not grieve for her properly."

I was determined to acknowledge her life and not her death. I got in the car and sat with my eyes closed, silently reprimanding myself for being a corny old man reminiscent of Edmund Gwenn's counterfeiting character in the movie *Mister 880.* Suddenly, I got back out of the car, closed my eyes, and held out my right hand.

"You okay, sir?"

I opened my eyes to see a Colusa County Sheriff's patrol car parked behind my car and a deputy standing beside me.

"Yes, Officer. I'm okay. I just stopped here to visit the gravesite of a girl I dated in high school. She died young."

"That's rough," the officer replied.

"Yeah. I'm a writer, and sometimes I try to catch an idea as it rides the wind."

The deputy nodded. "Very good, sir."

"The girl buried here passed over me like a spring breeze a long time ago." I lifted my right arm higher as though reaching to the sky.

As if he was caught in some wistful memory as well, the officer paused a moment and finally said, "I am sure she did, sir. I'm sure she did."

THE WALKING MAN

ANGEL STORK

The line between horror and humor can be paper thin when living with an alcoholic parent. My brother, sister, and I often resorted to the family-style ironic humor with snide commentary to hide our shame and powerlessness from our mother's disease. As we grew older, our reflections became more sardonic, a little bitter. Together, we exaggerated our tales from sublimely inane to ridiculously extreme as we recalled our mother's drunken antics, drinking-thinking, deep denial, and clever justifications for her addiction. We can still be reduced to belly-shaking laughter, tears streaming down our faces, annihilated by the perfect madness of our life with Mother. We rarely doubted her love for us but often questioned her attraction to dodgy people and situations and her utter lack of control.

Mostly, Mother was a happy drunk—friendly and generous with people. She held naive assumptions about everyone's grace and goodness and would jump at the chance to do a favor for almost anyone she knew. I have nearly forty years of "humorous horror stories" I can tell about my mother. "The Walking Man" is one example. If Aunt Shep had not been with us that day, this glimpse of my mother would have held no humor for me.

The Walking Man

Mother has a Walking Man. I have one too. I suppose they are everywhere if you look for them. The Walking Man appears to be in a trance or an ambling stupor. He is not lost, out for a stroll, nor on a trip to the store for a pack. He is compulsively walking. His years of committed drinking swell and flush his face and bloat his reddening hands regardless of his natural skin tone.

My Walking Man might be Asian with darker skin than mine, though it is difficult to discern his features through the poisoned distortions of his face. I have observed him for about twenty years—his small, quick steps, often talking and gesturing as if signing to underscore a private conversation. He never wanders in areas where other people congest the sidewalks. Often, he is seen along railway tracks or down avenues welcoming to cars but not to people. I see him several times each month in the outer districts, unvarying in his stride or manner.

If you have ever visited San Francisco, you will never come again without half your winter wardrobe in tow, regardless of what season is playing elsewhere in California. My Walking Man never dresses for wind, fog, or rain. On a trip to see my Mother in the eastern panhandle of West Virginia, it never occurred to me she would have an all-season walker of her own.

ଔ

"Well, I'll *be*," Mother says, staring up the street.

"What?"

"The Walkin' Man." She steps out of the car before I can recover my senses. We have never mentioned, compared notes, or discussed this subject. Yet, she not only *has* a Walking Man and calls him her Walking Man, she *knows* him.

"*Now* where's y'mother off to?" Aunt Shep's exasperation brings me back.

"She's got a Walkin' Man, Shep. There he is."

Shep and I follow Mother's weaving progress from the car, her arms waving, calling, "Hey, Steve!"

Steve, a bloated, red-faced white man, anywhere from thirty-five to fifty years of age, trudges stiffly forward. He stares straight ahead as if seeing nothing. Without contra-lateral arm swing motion, he moves like a robot though somewhat more relaxed—zombie is more apt.

Mother, determined to wake him, continues to wave her hands and yell. She has to cut right across his path before he stops. In his fixed state, it seems he neither sees nor wants to see her. It takes a few moments for him to pull his attention out of the middle distance and focus on her face, now about six inches from his.

"Haddayadoo, ma'am?" He regards her with dead eyes.

Shep and I gaze in amazement as Mother places her hands on Steve's shoulders, gets eyeball to eyeball with him, and tells him he needs help—meanwhile, *she* teeters from the wine she consumed this morning so we could leave the house. It is only by Shep's insistence that I am allowed to drive into town.

Shep and I shake our heads. Mother and the Walking Man sway together on the sidewalk, propped against each other by

Mother's outstretched arms, elbows locked to resist his forward tendencies.

Mother admonishes him to get sober, attend AA meetings, and keep his fists out of his wife's face until somewhere behind his hollow expression, a small recognition dawns and he mutters, "Yes, ma'am, I will."

Finally satisfied or just fatigued, Mother releases her hold and steps to his side. Seemingly relieved of the pressure against his shoulders, Steve stumbles forward a few steps then resumes his sleepwalk down the street. Mother polishes her knuckles in mock victory as she heads toward the car. She looks okay for about six steps, then one leggy leg crosses too far in front of another, and her saunter becomes a dangerous weave. She is forced to make a stride correction or fall.

Back in the car, Mother treats Shep and me to the confidential story of her Walking Man, his battered spouse, and his terrified children. She has high hopes for him, though, and believes he will follow her direction toward the nearest AA meeting.

"He just needs to get a few meetings under his belt; he'll be okay," she says.

"Maybe you should take him to a meeting y'self, Doris," Shep offers with a wink to me.

&#x03B #x8;

This little vignette typifies my mother's inability to see the absurdity, or possibly her arrogance, in being so insistent upon sobriety in another but not in herself. The keys to Steve's life problems could be found by attending AA meetings, but she ignored her own chronic drunkenness.

In much the same way, when I was a kid, my mother regularly counseled my girlfriends about their issues with their parents, school, or boyfriends. They revered her and thought it was cool that my mother was so wise. She *was* brilliant and could be down-to-earth about almost any aspect of living, yet she offered little guidance or support for her own children's development. My family lacked that "solid core" of those with parental leadership. We kids rarely experienced real togetherness and were mostly left to fend for ourselves.

My mother was one of the kindest people I have ever known, and she abandoned us all for her daily drinking episodes. Although she could be rational, cautious, and caring, she put us at risk many times because she was drunk. She was a loving person, but not of herself; giving but not *to* herself; humble, but often proud of her ability to have "handled" people who enabled her addiction and denial. She lied. She was maddening to live with, yet we loved her. This was the crazy-making, human complexity of alcoholism.

My sister saw only the dysfunction and dissipation of Mother's life. I saw the soaring spirit, the soul in torment, the artist, the intelligence, and the compassionate heart. There is no one truth. Blinded by darkness or by light is still blind.

Mother left a broad swath of scorched earth behind her: three broken children, one out of three alcoholic; six bewildered grandchildren, one highly addicted and dead at forty-nine; and at least two out of seven inwardly confused great-grandkids. Alcoholics may not be to blame for the lives their children lead, but the *disease* of alcoholism takes its toll on all generations—like fruit from a poisoned tree.

My mother's pain, suffering, and later life traumas engendered nearly sixty years of self-medication and solace seeking. She conducted a timid relationship with God but nursed a deep craving for grace. As Scott Peck aptly put it, "Alcoholics have a greater thirst for spirit."

My mother was quite a character: well known to many for her southern gentility, her enthusiastic talkativeness, her generosity, courage, and occasionally, her wisdom. She had been a volunteer with the Loudon County, Virginia Victim/Witness program for four years before she found the courage to stop her own drinking. By then, through her work with the county, she had influenced a dozen or more alcoholic men and women, including her Walking Man, to sober up. By the time *she* attended her first AA meeting, she walked into a room full of friends.

DELIVERANCE

MARY FOLCK

Andrew was three years old when he asked his great-aunt if he could live with her. His mother, a young meth head, could not escape her lifelong habits. Strange people came into her life to party, which left Andrew unattended for days at a time.

In 1995, Andrew met my son in their second-grade class and quickly became a sleepover buddy. They remained close friends, and I became another "auntie" supporting Andrew's elderly great-aunt in raising a child sixty years younger than she was.

As Andrew grew into his teens, young girls could not get enough of his good looks. Despite my efforts to keep him under control, girls constantly flirted with him. It didn't take long to realize that Andrew had no escape from the hormonal heat that shadowed him.

In high school, when they should have been in class, Andrew and a girl went to a secluded spot on campus where she performed oral sex on him. Afterward, she became overwhelmed. A school counselor found the girl weeping in the hall and asked her what was wrong.

According to the counselor, the girl said, "I think I was raped." The counselor did her job and reported the incident to campus police, who conveyed that story to a newspaper reporter. The next day's headline was "Truckee High School Rape."

ᙅ

In court, Andrew told the judge the girl had offered a blow job, and he accepted. Sadly, the young girl in the incident had sobbed her eyes swollen in court. She admitted she had lied to be part of a girls' clique and giving a blow job was her initiation rite. Her deceit had been encouraged by her friends.

In the windowless, wood-paneled courtroom, the judge looked up from his papers and said, "This is a case of teenage hormones run amuck." In that stale air, there was no conviction for rape, but Andrew was convicted of lewd behavior. It is against California law for those under eighteen to engage in sex.

Our son was Andrew's best buddy and helped carry the weight of that headline by defending him. The price of guilt by association with a "predator" was exclusion from the school community.

We became untouchables to some and had to cope with bullying voices, loud in a small community. A few people stayed supportive. Even though I lost friends, standing up to a community system when a lie was taking root was the "right" thing to do. The cost was isolation from the now cold and frightened people who had once smiled at me. This taught me much about righteousness and its inherent harm. In my experience, those who feel righteous have little awareness of other possible explanations or perceptions. There is no respect. My family felt victimized.

Andrew did group-home treatment required by the court, and my husband and I prevented the Nevada County Probation Department from creating another criminal by keeping him away from the California Youth Authority, an institution of ferocious predatory training. It took a lot of finagling.

Nightmares of darkened courtrooms filled with judging, hostile people plagued my dreams. I was restless and lost hours of sleep. Our house was mandated as a court-ordered temporary residence. It was up to us to get him on the right track.

Andrew was Andrew, and his charisma continued to attract women. To keep him from situations that could lead to problems, I set strict boundaries. These rules infuriated him.

Andrew began to hate me. I represented the surrogate-target mother for all his pain, anger, sorrow, and frustration. At least Andrew continued his private therapy and stayed out of trouble.

Once, I overheard him refer to me and say, "I would rather chew off my thumb than accept any help from her."

Teenagers. Sigh.

When Andrew turned twenty-three, he left a Mother's Day greeting of gratitude on our voicemail. He continued this annual practice, although he told loved ones that he was afraid of me. I smiled and chuckled deep in my soul.

His ownership of fear, which I suspected was based on my possible rejection of him, told me he'd had a breakthrough in his deep anger and sorrow. I was no longer the interfering target-mother. He had developed some accountability skills.

Then three years ago, he stopped by our home. I had not seen him in over ten years. Humbly, he apologized, and my angels and I rejoiced. He "felt" solid and well.

Today, Andrew is the devoted father of an amazing eighteen-month-old daughter. Hard working and responsible, he has bought a house. He does not have expensive material needs. He's a down-to-earth nice guy. This man, who asked his great-aunt if he could live with her to avoid his mother's unsafe web, escaped the road that could have left him in prison. And in the end, everything was worth it. I am a proud and contented mom.

SHE WORKS HARD FOR HER MONEY

PAMELA FENDER

One afternoon in the mid-1980s, I packed up my five cases of Mary Kay Cosmetics skincare samples and products and headed over to meet a new client. She could not find any friends to join her, so I booked an individual skincare class. I dressed impeccably: raw silk cream-colored suit, stockings, and matching high heels. Full makeup: foundation to bold berry cheeks, hazelnut eyes, and scarlet red lips. Then I topped it all off with Mary Kay's signature sandalwood fragrance.

To build my business, I placed small pink boxes around town in various stores for people to sign up for complimentary facials, picked them up a week later, then phoned whoever had signed up. This was a way to get people to book an appointment with their friends for a skincare class to learn about and then purchase the products.

I parked my car and took two of the five cases of products along with my purse. I rode the elevator up to the third floor of her building, easily found her apartment, and rang the bell. Jewel opened the door. I introduced myself, and she invited me in. The place was plain and ordinary with white walls and beige carpeting. The dining area was spacious for an apartment. Nothing distinctive in the furnishings or surroundings was memorable except for the enormous dining room table.

Politely, I asked where the most suitable place would be to set up. I released my cases and purse to the floor beside the dining room table and told Jewel I needed to make another trip to my car to bring the rest of my products upstairs. No problem.

I walked down the hall to the elevator and pressed the "down" button. I envisioned an exotic mango lip color complementing Jewel's complexion.

There were flecked mirrors on both sides of the elevator, which I found hideous and outdated, even for the '80s. Nevertheless, I glanced in the mirror to make sure my skin appeared flawless and I, presentable.

Unexpectedly, an unusual presence or force overtook me. I stared back at my reflection. A spiritual being spoke as though I had spoken to myself. The words inside my head were vivid: *"Right now, you are being ripped off."*

As if I had imagined it, I shook my head.

I hurried back downstairs to the trunk of my car to retrieve all that I could carry. After all, I was investing my time presenting the products I paid for to this young woman.

Who knew if I'd even sell her an eyebrow pencil?

I returned to her apartment, the mysterious feeling still with me—*she had stolen from me.*

Jewel tried all the skincare products and makeup line, applied and removed each product from cleanser to lip color.

After I presented the entire ninety-minute show, the whole *megillah*, I retrieved the order form. Predictably, Jewel loved the products but stated she couldn't afford anything. Then she asked about getting into the business. So much for the sell, sell, sell. I told her I'd get back to her the following day, packed up my products, and left.

ଔ

I dumped my stuff in the trunk and drove home, exhausted. After I trudged up to my apartment, I kicked off my heels, grabbed the wallet from my purse, and flopped on the couch. I needed to see the contents or lack of contents. I slowly opened my wallet. At that moment, my body went stiff.

All my cash . . . gone.

Where could it be? Did I spend it the night before? Did I lose it at the car wash? I phoned the last few places I'd been. Nothing. I didn't want to believe it was Jewel who'd stolen from me. Yet, I knew where the cash was. I needed to follow my initial intuition, that strange, unusual occurrence at the elevator. I made the phone calls and hoped my intuition was wrong.

When my husband got home from work, I told him what had happened.

"You should just forget about it. You'll never get your money back."

"No. I earned that money, and I want it back."

I tossed in bed all night. *What was that strange voice that had told me I was being ripped off?*

The following morning, I phoned the police and explained what had occurred the day before. "I'm a genuinely good citizen and honest person. I work hard for my money, and I want to know what *you* think I should do."

"Well, we can't advise you what to do, ma'am, and you can't accuse her because you have no positive proof. However, this is what I'd do if I were you . . ."

I thanked the officer, hung up, took a few deep breaths, and phoned Jewel.

"Hello, Jewel. This is Pam."

"Oh, hi, Pam!" She responded so enthusiastically, I thought I'd barf. "Have you thought about me getting into the business?"

Oh, absolutely, I thought. *So you can go into people's homes and steal from them too.*

"I'm phoning you, Jewel, because when I was in your home yesterday, I had money in my wallet. When I left, it was gone and I think you took it. If I don't get it back, I'm filing a formal police report."

Silence. Several moments felt like hours. I waited for her to tell me to go to hell. Or hang up.

"You can pick it up in a half hour. Meet me downstairs outside; I don't want my mother to see this."

What was her reason for committing this crime? Her motivation? Did she want to see if she could get away with it? Did she enjoy the challenge? Did she need the money? I never asked.

My husband insisted on coming with me. He wanted to see for himself if I was truly going to get my money back.

I got out of the car and walked to where she stood in front of her apartment building holding her two-year-old son. She handed me fifty dollars.

"I'm sorry, Pam."

I nodded. I needed no explanation from her, and I wasn't going to thank her. I felt betrayed, a victim.

I turned and walked back to my car.

"See, Paul? I'm glad I stuck to my gut feeling," I said as I flashed the cash before his eyes.

I OWE MY LIFE TO STEVE JOBS AND THE PRESS DEMOCRAT

Linda C. McCabe

The evening of October 8 and the morning of October 9, 2017, have been seared into my memory. It started normally with a touch of foreboding but devolved into a harrowing escape to safety.

My husband and I had a typical Sunday evening. We watched the movie *Hidden Figures* on HBO. The Diablo winds rattled our windows, sounding like distant thunder. I remember saying the winds were "wicked." Around ten o'clock, we smelled smoke. My husband, Scott, looked online and reported there was a fire earlier that day at the coast. Wind will carry the smell of smoke a long way, so we didn't worry about fires; we closed our windows and went to bed.

As I lay down, my biggest concern was whether I would get enough sleep. I had to wake up early for my 6 a.m. shift as a clinical laboratory scientist at Healdsburg District Hospital. Our nineteen-year-old son, Ian, came barging into our bedroom a little after 11:00 to say that the power had gone out. Was it the fire? Even though he was panicking, I remained calm. I told Ian to turn the radio to battery and tune into KSRO radio. During local emergencies, the station switches their broadcasting to exclusively cover the crisis. He came back a few minutes later to say KSRO was airing a show about UFOs. Since they were still broadcasting syndicated shows, I reassured him that the power outage was probably due to the wind.

The power was restored a few minutes later. My son was relieved; I rolled over and went back to sleep. At 2:45 a.m., Scott woke up from a nightmare. He had dreamt of playing with red-hot embers on our mattress. *Was the dream a premonition*? The thought raised the hair on my neck.

Our power was off again. This time I grabbed my iPhone and pulled up the Santa Rosa *Press Democrat* homepage online. The top headline read something like, "Fires Burn Across Sonoma and Napa Counties as Thousands Flee Devastating Flames." The story had been updated only nine minutes before. I clicked on the link and read about a fire destroying homes on Skyfarm Drive and Thomas Lake

Harris Drive. We live on Altruria Drive, less than half a mile from there. I put down my phone and announced, "Santa Rosa is on fire. We have to pack up and leave. Now."

My husband didn't understand my urgency. There were no sirens, no alarms going off. All was quiet outside. Scott suggested we could sleep a little longer, but I insisted we leave. Scott found our emergency flashlights so we could see in the dark, and I grabbed three suitcases and packed. Once I did that, my husband followed suit—I had the presence of mind to tell him to pack our passports because I knew they were difficult to replace.

I then went to our son's room. "Ian, wake up. Santa Rosa is on fire. We need to leave, right away. Here is a suitcase. Pack three days' worth of clothes. Your laptop. Anything else you need." One thing I made sure I packed was the working draft of my novel with notes from my critique group. My son took the manuscript for his fantasy novel as well.

Scott packed for our cat's needs—food, treats, the cat box and litter, and the cat carrier. Our kitty was not going to be left behind.

I texted my boss to let her know fires were raging all over Sonoma County, and that I was evacuating with my family. I wasn't sure if I would make it to work at 6 a.m. I learned later that my text alerted her to the tragedy that would soon engulf our beloved county.

My father-in-law, Roger, lived in a senior independent-living apartment on Round Barn Boulevard, and we were worried about him. I tried calling him on his cell phone, knowing that his landline would have no power. He didn't answer. I left a voicemail telling him we were evacuating and would try to get to him.

I was calm and focused. Scott and I used to live in the San Fernando Valley and had survived two other disasters that left long shadows on our psyches: the riots following the acquittal of LAPD officers in the Rodney King beating trial and the Northridge earthquake. I was mentally prepared to never see our apartment nor our possessions again. I wanted us to take what we needed and abandon the rest.

By the time we left, it was 3:15 a.m. Scott gave us damp dishtowels to wrap around our faces to help filter out the smoke in the air. As if everyone else had left before us, the parking lot was empty and quiet as a tomb. In hindsight, we should have pulled the fire alarm. We didn't even think about it at the time. We could have alerted others who were still asleep.

My husband wanted us to pile into one car. I disagreed. I felt we needed to have two cars. In the back of my mind, I was still planning to report to my job that day. I worked in healthcare and knew I would be needed, especially during this emergency. I even packed one set of scrubs. We were fortunate enough to have three cars to choose from. Scott moved our Subaru Forester to a spot closer to our apartment. It was at that point he discovered it had less than a quarter tank of gas. He decided against using that car, lest we run out of fuel during our evacuation. He pulled the emergency cord in our garage and retrieved his car. Our son and cat were going with him.

I left while Scott was still packing his car. I headed down Fountaingrove Parkway hoping to pick up Roger. I turned into the nearest entrance to Round Barn Boulevard but did not get far. A city bus idled, and a fire engine sprayed water on the hillside. I turned back around in time to see my husband's car. I called and told him we should try the lower branch of the road to reach Roger. Once we were near his street, we saw the iconic Round Barn ablaze with multiple fire engines on the scene. We did not want to interfere with first responders, so we kept driving. We hoped Roger and the residents had been evacuated.

The red glow from the fires was hypnotic and scary. Journey's End Mobile Home Park was engulfed as we passed by. I followed my husband's car as we crossed over the 101 freeway and sought an open road to go south. He had hoped to take the freeway, but it was closed because it was on fire.

My husband later told me that Ian had asked him if we were going to die. Scott said he tried reassuring Ian by saying, "I hope not."

We drove near Coffey Park on roads choked with cars that barely moved. I got separated from my husband several times and became agitated. I did not want to lose sight of him. We kept in contact with each other by cell phone, both of us listening to KSRO radio for real-time updates about the unfolding disaster.

At 4 a.m., I finally admitted to myself that I was not going to make it to work. My hospital was north of the fire line, and I couldn't navigate a safe path there. I had no idea where the fire ended and what roads were open. I wanted to reunite with my family in a safe place. The thought of leaving their side to drive through that area again was something I couldn't imagine. I called my boss to give her the news. She told me that Sutter Hospital had evacuated. I said that from what I'd seen, Kaiser would be next. When I then called my hospital and told the midnight shift tech I would not be coming in to relieve her, she understood.

It took my husband and me two hours to drive from Santa Rosa to Novato, a trip that usually would take only an hour during rush-hour traffic. We refueled, stopped for coffee, and developed a plan. After calling around for a hotel room in Marin County, we learned everything was booked and wound up staying in Millbrae at the La Quinta Inn. We were grateful to find a hotel that allowed cats. It was there my family finally relaxed and felt safe.

By the time we checked into the hotel, we had heard from Roger. He and all the residents were safe. They had been brought outside to an inner courtyard and watched as several fire engines "made it rain" around the apartment building. It was probably about the time we had driven by that he had been hustled out of his room without grabbing his cell phone. Once morning broke, they were taken to an evacuation shelter in Santa Rosa. Subsequently, they were bused to hotels in the Central Valley until power and water were restored, and some repairs from fire damage were made. They were out of their apartments for over a month.

We kept in touch with Roger and did not worry about his safety and well-being. I do not want to consider how distraught we would have been if we had gone through this emergency before cell phones and had to wonder about him for days until authorities could have matched us together.

That first night in the hotel, we worried if our apartment was still standing. We saw photos online of houses destroyed on our street. We were also concerned about whether the campus of Keysight Technologies, where Scott worked, had survived. Scott was practical and analytical. If we had no apartment to return to and he didn't have a place to work, he would still have a job with Keysight. He could transfer to a different facility. We contemplated our options and discussed which states we would consider moving to if necessary. Thankfully, we learned that same night that our apartment complex was standing and that Keysight had suffered some damage, but would survive. Our fears of losing our housing and my husband's worksite lifted.

We had sold the house we'd lived in for twenty years barely five months before. We had gone through "downsizing" from a five-bedroom home to a three-bedroom apartment and had put many possessions in storage. We'd planned to use the proceeds from the sale of our house to build on a lot we owned at Sea Ranch. I am unsure whether that dream will ever become a reality. The competition for construction crews to rebuild Santa Rosa and the increased cost of building materials may make this out of our reach. Months later, I still do not know the answer.

As days passed, I became obsessed. I followed the news on television, radio, and the *Press Democrat*. Watching as the evacuation lines shifted, threatening new areas, I called and texted friends warning them to evacuate. I hated seeing remnants of landmarks that were once our beloved haunts. We read harrowing articles about people who barely escaped with their lives. The fact that they weren't just names on a page—but friends of ours— disturbed us to the core. The running tally of families we knew who had lost their homes to the fires was over twenty. Thankfully, we knew none of the people who lost their lives to the fires.

My family was fortunate. We returned to our apartment in a neighborhood where many houses were destroyed. Our most significant loss was the vehicle we left behind. The car's charred remains, not fifty feet from our front door, told a story of a conflagration we were lucky not to have witnessed. We were displaced for two and a half weeks but returned to our home and our belongings. Thankfully, our insurance covered our losses and expenses. We were terrified for one morning, but we returned to our lives with minimal disruption compared to those who lost loved ones, homes, and all their worldly possessions.

My biggest debt of gratitude is to the late Steve Jobs for his leadership at Apple and bringing about the invention of the iPhone. I do not know what would have happened without having my smartphone, access to the Internet, and the reporting by Santa Rosa's *Press Democrat*. I might have shaken my head at my husband's prophetic dream and gone back to sleep. The fires scorched the hillside behind our apartment. Who knows what scene I would have awakened to a mere two hours later? And how safe would it have been for us to then evacuate? We might have tried driving away only to be caught in a firestorm, making it deadly for us to leave and unsafe for us to remain.

No one called us. No one texted us. No one knocked on our door. No one pulled the fire alarm to wake us up. We heard no sirens. We could have slept until 4:30 a.m. when I would have gotten up to get ready for work. I would have discovered we had lost power and seen an eerie orange sky. We could not have waited for doorstep delivery of a newspaper telling us Santa Rosa was on fire.

It was the combination of the smartphone, internet technology, and online reporting from the newspaper that gave my family the information we needed to leave when we did. For those reasons, I am forever grateful to Steve Jobs and the *Press Democrat* for saving our lives.

WELLNESS WARRIOR

Judy M. Baker

The serenity of yoga failed to soothe my body and brain that day. Jagged, stabbing pain rippled through my gut as I curled into child's pose. My breath caught in my lungs. My diaphragm seized up. The muscles in my upper back responded with sympathetic contortions.

For the weeks leading to this day, I rationalized my growing fatigue, lack of appetite, and my inability to eat as signs of stress and being overworked. I ignored the bloated feeling and ever-tightening fit of my clothes. I was over fifty. The symptoms echoed those in women past their prime.

Denial ended that day. The crisis in my body was like an ongoing siren—constant and shrill. The unrelenting pain within stole my peace. When I called my family doctor, he was on vacation. Panicked, I made an appointment with another physician in the practice. I ran through possible suspects for this terrible sensation: pancreatitis or an inflamed gallbladder. Both were common in my family.

Like a buzz saw carving out my guts, the pain cut sharply. My face, turning from technicolor to bland, the skin beneath my eyes translucent and nearly black, were harbingers of the battle ramping up inside me.

My face was gray. The most I could eat was a bit of food before feeling full. The substitute doctor refused to hear me. As I spoke, she tapped away on her computer like a schoolgirl writing an email. I gave her a vivid recounting of my complaints. She kept insisting I needed a test for my digestive system, which had nothing to do with my symptoms.

Overcome with frustration, I screamed, "Why aren't you listening to me?"

She passively ignored me, and I left with no relief to this misery.

When my pain escalated a few days later, I returned to the doctor. Crying and pleading, I repeated my ailments. Her solution was to send me to the hospital emergency room. I explained I had no insurance and was trying to tough it out. The dawn of Obamacare in two weeks was my goal.

The dismal gray of the skies matched my pallor. Nothing seemed to relieve the anguish of the demon twisting my gut. Two days before the new year, after another night without sleep, my husband drove me to the emergency room.

New horrors awaited me at the hospital. The week between Christmas and New Year's Day is one of the worst times to be in a hospital. Many regular staffers are on holiday. The lack of privacy in the ER smacked of one circle of hell.

Once in the exam area, a thin curtain separated me from a crazy man. He was a frequent flyer who ingested sharp objects. Razor blades were his snack *du jour*. I overheard the doctors and nurses discussing his proclivity and imperviousness to pain. This guy swallowed more than the blades. His mental health was in doubt. I was concerned that he may also be dangerous.

The ER was meat-locker cold. I lay there freezing. The nurse brought me another blanket, which did little to warm me. The ER doc came by, did a quick check, and ordered tests. The techs drew blood and sent it to the lab for analysis. To see what could be causing my pain, the doctor ordered a CT scan of my abdomen and pelvis.

Earlier in the week, my husband booked an interview with a prospective client for that Saturday. Not planning for a fun day at the hospital, I told Garry it was okay to keep his appointment. He called a mutual friend to come stay with me.

It's as if I had entered a different dimension—hospital time had a bizarre quality to it. The minutes stretched and contracted like silly putty. When our friend arrived, Garry left. I was taken away to the imaging department and returned to the same exam area.

ᦞ

I remember the ER doctor coming in and saying, "We don't like to say this, but you have cancer. We don't know what kind."

That couldn't be right. I exercised. I hadn't been sick in years, except for this. What was he saying?

I calmly asked him what was next. Like a switch flipping in my brain, it hit me—I had a choice—and I chose not to be a victim. In that instant, I knew I would be all right. I would do what I needed to defeat the enemy.

A week later, I met with my primary care physician. He had the results of my blood work. I had peritoneal cancer, stage 3C. Cancer is staged from 1 to 4. Stage 1 is the earliest point of detection. Stage 4 is the most severe and least likely to have a positive outcome. He made phone calls, and I was set to see an oncologist and surgeon in the coming week.

Two weeks later, I started my 60th year. Happy Birthday to me. A chemo cocktail was now on my list to celebrate the occasion.

Like an acid flashback, reality twisted into a weird hallucination. The players in this trauma: me at thirteen learning my father's diagnosis of breast cancer. Now, at fifty-nine, I plucked up the memory I'd tucked away from long ago. The promise I'd made to myself—I would *never* go through the medical nightmare my father endured.

My father fought hard through four cancers. At the time of his initial diagnosis, the breast cancer had invaded his lymph nodes and more than likely the migration to the later sites in his colon and pancreas had begun. His death came a few days before my twenty-first birthday. Maybe my milestone birthdays carried with them an invitation of bad luck.

Trying to process what the doctors said, my ears caught some words, flung others away. Like a spinning centrifuge, my brain roared into overdrive. Fear permeated every breath in, yet I exhaled a sense of serenity. I never thought of giving up or giving in to cancer. Instead, my engines revved up for the battle to restore me to wellness. Peaceful in my belief that my storyline had many chapters ahead, I had confidence in my ability to protect myself from the abyss.

In the coming days and months, I discovered how much of an impact I'd had on the community. It appeared with the assistance of a fantastic team of doctors and caregivers. People came to help me: long-time friends, family, community connections, traditional and alternative healers—singers of songs, the crew who packed our belongings two weeks into my first round of chemo and got us moved into a different house. I learned to let go and focus on becoming a wellness warrior.

I started chemo four days later.

Surgery was on April 17th. I fought with the anesthesiology team and dissuaded them from giving me an epidural, which I insisted I didn't need. I was right.

Post-surgery: four days in a room that could double as a sauna. It was furnished with a rubber, standard-issue hospital mattress that would have been at home at a Guantanamo Black Ops site. The kicker was the processed, nasty-tasting hospital food I couldn't stomach. I got out of there after my husband brought me a salad of fresh greens and veggies. Oh! The joys of a home garden!

I completed chemotherapy on July 8th, six months after starting treatment.

I am four years out from those troublesome days. Despite my years of trying to ignore the signals coming from my body, during my treatment something strange and wonderful took place. I could feel the cancer cells being gobbled up. Like ghosts in a Pac Man game, the chemical warriors chomped those cancer cells into oblivion. My CA-125 numbers (a tumor marker in the bloodstream of ovarian cancer patients) plummeted after my first infusion. My numbers have stayed in a healthy range ever since.

I learned to pay attention when my body speaks. I am stronger, calmer, and more in touch with myself. I came through a terrible battle.

I am a warrior.

I have won.

BIOGRAPHIES

Marlene Augustine-Gardini retired from the music industry as Senior Director/West Coast Promotion for MCA, a division of Universal Music Group. Her passion is animal rescue especially "TNR," the trapping/neutering/releasing of feral cats. After residing for decades in San Francisco, she, her husband, and pets live in Northern California.

Judy M. Baker is a creative ambivert who broke the gender barrier in high school by enrolling in a boys-only class to print her poems and drawings. She is a voracious reader who attributes her love of books to her father. Her life path is governed by communication: theater, graphic design, marketing, coaching, and writing.

Sandy Baker is immediate past president of Redwood Writers, past chair of two conferences, and chair of the 2017 and 2018 Sonoma County-Redwood Writers Fair Booth. In 2017, CWC presented her with the Jack London Award for "outstanding service to the club." Her passions are writing, reading, gardening, and traveling.

Barbara Beatie is a student of Margaret Caminsky Shapiro's Writing Circle. Her poetry has been published in *Sonoma: Stories of a Region and its People* and *Phoenix: Out of Silence...and then*.

Marilyn Campbell is a retired social worker who continues to marvel at the resiliency of the human spirit. She writes historical fiction, poetry, and short fiction. *A Train to Nowhere*, a sequel to *Trains to Concordia*, will be launched in the spring of 2018. She is a contributor to small journals and her work appears in the anthologies of Redwood Writers as well as in *First Press: Collected Works from Napa Valley Writers 2017*.

David Colin Carr has been editing fiction and non-fiction since 1988 with writers internationally. Collaboratively he brings forth their passion—with clarity, coherence, and distinctive voicing.

David values strong structure and lively, efficient language, and offers compassion, counseling skills, and creativity. His own fiction and non-fiction focus on End of Life. DavidColinCarr.com

Fran Claggett-Holland teaches poetry and memoir writing through OLLI and in her home. She edited *Stolen Light*, the 2016 Redwood Writers poetry anthology and is co-editor with Les Bernstein of their 2018 poetry anthology *Phoenix: Out of Silence...and then*. Fran has published many educational books, but most recently her third poetry collection, *Moments with Madge: Lux Aeterna,* in memory of her lifelong partner, Madge Holland.

John Compisi is a freelance travel/lifestyle writer focusing on California, Italy, and France. He is a published member of the Bay Area Travel Writers. He loves getting out there and experiencing the world, whether it's a destination close to home, a road trip, or a romantic international journey.

Tina Riddle Deason is a mystic and seeker. She writes about everyday magic as well as writing and performing ritual and ceremony. She has written newspaper features and has been published in *Common Ground* (Jan. 2016). She treasures her time spent with her family and her pets. Priestesstina.com

Roger DeBeers, Sr., BA, History, MA English, and MFA Creative Writing. His varied background as an English instructor, commercial pilot, flight instructor, government functionary, househusband, single parent, and years in two branches of the military as a Marine Corps enlisted man and Army Officer lends richness to his writing.

Jack Douglass Fender is a playwright, fictional writer, and occasional poet. He was born and raised in London, England. Jack lives in Sonoma County and loves to garden and practice yoga. He built a Free Little Library for the front of his home. Jack's been published in four Redwood Writers anthologies.

Pamela Fender, author of *Beside Myself: Recovery From My Family Betrayal and Estrangement*, received her Bachelor of Arts degree in English at Sonoma State. She is a notary public and certified signing agent. Raised in the suburbs of Los Angeles, Pamela returned to Sonoma County after losing her home in the 1994 Northridge earthquake.

Mary Folck writes to sort through her confusion. Her first submission was rejected for being "too hot" for *The Sacramento Bee*, but the editor suggested sending it to a psychology magazine. Her first published story called "A Tale of Two Charlies," was published in a newspaper called *Our Town Truckee* in 1993. More recently, her poem "Black Widow Moments" was included in *Stolen Light*.

Cristina Goulart writes fiction, poetry, flash memoir, and articles addressing environmental issues. Her work has appeared in several Redwood Writers anthologies, the *Windsor Times*, and other community newspapers. Her short story, "Spare the Rod," was selected for the 2016 Lucky Penny Productions' short story dramatic reading in Napa, California.

Alan Gould is a retired attorney who specialized in representing vets in disputes with the VA. He has self-published a novel and book of short stories, and is a recent resident of Santa Rosa.

Pamela Heck is an artist, writer, and special education teacher. She writes in a variety of genres including picture book, poetry, memoir, and short story. Her entry in this year's club anthology was her first foray into non-fiction. Pamela is a recent addition to the Redwood Writers Board of Directors.

Mara Lynn Johnstone grew up in a house on a hill, of which the top floor was built first. She lives in California with her husband, son, and laptop-loving cats. She enjoys writing, drawing, and spending hours discussing made-up things.

Jeanne Jusaitis has an MA in Education and has been involved in various writing groups since the inception of the California Writing Project. She is the author of two children's books: *Journey to*

Anderswelt and *Lilah Dill and the Magic Kit*. Her poems and stories are published in eleven anthologies.

James Kelly has been a long-time print journalist, writing for a number of publications over a thirty-year period including newspapers in San Diego, Sonoma County, Vermont, and Colorado. He is now working on his first novel based on his experiences in Marine medevacs in Vietnam and his uneventful return.

Jeanette Koshar, a Petaluma resident for seventeen years, retired from Sonoma State University as a Professor in the Department of Nursing. After years of scientific writing, she is now exploring a more creative aspect of the written word through memoir and travel writing. Follow her on her blog: travelinglifepaths.com.

Marilyn Skinner Lanier's life on a Wyoming ranch in the 1950s inspired her debut novel, *Hardpan*, published in 2015. Two short stories were published in the Redwood Writers 2016 Anthology, and she is now at work on a second novel and a children's book. Lanier has a Masters in English from CSU East Bay and has taken fiction and memoir courses through UCLA Extension.

Beth E. Lewis lives in Northern California with a variety of two- and four-legged creatures. She has written poetry and romance but her favorite work is in epic fantasy. She loves to lose herself in her writing, she can visit fantastical places along the way.

Roger C. Lubeck, Ph.D. is the president on the Redwood Writers board of directors. He was the editor of four anthologies and a memoir. Roger's published works include articles, poems, short stories, seven novels, two business books, and a ten-minute play. Roger is working on two novels and a screenplay.

Linda C. McCabe is the author of the award-winning novel *Quest of the Warrior Maiden*, an epic historical fantasy set in the time of Charlemagne. She traveled to France, Italy, and Germany for research and will soon release volume two in the trilogy.

Betsy Miller is a technical writer, the author of several books about children's health topics, and a picture book. Her short stories span several genres including mystery and suspense, magical realism, urban fantasy, and young adult. She is currently working on her first young adult novel.

Kay Mehl Miller, Ph.D is an eclectic author, currently writing novels and non-fiction. In her youth, she was a newspaper reporter, an English teacher, a columnist for LGBT media, and a psychotherapist. Her most recent work is *Ring Around Reality*, a coming-of-age novel focused on a woman's pathway to alcoholism.

Robin Moore has been writing since she was a child. A member of Redwood Writers for over ten years, she has published stories and poems in several of the club's anthologies. In the past, she served as a newspaper reporter and editor, including editing the Redwood Writers Newsletter.

Renelaine Pfister's stories, essays, poems, and articles have been published in the U.S. and in her native country, the Philippines. She is a physical therapist and a writer.

Linda Loveland Reid is past president of Redwood Writers and a Jack London Award recipient. She has published two novels, is a figurative oil painter and theater director. Linda holds two *cum laude* degrees from SSU and currently teaches art history for SSU's Osher Lifelong Learning Institute. More at LindaLovelandReid.com.

Belinda Riehl retired from her bookkeeping business in Simi Valley, California, in 2011. She has been an active volunteer in Redwood Writers since 2014. Her poetry and short stories have been published in several Redwood Writer anthologies, as well as in *Sonoma Seniors Today* magazine, and online at Medium.com. Her musings can be found at belindariehl.wordpress.com.

Elaine Rock is a former secondary history teacher and banking technology executive. After retirement, she focused on her photography and writing about women's rights. She is currently a vice president of the California Writers Club—Redwood Branch and co-chair of the 2018 Pen to Published Conference.

Robert Shafer is a member of Redwood Writers, lives and writes in Napa, California. He fulfills his desire to perform by reading books to his two grandsons.

Susanna Solomon is the author of *Point Reyes Sheriff's Calls* (2013) and *More Point Reyes Sheriff's Calls* (2016, Lucky Bat Books). She has had stories published in the *Point Reyes Light*, *The MacGuffin Literary Review*, online in the *Mill Valley Literary Review*, and in *Harlot's Sauce Radio*.

Laura 'LA' Sottile is a performer, humorist, composer, director, actress, and a certified creativity guide. She has close to two decades of experience in the entertainment and healing arts business. Since 2012, she has published her work in the *Foolish Times*, a monthly comic paper in Monterey, California.

Angel Stork is a non-denominational minister, writer and body therapist, designer of movement and spiritual practices for increasing our natural joy and enthusiasm for life. Her book, *Practically Perfect Wedding and Commitment Ceremonies* helps couples write their own wedding ceremonies. Angel's current project is part-memoir-self-help blog/book for children of alcoholics.

Bill Trzeciak is a retired librarian and current instructor of the Santa Rosa Junior College Older Adults Program classes in Readers Theatre. He writes novels, screenplays, drama, short stories, humor, doggerel, and essays.

Corlene Van Sluizer self-published *Resurgence*, a poetry book. Each poem is illustrated with her original artwork. Her poetry has been published in many newsletters and publications, including *A Moving Journal, Business World, Pegasus Journal*, and an article in *The Journal of Dance and Somatic Practices* on "Art and Poetry in Authentic Movement."

Christine Walker is a visual artist and author of *A Painter's Garden: Cultivating the Creative Life*, a narrative nonfiction, and co-author of *Wooleycat's Musical Theater*, a children's book. She has an MFA in Writing and Literature in Fiction and an MA in Creative Arts Interdisciplinary. She lives in Sonoma County.

Jane Wilder has published stories, poems, memoirs, and short plays in periodicals. She has written, and currently is editing her full-length novel. She also loves traveling, attending movies and plays, photography, and reading voraciously.

James Ellison Wills is a second generation Californian writer based in the Alexander Valley. He worked for thirty years as a guide in the mountains and cities of Asia and Europe. His second novel, *Annapurna Blues*, based on actual events on a trek in Nepal, will be released in 2018.

Marilyn Wolters has lived in Sonoma County for over thirty-five years. She spent most of her working years helping disabled college students develop essay-writing skills. Now retired, she can't resist writing regularly. Her poetry, short stories, and short plays have been published and performed.

JUDGES

Arlene Battishill, Ph.D. is the best-selling author of *Retail Shock Therapy: A Prescription for What Ails Your Online Sales*. She has spent years creating content marketing strategies for startup companies and entrepreneurs and specializes in writing ad copy.

Skye Blaine writes fiction, memoir, and poetry, developing themes of aging, coming of age, disability, and awakening. She received an MFA in Creative Writing from Antioch University. *Bound to Love: a memoir of grit and gratitude* was published in 2015. Her debut novel, *Unleashed*, came out in November 2017.

Daniel Coshnear works at a group home in Santa Rosa, teaches creative writing through UC Berkeley Extension, and facilitates workshops in the North Bay (often at The Sitting Room). He is author of two story collections: *Jobs & Other Preoccupations* (Helicon Nine 2001) and *Occupy & Other Love Stories* (Kelly's Cove Press 2012), and in 2015 he published a novella called *Homesick Redux.*

Barbara Cottrell is the author of *The Shadows of Miskatonic*, a series of supernatural thrillers based on the work of H.P. Lovecraft. Barb is a member of the Horror Writer's Association and presented her work at the 2016 Mystery Writers in the Mausoleum.

Anne Jordan is CEO of Popcorn Entertainment and President of the Northern California Writers. She has taught Creative Writing and Screenwriting at several colleges. Her literary career includes: a monthly column in four national magazines; two novels; and dozens of film and television scripts. Anne also works as an editor and script doctor.

Ferne Moffson is a retired teacher of English who enjoys assisting authors in the process of creating more meaningful and technically accurate written work.

Jean Wong, author of *Sleeping with the Gods* and *Hurtling Jade and Other Tales of Personal Folly,* is an award-winning poet, fiction, and memoir writer. Her work has been produced by the Petaluma Reader's Theater, Sixth Street Playhouse, Off The Page, and Lucky Penny Productions. Jean writes from the bottom of a well, always amazed to look up and see the sky.

EDITORS

John P. Abbott is a writer, editor, and marketing consultant based in Petaluma, California. His fiction has appeared in *Frisko*, *Fence*, and the *Vintage Voice Anthology of California Writers*. He served as editor for the 2013 Redwood Writers Anthology, *Beyond Boundaries.*

Inga Aksamit is an award-winning author who writes about adventure and exploration for the everyday person. She is the author of *Highs and Lows on the John Muir Trail* and *The Hungry Spork: A Long Distance Hiker's Guide to Meal Planning*.

Skye Blaine writes fiction, memoir, and poetry. She received an MFA in Creative Writing from Antioch University. *Bound to Love: a memoir of grit and gratitude* was published in 2015. Her debut novel, *Unleashed*, came out in November 2017. She teaches fiction and memoir in SRJC's older adults program.

Catharine Bramkamp is a writing coach and Chief Storytelling Officer. She has written 17 novels and 3 books on writing. Her poetry has been included in a dozen anthologies. She contributes to Redwood Writers through judging, editing, and organizing RW 2018 Pen to Published conference. She now lives in Nevada City, California.

John Compisi is a freelance travel/lifestyle writer focusing on California, Italy, and France. He is a credentialed member of the Bay Area Travel Writers. He loves getting out there and experiencing the world, whether it's a destination close to home, a road trip, or a romantic international journey.

Robert Digitale is a newspaper reporter and a member of the Santa Rosa *The Press Democrat* newsroom that won a 2018 Pulitzer Prize for coverage of the North Bay wildfires. He was editor in chief of the 2017 Redwood Writers anthology and has published two books in a fantasy trilogy.

Cathy Hollander is the author of Ico and the Sacred Cave, a middle-grade historical fiction set in the Caribbean when Christopher Columbus encountered the Taino Indians. When she's not working on a project, she teaches creative writing to high school students at Schilling School for Gifted Children in Cincinnati. Besides her popular novel, Cathy writes feature stories for magazines and newspapers and is an editor and ghostwriter of non-fiction, memoir, and fiction. Email her at csholland18@gmail.com.

Susan Littlefield is a notary and paralegal who enjoys spinning common occurrences into lively tales. She has published articles in a paralegal newsletter and *The National Notary* magazine. Susan dreams of reviving her unpublished novel, has published short stories, and has just started writing a memoir. Her website is strokingthepen.com.

Roger C. Lubeck is the publisher of It Is What It Is Press. He was the editor of four anthologies, and has designed covers and interiors for eighteen books. Roger's published works include seven novels, two business books, stories, poems, articles, reviews, a produced play, and a prize-winning flash fiction story.

Ana Manwaring coaches and edits through JAM Manuscript Consulting and teaches creative writing at Napa Valley College. She has completed two thriller/suspense novels set in Mexico. Ana is active in CWC and Sisters in Crime. Her book reviews can be found at Amazon, Audible, Goodreads, netgalley.com, and anamanwaring.com.

Ferne Moffson is a retired teacher of English who enjoys assisting authors in the process of creating more meaningful and technically accurate written work.

Belinda Riehl grew up in a family whose dinner conversation was punctuated with grammar corrections. The subject of the conversation wasn't always notable, but good grammar was required. Good grades in English followed. *Redemption* is the third Redwood Writer anthology for which she has enjoyed being an editor.

Natasha Yim is a children's author, freelance writer, playwright, and editor. She has published five picture books and written for Highlights for Children, Appleseeds, Faces, and Muse magazines as well as various adult magazines. She has recently completed a picture book project for Disney Publishing Worldwide. She is currently the Contest Chair for Redwood Writers.

PROOFREADERS

Sandy Baker is proud to admit she's a grammar geek. She rails at the TV and circles mistakes in newspapers and magazines. She earned a BA in English at Penn State and two years later went on to teach grammar to reluctant Army GIs in Germany—a fun and challenging experience.

Jane Bonham grew up in Healdsburg, enjoyed fishing at the coast, and exploring the countryside on horseback mostly by herself. With her B.S. from Stanford University and M.A. from Northwestern, she taught Educational Psychology and Early Childhood Education. During a college writing class, she discovered she wanted to be a writer. Now on her own after a lifetime down other paths, she will write.

Adele Layton became interested in court reporting while attending college. Her business expanded to offices in San Francisco and Oakland where she began a school for transcribers. She is currently working on two screenplays and has been published in *Sonoma: Stories of a Region and Its People.*

Connie Leap is a retired legal secretary who lives in Tennessee. She began as a responsive and thorough ARC reader with her kind and constructive comments to many authors. Now she is a dependable, efficient, professional copy editor/proofreader.

Arlene Miller, The Grammar Diva, has written ten grammar books, a self-publishing book, and a novel. She is the author of the Amazon bestseller, *The Best Little Grammar Book Ever!* She also writes the weekly Grammar Diva Blog, copyedits, and gives workshops and talks about grammar, writing, and words. TheGrammarDiva.com.

Belinda Riehl gained valuable experience as a proofreader while she was a legal secretary for a large law firm in Beverly Hills after graduating from California State University, Northridge. She enjoys contributing behind the scenes for Redwood Writers by proofing flyers, newsletters, and has worked on the last four Redwood Writers anthologies.

PUBLISHER

The name of the publisher is always listed inside the front cover, but we wanted to recognize Roger's contribution on yet another Redwood Writers anthology. Thank you, Roger.

Roger C. Lubeck is the publisher of It Is What It Is Press. He was the editor of four anthologies and a memoir. He has designed covers and interiors for eighteen books. Roger's published works include seven novels, two business books, stories, poems, articles, reviews, a produced play, and a prize-winning flash fiction story.

REDWOOD WRITERS

REDWOOD BRANCH OF THE CALIFORNIA WRITERS CLUB (CWC)

Jack London, George Sterling, and Herman Whitaker, among others, formed the Press Club of Alameda. In 1909, a splinter group of writers formed the California Writers Club. Early honorary members included Jack London, George Sterling, John Muir, Joaquin Miller, and the first California poet laureate, Ina Coolbrith.

In 1975, Redwood Writers was established as the fourth CWC branch. Informally known as Redwood Writers, the branch owes a debt to Helene S. Barnhart of the Berkeley Branch, who had relocated to the North Bay. She and forty-five charter members founded the Redwood Branch of the CWC.

Redwood Writers is a non-profit professional organization whose motto is "writers helping writers." The club's mission is to provide a friendly and inclusive environment in which members may meet and network; to provide professional speakers who will aid in the writing, publishing, and marketing of members' endeavors; and to provide other writing-related opportunities that will further the club members' writings.

In 2006, Redwood Writers published its first anthology. *Redemption* is the fifteenth in that series. From 2010–2016, Redwood Writers sponsored a short play contest in which winning plays were performed at 6th Street Playhouse in Santa Rosa.

Today, the club features professional speakers at monthly meetings that are open to members and the public. Every other year, the club holds a day-long Writers Conference offering seminars on all areas of writing, taught by area professionals. In addition, the club sponsors a book club at Copperfield's bookstores, public readings, salons, workshops, seminars, writing contests, a monthly newsletter, and a website. For more information about Redwood Writers visit redwoodwriters.org.

The Redwood Branch of the California Writers Club is indebted to its founders, charter members, board and club members, and volunteers who make the Redwood Writers a success. The Redwood Branch could not have developed into the professional and successful club it is today had it not been for the leadership of our Presidents.

1975	Helen Schellenberg Barnhart
1976	Dianne Kurlfinke
1977	Natlee Kenoyer
1978	Inman Whipple
1979	Herschel Cozine
1980	Edward Dolan
1981	Alla Crone Hayden
1982	Mildred Fish
1983	Waldo Boyd
1984	Margaret Scariano
1985	Dave Arnold
1986	Mary Priest
1988	Marion McMurtry
1990	Mary Varley
1992	Barb Truax
1997	Marvin Steinbock
1999	Dorothy Molyneaux
2000	Carol McConkie
2001	Gil Mansergh
2003	Carol McConkie
2004	Charles Brashear
2005	Linda C. McCabe
2007	Karen Batchelor
2009	Linda Loveland Reid
2013	Robbi Sommers Bryant
2015	Sandy Baker
2017	Roger C. Lubeck

HELENE S. BARNHART AWARD

Inspired by the first president of the Redwood Writers, the Helene S. Barnhart Award was instituted in 2010 as a way to honor outstanding service to the branch. It is awarded in alternating years of the Jack London Award.

2010 Kate (Catharine) Farrell
2012 Ana Manwaring
2014 Juanita J. Martin
2016 Robin Moore
2018 Malena Eljumaily

JACK LONDON AWARD

Every other year, CWC branches may nominate a member to receive the Jack London Award for outstanding service to the branch, sponsored by CWC Central. The following members received the Jack London Award for service.

1975	Helen Schellenberg Barnhart
1977	Dianne Kurlfinke
1979	Peggy Ray
1981	Pat Patterson
1983	Inman Whipple
1985	Ruth Irma Walker
1987	Margaret Scariano
1989	Mary Priest
1991	Waldo Boyd
1993	Alla Crone Hayden
1995	Mildred Fish
1997	Mary Varley
1998	Barbara Truax
2003	Nadenia Newkirk
2004	Gil Mansergh
2005	Mary Rosenthal
2007	Catherine Keegan
2009	Karen Batchelor
2011	Linda C. McCabe
2013	Linda Loveland Reid
2015	Jeane Slone
2017	Sandy Baker

COLOPHON

This book was produced using CreateSpace tools and services. The typefaces are New Times Roman, Myriad, and Trajan Pro.